WHEN THE SMOKE CLEARS

THE FALLOUT DUET BOOK TWO

AMANDA MARQUARDT

SILVER LANE PUBLISHING

Editing by Megan Carver

Proofreading by English Proper Editing Services

Cover art and design by KBG Designs

Paperback ISBN 979-8-9915280-3-0

EBook ISBN 979-8-9915280-2-3

CONTENTS

INTRODUCTION

Dear Reader,

I'm so excited for you to read the conclusion of Maci and Sutton's story!

As we dive deeper into ranch life and the local motorcycle club, I've added additional terms to the glossary. I've also included a special note there about an important location in the book. It's not necessary information to have beforehand, but may add some fun detail if you're less familiar with Texas and Spanish, and how they play together in this instance..

This book is intended for readers 18+. It includes on page depictions of sexual situations and mature language. I've included content notices on my website for those who would like to view them. Please keep in mind that this book does explore sensitive subjects and themes that may be triggering for some readers. Consider your mental health before reading.

To keep the story as authentic and accurate as possible, I received anecdotal insight, as well as professional feedback on many included themes and events. However, this is still a work of fiction and is not based on any specific event or occurrence.

Welcome back to Bull Creek!

GLOSSARY

Ranch Life

Ag - Agricultural education

Caliche - A white soil made of mineral deposits used for farm and county road paving

Blind – a concealed area used for hunting

Bull - intact male

Carhartt – brand of heavy duty clothing (in this context it references a jacket)

Cattle - ungendered plural

Cow - full grown female

Heifer - unbred female

Hog – a domesticated pig, often over 120 pounds

Pommel – round knob on a saddle rider's may hold

Springing Heifer - pregnant heifer in final weeks of pregnancy

Steer - neutered male

Tack – equipment or accessories used on horses

Motorcycle Club Terms

Church – club term for meeting

Cut - leather or denim vest (leather in this book)**Motorcycle Life**

Member - official members who have been voted into the club

MC - motorcycle club

Old Lady – club term for a female partner

Patch - insignia applied to cut to denote personal identity within the club

President/Prez - Club leader

Prospect/Probate - probationary member until fully voted in

Rocker - a curved patch that carries the club name(top) and area (bottom)

Irish Terms

Bake – (in context 'shut her bake') mouth

Da – dad/father

Mam – mom/mother

Note Regarding Nopal Vista

Nopal Vista is the name of the location where Maci and Sutton will be building their future home. The name is significant, as it represents an important moment at the start of their relationship. You may remember from When Sparks Fly, that Sutton propagates a portion of a prickly pear cactus from one at Strickland Ranch, to bring to Maci instead of flowers on their first official date.

Nopal is the Spanish word for 'prickly pear cactus'. 'Vista' is the Spanish word for 'view'. The prickly pear cactus is native to Texas and also serves as a food source. Other references to the specific cactus are nopales, which are the pads of the plant. Nopales, and nopalitos, are also a food item, which includes removing the spines and cutting the paddle into strips or dicing them. The plant can be eaten raw or cooked, and is also often pickled or canned.

DEDICATION

To my husband, my Sutton.

You broke through my walls of fierce independence and taught me

that just because I can do everything on my own doesn't mean I have to.

And to anyone who was ever made to feel shameful for choosing themself.

I'm glad you're here.

PLAYLIST

Peacekeeper – **Fleetwood Mac**

Fire Away – **Chris Stapleton**

Easy Silence – **The Chicks**

Buy Dirt – **Jordan Davis**

Every Storm (Runs Out Of Rain) – **Gary Allan**

Girl – **Maren Morris**

Beauty in the Struggle – **Bryan Martin**

Shake It Out – **Florence + The Machine**

DEVIL YOU KNOW – **Tyler Braden**

Sin So Sweet – **Warren Zeiders**

I Am Here – **P!nk**

He Set Her Off – **Emily Ann Roberts**

'Til You Can't – **Cody Johnson**

From the Ground Up – **Dan + Shay**

CHAPTER 1

SUTTON

"Goddammit!" My shout fills the cab of my truck as I drive recklessly into the night.

It's an effort to steady my thoughts and formulate a plan. My clenched fingers ache from the pressure I put on the steering wheel. Maci declaring her love and ending the call is not how our story ends. I will not allow those to be the last words I hear from her lips.

I press Nick's speed dial preset on the dash screen.

"Yo, man!" His carefree voice fills the cab.

"I need your help." There's no time for pleasantries.

His tone changes immediately. "What's up? What can I do?"

"Where are you?" I blast through the intersection of the county road and Main Street, the truck tires bouncing onto the city street thanks to my speed coming down the hill.

"Just coming back from the lake, checking for poachers."

"Can you meet me on Bluebonnet Cove? The address is twenty ten. Maci's there and that fucker that attacked her the other night showed up. I'm in town headed that way."

"Absolutely. I'll call it in." Some best friends might balk at being called directly into danger, but with Nick's career as a Game Warden, he doesn't even hesitate—though it's not why I call him first. Nor is it why I think he jumps into action whenever it's needed.

"Thanks. See you there." I don't wait for a response before disconnecting the call and dialing Maci back. My heart thrums faster with every unanswered ring. When I'm routed to voicemail, I hang up and repeat the process with the same result.

I ignore the possibility that I won't make it in time, instead focusing on the knowledge that we'll have backup, and being grateful that Nick has the sense to call this in, because I skipped that part. Meanwhile, every second spent not knowing what's happening makes the vise holding my heart squeeze tighter and tighter. Another frustrated yell fills the cab.

The engine roars, yielding to my increased force on the gas pedal. My focus turns to not driving off the damn road before I make it there. The police could attempt to stop me for any of the countless traffic violations I'm committing, but nothing will stop me from reaching Maci first. It's only been ten minutes since we spoke, but it's still ten minutes too long.

Her street is pitch-black, aside from the ray of my headlights. Since all the houses on this street sit on at least five acres, even if any of the neighbors are home, there's a good chance they won't have a clue what's going on tonight.

I whip into the driveway, taking the gravel drive between the symmetrical oak trees faster than usual. A black motorcycle sits near the house, and it's impossible to stop before smashing into it with my truck. Not that I try. Metal crunches loudly, but I'm not worried about damage to the truck, thanks to the grill guard.

The transmission jerks into park, still settling as I jump out.

The clear pop of a gun firing greets me.

A curse flies from my mouth and I start running toward the fire pit, lit like a beacon in the center of the backyard. Movement on the other side of the pit is obscured by the smoke and flames.A second round fires.

The dark mass of grappling bodies tips to one side. Maci's smaller figure is overtaken by Colt's taller frame. She falls backward and Colt drops awkwardly to his knees before falling forward.

Free of the smoke and firelight I take in the sight before me as I round the pit. Colt pins Maci down. Her head is thrown back as if her neck is hyper-extended. She's sucking in wild breaths and her eyes are closed.

There isn't a word for the panic cementing my body into place.

My voice breaks on the way out. "Firecracker?"

"Cowboy?" Her head lifts hastily from the ground, eyes shooting my way. "Oh my God." Relief coats her words, and she drops her head back to the ground. There's a catch to her breathing, like she might start crying.

"Fuck." I yank Colt off her, chucking him to the side, half expecting him to roll and face me. He doesn't fight back, his body limp. Maci attempts to crab walk backward from him, falling flat with a hiss. A pained grimace overtakes her face.

Colt's neck is warm underneath my fingers. I'm no medical professional, but I can't find a pulse. Maybe I'm in the wrong spot? "I think he's..."

Dropping my hand from Colt, I move back to Maci, caught between physically assessing for injuries and not wanting to add to any potential pain. My eyes pinball over her and start to travel in an erratic downward path. "Are you hurt? Did you get shot?"

"Sutton! Maci!" Nick yells from somewhere far off.

Neither of us responds as Maci says, "He stabbed me." Her left hand raises and loosely indicates the injured area on her lower torso before falling back to the ground. "It stings like a bitch, but I don't know how deep it is."

"Holy shit!" Nick yells, rounding the pit behind me. Both of our heads whip to him. "PD is right behind me."

"Maci's been stabbed," I tell him before looking at Colt's still body once more. "And I'm pretty sure he's...gone." It's the least descriptive thing I can come up with. A dark gun reflects the firelight, discarded on the grass.

I look back to Maci, whose stare is fixed on Colt.

Nick bends over Colt's body, pressing two fingers against his neck in the same way I did. He holds my gaze and after a moment shakes his head. "How long has he been down?"

I shake my head. "Not long."

"I don't think there's any coming back from that." Maci's tone is dry, and she reaches up with her fingers, brushing them over her sternum as if signaling something. I follow her gaze back to Colt's body.

Straining my eyes in the dim light, the wetness covering the back of his jacket becomes evident. *Did she shoot him right through the chest?*

"Let me see." I turn, refocusing on Maci, and reach for her sweater to check the damage around her wound. A flash of reflective light catches my attention, and I halt. The hilt of the knife protrudes from her body. My eyes fly up to hers.

"What?" Her mouth tightens. "Is it that bad? It fucking hurts." Her head drops back, and fire illuminates the wetness trailing down her cheeks.

It takes me too long to swallow and find the right words. "Maci, don't move. The knife is still in you."

"What!" Her body jolts as if she's about to sit up, but she inhales sharply and freezes. Her voice cracks. "Take it out! I don't want it in me. Please. Please."

"I don't think you should." Nick's calm voice comes from behind me. "It may be helping to stop the bleeding. You need to leave it."

"Please, Sutton." Her closed eyes pinch tighter and her fists clench at her sides. "I don't want any part of him in me."

My fucking chest hurts. I want to help her. I want to give her everything she wants and needs. But right now, I don't think those two things are the same, and I don't know how to tell her that she has to endure more than whatever I missed tonight. "I'm sorry. I can't." The words are painful.

She shakes her head vigorously, keeping her eyes pinned shut. It's hard to tell in the light, but I think she's getting paler. A fat tear rolls down her cheek.

"Fuck!" I look up at Nick. "How far is EMS?"

"Put pressure on it." Nick jerks his chin toward Maci before speaking into the radio on his shoulder. I rip my overshirt off, wad it up, and press it against Maci's injury.

A garbled voice responds and Nick echoes. "Five minutes."

How long have I been here? Five minutes feels like an eternity.

With my free hand, I cup Maci's face. Her green eyes pop open, shiny from tears. She's beginning to shake like she has a fever. Either from shock or her injury, I don't care. I just want her better already.

"You hear that, Firecracker? We'll get you fixed up in no time." I inch closer on my knees.

There's blood on her cheeks. I don't know who it belongs to. I don't know anything.

Her eyes fall closed and her jaw tenses.

"Maci..."

"I'm okay."

She's far from okay. I can't put into words that I need her to hang on. That she can't leave me.

This wait is taking forever. Checking my watch is useless; it's so dark I can't make out the tiny lines. I roll my neck to release some of the tension, but that doesn't help either.

Nick grips my shoulder from behind in solidarity.

Somehow, the blood thrumming loudly in my head, warring with the panic coursing through my veins, has ebbed, giving way to an eerie quiet. Logically, I know help is on the way, but right now it doesn't feel like anyone knows we're here. As the seconds tick by, my muscles continue to tighten bit by bit.

"You still awake, Firecracker?" I think she's trying to control her emotions, compartmentalize, but she's been quiet and still for longer than I'd like.

"Mmhmm." Her face maintains the same shielded expression.

Sirens wail from the main road.

Two police cruisers pull into the driveway, followed by an ambulance. Slamming doors and voices mingle from what seems like too far away. Flashlights bob in our direction. More vehicles flood the narrow driveway.

Will an ambulance even be able to leave?

Nick meets the first officer and leads them our way. Thankfully, the paramedics have a little more pep in their steps and overtake the officers quickly.

One drops down in the grass. "What happened here?" Her voice is questioning, not accusatory, and I'm thankful for that. I can guess there will be a ton of questions thrown at Maci, along with a full investigation, and I will do my damndest to keep myself in check while that process takes place. But if anyone so much as looks at her wrong, I may lose my shit.

"I have a stab wound." Maci's face is tight, her tone formal.

The chatter from the officers gets louder. Movement of people in the yard increases. A second paramedic pushes in near me, cueing me to move out of the way.

Releasing Maci is physically painful. "I'm right here, Firecracker," I say for her benefit as much as mine, as I stand and move behind the paramedics.

"Were you here when this took place?" One of the officers speaks to me from next to Nick.

I shake my head. "No. I showed up after."

He looks pointedly at my bloody shirt. My hands are also covered in drying blood. "I probably have both of their DNA on me. He was on top of her when I got to them, and I pushed him off." My breathing shallows and my gaze falls to Maci's firearm in the grass again. "I think he was already dead. Or close."

The officer nods. "Have you washed your hands?"

"Does it look like I've washed my hands?"

He presses his lips together and his nostrils flare.

Nick gives me a look from next to him.

"No. I haven't washed my hands," I say more calmly.

The officer bobs his head again. "What about her?" His chin jerks toward Maci.

I'm tempted to ask if this is his first day out of the academy, but I check myself. "No. Like I said, he was on top of her when I got here."

Newbie writes notes in a small spiral pad and peppers me with more basic information questions. "The medical examiner should be here shortly. And the detective. He'll want to speak with both of you," he says when he's finished.

He closes his notepad and sticks it in a shirt pocket. "I need to do a swab on your hands. Hang tight."

One of the paramedics jogs past. I lose sight of him and my focus turns to the officers beginning to tape off the backyard. This whole situation is completely surreal.

Newbie goes through the process of swabbing my hands and then Maci's. I may live on a ranch, but I've seen enough prime time TV to know he's looking for gunshot residue.

A gurney rattles through the yard, and I don't know what to do with myself. I'm the asshole standing around doing nothing while the woman I love is bleeding out on the ground.

Nick side steps closer to me. "She's in good hands, man."

I want to respond to him. He's my best friend and has the connections that got a fast response here tonight. But I feel sick to my stomach with guilt and fear. Somehow, I think he gets it when all I manage is, "Thanks."

He claps me on the shoulder.

Once Maci's secure on the gurney, the first paramedic turns to me. "Are you family?"

"Yep," I say, without question, and nod for them to lead the way to the ambulance. No one is separating me from Maci again. At this point, I'd consider drastic surgical procedures to adhere her to my damn body.

Chapter 2

Sutton

Maci dozes on and off on the ride. Several nurses descend on her the second we're in the ER, and I alternate between trying to stay close and trying to stay out of the way while they draw blood and start an IV. When they disperse, instinct takes over and I get closer, sliding my hand over hers.

I can't help but stand watch over her. It doesn't matter that Colt is no longer a threat. I almost lost her. I'm not completely sure of all the damage, and his fucking knife is still sticking out of her.

Her body stays rigid. She threads her fingers with mine but won't open her eyes, even though I know she's awake.

Maci's really good at creating walls around herself. To a fault even. So I stay put, rubbing her hand, letting her know I'm here on this side when she's ready to come out. Past that, it doesn't feel right to push her now.

Eventually, the doctor comes in and Maci opens her eyes, glassy and far from rested. He introduces himself and begins poking around her abdomen and side. She flinches and grits her teeth. Her grip on my hand tightens, but she stares vacantly at the ceiling. It's less reaction than we got at the house, and I can't help the nerves that race through me, wondering if she's losing feeling or just putting on a brave face.

I want to break something. To cause damage as retribution for what she's going through. Instead, my thumb continues to rub circles over the back of her hand.

It can't be more than thirty seconds before he speaks, even if it feels like a lifetime of anticipation. "We're going to take you back to surgery to remove this knife."

"Say what?" The words fly out before I can stop them.

The doctor looks at me blankly. "Safety precaution." He looks between Maci and me. "This wound has the potential to be painful but otherwise unremarkable, or we could be looking at something much more serious. We would see a lot more bleeding if it were an artery, but that doesn't rule out any organs being damaged."

Maci's eyes widen, and I add my other hand to the mix trying to infuse comfort into her. I know it's no use. I wasn't there when it happened, and I can't do anything now.

"What kind of organ damage?" Maci's words are measured, careful.

"Hard to say without seeing. Our biggest concern is going to be intestines. There's also a threat to reproductive organs."

Her eyes shift to me, wide and unseeing. They're full of tears again. If that motherfucker wasn't dead already, I'd kill him myself.

How did I manage to fail her both times she needed to defend herself?

The doctor continues, unphased. "You'll be under anesthesia in the operating room."

Maci's hold on my hand intensifies and I give her a softer squeeze in return, but I doubt it does anything to comfort her.

"Some more obvious side effects of anesthesia are confusion and drowsiness, but some people experience nausea and vomiting. There are some bigger risks. The nurses will go over everything, and you'll need to sign a couple forms before we get started."

His lips press into a bland, forced smile before he pats the foot of the bed and leaves. This is just another day for him.

"Paperwork, my favorite." Maci tries to grin at me, but it's tired.

"You afraid they won't like your handwriting, Firecracker?"

She gives me a half-smile and breathes a laugh. "No. I've just never had surgery to remove a foreign object before. Didn't know what to expect."

This woman is fucking amazing. She's laying on this shitty hospital bed with a psycho's knife sticking out of her body, and she's cracking jokes.

It doesn't stop me from wondering how this will affect us long term. Maci was just starting to open up with me. This has the potential to cause her to shut down in a big way, proven by her shields firmly in place right now.

The nurse pushes her way in with paperwork and a clipboard. "Hey sweetheart, let's get you ready for surgery."

The moment they wheel Maci to the operating room, the gravity of the situation overtakes me. I stand, alone, in the emergency bay, willing myself not to punch a hole in the wall.

Footsteps approach from the hallway. "Hey, man." Nick's voice is softer than usual.

I turn abruptly. He waves politely to another nurse, who gives a tight-lipped smile and walks away.

"I followed as soon as I could. They've sealed off the property for the investigation, so I got out of the way." He scans the empty space. "How's it going here? Where's Maci?"

"She's in fucking surgery." My head hangs, the words sounding defeated. If this goes sideways, I don't know if I can make it out the other side. Even thinking it to myself is crazy. I thought my life was full before Maci came along. I love my role at the ranch, have a wonderful family, and good friends. But now? I can't imagine life without her in it.

It was bad enough to consider her moving back to Austin for good.

Yesterday, I laid everything out for her. I wanted to give her time to process and decide what she wanted without my interference, so I let her be. The day got away from me, and we didn't have a chance to talk. I got up before dawn as usual and she slept in before lunch with her mother. I have no idea what the rest of the day held leading up to the incident with Colt. All I could think about was begging her to try long-distance if I couldn't convince her to move here.

I think she wants to be here. I know she wants me. Even if she's dancing around the decision.

And yet now...now I'm faced with the possibility that a scumbag who wanted her to himself may have done permanent damage to her, possibly stealing her from me forever, as his last pathetic act on earth.

My muscles all feel tightly wound, ready to strike.

"Sutton. Whoa, man." Nick has a death grip on my shoulders. "Come on. Let's go get some air." His eyes bore into mine, waiting for a sign that I've heard him.

I nod vacantly.

Maci's nurse stops at the open curtain. "I'll come get you when she's done." She starts to walk away but pauses. "You can wash up in the bathroom, if you want." Her chin jerks toward a door behind me.

"We'll stay close," Nick promises. I'm thankful, again, for his presence. He looks me over. "I have a spare shirt in my truck. I'll be right back." He waits for my silent acknowledgement before leaving.

I step into the private bathroom and take stock of myself in the mirror. My ruined white undershirt comes off first. Aside from my hands, there's also remnants of blood around my jaw and on my stomach where it seeped through the shirt. I wash it all down the drain. The mingled life force of the woman I love and the man who attempted to steal her from me.

Washing up isn't as refreshing as usual. I don't feel any better than I did with blood on me. None of it matters until I know what's going on with Maci.

Nick returns with a clean shirt, gesturing me into the hallway when I'm redressed. He starts talking, leading us away from the semi-private spaces in the ER. "Izzy and Leah are on their way."

My brows furrow.

"Must've been a sixth sense thing. They showed up at the house just after the ambulance left. I didn't give a ton of details, but they weren't taking no for an answer on where Maci was. I think they're packing her a bag and locking up the house."

"Thanks." I can't bring myself to say anything else.

Before long, we approach a small, enclosed waiting room.

"I know you don't think you're up for it, but we need to talk. You're gonna self-implode if I let you sit here and stew in whatever bullshit you're creating up here." He taps my temple.

"What do you want to talk about?" I shove open the door for us to walk through. The space is empty aside from us and a pot of coffee on a drab counter along the far wall. We both pour a cup, skipping the single-serve sweeteners, and sit in worn, leather chairs, side by side.

The free-standing ER location in Bull Creek is small. Unlike the hospital in the city, it's good for strep tests and ear infections, but I doubt they handle many knives in stomachs. My leg bounces anxiously at the thought of Maci lying in their sterile operating room.

"Tell me about Maci. You've been keeping a tight lid on everything, but this all happened fast. So, what's up?"

I grimace at the bitter brew. I don't even like coffee. Maci loves it. It's one of her greatest pleasures. I close my eyes and send up a prayer that I can make her coffee every day for the rest of her life.

"That. Right there. You're killing yourself." Nick's voice is firmer. *Is he pulling out the warden tone on me?*

I arch an eyebrow at him, and he smirks.

He is. And he's doing it on purpose.

"Start talking." He crosses his beefy arms over his chest. Maybe for the first time with him, I do as I'm told. He lets me rattle on for several minutes without interrupting, except to ask more leading questions, keeping me talking.

I share more than I ever have. Maybe in my entire life. I tell him about the day I met Maci after her grandmother, Ruthie, passed. How even in her grief and struggle to be composed, she was beautiful. About her pride at the funeral and how she held the community in her palm with her eulogy. About her determination to be all she needs for herself, because people have continued to fail her.

I was beginning to think I wasn't like the others—that I couldn't possibly be. Except I *did* fail her tonight.

"Dude, relax." Nick picks up where I left off. "Maci isn't dating you because she expects something from you. And you've been there every time she's needed you. You brought that dirty-ass trailer up to the Fall Festival. You were there after that asshole busted her window. You were there to calm her down after he accosted her on Halloween. And you made it tonight. You're here now. You don't need to be everything for her to prove she doesn't have to be everything for herself. You have to be *you* for her, because that's what she wants and needs. I promise you, man, that's enough."

I stare at my best friend in awe. In a mirror of my uncharacteristic sharing, he's spouted off some deep advice right when I needed it. My head rocks up and down while I wring my hands in my lap. "Thanks."

The ticking of the clock on the wall is too slow. I lean my head back on the chair, trying to ignore the way my lungs refuse to inflate completely. I didn't ask how long they would be. What's normal? Do I panic after thirty minutes or three hours?

We only sit quietly for a few minutes before Izzy and Leah barge into the silent room.

Izzy's ice-blue eyes are wild. "Where is she? Is she ok?" She clasps a hand tightly to Leah's. Leah looks less panicked, but her eyes bounce between Nick and I.

I rise quickly from my seat. "She's in surgery—"

"What!" Izzy shrieks and Leah releases her hand, wrapping her arms tightly around her friend.

Nick stands. "I know this is a scary situation, but Maci's in the best place she can be. You two can wait with us."

Both women visibly relax at his calm demeanor.

"What happened?" Leah asks, still deciding which of us to look at.

I take a deep breath. "Colt attacked Maci at Ruthie's. She had to defend herself, but he managed to stab her in the process."

Leah's arms fall from Izzy, whose hand flies to her mouth. I continue as calmly as possible, hoping that the more at ease I am, and the more information they have, the better they'll feel. But I'm dying second by second, so doing that for them takes everything I have.

"The knife was still embedded when I got to the house. We didn't want to cause any more bleeding, so we waited to remove it and the doctors said they would do it in surgery as a precaution. For the same reason."

"Oh my God," Izzy whispers.

"How long has she been in surgery?" Leah, usually the wild one, seems to be the levelheaded one tonight. Meanwhile, Izzy, normally practical, is on the verge of a panic attack.

"Maybe thirty minutes."

"There's coffee," Nick offers, and gestures to the long counter behind them.

"Thanks. Come on." Leah grips Izzy's hand and leads her over to grab their own terrible cups of coffee before they join us on the tattered chairs.

Chatter is at a minimum. We take turns pacing, sitting, checking the clock, commenting on the time, and asking each other questions none of us actually know the answer to, like, "How long do you think it will be?" or "Do you think something's wrong because it's taking so long?"

At some point, we all manage to sit at the same time. Leah and Izzy take up the lone extra wide seat, tucking themselves together. I stare, unblinking, at the water-stained tile ceiling. Nick's leg bounces in a slow rhythm next to me, bumping my chair periodically.

16

Around the two-hour mark, Maci's nurse swings the waiting room door open wide, causing me to jump up out of my seat. She gives me a soft smile. "If you want to come with me, I'll show you to her new room. She'll have a different nurse. I don't work in Recovery."

I nod. "Thank you."

She looks at the group of us. "Visiting hours are over, so only family." Her head tips my way as if to indicate me.

Izzy and Leah exchange a glance. Leah nods and Izzy says, "We'll wait here for an update"—I start to open my mouth, but she continues—"no matter how long it takes."

"I'll hang out, too," Nick adds.

I dip my chin in acknowledgement and turn to the nurse. She leads me to the elevator and down a long hallway. Maci's room is the last one, and she's tucked under several thin blankets. Her features are soft, her eyes gently closed. If I didn't know better, I'd think she was sleeping peacefully.

"She's been in and out a little already. She'll be groggy for a bit. The doctor will come in later and update you both."

"Thank you." I don't look away from Maci, pulling a stiff chair to the side of the bed. I wrap my hand around hers and hold onto her for dear life.

CHAPTER 3

MACI

Every part of me hurts. Which makes sense, considering a two-hundred-pound guy *did* fall on me after trying to slice and dice me.

The tension of the whole thing seeps into my bones. Peeling my eyelids open intensifies the dry burn. My throat hurts, but I don't know why because I didn't scream.

Sutton rubs light circles on my hand, sitting at my side. He perks up, realizing I'm awake.

"Hi," I croak.

"Hi, yourself." He stands and kisses me on the forehead. "Thirsty?"

I nod.

The warmth of his hands disappears as he moves to a small rolling table, filling a Styrofoam cup. He presents it to me with a straw. "Sips."

I roll my eyes. "When did you get a medical degree?"

"Real funny, Firecracker." Even through his sarcasm, he smirks. I appreciate the moment of normalcy. He waits for me to sip a few times before setting the cup back on the table and sitting at my side again. "How do you feel?"

Like I was hit by a Mac truck. "I'm okay."

Sutton's eyes narrow. "You don't have to—"

The room door swings open.

"Oh good, you're awake." A bright-eyed nurse smiles at me. "Are you thirsty?" She bustles around the bed.

"I'm fine, thanks." Her chipper attitude isn't as welcome as the calm nurse in the ER. My nerves are shot, an odd combination with how sluggish I feel.

"I'll let the doctor know you're up." She stands, staring at me expectantly, across the bed from Sutton. I blink at her. At first, I think she's waiting for a response, but it feels like she's assessing us. Judging us. Judging me.

Her mouth pulls into a smile that doesn't meet her eyes and she darts out of the room.

"This place is full of weird people," I mutter as the door closes.

Sutton chuckles. His presence is soothing, and I let my eyes close.

It's not the closed eyes of being at Nana's, wondering how long it would be until someone found me bleeding out.

The relief at hearing Sutton's voice almost instantly after the scuffle was unparalleled.

I'm not fully resting here, but having him near me is a reminder that I'm not the only one looking out for me. I don't have to be at one hundred percent now.

The door flies open again. This time, the nurse is followed by a man in his forties. She's still smiling widely, attempting cheerful, but it comes off more blinding.

"This is Detective Porter." She scans my face and Sutton's in turn.

"Hey there. I'm Detective Porter with the Bull Creek Police Department." He's dressed in khakis and a polo and carries a dark notebook in one hand.

The nurse eyes us once more before leaving.

Detective Porter walks further into the room as the door closes quietly. I'm not sure how such a large door can close without a sound. If only it opened the same way.

"I'd like to ask you a few questions about what happened tonight, if you feel up for it."

It's odd to think it's still the same night. I'm not even sure what time it is.

"That's fine. Whatever you need." I knew this was bound to happen sooner or later. My upbringing is fueling my ability to be pleasant right now, when I really just want everyone to go away and for things to be quiet. Not that it matters if it's quiet in here. Outside these walls, I can imagine all the whispered gossip going on.

Stupid small towns.

Now I remember just one of the many reasons I can't stand their oppressive nature. The last few weeks getting to know Sutton and spending time with my family and friends lulled me into a false sense of enjoyment.

"So you understand, we will be conducting a full investigation. I've collected the clothing you both had on earlier." Detective Porter doesn't make eye contact as he opens his notebook. The flipping pages jar my sensitive nerves, akin to scraping a fork on a plate.

I refrain from commenting that I'll never wear the sweater again anyway. "Fine by me."

"Can you walk me through the events of the night?" he asks, without acknowledging my response.

Sutton doesn't move from where he stands, his gaze burning into the side of my face.

I release a long breath. Reliving it all threatens to overwhelm my senses.

Just the facts. Stick to the facts.

"I was in the backyard when Colt showed up. On the phone with Sutton." I look up at him, and something flickers in his eyes momentarily. I focus on the detective.

There's nothing remarkable about him. He's a man of average height and weight with pretty, brown eyes. His face remains void of emotion and, as expected, he's writing in his book. I study the threads of the Bull Creek Police Department patch on the breast of his polo. I wonder how much this interrupted his weekend.

"Were you expecting him?"

"No." My lips are especially dry. I wet them before continuing. "The last I saw or heard from him was Halloween. He approached me at a Trunk-or-Treat event at the dental office. I filed a police report."

I pull my hand free from Sutton's, rubbing both over my face as the revelations from my conversation with Colt wash over me again. "Actually, there's another report, too. My Jeep window was broken last weekend, and I filed a report then. Colt admitted tonight that it was him."

Sutton shuffles on his feet and scrubs a hand over his face angrily.

The detective watches him for a moment before returning his focus to me. "Was that why Colt came over? To tell you about the window?"

A sardonic laugh bursts from me, and Sutton tenses. "No. Not even close. He came to kill me." I don't blink, daring Detective Porter to question my statement.

His lips purse and he scribbles more notes into his book. "You killed Colt Young because you feared for your life?"

It doesn't matter that his tone isn't accusatory. His bland use of "kill" sends fury rippling through my aching body. I grip the plastic rails of the bed with both hands and lean forward, gritting my teeth from the pain that shoots through my gut like lightning. "He threatened my life and stabbed me."

"And you shot him."

He's only stating facts, but after what transpired tonight, I feel reactionary, and it's an effort to school my emotions. He stares at me blankly.

Sutton takes a step forward. "With all due respect—"

I reach up and wrap my hand around his wrist. "It's ok." Except, it's not. "Yes. I shot him. Yes, I feared for my life." I thought I could, but I can't do this tonight. Not in a way that keeps me in control of my emotions. "Actually, I'm feeling kind of tired. If there's anything that you absolutely need to know tonight, please ask me that. Otherwise, I'd prefer to schedule a time over the next few days to discuss this."

He dips his chin and closes his notebook. "A gunshot residue kit was completed at the house, correct?"

Was it? I don't remember.

Sutton speaks up. "Yes."

"Good, good." He hesitates. "Were there any...other injuries?" He looks uncomfortably between Sutton and me.

I lift my left hand toward the hidden wound. "You mean, aside from being stabbed?"

He swallows. "No sexual assault?"

Sutton's head whips my way.

I close my eyes and work to keep my tone even. "No."

He nods. "I'll get out of your way tonight. No need to make an appointment. Just stop by the police department in the next forty-eight hours so we can discuss a few more details." He extends a card to Sutton. "Call me if you need anything in the meantime."

I can't bring myself to force a thank-you. I'm reaching my limit.

The door closes again.

"Cowboy." I wait for his perfect, steel-blue eyes to return to me, and he moves to the bed, reaching for my hand. "Can you please call—Oh, shit!"

His hand squeezes. "What is it?"

I shake my head. "I was going to ask you to use my phone to call Izzy or Leah to bring me some clothes, but my phone's at Nana's." I swallow. "By the fire pit."

"They're here already." He rubs a thumb over my cheek.

"Wha—" I'm interrupted by the door swinging open again. They just need to make these rooms with turnstiles.

Doctor Fields enters with the nurse behind him. "How are you feeling?" There's a disconnect between his question and emotion.

"Sore." A tiny part of my brain screams to apologize for my clipped tone, but I don't have it in me.

He stops at the foot of the bed. "That's to be expected. Surgery went well. You got very lucky. There was no damage to any organs. However, it did pierce muscle so you're going to be sore for a while. Try to limit lifting to only five to ten pounds for a couple weeks and take it easy." All the information comes at once, though he doesn't hurry through.

The half-smile he ends with does nothing to boost my spirits. I'm trying to wrap my head around the idea of layers of my body being infiltrated by a foreign object.

"Listen to your body. Increase activity each day, but don't overdo it. We don't want you popping any stitches, and quite frankly, healing muscles are pretty painful." He grins like he has first-hand experience. It's not comforting. "Any questions?"

"Do I need to come back to have the stitches removed?"

"No, but you'll want to be seen by your primary care provider in a couple of weeks for a follow-up."

"When can I go?" I ask eagerly.

Sutton gives my hand two quick squeezes. I don't have to look at him to know he thinks I'm being hasty, but I need out of this place.

The doctor focuses on his clipboard and turns to leave. "We'll monitor you for a bit longer. You'll probably be discharged in the morning." He pats the foot of the bed like he did earlier.

Nausea and exhaustion battle for control. The sensation of being under a microscope is wearing on me.

Sutton plants a long kiss on my forehead. "Izzy and Leah are downstairs. They weren't leaving without an update, but it looks like we're going to be here for a bit. You gonna be ok?"

I nod. "Yep."

He studies me for a few seconds while I stare stiffly back at him. Holding it all together requires me to maintain a distance I don't like.

Cold rushes through my body as soon as he releases my hand. I swallow to force back the emotion threatening to tumble out.

The lingering fog of anesthesia adds an annoying sensitivity to my nerve receptors. I blame that and the long-term exposure to adrenaline tonight for the weepy, fearful, overwhelmed way my body wants to react.

The nurse moves around quietly, her chipper personality absent. I wonder if she thinks I'm a cold-blooded murderer.

As Sutton reaches the door, I say, "You can go home if you need to. I'll be ok."

His sharp look tells me that won't be happening.

The nurse looks between us. As if the entire scenario isn't hard enough, we have to do most of this with an audience.

"I'm not going anywhere, Maci."

He may never understand the way I offer an out, hoping that he won't take it. And yet, every time he chooses me, a new thread of belonging ties us together.

My hearts flutters and I close my eyes to force the tears to stay in. Sutton shuts the door behind him and I will my body to rest, falling into a pseudo-sleep. What feels like seconds later, the door opens again. Only this time, it's the quietest it's ever been.

Through heavy lids, I peek at Sutton re-entering the room.

"Did they leave?" The words are hindered by my dry mouth and thick tongue.

He nods and offers me the Styrofoam cup to sip from, speaking while I do. "Visiting hours are over, but I gave them an update." His eyebrows reach his hairline for a moment. "They'll be back first thing to see you."

It sounds too easy. "Doesn't seem likely that they would've just left."

He sets the cup on the table, and a familiar half-smirk plays on his lips. "It wasn't quite that simple. They said they weren't going, and they'd just sleep in the lobby. I told them you'd just worry. They'll be back at eight." His last sentence is pointed and he smiles, situating himself back in the chair at my side.

I tilt my head closer to him. "So how are you still here?" My stage whisper draws his lips up.

"I told the paramedics I'm family."

"And now? No one's asked?"

He lifts our intertwined fingers between us. "Does this look like a lie?" His lips are warm as he kisses my knuckles like he's done several times before. The tender act sends those fiery little butterflies soaring through my veins.

His eyes roam my face, and I'm reminded of the state of my appearance. "I'll be right back."

He lays my hand on the bed and disappears into the bathroom, returning with a wet rag. "You have..." Letting the sentence trail off, he dabs at my cheeks and neck gently before rubbing a thumb along my bottom lip. "I don't care what you look like. Just removing anything he may have left behind."

It doesn't come across judgmental, but instead, thoughtful. Lying in Nana's grass with Colt's knife lodged in my body was the most violating thing I've ever experienced. Sutton's right that I want nothing left of him, however long the trauma of the event may last.

There's hardly any rest to be had in this place. How anyone is supposed to recover in Recovery is beyond me. People come in throughout the night to administer pain meds, check my vital signs multiple times, and draw more blood. They seem to think that because I still have an IV in my arm, there's no disturbance. They're wrong.

Sutton never leaves my side, despite the battered chair he occupies—which I'm certain isn't comfortable. At some point, he lays his hat upside down on the tiny rolling table in the room.

Sometime after seven I get a new nurse, and from that point on I'm wide awake. I'm not sure how leaving against medical advice works, but if someone doesn't produce discharge paperwork soon, I'll be finding out.

A breakfast tray arrives just before eight. I open the plastic dome on the plate, but that's as far as I get. Cold eggs and sausage links, and stale toast greet me. Breakfast of champions.

The next time the door opens, Izzy and Leah walk through.

It's an effort not to move. I want to wrap them both in my arms. Nick enters behind them.

Izzy's eyes glisten. "Oh my God, Maci. Are you ok?"

My friends rush at me from either side of the bed, wrapping their arms around my neck. I'm thankful to be in a somewhat seated position so I can wrap an arm around each of them, as well. My side tugs painfully, but it's muted.

When they release me, I pat my stitched side. "Better than new."

Sutton's face drops. "I wouldn't go that far."

I bite my lip through a smile. "I wasn't asking you."

"Seems normal to me," Leah says, grinning at Izzy.

"How long are you going to be here?" Izzy squeezes her tiny rear onto the bed with me. Leah replicates the motion, stretching her legs fully so they tuck under the chair Sutton was using.

"Actually, I'm being discharged soon," I say happily.

"Already?" Leah's voice is skeptical.

"Yep. Told you, better than new." My friends exchange a look over me.

Sutton interjects. "Our vehicles are at Ruthie's. Think you guys can lend some help getting them?"

"Already took care of 'em." Nick is posted near the bathroom, looking more like a warden than I've seen. Someone needs to tell these two men that the threat has been neutralized.

"Really?" Sutton readjusts his hat.

"Yep. We did some shuffling last night before we went our separate ways." Nick eyes Izzy and Leah in turn.

The nurse speaks from the doorway. "Discharge paperwork. Why don't you get dressed and we can go over everything?" She shakes a set of papers in the air.

Izzy holds up a small bag. "I got you."

My heart is full. After everything, my friends are here to help me through. I can't decide if I'm annoyed with this stupid small town and all the trouble it's caused, or happy that I've fallen in love and my best friends have easy access during my time in need.

The nurse sets the paperwork on the rolling table with my Styrofoam cup, swapping it for my untouched tray of food, and shuts the door on her way out.

"We'll wait outside." Sutton motions to Nick, who departs without question.

"Did we wake you?" Izzy sets the bag on the table.

"No?"

Leah plops into the chair Sutton occupied. "So, why the radio silence? Anesthesia fog? Sutton told us about the…" Her tanned face darkens, and her eyes drop to the floor.

"Actually, I need to get a new phone. I assume the police department has mine," I say mostly to myself.

Izzy studies my face. "How are you really?"

I squeeze her hand tucked into the blankets by my hip. "I'll be fine."

"You're so damn stubborn, Maci Grace. Can't you just let people take care of you?" Leah huffs, while Izzy yanks a shirt out of the bag she's holding in half-hearted annoyance.

I grin. "I love you. Thank you for being here."

"Oh, honey, we wouldn't be anywhere else." Izzy brushes some hair out of my face. "Come on, let's get you dressed so you can go home with your cowboy." A faint smile passes her lips.

Moving is an effort, but I'll do whatever is needed to get out of here. After Izzy helps me dress, I sit at the foot of the bed.

Izzy's voice comes out in a whisper. "You had us worried."

I don't dismiss her emotions by telling her that nothing compares to thinking your one-night-stand-turned-stalker-stepbrother is going to gut you in your safe haven. Instead, I say, "All good."

"Sure. I'm gonna grab the nurse so we can get you out of here." She gives me a gentle hug before standing. "I love you. I'm really glad you're okay."

I release her quickly. I can't get into all this emotional stuff right now.

The nurse makes me agree not to drive for twenty-four hours since I was under anesthesia. I doubt anyone around here would let me even if I wanted to at this point. She goes over how to take care of the incision and promises to return with a wheelchair.

Izzy addresses Sutton in a friendly tone. "Before you hold our bestie captive, why don't you let us run her for meds and a new phone?" She's not really asking even though she's asking.

Sutton's eyes bounce between us. "I don't mind taking her, but that's her call."

The nurse returns with my metal chariot. "All set?"

Everyone looks at me. "Yep."

As Sutton helps me into the chair, I say, "Why don't you let the girls take me? You've been here all night."

His face is tight, but he nods before pushing me out to Izzy's car and helping me in.

CHAPTER 4

SUTTON

Leaving Maci with her friends is almost impossible. Not that it's up to me or I don't trust them. But after everything that's happened, I just want to bring her home and let her rest.

At home, I shower, but it does little to release the tension lining my body or wash away the images of last night from my mind. It's past nine when I head into The Big House.

"Hi, sweetheart." Mama hugs me as soon as I enter the kitchen. "How's Maci?"

I shake my head and lean against the doorframe. "She's acting mostly normal. They stitched her up and there was no organ damage, but the muscles took a beating, it sounds like."

Last night, I made a brief call to my dad to let him know why I wouldn't be out at first light this morning. He may not be keeping tabs, and Mama is first on my presets, but she would panic and ask me a hundred questions. I shared as little as I could, but in typical form, Mama wants answers now.

"Oh no. Where is she? Should I make her some breakfast?"

"No. Her friends are helping her pick up meds and a new phone in town. They'll bring her out here after."

Mama pats my chest, her tense frame relaxing. "I know I don't have to tell you to take good care of her."

"No, you don't." I pour a glass of juice and lean my back against the counter, mulling over the last eighteen hours.

"What is it?" Mama stares at me.

"Nothing. Just...something's off with Maci."

"Well, of course something's off, honey. She was attacked."

"That's not it." What if she pulls back from me now? What if I can't help her through this? She's acting similarly to usual, but that's just it. It feels like an act. Fuck. I'm in way over my head and I *need* to make this better. "She's trying to be her stubborn, independent self like nothing happened."

"Maybe it's a safety mechanism." She gives me a faint smile. "She'll come around, honey. You just keep being there for her. Even if she hasn't said it, she needs it and she appreciates it."

She continues after a beat. "This may not be easy, son. Not by a long shot. In fact, it's probably going to be really damn hard, but everything worth having is worth fighting for."

I twitch at her use of "damn." She's cussed on occasion, though it doesn't fill her vocabulary like many. It's reserved for the most enthusiastic responses. She's right, though.

There's nothing else I can say right now. I kiss Mama on top of the head and take a fresh muffin with me on my way to the truck.

I park in front of the open stable door, which gives me a clear view of Jason and Cody saddling the horses inside. Kelly is checking supplies in the back of the Defender, parked at the corner of the building.

"Hey, man." Kelly looks me over. "Heard through the grapevine that you were in the ER last night. Everything okay?"

I've worked with our current three ranch hands for about three years, and we get along fine, but it occurs to me now that although I've been courteous with them, I haven't been especially open. Doing so feels foreign. "Yeah, thanks. It's a bit of a story. I was there with Maci."

Cody's eyes widen and he turns from the horse. "Is she ok?"

I nod. "Yeah. She's resting. I may be a little more in and out for a bit while she heals."

"No worries, boss." Kelly claps me on the shoulder. "Family first."

I clench my jaw and swallow. Either they know more than I've let on, or I've let on more than I realize.

"Let us know if we can help." Jason leads Dusty, my dad's horse, out of the stables.

"Yep." My eyes linger on the items Kelly gathers up. "What are you three getting into this morning?"

"Checking calves." Kelly shows me a folder of paperwork in the front seat. Cattle are extremely intelligent, contrary to what some may think. Unfortunately, that means they get into some precarious situations. They're also prone to certain illnesses, especially after birthing, so we monitor the herd daily. Even a little gash on a leg if they run into something or get too rough with each other can turn into a big issue quickly.

"I'll come with."

"Johnny's in the pasture." Cody motions behind the building. The stables are complete with matching front and rear doors that slide open. On the backside is access to a fenced-in area, which leads to a pasture if we open a gate inside. "We weren't sure if you'd be out."

"Thanks for putting him out. You guys go ahead; I'll catch up."

I wait for Jason and Cody to mount Dusty and Boots, and the three of them to head out with Kelly in the rear. Life on the ranch can be hard and unforgiving, and I don't expect this team to stick around forever, but having them here is reassuring in a way I wasn't expecting.

Maci's time in town is shorter than expected, but I can't say I'm disappointed. Before lunch, Izzy's car heads up the drive. After they park in front of The Big House, I open the back door, where Maci peers through the window. She extends a hand, expecting me to help ease her out. Instead, I scoop her into my arms.

"I can walk," she grumbles.

"Just let me do this, Firecracker." I press my lips to her temple. "Thank you," I say through the backseat to Leah and Izzy, who wave our way before I knock the door closed with my hip.

Inside, I set Maci gingerly on her side of the bed.

Her cheeks warm with color before it disappears. "You can't keep me locked up here for the next two weeks."

I stuff another pillow behind her and fluff them to prop her comfortably. "I don't plan to. But even if I have to tie you to the bed, your ass is chilling out today."

"That could be fun." She grins with a coy tone.

The corner of my mouth tugs but I push it away, sitting on the edge of the bed. "Not what I mean, and you know it."

"I know playing protector comes naturally to you, but in case you haven't figured it out by now, I can't sit here all day. It's not possible." She runs a hand through her hair, but it gets stuck and she makes a face, untangling her fingers from the knotted strands. "I need a shower."

"You weren't listening during your discharge, were you?"

"Oops. Must have left those instructions in Izzy's car." Her lips pull together in a tempting purse, and she blinks rapidly at me.

Again, I try to smother a smirk. Her safety is important, no matter how frustrated she is or how irresistible I find her. "No problem. I was listening for the both of us. No showers 'til tomorrow night."

Her green eyes go vacant for a split second before they scan the bed and side table. She leans to her right, reaching for a hair tieshe's spotted. A tiny grunt follows as she gets stuck trying to sit upright again.

I'm already moving and grip her ribs, adjusting her back onto the bed. "You trying out diving, Firecracker?"

She breathes a small laugh, even though her face drops in annoyance. "I just want to pull my disgusting hair up."

I keep my hands to myself. They itch to help her, as stubborn as she is. I don't want to reiterate that she's had surgery and it's ok to accept help. "Let me guess; you don't want my help with that either." The weight of my feelings for her settles on me, and this time I don't hide my gentle smile.

"It's gross, but if you insist." She presses the black band between her pointer and middle fingers and lifts it to me.

An unexpected win, but I maintain my stoic face. "Ponytail or bun?"

She stares at me with her mouth slightly agape.

"They're the only two styles I've seen you wear besides a braid, and I'm not going to embarrass myself by attempting that," I explain.

A light blush dusts her skin, reaching up her neck to her face. "A bun."

"Full disclosure," I stand and move to her side, "I've never actually done this before. This may come as a surprise to you, but my sister never asked me to help with her hair."

She breathes another laugh. "I wouldn't know if that's normal or not. But don't worry. Nothing can be worse than it is now."

"Good. You're setting your standards low." Dirty or not, her dark hair still feels soft between my fingers, which I use as a makeshift comb, transferring everything to one hand. I'm not actually sure what to do from here. "Now what?"

Mirth coats her voice. "Twist it and then wrap it around itself. Like...like you're making a cinnamon roll."

My brows tighten. "A what?"

"Ok, that wasn't a great analogy. Sorry, I've never taught anyone how to do this before."

Gently, I pull the fist full of hair back, encouraging Maci's face to look up at me. "We need to work on your teaching abilities." She swallows.

I grip her hair tighter, keeping her in place as I plant a soft kiss on her lips. "Don't worry, I think I'm good."

"You are," she mumbles as I right her head and begin twirling the hair. Her posture softens, and she seems to relax as I work.

"How's that?"

"Perfect." She doesn't touch the bun. Maybe can she tell some other way.

"Good. Are you hungry? I can grab some lunch."

"Not really." She chews her lip.

"Ok. Well, you're on bed rest. Stay put. Play on your phone, text your friends, take a nap...I don't care, but stay here." I pin her with my don't-try-me look.

Her eyes hint that she's considering an argument. "Fine. But I'm not going to like it."

Before turning to go, I kiss her softly once more. "I'll make it up to you later." I'll never be able to put into words how glad I am that she's still here.

35

Her returning look is hungry. It's hard to leave, but I do.

CHAPTER 5

MACI

I do as I'm told and rest, napping off the remaining anesthesia and running through tasks on my phone. I text Randi and Liv to give them a short version of what happened.

Thankfully, I'm not a complete invalid, because I can get to and from the bathroom on my own, and I walk up and down the hall twice before falling back into the bed.

Sutton comes in periodically, and for good around dinner. "Do you want to head into the house for dinner, or eat here?" He stands in the bathroom door, drying his hands.

"This is you saving me from questions, isn't it?" I dangle my legs from the side of the bed.

He doesn't respond.

"Are you going to feed me?" I ask, quirking an eyebrow and trying to elicit some sort of reaction.

His eyes flash, and I press my lips together to squash a grin. "I have a better idea," he says. "I'll be back in a few." He winks and exits the room before I have time to ask any questions.

My phone vibrates on the nightstand.

How's our favorite patient?

Me:

I think I'm already going stir crazy.

I could never be bedridden.

If that ever happens, please help me with assisted suicide.

Izzy:

Well that escalated quickly.

Leah:

I'll help.

Me:

Ride or die. >kiss emoji<

Izzy:

We'll stop by with breakfast tomorrow.

Leah:

Taco Tuesday!

Me:

I'll be the one with a limp and dirty hair.

And tomorrow is Monday.

I set my phone on the nightstand and head into the bathroom to clean up. When I open the door, Sutton is waiting for me. His shoulder is pressed against the doorframe, and he extends a hand to me.

It's warm around my own. "Where are we going?"

"Not far." He already looks proud, and I have no idea what's going on. Thankfully, I don't have to wait long. Outside of the hallway entrance is a tiny card table and two folding chairs.

I gape. "Is this a date?"

"Just thought you could use some fresh air." He helps me to a chair before sitting across from me.

For now, we seem to be skirting the big issues because he asks, "How was lunch with your mom?"

Lunch with Stephanie may have only been yesterday, but it feels like a lifetime ago.

The bite of meatloaf I take gives me a chance to organize my thoughts. Sharing how she told me that her love was clouded by pain and that my life isn't in Bull Creek makes me tense. I'm good at compartmentalizing most of the time, something I'm realizing more and more that I got from my mother. Discussing it just makes everything raw and real.

"Not great, but that's no surprise. She tried to convince me not to stay in Bull Creek."

His focus turns wholly to me. "Do you need convincing?"

"I don't make my decisions with input from her. I do plan to stay, though. She told me that she's not contesting the will, and Randi's already told me she isn't keeping Nana's house. So I talked to her about turning it into a bed and breakfast, and a photography studio."

A new kind of smile fills Sutton's face. It's soft, bringing a youthful innocence to him. "That's a great idea."

"Yeah?" I didn't make the decision out of a need for Sutton's approval, but knowing he thinks it's a good idea does increase my confidence. "I don't need the whole house, no one does apparently, but it has so much love left to share."

His lips purse. "You plan to live there?"

"For now. Well, once I'm healed."

He hums an acknowledgment, but the guarded look in his eyes tells me there's something I'm missing.

After we finish eating, Sutton helps me back into the bedroom and onto the bed, leaving to break down our dinner space. I lean against the handmade bedframe, taking in its woven cedar branches again.

I wonder what else he's made here.

I'm silently jealous when Sutton comes back and disappears into the bathroom to shower. Partly because I'd rather he at least leave the door open so I get some eye candy, but more so because I feel disgusting and I'm ready to be fully clean again.

Instead, he surprises me, returning from the bathroom with a large bowl of warm water and a washcloth. He sets both on the side table. "I know you feel dirty. It's soapy water. Do you want some help?" He studies me cautiously. Like I'm breakable. I'm equal parts touched and frustrated. I worked so hard not to be a victim again.

My heart aches at the kindness, but I'm not prepared to let him help me. "I'll work on it while you shower."

He purses his lips to one side. "Sure. Just don't overdo it."

While Sutton enjoys the shower, I wipe down my face and neck before sliding my thin sweater off, cleaning up my arms and chest. The rest will have to wait for a full shower.

When he's dressed, Sutton brings a shirt to my side of the bed. His eyes linger a moment on the gauze taped to my side, his jaw ticking. Whatever he wants to say doesn't come.

"This will be soft to sleep in, if you want." He waits for my nod and helps me into the fresh black tee, dousing me in his signature leather and hay scent.

"Lay back." As usual, all of his instructions are short but thoughtful. He removes my pants and tucks me into the plush bed. My eyes fall closed as I slip into the familiarity of the many pillows.

There's a click, and then darkness covers the room. The bed dips as he slides in next to me. One strong arm reaches beneath me gently, and he pulls me into him, wrapping me up in his heat. His lips are warm against my temple, and before long, the combination of his steady breaths and the overwhelming fatigue in my body lull me to sleep.

Unlike previous nights curled into Sutton's arms, my rest is fitful. The throbbing from my wound wakes me occasionally, and when I'm asleep, nightmares plague me. Colt's angry face as he lunged, the sound of the gun going off, the moment his knife pierced my abdomen; all of it plays out on a movie screen in my mind.

Each time I startle awake, I have to remind myself where I am as I search the darkness for a threat. The rapid beating of my heart is nearly painful. Repeatedly, I snuggle deeper into Sutton's chest and work to right my breathing.

The final time I fall back asleep, I'm once again telling Colt it doesn't have to be this way when he lunges at me. The gun goes off high and to the right of him. He smashes into me, the knife penetrates my side, and vile things spill from his mouth against my ear. I fight through the searing pain of the blade to wrestle my arm free. Somehow, the gun goes off again, and I'm crashing backward to the ground. Colt grunts loudly and stumbles my way before falling partially and then collapsing atop me. His hands scrape feebly on the ground, but he never gains traction. He stills and I drop the gun, trying to push myself out from under him. His limp body seems to gain weight the longer he lays on me.

I wake soaked in sweat and panting. A warm hand cups my face, and I shove away from the source, scrambling backward on the bed.

"Maci, wait—" Sutton grunts as one of my feet makes contact with his ribcage right before I fall off the bed onto the floor. "Shit!"

The amber light of his bedside lamp illuminates the space. Before my eyes have adjusted, he rounds the bed quickly and drops to the floor in front of me. "Maci, it's me."

"I know." I pant and lean against the wall of the closet. "I'm sorry." My throat feels thick, my side is screaming, and I just kicked the man I love in the ribs.

He cradles my face in his hands, studying me. "Why are you apologizing to me?"

It's an effort not to shriek at him when I respond. "I just kicked you!"

My favorite twitch at the corner of his lips hints that he's hiding a smirk. "It's ok, Firecracker. Don't apologize." His hands leave my face to grasp mine, which rest on my drawn knees. "I'm going to put you back where you belong now."

I nod with a sad smile. Gently, he slides one arm under my legs and one behind my back, but he's on the wrong side to put me into the bed. Instead, he carries me to his side and crawls in on his knees, tucking me against his warm chest.

He's quiet while our breathing settles, playing with my hair. Hair that's probably covered in the mixed blood of myself and my attacker. Bile fills my stomach.

"Do you want to talk about it?"

I don't respond at first. I can't.

In true Sutton fashion, he just waits. My eyes burn with unshed tears and my throat begins to close again. I untangle myself from his arms and slowly push up to sitting. Somehow, I manage not to wince or audibly complain about the ache in my side, but it's at the expense of my teeth, which are firmly clenched together.

Sutton very obviously wants to help me but refrains. He adjusts the pillows behind me and rolls onto his side, watching me.

"Nightmares." It seems like such a childish response. Images from my dreams, from my experience, loop in my mind.

His hand rubs over my covered legs.

I lick my lips. "I need to take a shower."

"Let me help you." He sits up quickly.

"Sutton."

"Maci." His tone leaves little room for negotiating, and I love him all the more for it, but I need to be alone. "You're not even supposed to be showering yet, but I know better than to think I can talk to you out of it. At least let me help you."

"Please." I caress his face, the stubble there a familiar sensation, soothing in its scrape against my hand. He leans into my touch. "Please," I repeat.

He scrubs a hand over his face and pushes back his disheveled, sandy hair. "Ok, but I really don't like this. I'm going to help you into the bathroom and be waiting out here when you're done."

"I wouldn't expect anything less, Cowboy."

The tightness in his face softens minimally.

I'm grateful for his assistance as my body has gone somewhat stiff, and the ache in my stomach muscles makes it hard to stand fully. A whisper of doubt creeps through my mind, but I ignore it. It doesn't matter that it's only been a day since someone tried to kill me. I need to do this.

Sutton turns the shower on before he leaves the bathroom, hanging a fresh towel on the rack closest to the glass door. He pauses, looking me over with a pained expression before he departs.

I'm motionless at first. Steam fills the enclosed space. Using as few movements as possible, I slip my underwear off my hips, and they fall easily to the floor. The shirt is going to be another beast.

Getting my right arm loose isn't a problem, but the left tugs at my wound and I hiss, pulling it into the shirt. I focus on my breathing as emotions and pain war within me, shoving the tee off my head.

Through the mirror, I examine the gauze. It's easier to look there. A soft entry to visualizing what's happened to me. My chest tightens, an unpleasant electric energy pulsing through me. I shut my eyes to calm my rolling stomach.

Colt's heavy breathing crashes through my head. I can practically feel the flames from the fire pit licking the air. A phantom twinge yanks at the sutured area, like being stabbed a second time.

I drop my head forward, bracing myself against the cool countertop with both hands, before finally giving in and looking directly at the covered space on my body.

It isn't bloody from the outside. The adhesive from the tape holds strong, tugging as I slowly peel it from the sensitive skin. Although I would love nothing more than to rip this shit off and get it over with, something tells me that won't help the pain any, and it may risk the stitches.

When the bandage is fully removed, I take in the damage. My skin is red and puckered around the stitched puncture, but it's nothing worrisome.

Leading with my back into the water, I finally step into the spray. The warmth is appreciated, but the water trickling over the front of my body stings when it reaches the stitches. Another hiss escapes my mouth.

Apparently, I'm part snake now.

I fill my lungs almost to the point of discomfort before I lean my head back, soaking my hair through. When I right my head and glance down, pink swirls in the water and disappears down the drain. My stomach turns. Again, I push it away and focus on one task at a time.

The comfort that fills me when I pop open Sutton's shampoo and inhale his scent is instant. Relief, like coming home. Ironically, this all started with a homecoming. One that was painful in a different way.

It's a feat to wash my hair with mostly one arm, but I use my left when entirely necessary and eventually manage to rinse. The soapy water runs over my healing wound, and I scrub too hard and for too long over the rest of my body, trying to rid myself of the shame and disgust that live inside me now.

I would love to scrub the stitched area from the inside out. To eradicate any part of Colt that managed to infiltrate my body without my permission, and even the parts that I allowed willingly.

Another wave of nausea passes through me. Disgust at myself, disgust at the situation, disgust at the revelations.

When I finally exit the shower, I pat softly at my tender side before drying the rest of my body.

All of my clothes are sitting in the bottom of Sutton's closet. Something I think he's been counting on while I've been hiding in here. I wrap the towel loosely around me, not bothering to dry my sopping hair, and open the bathroom door.

As promised, Sutton sits on my side of the bed, facing me. He's always been attentive, knowing just what I need when I need it, or even before I've realized. But in this moment, he looks hesitant, and that's painful in a new way.

"Hi." I lean against the doorframe.

He smirks and moves toward me, wearing only his boxer briefs. "Hi, yourself."

I take my time looking him over.

He toys with the tangled strands of my hair as it drips onto the towel around my body. "I guess you want to get dressed now."

"Were you planning to hold my clothes hostage?"

"No. Just making sure you behave."

I cock an eyebrow. "Are you sure that's what you want?"

His face turns serious, and he encroaches on me against the doorframe. "Yes."

His lips brush mine in a whisper of a kiss, and I immediately want more. I know better, though. He's not giving in.

"I'm going to help you with a fresh bandage and clothes, and then I'm going to get you coffee."

My right hand flies to my chest dramatically and I gasp. "My hero!"

Something crosses his face, but he schools it quickly and shakes his head. "Come on."

He chaperones me to the bed, seating me near the head so I can point out clothing for the day. Despite my firm belief that it's unwarranted, I allow him to dress me. Something in his worried eyes tells me he needs it more than me.

Then he sets to brushing my hair, ignoring all of my refusals, before situating me back onto the bed with the excessive pillows stuffed around me.

"Now coffee," he says quietly.

I need no more explanation than that, letting my eyes fall closed as he kisses my forehead. I'm so lucky he's mine.

CHAPTER 6

SUTTON

M aci clings to the mug when I hand it over. "Thank you. This smells amazing."

Color has returned to her cheeks, though her eyes are darker than usual. I sit on the edge of the bed.

She sips from the mug. "You probably have things to do."

"Why do you do that?"

"Do what?"

I readjust my hat. "You always act like you're keeping me from something."

Her lips purse briefly. "I usually am."

"You're not."

One eyebrow quirks up. "Oh? So you don't have springing heifers and calves to check on?"

I can't help the grin that overtakes my mouth or the way my heart thuds even harder for her. "That's sexy as hell."

She shifts the mug to her right hand and reaches with her left to pull my hat off my head and place it on hers. "You're not the only rancher around here."

"That so?" I snatch her coffee and set it on the side table before grabbing her face in both hands and pressing a furious kiss to her lips. She fists both

48

hands into my tan button-up, holding on tightly, and meeting my movements eagerly. "I told you I don't share."

"Good thing I'm not straying." She kisses me again. Her hands release my shirt, sliding into my hair instead. She gives a little tug. "I'm trying to learn all I can. Want to impress the boss." She grins against my lips.

She's made for me. I'm never letting her go. Whatever shit she needs to get through, I'm here every step of the way.

Our next kiss is gentle. Then, she places my hat back onto my head.

My lips ache for more and I kiss her neck gently. "For the record, nothing is more important than you. Not a single thing. This entire ranch could burn down, and my only concern would be for you."

"That's foolish," she chides. She's terrible at taking compliments.

"Then I'm a fool for you."

The blush that rises to her cheeks threatens my resolve, but she's had enough done to her body in the last forty-eight hours.

"I know you're trying to get rid of me, so I'm going to check on everyone."

She drops her chin and pins me with her gaze while sipping her coffee. "Izzy and Leah should be here soon with tacos," she says after swallowing.

The excitement that lights her face is hard to miss, and that simple change makes it easier to leave her in here. "When they get here, they'll need to use the keypad to call to The Big House." I squeeze her thigh and stand. "I'll be back to check on you in a little while."

"I'll be fine." She tries to wave me off again.

I lean over the bed, caging her in. "Indulge me." Her lips taste like caramel apples when I kiss her—I'm going to buy stock in that lip balm—and I want to savor every inch of her. To show her how much I need her. How thankful I am for her.

CHAPTER 7

MACI

When Sutton heads outside, I'm too wired to go back to sleep. I don't have a fighting chance with coffee on board, anyway.

Nervous energy zings around inside me, and a localized throbbing starts behind my eyebrow. I rub at the spot with two fingers.

I throw the covers back, shifting so my legs dangle off the side of the bed. My house shoes are easy to find in the bottom of the closet. My pajama pants will likely drag on the ground, but I don't care.

The bedside table is cool under my hand as I use it to help me stand. The increasing pain in my side reminds me that it's time for another round of pain meds.

Taking my half-full mug with me, I make my way into the bathroom for my pills before heading into the hallway. The stiffness begins to ease from my muscles, even if the wound aches. Moving helps somewhat.

It's a short distance between the bedroom door and the entrance, and I rest my hand against the wall on my left side as I take my time getting to the exterior door to venture outside.

The gravel drive crunches underfoot. I'm not sure where I'm going. I don't really want to be with anyone; I'd be shit company right now. I also silently hope that Daisy doesn't come boop me in greeting.

Despite the dark, the silhouette of the Defender calls to me. With measured steps, I cross what I guess to be twenty-five feet to reach the backend of the machine. The tiny tailgate is open and just above ass height. It takes effort, but I slide my way onto the bed of the off-road vehicle. My feet dangle in the cool November air and puffs of smoke escape my mouth.

I did it on my own. I sip my coffee with pride. Success feels good.

Enough time passes for the sky to change colors as the ranch awakens. Intermittent moos sound and occasionally a bird calls. Faintly, voices shout back and forth. The nearest building is down the hill a ways. I wonder if there are any new calves this morning.

The ceramic mug is cool against my lips, chilled by the morning air.

Crunching gravel draws my attention toward the corner of the house, just before Sutton rounds my way. I perk up.

"Firecracker?" His pace picks up.

"Hey, Cowboy." I cock my head at him playfully.

"What are you doing out here?" When he reaches me, he rubs my arms up and down. "Are you cold?"

I shrug. "It feels nice."

The pad of his thumb is rough as he runs it over my cheek, eliciting goosebumps across my body. "Why didn't you call me?" His voice holds less frustration than anticipated.

"I couldn't sit still, and you hadn't been gone long."

He holds my gaze for a long moment. "How are you feeling?" I open my mouth, but he interrupts. "And if you even *think* about saying 'fine,' I will haul your ass inside so fast your head will spin."

A small giggle bubbles out of me. "I'm a little sore."

"Do you need more pain meds?"

"No, I took a dose before I came out. They don't get rid of it all, though."

"Stay put." He grabs my mug from beside me on the tailgate. As he turns to go, he gives me a sharp look. "I mean it. Your stubborn ass better be right fucking there when I get back."

My eyes widen and my cheeks heat. Sutton being a man of few words has never bothered me. He conveys plenty through looks alone. Coincidentally, he also has a certain way with words, and as usual, I'm immediately on fire when his commanding side comes out. "Yes, sir."

It's wildly satisfying when his eyes flash before he walks away.

As promised, I stay put until he returns carrying a full mug.

"Thank you." I sip my coffee. A low groan rises from me at the renewed warmth. "Any new calves this morning?"

Sutton hides a smirk. "Not today. Do you want me to help you in? I have a few more things to do."

I shake my head. "I'll head in soon and get dressed." I'm reminded of the day I met him as he continues to stand silently. He stood on Nana's porch while I came close to a mental breakdown, just letting me go through whatever I needed to. I wonder if he knows he was a safe haven for me then, just as he is now.

"Ok. I'll come check on you in a bit." He kisses the top of my head before heading around the front of the house and disappearing, giving me one last look over his shoulder.

When the sun is fully up, I slide off the tailgate slowly and make my way inside. The painkiller has kicked in and my side is only a little sore for the time being. It makes getting out of pajamas and into clothes for the day easier. I know I'm supposed to be taking it easy, so I assume healing is going to take a bit longer than they suggested because I can't possibly sit still.

Someone knocks on the door. Anticipation floods my system. No one has ever come around when Sutton isn't here. Not that I've spent much time alone here. I enter the hallway to open the door.

"Jesus, it took you long enough, gimpy," Leah says, grinning wildly, and Izzy shoves her with a shoulder. "Too soon?"

"It's barely seven thirty; I didn't expect you so early!"

"Well, you'd have known we were coming if you'd bothered to check your messages." Leah pushes her way through the door.

Izzy holds up a take-out bag. "We brought tacos!"

"Come on, we can eat in the office," I say, leading the way to Sammie's old room. I've yet to meet Sutton's sister, but with any luck we'll make the trip soon.

Izzy points to the couch. Because of course, she's forcing me to sit. I do, with an added look of annoyance. "I already know you haven't been resting," she says.

My jaw drops. "Excuse me, I am—"

She pins me with the face of a teacher instead of her true dental hygienist nature. "Don't even try it. We saw Sutton on the way in."

"Traitor," I grumble, crossing my arms over my chest.

"Even if we hadn't, you never listen to anyone."

They both ignore my half-hearted glare. Leah finds everything she's looking for and falls onto the couch next to me with a stack of tacos. "Ow. This thing hasn't been used much."

I snicker. "I don't think it's a common office. It's just Sutton's."

She looks around the rustic space. "You guys break in that desk yet? Eh?" Her elbow makes contact with my ribs, and I'm thankful she's seated on my right.

"How are you?" Izzy leans against the desk, ignoring the tinfoil-wrapped goodness behind her and Leah's joke.

I unwrap the first taco Leah sets on my leg. "I'm fine."

"Liar." Leah takes a huge bite of taco to hide her quip.

"Just sore and a little tired. I didn't sleep great."

"Why?" Izzy asks. "Is the pain waking you?"

This time, I take a bite to buy me time. She continues to stare at me, waiting. A habit that she and Sutton share.

"No. Waking up a lot, but it's not pain."

Her face softens. "Nightmares?"

I fold the aluminum foil back over the taco and pinch it closed without responding.

"You didn't tell the cowboy, did you?"

It's not lost on any of us that he's actually a rancher, but he never corrected me, and the name just stuck. I shake my head.

"Why?" Leah's mouth is full of egg and tortilla.

"He's so busy trying to take care of me, he's not focused on the ranch. And I think something is bothering him."

My friends exchange a look.

Izzy drops down from the desk. "He's probably freaking out a bit."

"Exactly. So I don't want to pile on another thing for him to worry over."

"Maci Grace, you both had a scare. It's going to take some time for things to right themselves. But you keeping things from him isn't going to stop him from worrying."

"I know." I study the tinfoil intently.

"Eat. Then we can go get the rest of your stuff from Nana's." She stands and picks up a taco from the desk.

Nana's? It's true, the only things I have are items I accidentally left after the first weekend I stayed here, and the couple of items my friends packed. Still, I hadn't considered going over there.

"It's ok. I'll just run some laundry here. I'm sure you two have things to do today."

"I'm off," Leah says, opening another taco. She watches me blankly while she chews, but I know better.

Leah isn't pushy in the way Izzy is. She doesn't ask the hard questions or push me toward the things that make me uncomfortable. But she still makes a point in her own bold way.

I scowl at her. "How's Lily?" Two can play that game. She's made a point to use Nana's passing and the things going in my life as an excuse not to talk about her own, but I know better.

She swallows and sticks her tongue out at me. "I'll manage my sister. Quit deflecting."

Izzy sighs. "Well, I'm not off today. I have time, but if you don't want to go over there, I'm not going to force you." There's an unasked question hanging on the end of her sentence.

I blink. "I'm just not ready."

"Ok. I understand."

An angry part of me rears up, saying she doesn't understand—she can't possibly—before guilt creeps in. None of this is her fault, or anyone else's who's looking out for me. And it's not like she's pushing.

"So, what's the plan? You're staying here?" Leah wads up her taco wrappers.

"For now. We haven't set a date on me leaving, but when I'm healed, I'll head back to Nana's."

"Mhmmm." Leah's drawn-out hum rings with skepticism.

"What?"

"Oh! Nothing!" Leah feigns surprise, her eyes huge as she blinks repeatedly at me.

This time, I stick my tongue out at her.

Izzy snickers from her place near the desk.

We finish our breakfast with discussion of Thanksgiving, and I'm grateful for the topic change, even if I have no idea what the holiday will look like for me.

We clean up our trash and head to Izzy's car parked in the drive.

Daisy rounds the other side of the house as we near the front porch steps. She beelines for me, albeit slowly, because she's a cow. I'd be lying if I said I didn't experience a flutter of warmth at her memory.

"What the fuck?" Leah nearly screeches next to me.

"It's just Daisy." I smile and meet Daisy halfway.

"Of course Sutton's cow is named Daisy."

Daisy boops me with her cold, wet muzzle. I giggle and rub the bridge of her nose. She's gentler than the last time she greeted me, which I'm thankful for given the circumstances.

"I doubt he named her," Izzy chimes in.

Hoofbeats thud along the ground, drawing all of our attention. Sutton comes around the house from the same side Daisy did, astride Johnny Walker, his red gelding.

My cheeks rise as a wide smile overtakes my face. I've always joked about him being a cowboy, but I've never seen him ride before. The sight does things to my insides.

He grins and hops down effortlessly.

"I was beginning to wonder if that hat was all for show." Leah smirks at Sutton from next to me.

He smiles. It's not the smile he gives me. In fact, I'm not sure I've seen this one before, and I wonder if it's for show, given everything that's going on. "Thanks for coming out with breakfast. Looks like you found her ok."

"Yeah. She was where you told us," Izzy says. She looks between us. "We'll talk later. Call if you need anything. Either of you."

"What she said." Leah hugs me. "Love you."

"Love you, too." I release her after a quick squeeze and wave as they walk to Leah's car.

Before they've disappeared at the fork in the drive, I have a text.

Don't forget to talk to the cowboy.

> **Hands free. Eyes on the road.**

I'm not driving.

> **And don't tell me what to do.**

Izzy:

Someone needs to.

Sutton slides an arm around my waist and kisses my temple. His voice is low, and his breath tickles my hair. "You look beautiful. How are you feeling?"

Heat fills my cheeks at the compliment. "Good."

His lips press together, no doubt analyzing my every word.

I breathe a laugh. "I'm fine. You don't have to keep checking on me."

He grips my chin between his thumb and forefinger. "Yes, the fuck I do. And the sooner you figure that out, the better. I don't check on you out of responsibility. I check on you because I want to know how you are. And I want to help you when you need it."

My throat thickens as I stare into his stormy eyes. With both hands, I reach around his neck and pull his head down to kiss me. It's tender at first but quickly turns hungry, giving into a need we share fueled by fear.

Breaking the kiss, he rubs his nose against mine. "Stop fighting me all the time, Firecracker."

"But it's what I do best." I give him another peck.

"That's true. But you don't have to work so hard at it."

Rumbling fills the air, speeding closer. The front door of the house slams open. Sutton and I look up to the porch, where his dad, Michael stomps out. He cocks a rifle, and my eyes widen.

"Dad, what the hell!"

Behind us, the noise draws nearer. Several motorcycles travel up the drive together, pulling into the circular space in front of the house.

Mr. Strickland gestures their way with his chin and projects his voice. "Said they want to see Maci."

Sutton looks at me as I eye the bikes.

James leads the group.

"Everything's okay." I raise my voice over the engines.

They park in a sort of pod and cut their engines. James is the only one to get off his bike.

Sutton and Michael stare at me. "It's my dad," I manage.

"Pardon?" Mr. Strickland says, lowering the gun he's holding, as Sutton says, "Come again?"

I'm sure Sutton's remembering the night on Nana's porch when I told him I wouldn't know my dad if I saw him. I rub a hand over my face. "I haven't had a chance to tell you. He came by after lunch on Saturday."

Sutton looks between us as James approaches. "You're sure?"

I nod. "Yes. It's fine. I promise."

"Gracie," James says, his Irish accent only hinting through the nickname.

My upbringing tells me to smile and be polite, but with the way he keeps showing up unannounced, it's hard. "Hi. I didn't expect to see you here." Sutton's posture is stiff as he studies the group. "This is Sutton. I told you about him."

James shakes Sutton's hand and they hold each other's eyes for a moment. I don't know what kind of role my estranged father wants in my life, but I'm hoping he and Sutton start off on the right foot.

"This is his father. Michael Strickland." I gesture to where Michael stands on the porch. James nods in his direction.

Sutton holds my eyes. "I have some things to do. I'll let you two talk." He kisses my head and surveys the rest of the bikers before mounting Johnny Walker and riding off behind the house.

The front door closes. I don't bother looking to see if Michael went inside.

James looks me over, his appraisal intentional. "Your rancher is awfully keen on you."

"It's mutual."

He nods. The sleeves on his white dress shirt are rolled up again. It doesn't look windblown despite the ride. His dark jeans and riding boots look the same as before. "Heard there was an incident. Needed to see for myself."

Instead of responding, I look behind him to his companions. Four other men sit on or mill around their motorcycles, their eyes scanning and bodies tense. Two study me openly, one my age and one James'. The other two scan the property.

I trail the lines of the large bird patch on the back of one of their leather cuts. The wings are spread wide like it's landing.

"Hawks?"

"Falcons," he corrects, calmly.

I frown, returning my gaze to him. I'm sure there's symbolism there, but I don't question it. "Why did you bring all of these guys with you?"

He stuffs his hands in his pockets, but it's not a sheepish move. "Habit." He smirks. "Were you hurt?"

Even though he's very good at casually directing the conversation, the hint of fear over potentially losing something he only just got back isn't lost on me. His face remains composed, a little cocky even, so I don't know how I know he feels that way, except that *I know*.

My side throbs as if pain has been summoned. "Stabbed. It was Colt." I motion around the wound with my hand.

He looks toward my hip and his face tightens, but he doesn't seem surprised at the mention of Colt.

When he draws his eyes back up to mine, his features smooth over. "You finished him."

He's direct but not callous. I press my lips together and give the smallest nod in affirmation. No one else has said it. We all know, but we skirt the issue. I clear my throat.

A twitch in his cheek and the gleam in his eyes hints at pride. "Good. Does your mam know?"

"Not yet." The words are clipped.

"What was all this about?"

I shift on my feet. "Colt's dad."

James' full eyebrows pull together.

"Long story short, his dad is my stepfather. Somehow, he blamed me for that."

His eyes darken and several beats pass before he responds. "I'm sorry you had to handle that on your own."

I lack what feels like an appropriate response. I don't blame anyone for what happened, nor do I wish anyone else had been there. The situation was shitty, and I did what I had to do. Anyone else being there would've escalated everything and made the whole thing that much more dire.

"Lots of people lookin' out for you here." He removes his hands from his pockets and scans the front porch. "Hope it didn't cause a problem, me coming by."

I can't determine if he's being authentic or not, and I realize there's so much about him I don't know.

"I think everyone is just on edge after what happened, and Sutton and I haven't had a chance to discuss much." A painful breath escapes me. "I'd like if we could all have dinner together or something."

"We can. You know where to find me." His face softens. "You did good, lass."

As he turns to go, I swallow again, pushing down all the emotions rising to the surface. I don't have time for all that right now. To uncover his meaning, or to decide whether or I not I think he's right. I need to get off my feet.

CHAPTER 8

MACI

Sutton's weight causes a dip in the bed. When I peel my eyes open, he's lying on his side, watching me. "I didn't mean to wake you."

"It's ok. What time is it?" My voice is croaky again.

"About six. I came to see if you were hungry."

My eyes widen and I push up to sitting, wincing at the ache in my side. "Wow. I just sat down to rest for a minute."

"You're amazing, Firecracker, but you don't have to push yourself so hard." He twirls the hair that's fallen on my shoulder around in his fingers. "I'm glad you finally got a little rest."

"Should we clean up for dinner?"

He exhales heavily. "Yeah."

I swipe my phone off the side table as he heads into the bathroom to wash up. There are several notifications in the group thread with Izzy and Leah.

Izzy:

Did you talk to the cowboy?

Leah:

Hello?

> **Quit the radio silence.**

Izzy:

> **You can't avoid this forever.**

> **Or us.**

Leah:

> **That's it. We're coming out there if you don't message by dinner time.**

Izzy:

> **I'm leaving in five to pick you up, Leah.**

I roll my eyes at their wholly unnecessary escalation.

Me:

> **Jesus, calm down. I took a damn nap.**

Leah:

> **You don't have to be so snappy.**

> **>devil face<**

Izzy:

> **Did you talk to the cowboy?**

Me:

> **OMG MOM, I will!!**

> **And do not show up out here. I can't be held responsible for my actions if you do.**

"Everything okay?" Sutton's warm voice draws my attention.

I lock my phone and lay it back on the table. "Yeah, just Izzy and Leah being overbearing as usual."

He smiles softly. "You could do worse than a couple friends who check in on you."

Raising my eyebrows at him, I slide my feet into my boots. "So could you."

He grunts in response.

Dinner with Sutton's parents is quieter than the last time we dined together. Andi is always one to fill the silence with words, but even she falls quiet a few times. Despite her protests, I help clean up after we eat.

"I won't break if I load a few dishes into the dishwasher," I promise her with a wink.

She shakes her head at me in that loving way mothers do. At least, the way I assume mothers do, because it's a habit Nana had. Stephanie has never looked at me that way, with crinkled eyes and a tight mouth.

Michael retreats to his office after dinner. I don't know what he makes of everything, but despite his quiet nature, I don't get the impression he's judging me.

As soon as the last dish is clean, Sutton whisks me back to his private area of the house. He showers while I change into his shirt from last night and apply a fresh bandage to my stitched body. I crawl into bed and wait for him to emerge, hoping that he'll come out in just a towel, shaggy hair still dripping.

He does not.

He returns from the bathroom in dark, cotton, drawstring pants hung low on his hips. I've never seen him wear them before, and my mouth immediately begins to water. His perfect torso is dry, and each sculpted line is on display in the amber glow of the lamp as every shadow points lower to what's hidden in his pants.

He pauses at the foot of the bed. "Behave."

My cheeks heat and my lips part. "I'm just lying here, broken and helpless." This elicits the most beautiful laugh from him, and his face lights up in the way I love. He's truly an exceptionally handsome specimen of a man.

As he crawls under the covers, he opens his arm up for me to snuggle closer. "You are far from helpless, Firecracker."

If he knows about the ache between my thighs, he doesn't show it. I blame my stupid stitches. He crushes me to his side and neither of us speaks as we rest against each other. Like last night, it isn't long before his even breathing has me on the verge of sleep. I wrap my arm over his warm body, desperate to stay in this moment, in this perfect safe space, for a little longer.

By Tuesday, my brain seems to have cleared enough to handle all the things I've been avoiding at Strickland Ranch.

After coffee, I make my way onto the front porch of The Big House and settle into a creaky rocking chair. I wonder if these were also made by Sutton's grandfather.

I make my anticipated first call of the day. As Nana's lawyer and executor of her will, if Hank hasn't been notified of what took place at the house, he needs to know. He answers on the second ring.

"Hank Campbell speaking." He has such a smooth voice. It's not as deep as Sutton's, but still just as comforting.

"Hi Hank, this is Maci McCullough, Ruthie's granddaughter." My feet press harder onto the wood planks of the porch, picking up speed in the noisy chair. "Unfortunately, I'm calling with news on the house."

"I wondered if I was going to hear from you all."

I pause. "Have you already been notified?"

"Yes. The detective came by my office yesterday morning." He lets a breath pass. "Are you alright?"

What a loaded question. "I'm healing."

"Maci, I can't imagine what that was like for you. I know we aren't exactly friends, but if you need some legal assistance, let me know and I'll point you in the right direction."

My throat threatens to close. "Thank you."

"I've scheduled crime scene cleanup, and I'll handle all of the behind-the-scenes items."

"We don't deserve you." I hadn't even considered crime scene cleanup or anything else that needs to be done.

Hank lets out a chuckle. "There's nothing to deserve. For one, this is the role I signed up for and I'm the most qualified to handle it, anyway. But also, Ruthie was a very kind person and I'm glad to help her family where I can." He sighs. "It's not my place to say, but I couldn't help but notice all the tension in the house while I was there—and I know what the will entailed—so I imagine it didn't get any easier."

"That's a bit of an understatement," I say, wryly.

"Well, I meant what I said. If I can help in any way, I will."

The thought of having someone on my side who isn't family or my boyfriend brings me a sliver of comfort. Someone who has connections and knowledge of the laws. "Thank you."

"I have a meeting to get to. Was there anything else?" Hank's voice is soft instead of dismissive.

"No. I really appreciate you, Hank."

"You bet. Talk to you soon, Maci."

One call down, two to go.

My second is to the Bull Creek Police Department. I'm surprised I haven't heard more from Detective Porter about not coming in yet. I leave a message with the officer that answers that I'll come by tomorrow. He seems unphased by my call.

My final call is the one I'm looking forward to the least: Stephanie.

CHAPTER 9

STEPHANIE

D read sits heavy in my stomach since Mother died. It never occurred to me that we wouldn't get the chance to mend things. Now, Alan wants to contest the will. I want nothing from my mother's estate, aside from the few items I brought back after the funeral.

Before James, I thought she'd never be happy with me. I spent so much time as the rebel, I just assumed it wouldn't happen. After I left him, I was embarrassed. Ashamed. It was then that I decided I needed to shape up. I could be poised and put together. But it didn't help our relationship. A stable husband who could provide for Maci and me didn't either. We never could get on the same page.

Contesting the will after all of that just seems like a slap in the face to her. I could never do that.

So, the dread deepens. I contemplate if I'm getting an ulcer. When Alan returns from his work trip, he'll want to know where I stand. He'll want to know I stand with him. I'm not sure I'm prepared for his response when I tell him no.

Maci's name lights up my phone screen just as I'm getting back from the gym. I can count on one hand the number of times she's called me in the last six years.

I swipe the green button, noticing the state of my nails. I haven't gotten them done since before the funeral. He will have something to say about it if they're in this condition when he returns. Alan used to tell me the nail care was for my benefit. To be pampered. But the sweet gesture became frustration whenever I would decline or allow too much time to pass.

"Maci? Is everything alright?"

Her tone is formal, but less confident than usual. "Do you have a few minutes to talk? There are some things we need to discuss."

"This sounds serious." Normally, I'd go straight for a shower after the gym, but Maci has me curious. Eyeing the security camera in the ceiling corner, I tuck my legs against the couch, crossing them at the ankle.

"It is."

"Well, you caught me at a good time." I wait for her to continue. I would've assumed she said all that was needed at our lunch over the weekend. She has my propensity to lash out, though I tried to curb it in her. Her will has only grown since leaving home.

"I don't even know where to begin," she says quietly. I'm not even sure she's talking to me.

"For heaven's sake, you've got me on pins and needles. What's going on?" My annoyance is more about a lack of control than not wanting to hear what she has to say. From the jump, she was a dramatic child.

"I met my father."

"James?" His name sticks in my throat. I haven't said it aloud in too many years, though I used to sigh and scream it for so many reasons.

"Yes. He came to see me on Saturday, after you left."

"Oh?"

She continues, "He saw us together at lunch and decided it was time to clear the air. But you had already left and since the cat was partially out of the bag when he showed up at Nana's, he told me the rest."

"The rest."

"He told me how in love you both were. How you eloped to Vegas." Maci's words come across kind instead of smug. Maybe she hasn't seen me spontaneous, but she doesn't seem cynical.

James lit liquid fire in my veins with his touch. I thought nothing could ever come between us. Every day without him has sent me deeper into a cold cavern of despair.

She continues when I can't bring myself to speak. "Told me that you found out about his brother—his family—and got scared. That you left him a note."

When the news of Corbin's death reached us, the fear was overwhelming. Would they come for James, too? Maci? Would he want us to move to Ireland? "I did what I could to protect you."

"I know."

"I—what? You know?" For the first time in too many years, she believes me. I expected more disdain.

"Yes. James confirmed that the way you handled things was probably the safest option. And based on what he said, I would've been scared shitless and run with my daughter, too."

"Maci." Even as I half-heartedly reprimand her for her language, I don't fully believe what she's saying. Maci has the kind of strength I wish I could have held onto. She's tenacious, untamed. But I'm not convinced James would have thought me leaving with our daughter was best, so I wonder why he would've said it.

How could he think what I did was right when we hardly had a conversation about it? And why is she so quick to believe a man she's just met?

"That's not all." Her tone changes abruptly, like she's leading into something else. Meeting James is a pretty big event, given that Maci hasn't seen him since she was almost four. I can't imagine what could be bigger.

"Go on."

"There was a guy I met right after Nana passed. Here in town. At a bar."

Seriously? We may not have agreed on much, but surely I taught her better than to get knocked up by some small-town hillbilly. "Oh, Jesus, Maci. Please tell me you're not pregnant."

"No!" A shocked anger infuses her words. "Wow. That's the worst you could think of?"

I recall my conversation with Mother when I called to tell her James and I had eloped. She'd asked if I was pregnant and I was horrified that she thought so little of me, despite my wild nature. Then I got pregnant with Maci during our honeymoon and all but confirmed her initial thoughts. I'm not sure she ever believed me. No wonder they say you become your parents. "I just want you to do things the right way."

"That's a conversation for another time." She brushes me off, annoyed, and redirects the conversation. "The guy...he's not very nice. Well, wasn't."

I tap the side table with my nails.

"Has Alan gotten any bad news lately?" she asks abruptly.

I steal another look at the camera. Nothing blinks, or otherwise changes, to indicate if he's watching. I'm suddenly thankful there's no sound included. "I haven't heard from him in close to a week, since he left town for business."

Early in our relationship, we worked out the kinks of me calling while he's away. He can't usually get out of meetings, so it always made more sense for him to call when he's available. He's usually quite busy when he's gone though, so the calls are rare. I don't pretend to be interested in pharmaceutical sales, and he doesn't attempt to tell me much about work.

Silence from Maci is usually an indication of worry. Or that she's ignoring me, which she does well. I'm about to tell her to get on with it when she continues. "This man...he was Alan's son."

"Colt?" Two estranged family members in one weekend? That seems too coincidental.

I seem to have unknowingly confirmed something for her. She grunts a "Yes."

"You know him?" I ask, despite her saying as much. I never met Colt. While Alan and I dated, their relationship was strained. After we moved, Alan all but forbade me from speaking of him. Once, I asked one too many questions and Alan gave me a bruise that lasted for a long weekend after his temper got away from him. Colt never came up in conversation with Maci for that reason.

Maybe she could've asked about him more, but she avoided Alan and anything pertaining to him like the plague. She has always been on edge with him, like a dog that distrusts someone based on something only it can sense.

Her breathing is audible now. "I knew him."

My eyebrows pinch. "Maci, get on with it. Tell me what happened. I don't understand." Her rising panic is fueling my own, dredging up too many unwanted memories.

"Colt and I met after Nana passed. Let's just say, he was a Class-A asshole. Unfortunately, his behavior escalated. He attacked me at Nana's house."

I stare at the plush, beige carpet, trying to process what she's said. Maci quiets, but I can't bring myself to respond.

"He stabbed me. After a very lengthy discussion where he told me that he was the person who attacked you and me in the parking lot ten years ago."

The pounding of my heart in my ears threatens to drown her out, and the room begins to spin.

Maci prompts, "Are you listening?"

"I..." Is this a heart attack? My arm doesn't hurt, and I think I'm too young, but something low in my chest threatens to burst. "Colt attacked us?"

"Yes." Maci's voice softens. "He thought you and I were taking everything from him. But his plan to teach us a lesson backfired. I'm not even sure what he wanted to achieve. Anyway, he claimed that Alan knew he was the one to attack us and that Alan told him off and never contacted him again."

My marriage with Alan wasn't exactly a love match, but surely he would've told me if his son was disturbed. Right?

"Did he ever say anything?" Maci's tone is insistent, pressing for answers. Answers I don't have.

Something breaks in me. How do I always manage to choose wrong? Every single choice I've made. "No! Nothing!"

"There's more to this story, but I need to know you can get out of there." Maci's voice is muddled.

"What? Get out of where?"

"I'm worried for your safety, Mom."

Mom.

"Maci?"

Her voice is laced with tears. "He was going to kill me. I shot him. It was the only way..."

The room is a spinning blur. My hand flies to my mouth. "Oh my God. Is he dead?"

"Yes. I think you need to leave Alan. He may retaliate."

Has he heard? Would he come home without telling me? If he could hide that his son attacked me, anything seems plausible. "I'll think about it." What would I even do if I left? I gave up my tiny career to be a useless trophy wife for him. "Are you ok?"

"Yes. I was seen by a doctor and I'm recovering fine."

Our conversation ends with a promise to follow up. I get the impression Maci's not told me everything yet. I can't tell if it's her usual guarded nature with me, or something else.

After we hang up, I contemplate everything she's told me. Once again, I'm faced with leaving my husband out of a necessity for safety.

Was it all for nothing? It feels like it. Can you feel betrayal from a man you never loved?

So many moments from the last ten years spiral through my brain. Indicators that something was really off. My panic gives way to anger. Rage. That I've allowed so much to transpire while I sat passively by, just seeking Mother's approval, just hoping to bury my head in the sand.

I had a husband who cherished me, who was a wonderful father. A husband I left at the first sign of trouble, without even a thorough conversation.

Chapter 10

Maci

Sutton kisses me on the forehead when he slips out of bed before dawn. I doze on and off for a while before deciding to get back into the swing of things. Unlike the night at the hospital when the anesthesia suppressed my dreams, nightmares continue to plague me now and my sleep is broken at best.

Moving around is minimally easier today, and I speed up my shower process by skipping a hair wash. After applying a fresh bandage, I get dressed in leggings and a thin, oversized sweater, then pull out my computer. My heart swells. Between the clothing and photography items I left here, and Izzy picking up my computer and a few more items from Nana's, I have all the most important things.

After shoving my feet into my slippers, I grab my computer and coffee mug and head out the exterior door. Maybe Andi will be up for some company.

As the front door closes behind me, I call out, "Knock knock," then roll my eyes at myself. One hospital stint and I've turned into a forty-year-old.

"Oh, Maci! In here," Andi calls before her head peeks out of the kitchen.

The trek up the hall doesn't feel as long as yesterday.

"Good morning, sweetheart. How are you feeling?" She kisses me on the cheek with more sound than lips. "You look good."

My skin warms in a blush. "Thank you. I feel better today. Still sore."

"Oh, yeah. I bet." She points to the half-full coffee pot as she turns back to a bowl on the counter. "Coffee's still hot."

"Perfect. That's just what I came in for. And to see you, of course." When I open the fridge door, I see a bottle of caramel creamer sitting in the door shelf. *Do not cry. Do not cry.*

Andi smiles brightly over her shoulder. "Oh! Sutton mentioned you prefer caramel, so I picked some up while I was out yesterday."

"I—" There are no words. Heavy tears fill my eyes. "Thank you."

"Of course. You let me know if there's anything else you need."

I hum a response and set my computer in the dining room. With a full cup, I lean against the far counter, watching her work. "What are you working on?"

She dumps the contents from the bowl onto the butcher block counter. It's a dough of some sort. "It's an easy bread. I have a soup in the crock pot, and I thought fresh bread would go nicely."

It always feels like home in here. I'm reminded of cold days spent in a warm kitchen with Nana. "That sounds delicious. Is there anything I can help with?" Her glance my way is quick, and I anticipate she'll tell me no as usual. "And please, don't tell me no. I'm starting to go a little stir-crazy." I grin.

Her eyes squint, but she smiles on the backside. "I'm sure I can come up with something."

Sutton is so much like her. A man of few words like his father, sure, but his hidden heart of gold is all from this amazing woman. She's become so special to me in such a short time.

We work quietly, me following her instructions to the letter, until there's a lull. "I loved spending time in the kitchen with my Nana."

"I bet." Andi beams. "She was so special. You know our family holds her in our hearts."

"I do." I finish washing my hands and turn to face her. "I don't know if Sutton told you, but my mom and I aren't close. Haven't been for a while."

"He didn't. You know he doesn't take to talking about people much. Or himself, for that matter."

"No, he doesn't." We share a smile. "He's been so amazing. Even before my injury"—I clear my throat of the catch—"always so patient and kind. I'm lucky to have found him."

Andi wraps her arms around me, squeezing me tightly and speaking into my ear. "Oh, honey, you are the best thing that's ever happened to him." She pushes back to arm's length. "He's always been intense, but he's lighter with you. I know you two will take things on your own terms, but he does it because he cares."

Her eyes turn glassy and she swallows hard. "I hate that you haven't had enough people love you unconditionally. But I am so happy, *so* happy, that my son gets to be the one to show you how it's done."

Tears trickle down my face.

The front door closes firmly and we both jump, though a shared happiness flows between us. I use the back of my hand to wipe at my face, trying to get myself in order before whoever it is comes walking in.

As if I don't know. I'd know Sutton's steps anywhere.

He rounds the corner and grins broadly at me before his face drops.

"Hey, Cowboy." I smile widely.

His eyes flit between Andi and me. "Mama, why is Maci crying?"

"I'm standing right here." I tip my chin down indignantly.

Andi smiles. "We were just having girl talk. Don't you worry." She pats his arm.

He considers for a moment before relenting. When he wraps me in his arms, I melt into his chest, wrapping my own arms around his middle and trying to cover my wince at the stretch. He kisses my forehead. "I saw that."

"I have no idea what you're talking about." I pull back and open the oven, sliding in the muffins Andi had me working on.

He hums a response and grabs a glass for water, as usual. "Just came in to check on my two favorite ladies." He smiles at us and I swear his mom blushes. She's adorable.

"I'll walk you out," I say, once he's downed the glass.

"Walking me out of my own house?" He raises his eyebrows at me.

"It's not your house," Andi says, as we head down the hallway. "You're building your own."

Sutton opens the door for us, following me onto the porch. Once the door is closed, I speak again. "Do you think you'll have a late night?"

"Actually, no." One hand slips around my waist, pulling me to him, and the other pushes a strand of errant hair behind my ear. "Missing me?"

I place my chin on his chest and look up at him. "Yeah. A lot. And I think we need to talk."

"Sounds serious." His tone is playful.

"Important."

"Ok. I'll be in for dinner and we can talk after. That ok?"

"Yes. Actually, I need to head into town."

Sutton pulls back and looks me over. "Everything ok?"

"Yes," I give him a faint smile, "but I haven't been in to speak to Detective Porter, and the last thing we need is more people coming out here to look for me. I'd rather go to him on my terms."

"I'll come." He shifts his hat.

"No." His jaw tightens. "Please. I can't feel like I'm always pulling you from other things. I'm fairly certain the worst that can happen already has. I'm just going to have a conversation with him."

He doesn't look convinced. Several silent seconds pass. "I think you should have a lawyer with you."

"If they were going to arrest me, I assume they'd have done it by now." I'm aware of my right to protect myself on Nana's property. I'm also aware the police department is taking the investigation seriously.

Sutton scrubs a hand over his face and lets out a long, heavy sigh. "I do not like this. You have no legal protection on your own."

I press up on my toes. "I'll be fine." I brush my lips over his.

Something breaks in him, a wall he's kept up for the last few days. He grabs my head with both hands and kisses me powerfully, possessing my mouth and infusing so many emotions in every press of his lips and swipe of his tongue. Wetness gathers between my legs, and I ignore my side yelling in protest as I reach up to wrap my arms around his neck.

As if he knows, he releases me gently and I stand firmly back on my feet. He gives me one last tender kiss. "I'm sorry."

I fist his shirt in my hands. "Why are you sorry?"

"I know you're sore."

"You kissing me the way you're supposed to isn't doing anything bad to my body."

He smirks. "The way I'm supposed to, huh?"

"Yes," I breathe.

His eyes bounce between mine for a moment, and he leans in once more to kiss me softly. "Just be careful."

Eventually, Andi disappears into her bedroom. I seat myself at the dining room table and pull up my email on my laptop. My thoughts are distracted, and instead of sending many responses, I start researching laws around self-defense, which leads me down a rabbit hole of survivors and their experiences.

Many of them talk about the legal ramifications, and what they went through to be considered "not guilty" of murder, even discussing the financial impact. Few of them share what the emotional experience was like.

Removing my hands from the keyboard, I lean back in the chair and stare out the back window of the dining room. Owning my own business means I can't afford health insurance. I don't have the funds for therapy or anything like it. I hardly know how I'm going to handle all of the hospital bills from this when they start to come in.

At the same time, I suspect I'm going to need some outside help. Help that doesn't come from my friends and family, and certainly not my new boyfriend, who has already taken on so much.

My fingers drum idly on the keys. There are enough online forums about the legal aspect of these situations; there has to be something for the emotional side. After a few more searches, I manage to find a few articles on post-traumatic stress disorder.

Do I really have a disorder? It feels damning. Unfortunately, the symptoms fit.

One person shares their experience with exposure therapy, and how it helped them to cope. I read through more articles on the technique, which involves confronting the memories and triggers of the emotional responses in a gradual manner to lessen the anxiety and other symptoms. It's meant to be done with a therapist, but as that's financially not an option, I decide to try it out myself.

I can face these things slowly and incrementally. I can do this.

I'm pretty sure I've used up all my energy reserves. I manage to climb into the Jeep on my own, then sit idling while I compose myself from exertion before leaving.

This is fine. Everything's fine.

It feels surreal to be driving to the police department. People in town are going on their merry way, and I'm about to walk into a building I may not walk out of.

I might have convinced Sutton to calm down, but it doesn't lessen the severity of what I know is about to happen.

After a final cleansing breath, I grab my purse and head inside. A man in uniform sits at the front desk. He doesn't speak, just looks at me with a bored expression.

"I'm here to see Detective Porter." The confidence I'm going for is lacking.

"Name?" There's no change to his stiff face. His voice is just as blank.

"Maci McCullough."

If he's aware of who I am, there's no outward indication. "Have a seat."

I don't bother to respond, making my way to the row of hard-backed chairs. The first one I come to has something sticky on it, so I skip a few before sitting down.

The officer picks up the desk phone and starts speaking quietly, my name falling from his lips. His head bobs in acknowledgement of something, even though the person on the other end can't see him. The receiver smashes into the cradle and I jolt, but his face is still impassive.

"This way." His volume hardly increases as he stands. There's a door to the right of the desk, and I move hesitantly toward it. "I'll meet you on the inside."

That doesn't sound good.

A buzzer blares and a lock clicks as it disengages. I pull open the metal door with effort. The officer stands at a similar door just inside the small hallway.

"Follow me." He rounds a corner and I work to keep pace. He doesn't have an incredible height on me, but my tender steps make it hard to move quickly. Voices float through doors, although I can't make anything out.

We stop at two black doors, side by side. Nausea washes over me. I imagine that inside these doors there's an adjoining wall with a one-way window. This suddenly feels far more real than I anticipated, and I'm second guessing if Sutton was right about bringing a lawyer. One of these days my fierce independence is going to do more harm than good. I may have reached that time, actually.

The officer shoves one of the doors open and I'm happy to find there is not, in fact, a window of any sort. A table and three chairs butt up against one wall.

"Detective Porter will be here in a minute." The officer closes the door behind him without waiting for me to respond.

He's pleasant.

Claustrophobia creeps in as my stance on the lack of windows changes. I'm not shut in for good, but there's an element to being closed off that doesn't sit right.

I choose the chair in the corner, pulling it farther from the table, and facing the door. Almost immediately, Detective Porter walks in.

"Hey, how are ya?" He closes the door behind him and plops down in the chair opposite me, his notebook in hand. I don't have a chance to respond. "Thanks for coming in."

His voice is relatively welcoming, even as he looks me over with narrowed eyes.

I stare at him. Am I supposed to say you're welcome? I'm not feeling especially cordial.

He smiles at me. It doesn't meet his eyes. There's a too-long moment of quiet between us.

"So, I want to start with what you told me at the hospital. Mr. Young came over to the house on Bluebonnet Cove without your knowledge."

I nod. "That's correct."

"How did you and Mr. Young meet?" He tosses the notebook onto the table loudly, clasping his hands and looking directly into my eyes. It's open to a page where notes are scribbled on the top section.

If he thinks he's going to intimidate me, it won't work. "We met at The Spur."

"When?"

"October 6th."

"October 6th," he repeats, as if mulling it over. He yanks a pen from his shirt, clicks it loudly to extend the ink chamber and jots the date down. "What was the nature of your relationship?"

I consider for a moment. "I wouldn't really call it a relationship. He bought me and a friend drinks. We talked with him and a friend of his—"

"What friend?"

"Pete."

"What's Pete's last name?" He looks up from writing, waiting.

I shrug. "I don't know."

"You don't know." His tone isn't accusatory, but his gaze is still hard.

My jaw clenches. "Listen. I told you at the hospital, I'm willing to help you. I have nothing to hide. I'll answer your questions, you can check my phone records, pull whatever surveillance from wherever, I don't care. But this will go a lot faster if you stop repeating me and assume that I'm telling you the truth."

He gives me a sarcastic smile from one side of his mouth. *Click.* He tosses the pen onto his notebook.

Does he think that's a power move?

"Ms. McCullough, I don't have the luxury of assuming people who come in here are honest with me."

"Fair enough." I sigh and set my purse on the table. "Colt and I had sex in the alley behind The Spur."

His eyebrows jump before he hides the response.

"I was intoxicated, and he was a pig. It was a lapse in judgment." I press my back firmly into the chair and cross my arms, annoyed at my decision and how I got here, and aggravated at having to face it head-on again. Raised to value perception so heavily, admitting my shortcomings to a stranger doesn't come naturally.

"I thought there was nothing more to it." I shrug. "A one-night stand. My friend got Pete's number, and I planned never to see Colt again."

He nods, clicking his pen again. The sound is a zap of annoyance down my spine on delayed repeat. After a few notes, he continues his questioning. "So, you didn't see him again until Halloween?" This time, his tone is curious.

"Not exactly." I release a heavy breath. "Sutton and I—"

"That's your boyfriend?" I try to overlook his habit of interrupting me as a product of his career.

"Yes. Sutton and I were eating at Granger's a week or so later and Colt was there."

"You talked to him?"

"No. He was leaving and revved his motorcycle in the parking lot. I happened to see him."

He waits. "Nothing was said?"

"No, he was outside. He just gave me a creepy look."

"A creepy look?"

"Yes. A creepy wink." I stare at him.

His face is blank. I don't bother explaining further. He knows as well as I do what kind of expression I'm referring to.

"After that was when your window was broken?" He fidgets with the pen.

"Yes, at the Fall Festival."

"And he admitted this was him?"

"Yes, when he came to my grandmother's house."

He drops the pen again and sits back in the chair. "What happened on Halloween?"

I dip my chin. "He approached me during the Trunk-or-Treat at the dentist's office on Main Street. He was antagonizing me, grabbed my wrists and wouldn't let go, spouting off. I ended up head-butting him."

His eyebrows rise slightly. "Did you receive any injuries?"

I hold my breath on an inhale. All of these pieces sound pretty trivial based on the way he's asking. "A nasty headache. He didn't leave any marks. There's a report." I told him as much at the hospital.

"During any of these instances when you two were together, did he hurt you?"

A rock sits heavy in my gut. Colt managed to make me look like the aggressor, intentionally or not. My words come out quieter than I'd like. "It was self-defense."

Detective Porter says nothing. He continues writing. I assume being evaluated by a psychiatrist feels like this.

I chew my lip. "There's more."

That catches his attention. His eyes pop up to mine. He motions with the hand holding the pen for me to continue. "Go on."

"Colt is my stepbrother."

Licking along his upper teeth doesn't compose his face the way he thinks. The cogs are turning, but he's not speaking.

"We didn't know," I add. A new wave of shame washes over me. This sounds like some country bumpkin bullshit. I can't believe I have to say it aloud. I shift in my seat. "His father married my mother ten years ago. Shortly after, my mom and I were attacked in a grocery store parking lot. Here in town. I'm sure there's a report on that, too." Who knew I had such a paper trail here?

I continue, unprompted, "The man was wearing a mask, and it was unclear what he wanted. Anyway, Colt admitted to me when he was at the house two nights ago that it was him. He thought that I stole his dad, and he was angry."

Detective Porter's raised eyebrows and flat mouth indicate he thinks this is a stretch, and I can't help but agree. "You never met him over the ten years your parents have been married?"

"No." I shake my head. "In fact, I didn't even know his name. Alan, his dad, never talked about him. Look, my mom and I don't have a great relationship. My relationship with Alan is toxic, at best. My high school years were spent in a very cold house. We didn't have pictures up or family dinners or talk about our feelings. In fact, most things got swept under the rug for the sake of saving face."

Detective Porter takes a moment to assess me again. He rubs a hand over his mouth. "Alright, walk me through what happened when Colt came to the house."

I take a Guinness Record-style breath before summarizing the conversation and Colt's odd behavior as best as I can, explaining that I waited as long as possible before pulling out my gun. I let him know how the first shot missed, and how Colt stabbed me in between that and the second shot. "I *was* trying to protect myself. I had every intention of shooting him at that point, but I didn't mean for the gun to go off when it did the second time. It could have easily been me."

He writes furiously in his notebook. "How did your boyfriend come to be there?"

"He was already on his way."

"And the game warden"—he checks his notes—"Nick?"

I blink. "Actually, I don't know."

"Your boyfriend call him?"

"Probably. Sutton is a rancher. He works long days, and we haven't had a lot of time to talk since the incident. But they *are* best friends." I drop my head, realizing how much we really need to discuss.

Probably because Sutton is trying to be patient and supportive while I sweep shit under the rug, as usual.

"Seems like you two would've discussed this quite a bit." He stares at me, waiting for a response. I don't bother. I don't owe him a personal view into my romantic relationship when it doesn't pertain to what's going on.

"You mentioned phone records. We will be checking them." He looks at me as if I'll recant.

"Yep."

He presses his lips together, but the comforting smile he's going for misses the mark. "I appreciate you coming in. We'll be in touch if we have more questions. You have plans to leave town anytime soon?"

My brows inch closer together. "My apartment is in Austin, but I gave my notice Saturday afternoon. I have work up there, some appointments scheduled."

"If you make any other travel plans, keep me posted. It may seem questionable otherwise, given the circumstances."

I rush to stand. "Happy to."

Detective Porter walks me to the door with the buzzer before he lets me exit alone.

On the steps of the police department, I suck in a huge breath. Somehow, I managed to keep it together inside, but my veins feel electrified—and not in a good way. I adjust my sweater and bag and make my way down the steps toward the parking lot.

A middle-aged woman approaches on the sidewalk. I don't pay her much attention, instead absently rubbing my aching side. The woman stops walking and stares at me.

I side-eye her as I pass, adding more space between us.

"You're Maci, aren't you?" Her voice is quiet, but not timid.

"Yes? And you are?" I halt. My heart rate kicks into overdrive.

"My name is Melissa Garrett." Her face is blank, pale. Her dark hair falls to her shoulders, cut bluntly like she took a set of kitchen scissors to it, and her hazel eyes lack emotion, though they're somewhat swollen. "Colt's mother."

Adrenaline surges through me and my meager breakfast warns at reappearing. This day is getting more and more difficult by the minute. Why have so many of my days gone this way lately?

Stupid fucking small towns.

My mouth opens, but I don't know what to say.

"You probably think you need to apologize right now. You don't need to," she says.

I assess her more closely. The dark circles around her eyes, the translucent tint of her skin.

"I'm not angry with you. I forgave you as soon as I got the news."

My face scrunches. "That's a very selfless thing to do. You don't even know me. Or what happened."

"I don't need to. I knew my son. And he was just like his father." This suddenly feels like a much deeper conversation, and a latent validation of my distrust of Alan all these years.

I look around the sparsely populated lot. "I get the impression you came here for a reason that wasn't to talk to me."

Her eyes pass momentarily to the front door of the police department. "I came to speak with the detective."

"I see." I study my boots.

"You look like you're in pain." She motions to my midsection. "They said you were injured during the incident."

I don't know how much I'm supposed to say. Once again, I feel like I'm in over my head. Yet another reason I should have a lawyer. I hoped by helping with the preliminary process that this would all go away.

Melissa seems to be genuine, though.

"Colt stabbed me."

"Was it serious?" She takes a half-step forward, realizes her movement, and pauses. "This is all so surreal."

"It is," I agree quietly. "It could've been worse." The fact that I'm saying as much to the mother of the man I killed makes me feel ill. I could be dead, and hinting that his death was a better option than mine feels selfish to say directly to her.

"I'm glad it wasn't." Her face twists into a grimace.

"Ms. Garrett, glad you could make it!" Detective Porter calls down to her from the open front door.

Both of us look his way. She waves politely before turning back to me. "Would you be open to speaking again? It can be in public."

I weigh the options. "I'll think about it." I hand her a card from my purse. "You can reach out and I'll let you know how I'm feeling."

She nods solemnly. "That's fair. I hope you have a smooth recovery, Maci." She presses her lips together in an awkward, tight smile.

I can't bring myself to say anything. I only watch as she climbs the steps to meet Detective Porter, whose eyes stay pinned on me.

CHAPTER 11

MACI

After dinner, Sutton and I take the truck to the future site of his house. The sun sets earlier and earlier these days, and the sky is a deep indigo when we park. Still crisp, the gusty wind from earlier has left the air. Dim stars begin to dot the sky.

Sutton pulls a blanket from the backseat and opens the tailgate. I don't move until he comes to my door, swinging it open wide and leaning his front against my seat. Warm breath teases my ear as he tucks his head in close. "Tonight, you're going to let me help you into the truck, Firecracker."

"I'm in the truck." I bite my lip to hide a smirk.

His voice is intoxicating. "The truck *bed*, Maci."

"Are you going to lay me down in it?" I tip my head up, subtly giving him more access to skin. Needing more touch, more fire.

"I am not." He indulges me, kissing down my neck with featherlight lips. "And you're going to behave."

"Yes, sir." I barely manage a whisper. I'm flooded with arousal. With him treating me delicately these days, I don't see a remedy for that anytime soon. Being near him is almost painful.

He pulls back enough for me to see that wicked look cross his face, before he grips my jaw softly in his hand.

"I'm positive you know what that does to me by now." His breath skates across my lips. Despite his grip, I press my chin forward, trying to reach his perfect mouth. His grip tightens. The whimper that escapes me is all need, no pain.

"Don't tease me, Cowboy."

His smile precedes his lips ghosting against my own. I want more. *I need more.*

"You said we need to talk." Like a flipped switch, he pulls back and slips one arm under my legs and one around my back, lifting me from the seat. "Don't get any wild ideas. I don't need you pulling a stitch and bleeding all over my truck."

I'm glad he's feeling comfortable enough to joke.

He deposits me gingerly onto the tailgate and lifts himself to sit beside me. With his weight back on his hands, he's too kissable. Before he can protest, I straddle him, slip his hat onto my head, and glide my hands into his hair. His eyes flash.

"You know what they say about wearing the hat and riding the cowboy." I tease him to disguise the pain.

He groans into my mouth, accepting my soft kiss. The next kiss is firmer, nipping his bottom lip as I pull back. His body is rigid beneath me.

"I feel a little like I'm taking advantage of you," I whisper against his mouth.

Leaning his weight forward and sliding his hands up my back, he kisses my forehead. "It's hard not to worry about you, especially when you don't worry about yourself."

"I'm okay." My response is too fast, and we both know I'm lying.

His eyes darken and he studies every bit of my face. "I thought I might lose you before we got the chance to even start."

93

My hands slide forward to cup his face, the stubble sending a welcome electricity zinging through my body. His steel eyes fall closed and he leans into my touch. "Sutton." He reopens them, holding my gaze. "I'm not going anywhere."

He shifts quickly, gripping my cheeks firmly between his warm hands and kissing me hard. A second one follows, which says so much more than we ever manage between us. It's equal parts soft and strong, give and take. An agreement. A commitment. A need to heal something that's been broken. To push away the fear and try to infuse some hope into our future.

It turns hungry without warning, and we're all tongues and teeth and heavy breathing as our hands roam over each other.

Without warning, Sutton grips my hips and slides off the tailgate to stand, placing my feet on the ground. "We have a habit of getting carried away on this truck bed. One of these nights, I'm going to watch you come undone under the stars, but not tonight."

I refuse to admit my disappointment when he shuts me down and starts me up at the same time.

"Tonight, I'm going to dance with you. We're going to build new memories where we'll build our home and our life. Is that ok?" His fingers tangle with mine as he waits for a response.

"*Our* home?"

His eyebrows dip momentarily. "Of course it'll be ours. Why else do you think I brought you out here before?"

"I just thought you were sharing then." Even as I say the words, they aren't entirely true. I knew there was something he wasn't saying before. A way he was assessing my response.

With our hands still clasped, he wraps both arms around my waist, trapping my hands behind me like he did after our first dance, and drops his chin, bringing his mouth closer to me. "Yes, I was sharing. Intentionally. I wanted to know if you wanted it, too."

"Why didn't you just say that?"

He exhales a silent sigh and one shoulder sags. "I didn't want to push you. I never do. I want everything with you, Firecracker, but I don't want to take it from you. I want you to want it just as badly."

I untangle my fingers from his to place them against his torso. Stretching up on my toes, the pain of the movement eased by his supportive arms still around me, I place a soft kiss on his mouth. "I want it."

"You want this ranch life?"

Why does he seem so surprised? "Yes." I've thought on this considerably.

His hands return to my face, thumb tracing my lips. Something plays in his eyes and his touch stiffens. "That night, there was a moment where I thought the last thing I would hear was you telling me you love me."

I replace his hat. "I didn't say it because I thought I was going to die. I said it so you would know I want to live. That I was going to fight."

His hands come to my hips, and he brushes a kiss over my lips. "You didn't wait to hear it back. You wouldn't know what you mean to me."

I blink to clear my vision. "I was hoping that you were genuine the day before. When you told me you were all in."

His voice is thick. "I was. I am."

"I love you, Sutton. I want this life with you."

He kisses each of my cheeks. " I love you, Maci."

"I'm not always really good at talking about my feelings, but you need to know: I want you. I need you. You make me feel light, and free, and happy. So damn happy. And you are where I feel safest. Even when the entire world is crashing down, it's not as scary with you."

I'm unable to continue when he slams his mouth into mine.

His kiss is all consuming and I let him devour me, needing this connection. The last few days have been tense and painful in more ways than one. Whatever it takes to get us on the same page again, I need it.

"That's good. Really good. Because I was considering attaching you to my body to keep you from leaving." His boyish grin soothes my tired heart.

"So, I guess that means I'm not going back to Nana's when I'm healed?"

"Not if *I* have anything to say about it. You belong here. With me." His arms tighten around me. "And don't even try to get up in your head about it. It feels right and you know it."

"It does."

"So, can you please unpack your stuff? There are plenty of hangers and space in the closet, and I'll clear some drawers."

My heart flutters and I nod into his chest.

His lips press softly to my cheek, before lingering by my ear to say, "By the way, I really fucking like how you look in my hat. Expect one soon."

Heat rushes into my cheeks as I grin.

"I blamed the tailgate, but it's your fault."

I laugh. "What's my fault?"

"Did you just laugh?" Sutton pulls me close to him, swaying us gently back and forth.

"I guess I did."

"It's an amazing sound," he says into my hair. "I blamed the tailgate for our inability to have a conversation, but it's just us."

"We do have good chemistry," I murmur into his chest.

He kisses the top of my head. His tone softens as he changes the subject. "How did it go at the police station?"

I grunt. "I'm not convinced Detective Porter believes me. Even though there are reports, only one actually implicates Colt. Everything else is just my word. And it's a tangled fucking mess anyway, so..."

Sutton's arms tighten.

"I think if they had enough to prove I was out of line they'd have arrested me already, but I don't like not knowing where this is going." I listen to the rhythm of his heartbeat and let his warmth seep into me.

After a minute, he speaks again. "I'm not going to push you to talk about what happened with Colt. Not when you first met, and not on that night. But the moment you're ready, even when you don't think you are, I'm here."

I can't bring myself to respond. My grip on his waist tightens.

"It's okay if it's messy. Or ugly." His voice is quieter, even though there's no one around except us. "Nothing you could say or do will make me feel differently."

Keeping myself tucked against his body, it's an effort not to hide my mouth against his chest when I speak. Instead, I hope the chill breeze will carry my words away. "He was Alan's son."

The steady thrumming in my ear picks up.

"He was the one who attacked Stephanie and me before, in the parking lot," I whisper.

"Fuck."

"Yeah, fuck." The temperature seems to drop around us. "How wild is it that he was connected to me in so many ways and we just happened to run into each other at The Spur?"

"Do you think it *was* coincidence?" Sutton's question hangs between us for a minute as I consider.

"I think so. That night, he was different from any other time I saw him. All the other times, it was clear he knew me. I don't think he could've hidden some evil scheme. He was too smug."

"That is wild, then."

I don't go into anything else. The moment is too peaceful to tarnish with the ugliness of *that* night. I just want to enjoy being wrapped in the arms of the man I love, who loves me, and exist quietly in the world for a while.

CHAPTER 12

SUTTON

Johnny Walker grazes in the corral behind the stables as I approach. When I was younger, we didn't have any permanent staff. None of them lived on the property, so the only people caring for the horses were our family.

I was a teenager when Mama and Dad expanded from one herd to two. It took everything they had—a risk similar to what I'm about to make with this potential expansion. The biggest difference is that, for the most part, their growth was incremental. This change is on a much larger scale, and we have a lot to lose if it goes badly.

All of this sits at the forefront of my mind, right beside my worries about Maci and all that's going on with her. I'm torn between doing what I think is right for her and letting her do what she thinks is best because she's a grown-ass woman. But she's a grown-ass woman who I fucking love, and I don't like thinking she's in danger or being painted into a corner.

Johnny Walker lifts his head and studies me, as if knowing I could use a long ride.

My phone buzzes in my shirt pocket as I step into the tack room. I doubt it's Maci, because she's too damn stubborn to actually call if she needs something, but I check anyway.

Sammi.

Now there's a voice I haven't heard in a while.

"Hey, sis," I say, pressing the phone to my ear and leaning against the door frame. "Everything okay?"

Sammi chuckles. "Of course. Can't I call my big brother?"

I frown. "Ok, well now I know somethin's up." The door of the stable office is open and the room is empty. No one uses it. I slide open the window to let in a breeze and plop down in the swivel chair.

"I heard you have a girlfriend, and I want to know when I get to meet her."

My boots thud on the desk as I kick them up. This is going to be a long conversation. The chair protests beneath my weight. "So, you've been talking to Mama."

"Of course I have. Unlike you, she knows how a phone works." Her tone is only half playful. "Anyway, when do I get to meet her?"

I clear my throat. "We plan on coming up soon. I was actually going to reach out and see how your calendar looks coming up."

"Really?"

"Yes, really. Mama overheard that conversation, too. I'm surprised she didn't tell you." I hike an eyebrow, even though she can't see me.

"Well, when are you thinking?"

I sigh. "I'm not sure. I need to talk with Maci more about it. Some things came up."

Sammi hums a non-committal response. She's like Mama. When they're quiet or blank in the face, you know they're up to something or looking for information. "How are you?"

I breathe an exasperated laugh. "I'm fine."

Her beating around the bush isn't doing anything. She's talked to Mama, and that woman can't keep a secret from her daughter to save her life. I wouldn't be surprised if she told Sammi that I said Maci's my future wife.

My fisted knuckles rub against my chest.

"You know, you don't have to handle everything on your own."

"I'm not sure what you mean."

Sammi sighs, and I can see the sister of our teenage years rolling her eyes in an exaggerated manner. "I'm still here for you."

"I love you, but you have a life that isn't here—"

She interrupts. "I'm still your sister. It doesn't mean I don't care just because I'm somewhere else."

"That's not what I mean. I don't need to call you about what I have going on. You have enough going on with a baby, a marriage, and your job." Quite frankly, I wouldn't call even if none of those things were true. I'm not in the habit of talking through things with my sister.

"Sutton, I know you think you need to be the hero, but you don't."

I kick my feet off the desk and sit upright. "I never said that."

"You don't have to. A wall barely separated us for eighteen years. I also saw it first-hand..." Her voice trails off.

Ok, so I beat the shit out of her high school boyfriend when he got too handsy at a party and wouldn't take no for an answer. That wasn't being the hero, though. It was doing the right fucking thing.

I don't bother with a response.

"It sounds like you have a badass girlfriend who was put into an awful situation, and she did what she had to."

"We aren't getting into this." This is the last thing I want to deal with this morning. The exact opposite of what a relaxing ride provides for me.

"You don't need to feel guilty. I highly doubt Maci blames you in any way. It's just a shitty situation."

"Yep." She knows as well as I do that my curt response is an end to the conversation, not an agreement.

101

"Just think about it. And seriously, call me."

"Mmhmm." The office door slams closed against the trim behind me as I head back outside.

"I love you, bubba."

"You, too." I end the call before she can say anything else. I pinch the bridge of my nose to counter the headache coming on.

Having saddled and mounted Johnny Walker, I'm about to head out for my anticipated solo ride when my phone vibrates in my shirt pocket. There's no stopping the heavy sigh that escapes my lips.

I answer without checking the caller ID. "Yeah."

"Boss man, we got a problem," Jason says. There's a hint of concern in his voice. "One of the cows has her head stuck in the fence."

I frown. "The fence?" The majority of the fencing where the herds are is cattle fencing. It's specifically made to avoid animals getting snagged on or stuck in it.

"Well, the gate to the southwest pasture."

"What the fuck." The exasperated words are meant for me only. Our panel gates are definitely large enough for a cow head, and a lot heavier than the fencing, too. "Alright, I'll be down there in a few minutes. Who's with you?"

"It's me and Cody. Kelly's fixing part of the fence line along the road. She's starting to thrash around."

"Do either of you have a jacket?"

"Yeah, I've got one."

"Okay. Toss that over her head to calm her down. I'll grab the cutting torch and head that way. I need to put Johnny back in the pasture. Call Kelly on the radio and have him call the vet. We'll have them check her out after she's loose." There are a few vets in town, but only one that handles cattle. They're familiar with us, and we don't usually have trouble getting them out the same day to check on animals when it's needed.

"Yes, sir."

I move as quickly as possible, removing Johnny Walker's saddle and tack, and put him out to pasture. He paws at the ground and swishes his tail at me in annoyance. Unfortunately, I understand all too well that he was craving this ride.

"Sorry, big guy. Duty calls." I reach for him, but he grunts and takes off before I can pat him. I don't have time to deal with a moody horse, too, so I focus on the task at hand, hurrying to grab the welding torch and get into the truck.

The ride to the south pasture is bumpy, especially after the caliche road ends. By the time I make it to the gate in question, Kelly has also arrived. The cow seems reasonably settled with Jason's Carhartt jacket draped over her head.

I set my hat on its crown in the passenger seat, exchanging it for the welding helmet.

Cody and Jason turn to me as I approach with the torch in hand. Cody grins. "I got a photo in case you want to turn this moment into a meme later."

My brows pull together. "A what?"

Kelly, on the other side of the fence, drops his head and shakes it slowly. I think the reaction is directed at Cody, not me. "Not the time," he mutters, but there's no anger in his tone.

Cody's smile turns sheepish.

I blink and shake my head. "Alright, I'm gonna start cutting. Just try to keep her calm, but watch out for legs." I'm preaching to the choir; these guys know what to expect from the cattle, but it doesn't stop me from reminding them.

When the torch is ready to go, I flip the helmet down, after clocking Kelly once more. I won't have much visibility aside from what I'm doing, so hopefully he's ready. The cow has a soft disposition and stands mostly still while I work. I lift the lid to find her back feet dancing.

Once she's loose, Jason pulls the jacket off her head quickly and she runs the opposite direction of us, finding some shade to settle in.

"You get her earring number?" I ask, referencing her ear tag. We spend quite a bit of time with the cows, giving us a chance to learn their varied personalities. But having the number ensures we know we're handling the right one.

"Yep." Kelly nods. He turns to Jason. "You did good. She was settled. That went better than it could have."

He's right. Once, before this crew, we had a cow get herself stuck in one of the paddock fences and she was as mad as a bull, whipping back and forth. She tore the entire panel down to free herself from it, shaking wildly. It was a risk not only to herself, but all the cattle and ranch hands in the area. Everything turned out okay, but it's better all the way around when things go smoothly, like today, if it has to happen at all.

"Alright, I'm gonna load this up. You guys need any more help down here?"

Kelly looks to Jason and Cody. They all shake their heads.

I nod. "I'm going to head up to The Big House for a bit, after I drop this off."

"We're headed up to the stables." Jason follows behind me. Kelly climbs into the Defender while Jason and Cody mount Dusty and Boots.

Despite our varied modes of transportation, we make it back to the parking area in front of the stables and barn about the same time. I climb out of the truck, replacing my hat. A loud moo greets me, which wouldn't be that extraordinary if it didn't sound close and high.

My eyes rise to the open hay loft of the barn, where Daisy stares out at us.

"Sonofabitch!" I yell. I whip around as Jason and Cody jump down from their respective horses, running up behind me, and Kelly pulls to a stop, cutting the Defender's engine.

Cody's eyes are the widest I've ever seen, and his face turns a bright red.

"Who left the damn barn door open?" I don't bother hiding my annoyance.

Cody doesn't need to say anything. His grimace, which turns from red to green, says it all. "That'd be me."

I press a hand against my forehead, which is beginning to throb.

The barn has entrances on both sides of the building like the stables. The front doors are shut, but it's clear the back door must have been left open for Daisy to enter from the pasture side. Although, it's Daisy. I wouldn't put it past her to open the front damn door and walk right in.

Kelly speaks up. "Jason, go grab some oats and we'll lead her back down the same way she went up," he says.

"Sure, give her a treat," I mutter.

Kelly ignores me, because we both know it's the easiest way to get her down.

"This damn cow is going to market. Like, yesterday." I stalk into the stables to re-shelve the torch and helmet.

"Don't think Mrs. Strickland would be too happy about that," Jason calls behind me, not doing much to hide his snicker.

"Well, she can come get her down from the damn loft then!" My annoyed shout carries out the open doors.

CHAPTER 13

MACI

Aside from the afternoon I spent at the police department, I've been laying low at Strickland Ranch. Spending time on the ranch is beautiful. It's peaceful, and everyone has been welcoming. Loving, even. But even though it has plenty of fresh air, I'm starting to feel shut in.

Despite the numerous check-ins from most of the women in my life, there's still so much I haven't told them all, and doing so is the perfect excuse to get off the ranch for a bit.

I don't exactly have a desire to discuss my personal business in public, especially in this little town. However, Nana's isn't an option since I still can't bring myself to go over there, and I'm not ready to have everyone out to the ranch. So, I come up with Plan B.

Once everyone responds to my mass text, I set up pedicures for all of us in town on Saturday.

Since Sutton is working, I let Andi know I'll be back later. I've decided to try step one of my exposure therapy, so I'm leaving a bit early. Not that anyone needs to know.

So far, the thought of revisiting Nana's and what happened there causes anxiety to barrel through me. My stomach turns, my muscles tighten, and breathing becomes difficult. It's not that I'm afraid that anything is going to happen again. But I've made a point not to revisit the images, and coming face to face with the house will put me front and center of that show.

Maybe if I can just sit outside. On the street even.

But I can't.

I make it as far as the turn off from the county road before the pressure on my chest is too painful, and I pull off the road onto the shoulder. Phantom sirens wail loudly in my head.

Sutton may not have realized how alert I was that night. I'm not going to share the gory details with him, but I remember every second of lying in Nana's yard with Colt's knife protruding from my body—willing myself into a fixed state so I wouldn't completely freak out, even though that's what I wanted to do.

Inside I was screaming, thrashing, kicking. I wanted that fucker's last action done, and nothing left of him attached to me.

The residual feelings of fear are just as prevalent. That I wouldn't make it. That I'd have permanent damage, even if I did. The siren wails should've been a welcome sound, but they caused my heart rate to skyrocket. Not having answers is sometimes easier, because you don't know the worst of things. Sirens meant medical personnel, and a chance that someone was going to give me bad news.

After taking a few minutes on the shoulder, I right my breathing and settle my nervous system. I stare up the road to where I know the house is. I can't go there today, and I'm not sure when I'll be able to.

This is harder than I anticipated.

I swing the Jeep around and head to the nail salon.

The place isn't very big, and it sounds like we'll be mostly alone with the five of us in there at once. I'm a little surprised they had enough openings last minute. The few times Leah, Izzy, and I have gotten pedicures together, we've gone into the city where the salons are bigger and there are more options.

Liv and Randi stand waiting out front by the time I arrive.

"How are you, sweet girl?" Randi asks, smiling, as I climb out of the Jeep.

It doesn't matter that I'm in my mid-twenties; Randi is still just as doting as ever.

"I'm doing better." It's the most truthful I can be.

Just as I'm about to continue, Izzy and Leah pull in. After greetings and hugs, we make our way inside and get seated. The smell of acrylic and nail polish invades my nose, but it's quieter than most salons.

"I'm sure you have a lot to tell us." Liv doesn't waste any time coaxing me into talking.

"I do." Somehow, I've been seated between my two friends on one side and my family on the other. "A lot has happened, and I'm sure you'll have a ton of questions, so..."

"You just say whatever you need to, honey." Randi pats my hand from the seat next to me.

I take a deep breath. The warm water on my feet is soothing, and the ladies in front of us are talking amongst themselves, mostly ignoring us as I begin. I turn to Izzy and Leah. "I'm still planning to move here for good."

Leah does a happy dance in her seat.

"My goal of opening a B & B at Nana's and turning the garage into a dedicated photography studio is still on track. I want to set up some areas around the grounds for photos, but it will give me the option of an indoor space, as well."

Izzy's mouth purses. "Are you going to be living there?"

Leah grins beside her.

I settle deeper into my chair, enjoying the feel of the massage chair balls roaming up and down my back. "Sutton and I had a long talk, and I'm going to be staying with him permanently." I blush as my friends squeal and squeak. "It's just so weird to think that six weeks ago we didn't even know each other, and now he's talking about building a house with me. We haven't made anything official, so if I need the space at Nana's, it's there. But it doesn't seem like I will."

"You move at whatever pace you want." Liv's calm voice carries over the bubbling water of the foot spa. "Don't worry about what other people think. People get married after short courtships all the time. Nana and Pop did. And they were really happy."

Randi smiles softly in agreement.

I chew my lip, considering if it's the opinions of others that make me question making things official with Sutton. "Sutton's been great. His whole family has. I haven't met his sister yet, but I know we'll be headed up to Dallas soon to see them." I take another deep breath. "You may be right, though. No one seems put off by me being there."

Randi wiggles in the seat as the nail technician scrubs her foot. "Does Stephanie know what's happened? Where you are?"

"I only talked to her briefly. She isn't aware of any of this, actually. But she is aware of the incident with Colt and my conversation with James."

"James?" Randi's brows are furrowed.

"Yes, James. My father." Liv and Randi's eyes pop open, creating mirror images. I turn to Leah. "Remember the President of the motorcycle club we saw at The Spur?"

Her eyes widen and she grins. "Does this mean I get a new Daddy?"

I can't help snickering at her joke.

Izzy blushes for her. "You are so inappropriate." But any real chastising is missing.

I continue with a sideways smile, facing Randi again. "That's who stopped by when you were leaving the other day. Before the situation with Colt. He saw Stephanie and me at lunch and wanted to come clear the air." I'd nearly convinced myself that my mother was having an affair she hadn't mentioned to me, which knowing that they were together at some point doesn't seem so far-fetched.

"Did he want anything else?" Izzy is obviously still concerned.

My head snaps back her way. "He wants to get to know me. I think he genuinely cares. In fact, once he got wind of what happened with Colt, he came by the ranch. That was awkward for a minute." I choke on a laugh.

"What happened?" Liv prompts.

I let out a heavy breath. "James showed up with a few club members—"

Izzy's eyes go wide. "A bunch of bikers?"

I don't know why she says it like they're street thugs. I guess Colt didn't help whatever image she had in her mind about them. "He was worried about me. I hadn't had a chance to share who he was yet, and Sutton's dad didn't know what to think. Michael came onto the porch with a shotgun."

"Oh my God!" Izzy's half-panicked. "Sutton's dad?"

I nod through my words. "It turned out fine. But everyone was a little on edge for a moment."

"Why do I get the feeling this isn't why you called us all here?" Randi's legs jerk intermittently from the attention on the soles of her feet.

"There's something I haven't had a chance to share." I exhale a long breath. "When Colt came over, he didn't just start swinging. He had some interesting things to say."

"We're all waiting with bated breath." Izzy smirks.

"Colt is Alan's son."

Her smirk disappears.

"Alan, as in Stephanie's husband?" Randi's face contorts. "How can that be? Wouldn't you have known him?"

I shake my head. "Believe it or not, he and I never met. Stephanie also shared some things with me while she was here for Nana's funeral. If I'm being honest, it's like putting a puzzle together without a reference picture. So, I think I'm still missing something, but I don't know what it is. It all feels a little wild."

"I'll say." Liz is staring off at the wall of nail polishes.

"Did you ask Stephanie about this? Has she met him?" Randi asks, still trying to piece it all out.

I nod. "I did. Do you remember when she and I were attacked at the grocery store?"

"Yes, that's the whole reason you all moved to Austin."

"Yes. That was Colt."

A collective "What?!" passes through the other women. The technicians seated before us all stop talking momentarily to scan us.

A flush rushes from my chest into my face and I clear my throat. "He told me. Alan knew, but he never told Stephanie."

"What do you mean he knew?" Leah scrunches her face as she studies me.

"Colt said that Alan knew he was the one to attack us. That Alan never spoke to him again."

"So then he won't be upset?" Liv doesn't sound sure of her logic as she poses the question.

"Oh, I think he'll be upset. He was like a landmine while I lived with him. I never knew what was going to set him off. He kept himself mostly controlled, but I swear that man is evil. I'm just thankful I didn't see more of it." I pause for a beat. "He got aggressive with me once. Grabbed me and got really demanding. I left after that."

Izzy speaks more to herself than us. "I still can't believe Stephanie didn't do anything then."

Randi looks very concerned, a mirror of what I felt talking to Stephanie about the entire situation. "None of this sounds good, Maci."

"I know." Her echoing my own concerns doesn't make me feel any better. "I told Stephanie I think she needs to leave Alan."

Leah snorts. "Is she going to?"

I shrug. "I'm not really sure. She said she would think about it. I need to call again and see what's happened. It seemed like when I called he wasn't even aware that...well, he hadn't been notified about Colt." My throat tightens and I push down all the emotion threatening to rise.

"I know my sister hasn't been the easiest to deal with, but I wouldn't wish harm on her." Randi's gaze is somewhat vacant as she muddles over what I've shared.

"I wouldn't either," I agree vehemently.

Our group falls quietly contemplative, and I shift the conversation to Liv's classroom.

There's only so much information I have at this point, and I've shared all that I can. I can't bring myself to mention meeting with the detective, or that I happened upon Colt's mom at the same time. My friends and family are concerned enough, and it will only add to that.

CHAPTER 14

STEPHANIE

I sat with the news Maci dropped on me for hours. When another day passed without hearing from Alan, my nerves were at an all-time high. Surely, he'd been notified by now. Colt may have been a taboo subject, but he'd let me know about his passing...right?

Would he take out his emotions on me, as Maci predicted?

It wouldn't be the first time.

Most of the time he takes it out on me in the bedroom. He's never been a great lover, especially where my needs are concerned. Unfortunately, he's not working with much to begin with. But when he's angry, he turns brutish. Rough-handed, impatient, degrading.

What must it be like to make a decision without fear of consequences? I used to. I was the "wild child." Mother was always mad at me, and Dad was always disappointed. Randi could do no wrong. It became our thing, so I continued to do what I wanted.

When I met James, I finally felt seen. He met my wildness with his own calm nature, accepting me completely as is and setting my soul at ease. I thought our marriage meant happily ever after.

I should've known better.

We needed to be close to family after I left James, so I got Maci and me a little apartment in the city. I hoped that keeping us out of Bull Creek meant we wouldn't run into James. And even if anyone did come after him, maybe they'd be just as happy that we were gone.

As if the fear and shame of my decision to leave wasn't enough, I was terrified Maci would see through me. Looking at her daily cracked my heart bit by bit. I still tried. I tried to be the perfect model for her.

Instead, Mother undermined me, and Maci all but disowned me.

Not when she was little. Those first few years she clung to me, her little arms a vise. I couldn't keep her out of my bed; she was terrified I'd be gone in the morning. Talking her through her worries never seemed to help.

Then one day, the pendulum started swinging the opposite direction. She didn't crawl into bed with me. She made herself breakfast in the morning. I thought she was starting to feel steadier, comfortable. It wasn't until later that I realized she was burning our bridge, plank by plank.

Maybe I started the fire.

I tried to be everything, but without James I was nothing.

With Alan, I'm still nothing. A permanent trophy wife who acts as a secretary or a mistress as it suits him.

The more I sit with everything tumbling around in my head, the more convinced I become that Maci's assessment has always been accurate. I'm not blind to Alan's shortcomings, but I did think we had some sort of unspoken agreement.

I'm convinced now that I've allowed myself to be a pawn instead of a queen.

Not anymore.

I'm calling Maci before I've thought things through. She picks up on the second ring.

"Maci." My tone is once again tight. She thinks it's because I don't care, but I do—it's just habit out of need for control. Not that I've had it for a while.

"Stephanie. Are you ok?" Her voice is cautious.

"Yes. I'm calling to follow up on our previous conversation." Everything comes out stiff, so I hurry through. "I'm leaving Alan."

A puff of air hits the speaker on her end and she's quiet for a moment. "I think that's the best idea." She doesn't elaborate. I'm not surprised.

"I'm going to be staying at Nana's house."

"You're coming to Bull Creek?" She sounds like a teenager who got in after curfew.

I huff. "For a short time. I'll need to get affairs in order."

"And then?"

By now, I should be immune to her emotional shields, but her words hurt. She warned me, encouraged me to leave, and yet now she's back to being guarded. Will we never be able to mend our relationship? I never did with Mother. I have only myself to blame.

I don't have all the answers. In fact, I have close to none. "I haven't decided."

"Ok. Well...is there anything I can do?" She's genuine, even if it causes her discomfort.

Suddenly, I wish I was the mother who taught her to be herself no matter what others think, instead of always worrying what they do. Maybe she's become that anyway.

"I don't think so. I just wanted to share that I'll be in town."

After a pause, she continues. "Ok. Well, I'm staying with my boyfriend at his ranch. It's not very far from Nana's, so if you need anything, let me know."

"You have a boyfriend already?" Jesus, she's only been in town a couple of weeks.

She inhales deeply. "I have a boyfriend. His name is Sutton. He was at Nana's funeral, so you may have met him then. Either way, I'll be happy to introduce you."

"You had a boyfriend at—" I'll deal with this later. "How are you? Your injuries."

That's when the front door opens and Alan walks in.

CHAPTER 15

MACI

Sutton opens my Jeep door and I jump, focused on the phone call from Stephanie. He smirks, gripping both sides of the door frame and looking me over without speaking.

"My injuries are healing as expected. Thanks for asking." I manage to answer Stephanie, even though my mouth has gone dry.

He quirks a sexy eyebrow at me. I'm immediately ready for him to bury himself inside me. "We should be hearing from Ha—Mr. Campbell soon with a probate update. If I hear before you, I'll let you know."

"Very well. I'll talk to you soon," she says, her voice floating through the Jeep speaker, then disconnects before I can respond.

Sutton looks me over. He has yet to share whatever opinions he has about Stephanie. He may think it would bother me, but it won't. People are entitled to their opinions, and I'm sure most feel strongly about her. I certainly do.

"How was the salon?" He extends his hand, and I accept it after unbuckling myself.

"We had a nice time. It was good to spend time with them."

"Good." He kisses the top of my head.

I wrap my arms around his torso as he winds his around me and buries his face in my hair. It's hard to believe how different life looks after a few short weeks. If someone had told me six weeks ago that I'd be dating someone, moving in with them, and planning a future together, I would've laughed in their faces. Now, I can't imagine my life without Sutton in it.

If they'd have told me I'd be facing charges for murder in self-defense, I would've assumed they were unhinged. Yet here we are.

"How's your mom?" he asks softly.

I shake my head against his chest. "Difficult as usual. She wants to move into Nana's temporarily."

He doesn't respond at first. "Does that mean she took your warning seriously?"

"Maybe? If she has a plan, she didn't tell me much." Tucked into Sutton's arms feels like home. I don't even care how dirty he is, or what he has on him.

"Are you going to go over there?"

I pull back to look at him. "To see Stephanie?"

"In general."

Every step I take not to be a victim seems diminished by my fear of revisiting the site of my altercation with Colt.

"Maci..."

"Sutton." My face remains composed. At least, I think it does.

He smiles softly. "Fine." His lips brush against mine and I lean up to deepen the kiss, but he pulls back before I gain much purchase.

"I know you just got back, and if you're tired it's fine. But I think we need to get away for a bit."

"Ok." I assess him, trying to figure out what he has in mind.

"Our first date didn't go exactly to plan." He smiles softly when I scoff.

"You mean because my psycho one-night-stand slash mystery stepbrother interrupted us by being even more of a creep?"

His smile stretches into a grin. "Yeah. Something like that."

"What do you have in mind?" I press my chin against his chest and peer up at him.

"How do you feel about bowling?"

A laugh bursts from me as I back up. "Bowling? You bowl?"

"Why is that so hard to believe?" His jaw sets but his face is otherwise soft, and he still hangs on to my hands.

"It's not really." I study him for a moment. "Oh shit. You're really good, aren't you? That was your plan to seal the deal on our first date?" I can't hold in my laugh.

He chuckles. "I like to bowl."

"You like to bowl. Mm-kay." He's right. We need a break from the constant tension. "You don't get to make fun of me."

"So what I'm hearing is you need some lessons."

"Oh no. We haven't even gotten there and you're already getting a bigger head." I feign annoyance and walk around him to go around the house.

He trails behind at a slower pace, and at first, I think he believes my faux anger, until he starts speaking and his tone is taunting. "Are you afraid you're too weak? The ball will be too big, right? Especially since you're injured."

I gape and whip around. His hands land on his hips and he grins at me. I want to photograph him again. I need to start carrying my camera like I used to.

"I'm not afraid."

He drops his hands and approaches even slower than before. "You should take it easy. I don't want you to break a nail."

My eyes narrow. "You don't have to push so hard. I was going to say yes."

He grabs the seam of my sweater on each side and yanks me the last couple of feet to him. My arousal is immediate. "I hope you always say yes," he says, dropping his mouth to my ear. "But you always have the option to say no."

As if I need more reassurance, he adds, "The ball is within the weight limit the doctor said, and you're right-handed, so it will be on the opposite side. First sign of a problem and we're done."

Those fiery butterflies he often releases in me take flight. He's so fucking good.

"So, Firecracker, do you want to go bowling with me?"

I just nod, chewing my cheek.

"Words."

I pull back and look up into his eyes. "Yes, Cowboy. Take me bowling." I press on my toes and kiss him on the corner of his mouth.

The bowling alley sits in the tiny area of Bull Creek that can be considered industrial. It looks like an abandoned building, and I wouldn't be surprised if we walked in and there was a giant hole in the roof. From outside, the place looks like it hasn't been cared for in years. And yet, there are a good twenty cars in the parking lot when Sutton parks near the front.

There's something nostalgic about the sound of a ball rolling down the lane, crashing pins, and a jukebox playing. The air holds the scent of communal shoes that shouldn't be comforting, but somehow is. I haven't been bowling since I was a teenager. Rainy summer days in Bull Creek were for bowling, back when Izzy, Leah, and I were teenagers.

A group of women Nana's age occupy the two lanes farthest from the entrance. My feet plant as we get to the carpeted walkway, worn from years of use, and I take them in.

Sutton's warm arm encircles my waist as he stands to my side. "All good?"

"Yep." I turn to him with a grin. "Let's do this. I'm gonna kick your ass."

His eyebrows jump. "Well, this should be good."

After grabbing shoes, we go our separate ways for a few minutes, searching through rows and rows of dirty, dented bowling balls for the perfect method of destruction. Mine is bright pink out of pure coincidence, but I don't miss the laugh that Sutton suppresses when I carry it back to our lane.

"Do. Not." I pin him with a stiff look and drop the ball onto the ball return.

That does him in and he snickers like a teenager. His ball is blue. How typical.

"Ladies first." He gestures to the lane, having already put our names into the computer.

My cheeks heat at the letters on the screen. Firecracker and Cowboy are playing.

The pink ball glides into the gutter. Defeated, I turn back and wait for the ball to make its trek through the return. The second attempt isn't much better, but I manage to knock down two pins on the left.

Sutton stands, dragging his fingers along my side as he steps by to get his own ball. I plop down on the plastic chair. I have a feeling I'm about to get schooled.

Sure enough, Sutton has beautiful form and his ball direct hits the center pin, knocking them all down in one swoop. I cover my face with my hands and peek at him from behind my fingers as he returns, grinning at me.

"Well, that was hot." I cock my head to one side, watching him.

The computer screen highlights my name again. When I approach the ball return, Sutton doesn't sit. Instead, he leans his head down toward me and asks, more seductively than I would have thought, "Do you want a pointer?"

I turn my head to the right, toward his chest, but don't look up. The tension is killing me and my breathing shallows. After a short hesitation, I nod.

He gestures for me to approach the lane but follows me this time. I prep the ball for release but don't pull my arm back, keeping it cradled to my chest.

His warm hand presses against the underside of my arm. "Your follow-through is off." I want to melt backward into his chest but force myself to remain standing still.

He glides his hand up my forearm, aligning his fingers over mine. "When you let go here," he pulls my arm down to show where I released the ball previously, "your wrist is twisting. Like this."

I'm a little disappointed when he releases me to demonstrate with his own arm. "Instead, you need to keep your hand moving upward. Like this." He extends his arm higher than I did, as if reaching for the ceiling.

I nod, debating fucking up on purpose so I can have another hands-on tutorial. He retreats to wait near the ball return.

Focusing on the arm adjustment, I swing the ball forward. It rolls much closer to center, knocking down a middle section of pins. Elated, I spin around with a jump, immediately regretting the maneuver, which tugs at my healing wound.

Sutton smirks.

After the next frame, I manage to knock down all but one of the remaining pins. We get into a rhythm where Sutton gets a strike and I try for a spare each time. I'm only successful a few times, but I still manage to avoid the gutter more than not.

"Tell me about your dad," he says as I walk back after a turn.

Oh yeah. "James showed up after my lunch with Stephanie. He saw us while we were out and thought it was time to address things. Long story short, he and Stephanie were stupid happy and eloped. When I was a few years old, his brother was killed in Ireland and he came clean that he has ties to the mafia. Stephanie freaked and ran away with me."

Sutton and I stare at each other. The pins are reset and waiting.

"That's not where I thought that was going," he says, grabbing his ball.

"It caught me off guard, too. I really don't know where we stand. Him showing up here was out left field."

"He obviously wants to be in your life." He takes his turn, earning another easy strike, and returns. "And he's keeping tabs enough to know where you are."

"Somewhat. He saw me the night I met Colt. He was surprised, said he knew it was me even though I never ran into him growing up. My family never mentioned him, although according to Randi, she and Nana tried to get him and Stephanie back together." I roll the ball and return before I see what's been knocked down. "There's still a lot I need answers for."

My heart aches for the years that were stolen from us, anger filling me at my mother's inability to handle conflict. She always chooses to dismiss emotion because she can't deal with the repercussions of it.

Maybe dealing with them hurt too much in some of her most important moments. Maybe that's what she meant when she said I look like him and it was painful. I can't forgive her for her treatment of me, but a part of me is at least starting to piece her together.

"I'd like to spend more time getting to know him. Our conversations have been very brief—he's open and vague at the same time. I don't know much about the club or his life, or what type of person he really is. I'll never know for sure, but I think he would've been a good father. I think he was while it lasted."

Sutton nods, looking over my face. "I think that's fair. You just need to be careful. I've never heard anything bad or criminal about the club. A few bar fights, but that could be anyone around here." He smiles gently. "Still, club life is a whole different ball game. And just because I haven't heard of it, doesn't mean it's not happening."

"I'll be careful," I promise.

He gives me a skeptical look I ignore, and I grab my ball for the final frame.

CHAPTER 16

MACI

When I wake in the morning, I don't feel like crawling out my own skin and my incision isn't as tender. Following doctor's orders isn't my forte, but at least my body is healing appropriately.

After a steaming shower, I turn on the bathroom fan to remove the humidity as usual. Today, the noise is overwhelming. I flip the switch off and open both doors to the Jack and Jill bathroom to let the air circulate.

A gun case in the corner of the office catches my eye as I swing the bathroom door open on that side. I haven't spent much time in here. Aside from the desk and some seating, there's a mini fridge and the spectacular map of Texas on the wall that I noticed the first time I came over.

Several rifles and shotguns are on display through the glass door of the gun case, though it's not full. A small handgun sits on one of the wooden shelves inside, alongside some medals in velvet cases and other memorabilia.

My own handgun is now locked away in the Bull Creek Police Department, assuming that's where they house evidence. I don't anticipate ever getting it back, not that I asked about procedure.

I pad into the office, the wood floors cool underfoot. Compulsively, my fingers trace the dark mahogany before I try the door. It's unlocked and opens with a loud click into the room. With a sure grip, I pull the gun out and examine it. It's a similar size to mine, a little heavier, and unloaded. I slip it into the holster in my jeans before opening a low drawer to find the magazine.

Even with the new weapon in my possession, I don't feel any better. I should. With or without it, my villain is gone. Right?

It wasn't supposed to be this way.

When I started carrying a few years ago, I hoped it would help me feel protected. Maybe falsely for a while, I did. Now I feel stuck in a deeper, darker place than I did back then.

I never wanted to be a killer. I just wanted to be safe. Aside from being tucked into Sutton's arms, I don't know if I'll ever feel that way again.

I close the door on the case and make a mental note to tell Sutton I have the gun for now.

The sun hasn't fully risen as I make my way inside The Big House. It's oddly quiet when I enter. The usual kitchen noise is missing.

"Oh, Maci." Andi greets me with a signature smile. "I didn't expect to see you so soon."

My cheeks flush. "I don't think I'd like to get a reputation as a late riser around here."

She laughs. "Nonsense. You sleep as long as you want." She's busy cleaning up from breakfast and I check the dining table for anything else that needs to be washed or put away. Her voice follows me. "If you're looking for some of the muffins you made, I'm afraid you're out of luck. The hands finished them off right quick and in a hurry."

A breathy laugh leaves me. "I wasn't, but I'm glad they enjoyed them."

"They were singing your praises," she tells me with a smile when I re-enter the kitchen.

My brow furrows. "I hope you didn't give me all the credit. All I did was follow instructions."

"I didn't say anything. Actually, they were talking about your photos."

"My photos?" I haven't held a camera in too many days, which creates a different kind of ache.

"Yep. I didn't hear it all, but sounds like they saw your work from the Fall Festival."

For what feels like the first time in too long, pride races through my body. Photography is important to me, and documenting special times for families genuinely makes me feel good. I love sharing in those special moments with them. So hearing that people I don't really know enjoy my work, versus my biased friends, is a welcome form of flattery.

"Speaking of that..." Andi looks at me where I'm washing a casserole dish in the sink. "The Jingle Bell Bash is coming up soon. Are you interested in an appearance?"

"Is your other photographer unavailable again?"

She grabs a towel and takes the dish to dry it. "I haven't checked, to be honest. We didn't book her in advance for this event and she hasn't reached out since she had to pull out of the Fall Festival."

"As long as you don't think it will cause drama, I'm happy to do it." The last thing I need right now is more small-town drama. "Maybe my window won't get bashed in this time."

It's an ill-timed joke and Andi looks at me with a sad smile.

"Actually, the ranch hands asked after you, too." She looks at me from the corner of her eye. "I think you and Sutton have more in common than you think."

I'm unsure what she means and turn fully to face her, shutting off the water.

"I don't know why, but you two both seem content to take care of others without letting them in. The ranch hands respect Sutton, and I think they'd like to think of him as a friend, but he keeps them at arm's length." She mulls over her words. "But maybe that's changing. They've shown concern over you, and that may be enough to set him on the right course."

I cock my head. "Why are they worried about me?"

She raises an eyebrow at me, in a way I suspect she looks at her own children. "You two sure are cut from the same cloth." She breathes a laugh and shakes her head. "They're aware something happened last weekend. This ranch is home to them, and we take care of our own around here."

Once again, I'm struck by being surrounded by people who are genuine in their care for me. People I barely know who worry about me, while my own mother kept the Great Wall between us.

I sigh. "I have close friends. Not many, but I do."

"I'm not judging you, sweetheart," she promises. "Sutton has friends, too. The fact remains that you two could stand to let some others into your circle. Or let your circle in more, for that matter." She's not the first person to say something similar.

She scrubs the long counter close to the dining room and starts pulling out ingredients.

"What are you working on?"

"I'm going to make some pasta. I haven't made homemade pasta in a while, and I'm in the mood for some." The smile on her face is serene, just for her.

"Sounds delicious."

She dumps an ample amount of flour onto the counter, creating a large dome. It reminds me a bit of making a volcano in school. She spreads a hole in the middle. "Have you ever made homemade pasta?"

I shake my head, even though she hasn't looked away from her new creation. "No. Nana taught me her chicken noodle recipe, but we never made pasta from scratch. Just bagged egg noodles."

Andi smirks at me. "I know she knew how to make pasta from scratch." She's steadily cracking eggs.

"I'm sure. We were teenagers during the lesson, so as special as it was, she probably took a shortcut on that step." I smile, thinking about my best friends and me in Nana's homey kitchen; the distinct scents of fresh vegetables and chicken stock are almost close enough to be real again. "Actually, I'd love to make a large batch for everyone. Whenever it would be helpful to you."

Andi beams over her shoulder. The flour puffs and kisses her cheek as she turns. "That would be lovely!"

A shrill ringing fills the air and I jump. Andi, elbow-deep in the dough she's creating, peeks over her shoulder again. "Would you mind grabbing that, dear?" She nods at the aging phone hanging on the wall.

"Uh, sure." The phone trills again before I can remove it from the cradle. "Hello?"

"Uh...hi? Did I—" A young female voice hesitates on the other line.

"Are you trying to reach the Strickland residence?"

"Yes." Her statement is almost a question, and her tone changes from confused to suspicious. "Who is this?"

"This is Maci." Eyeing Andi from where I stand, she hums as she presses the dough. I shift on my feet.

"Maci? This is Sammi. You're Sutton's girlfriend." Excitement sneaks in at the end, and a blush coats my skin. My heart rate picks up and I smile stupidly.

"Yes. Hi, Sammi."

"Hi, honey!" Andi yells from her place but doesn't clean her hands. Apparently, she's not in a hurry to chat.

"My parents are the only people I know who have a landline; I'm not used to hearing a different voice on the line. Sorry."

"No apologies necessary. I should've announced the house name."

Sammi chuckles. "Don't worry about it. What are y'all up to today?"

Is this small talk? Shouldn't she be asking for Andi? "Um, well, your mom is currently elbow-deep in pasta dough." Gripping the dangling cord in one hand, I twirl my pointer finger in and out of the permanent ringlets.

"I'm so jealous. Mama's pasta is to die for."

"I haven't had anything that's less than amazing," I agree. "Did she teach you, too?"

"Oh, no," Sammi laughs. "I'm helpless in the kitchen."

That's a twist I didn't expect. In my head, Sammi would've naturally followed in her mother's love for the kitchen, but it's an outdated assumption. "Oh."

"Are Daddy and Sutton out?"

Daddy. It's sweet. I didn't have the opportunity to be a daddy's girl, but I wonder what that would've been like. "Yes. They started early this morning."

"I know *that's* the truth." There's a note of sarcasm in her voice. "They're always up before the rooster crows. I never had it in me. I'd be in so much trouble if I had to stay on the ranch."

I laugh knowingly. "I've never been a morning person either, until now."

"Oh no! Did Sutton rope you into ranch life? You tell my brother he can't make you get up if you don't want to. You're an independent woman and he can't force you into cow manure and forced baby-making."

"Are we still talking about the cows?" The playful question tumbles off my lips as I take in her short rant.

"Ohmygod!" That sets her into a fit of laughter, going until she can't breathe. I check on Andi at the counter, but she doesn't seem to care what's happening on the phone as she makes a neat ball of dough, wrapping it in plastic wrap. Sammi manages to compose herself. "Yes, I was referring to the cows being forced to breed." Her words are almost breathless.

I chuckle. "Well, no worries. Sutton has never asked me to get up with him. In fact, he's really quiet in the morning. He always leaves me coffee, though."

"Coffee?" She contemplates this for a moment as I hum affirmation. "He doesn't even like coffee."

A wide smile splits my face. "I know. He prefers water. Or juice, sometimes."

"Wow."

Andi sets the dough away and I gesture the phone in an offering. She waves me away and works on cleaning up the counter. I decide, without a doubt, this was a setup. She quietly hums a song I don't know.

"So, when are you two coming up here?" Sammi's words come out in a rush.

"Um, I'm not sure. We've had..."

"It's ok," Sammi says, softly. "You don't have to explain...I kind of heard."

That doesn't really come as a surprise. "Yeah." I inhale deeply. "Well, Sutton mentioned coming up soon, so it's a definite. I'm sorry we haven't scheduled something already, but I am looking forward to meeting you and your family."

"I am, too." A baby cries. "That's Vivi. I have to run. Tell everyone I love them. Nice talking to you, Maci."

"You, too. Bye." I wait for her to hang up, standing with the phone against my ear for longer than necessary. A new ache infiltrates my chest.

I assume most only-children always want a sibling. Someone to play with. I didn't. I did want that connection, though. More so since my dad was out of the picture and Stephanie was so distant.

My best friends filled that for me in many ways. Still, I can't help but hope that Sammi and I could form a strong bond someday.

CHAPTER 17

SUTTON

Getting going in the morning has always been easy for me. But now that Maci occupies the bed, it's been hard to start my day. She isn't talking about it, but her sleep is restless. Sometimes she wakes in the middle of the night and doesn't fall back asleep until the early hours of the morning. My touch doesn't provide all the comfort she needs right now. Laying next to someone you want to help and not being able to do anything is a really fucked-up feeling to have. Knowing there are some things she's going to have to work through without me sucks.

Thankfully, all of the fall calves have been delivered and the herd is in good shape, so if I'm the last one out, no one says a word. Not that they would. There's still plenty to do around here, and I want to focus on getting the ranch team as organized as possible. It's time for me to start determining who fills my shoes. The potential addition of the property next door has me thinking of all the ways we need to increase our efficiency, and how I can't be the only one holding on to all the information. Which is why I've asked the ranch hands to meet me for a sit-down meeting. Hopefully I haven't scared them, seeing as how we don't really have these very often.

During the meeting with my dad, just before I met Maci, we discussed a slow transition. Yet somehow, we've fallen into it faster than I expected. I still keep Dad updated, but even with everything going on, he hasn't been as present.

I know him too well to think it's anything more than him letting me do things my way. Come into my own or some thoughtful phrase like that.

I've just stepped into the bunkhouse to meet with the crew when my phone rings. I have no reason to think it's anything serious, but that doesn't stop me from checking, and I'm surprised to see Terrence's name flash on the caller ID.

"Good morning, sir." I step back outside the door and shut it behind me.

"Sutton, good mornin'." Terrence's thick accent is so stereotypically Texas. "Wanted to let you know I've considered the offer you and your dad gave me."

I try not to hold my breath. It's not that we can't go higher if Terrence comes back with a counteroffer, but I'd prefer to avoid it if we can. Before meeting with Terrence, Dad and I had a sit down with a financial planner in town. After getting a hold on what we have going on and what we want to accomplish, specifically to allow growth without my parents being financially tied down, he was able to set a plan and advise how to move forward with the purchase.

Just one more thing Maci and I haven't had a chance to discuss.

"I'd like to accept."

I blink. "Well, that's wonderful."

"I'd appreciate sixty days to get things in order here." I don't get the impression that he's asking, but the timeline works for us, too. I hope.

"Yes, sir. Not a problem." That will put us just into the new year. My mind is already running through what the next few months look like on our calendar, adding in what we need to accomplish to be ready for an expansion.

Something Maci said previously about our role in the community stands out in my mind.

"Sounds good."

I rub a hand over my mouth. There are a lot of people's livelihoods involved here, and not just the people Strickland Ranch employs. "Is your team aware of the transition?"

"Yep, yep. They're aware I'm sellin'."

"Well, we'd be open to considering some staying on if they'd like to. I'd want to meet with them and gauge everyone's expectations." I'm working on the fly.

"Ok. I'll let 'em know you're open to it."

"Thank you. We'll be in touch to coordinate further. You let us know if you need anything in the meantime."

"Same to you, Sutton. I look forward to seeing what you do out here."

A little pride joins the mixture of emotions swirling within me.

After hanging up, I step inside the bunkhouse again. The ranch hands sit at the dining table, looking expectantly at where I stand at the door.

"Sorry about that." My steps echo on the pier and beam floor. The fourth seat at the table is open and I sit down. "I have several things I want to go over this morning, but I'd like to start with anything you want to discuss."

The three men exchange looks.

"Nothing's come up on our end. How's Maci?" Kelly asks. I don't miss Cody and Jason deferring to him.

My knuckles tap twice on the dining table, thumping hollowly, a distraction for covering my surprised emotion. It's odd to have them interested in my personal life. I haven't had much of one worth discussing until recently, so it isn't commonplace. "She's doing better. It'll take time."

"Some wounds don't heal. Not completely." He holds my gaze. Something tells me he knows more than he's letting on. Maybe not about what happened, but the aftermath of something like this.

I nod. "It's true. I don't expect she'll ever be the exact same Maci she was."

"Just love her through it." We don't speak for a few moments.

Well, this went differently than expected.

There's a lot of that these days.

I clear my throat. "Alright, let's get started on the news." I rattle my phone against the table in my other hand. "That was Terrence. We're going to be acquiring the property next door."

Cody's drops his chin as he speaks. "The whole ten thousand acres?"

"Yep." I give him a gentle smile. He's the youngest of the group, and sometimes I forget how green he is. He removes his hat and runs a hand through his short blond hair. "Some things will be easy transitions, and some may be hard. We have sixty days to get things in order over here and have a solid plan in place for what needs to happen over there."

"*Is* there a plan?" Jason is seated across the table from me.

"Somewhat." I grin. "First things first, I'm going to need one of you to manage cow-calf operations for Strickland Ranch as we expand. We'll also be making decisions on how we're going to reorganize the land, if we're going to grow the herds or add more, and what other endeavors we'll be exploring out here."

"What kind of things are you thinking?" Kelly perks up. He's the oldest of the group, and the steadiest, too. I know he was injured when he was younger running the rodeo circuit, but I've never asked for details. I'm not sure what else he's gotten into.

I share with them some of the things I've brought up with my dad, including guided hunts. "Maci also thought it could be beneficial to add opportunities for the public to stay on the ranch in private areas, and possibly participate in what we do."

"Like a dude ranch?" Jason asks, brows furrowed.

I chuckle. "That's what I said. But she had some good points. It makes us a destination and gives people a better idea of what we do. They pay us to be manpower. Granted, each time would be new for them, and more like teaching than actually having efficient help."

Kelly hums. "I don't think it's a bad idea. There'd be things to figure out, for sure." As an afterthought he adds, "What about a venue?"

I cock my head in question.

He continues. "Special events. Terrence has several semi-permanent structures set up. They have power and sound systems. I think a couple have big-ass fans, too. If you aren't planning to take on horses, we can repurpose what's there for special events. Weddings, team building, corporate events. It could tie into the dude ranch idea or not. It may compete with the fairgrounds, but that's their problem."

"Fuck, that's genius." Cody stares ahead vacantly.

I breathe a laugh at his response. "I hadn't thought of that. I like it. Certainly something to work with."

Kelly nods a thanks.

As the meeting continues, I feel better having them actively participate in planning for the future. After we finish, I'm torn between heading into The Big House or finding Maci. She's the first person I wanted to tell the good news to, despite already being at the bunkhouse and diving straight into our meeting.

Fate works in my favor, because as soon as I step inside, still undecided who I want to talk to first, Maci's voice floats down the hall. She and Mama are talking in the kitchen.

A few steps into the hallway, Maci's beautiful head pops out from the kitchen. She grins and my heart beats faster. I will never tire of seeing her throughout the day.

"I thought I heard you come in."

"Came to see my favorite women." I wrap her in my arms and plant a kiss on her head. She wraps her own arms around my midsection, holding snug.

Mama smiles proudly behind her.

"Where's Dad?"

"Right here." My dad steps into the hallway from the living room.

Maci pulls back, but I keep hold of a hand.

"Good. Everyone got a minute?" I look between the three.

Mama's eyebrows jump.

"Sure. We need to sit down?" Dad gestures to the dining room.

"Yeah, let's talk for a few." I motion for Mama to lead the way, and Dad follows suit.

Maci smiles softly at me. "I'll let you three chat." She shifts toward the kitchen entrance, but I squeeze her hand, drawing her attention back.

"Where do you think you're going?"

She freezes. "I thought—"

"This pertains to you, too. You said you want to know more about the ranch, that you want this life." My chest aches at her pleased face. I jerk my chin toward the dining room and pull her before me to the table.

"You're doing that thing again." Her voice is quiet. I'm not sure she meant for me to hear.

"What thing?"

Her green eyes meet mine over her shoulder. "Leading by following."

I furrow my brows. "I have no idea what you're talking about."

She gives our intertwined hands a little shake where they hang together in front of her shoulder.

"Hmm." It's an interesting concept. I think about its application to other areas.

We sit, and I relay the phone call from Terrence.

"That's great news!" Mama clasps her hands in front her, her bright smile lighting the room.

"There's still a lot to nail down."

Mama gives me a flat-lipped smile. "Don't diminish this. You have big plans for the ranch, and this is where they begin."

She's right, but I'm still trying to manage my nerves. "You're right."

Maci grips my hand, her cool touch a reprieve.

"I had a meeting with the hands before I came in," I continue. "They're completely on board and they have some great ideas, too. And I told Terrence that if anyone wants to stay on from his crew, I'd like to speak with them."

"This is gonna be good, son." Dad's steady tone almost does me in. He doesn't have to say anything else. His lit eyes and soft smile say it all.

I clear my throat.

Maci's phone starts ringing. "Shoot, sorry." She jumps up and yanks her cell from her pocket, hurrying into the main hallway.

"You'll get it all organized. Let the guys help. Y'all make a great team. They'll grow with the ranch if you let 'em. So will Maci." Mama threads her fingers with Dad's on the tabletop as she speaks to me.

"Your mom's right," Dad adds. "The crew is loyal to you. Just because we had part-time or short-term employees in the past, doesn't mean that's how things should go now. Trust these three, let them in, and they'll be with you for the long haul."

I study my dad carefully, imparting a rare bit of wisdom on me. His encouragement means everything.

Maci reseats herself next to me.

"Everything okay, sweetheart?" Mama can't help but check in.

She nods, an unsure look on her face. "That was Melissa. Colt's mom. She wants to meet."

The tension from my parents is immediately palpable. Wife or not, they already care deeply for Maci. Especially Mama.

I lower my voice. "Are you going?" It doesn't matter; they can still hear me.

"Yes. I don't have anything to hide, and she seems genuine."

Mama pats Maci's hand. "She sounds like a grieving mom, from what you've said. Maybe she just needs a little closure."

Maci pulls her bottom lip into her mouth. "I think you're probably right."

CHAPTER 18

MACI

Before my meeting with Melissa, I decide to try my hand at some more self-help. It's been two days since I attempted to go to Nana's house. Nothing seems to have been made worse, even if I'm not sure if it did much good.

This time, I make it to the turn off with no problem. I stop anyway, easing into what's to come. At least, that's what I try to convince myself I'm doing.

In truth, I can't bring myself to move. It's like some weird form of compulsive magic. My hands won't steer the wheel onto the street, and my foot won't push the pedal if that's where I'm trying to go.

This time, there's no additional sensory input. Just an overwhelming pressure not to move forward. Maybe this is a positive reaction? I convince myself to take the win and head to my meeting with Melissa.

Instead of parking at the cafe where I'm meeting Melissa, I park less than a block away in the bank lot behind Town Square. It's a two-fold decision; for one, I'm shit at parallel parking, especially on Bull Creek's narrow Main Street. More importantly though, the short walk will give me a chance to fortify my nerves against whatever may be coming in this meeting.

The green space in Town Square hosts a central gazebo, which is often used for live music like during the Fall Festival or for farmer's market events. Today, families mill about or pass through on their way to visit shops on the next block.

Melissa is already seated at a bistro table outside of The Jim-Dandy where the original library used to be. The floor-to-ceiling windows expose the mostly empty interior. She has a takeout cup before her and watches people passing by.

I've never eaten here. In fact, the only times I've stopped in were with Leah and Izzy during past Jingle Bell Bash events, when we ordered their spectacular hot chocolate.

Melissa smiles timidly at me when I approach. She stands awkwardly, as if she's unsure if she should shake my hand or not.

I gesture at the chair across from her and we both sit.

"How are you?" I can't begin to imagine what she must be going through, no matter how we got to this place.

She takes a deep breath. "Disappointed. Ashamed. Hurt, obviously. I love my son, despite his faults."

"I'm truly sorry for your loss. I had my own, recently, and though it's not the same, it was also very painful."

One of her hands moves to rest around the base of the cup. She fiddles with the textured outer layer. "How well did you know Colt?"

I clear my throat as a cover for determining how forthcoming to be. "I didn't know him very well, honestly. In fact, I only met him a few weeks ago."

She presses her lips together. "Whatever happened between you two, I know it was because you were defending yourself."

My brows furrow. "That's a bold statement for someone to make about their own child." I can't help my curiosity.

"I told you. I know—knew my son." She swallows. "I'm going to assume you don't know much about his past. Or if you do, it came from Alan and not him."

Adrenaline spikes through me at the mention of Colt's father and my stepfather. I'm still disgusted every time I think about it. Another scalding shower to scrub off the outer layer of my skin sounds preferable right about now.

"I don't know much about him. Alan never spoke of Colt—at least not to me—and when we met, we didn't realize the connection. Colt figured it out after."

"I'm not surprised Alan never mentioned him." She shakes her head. "I won't go off on a tangent, because we aren't here about him. I am sorry for what you went through, though. I feel partially responsible."

"Responsible?"

Her fingers tear at the sleeve on the cup as a cold wind rushes through the covered sidewalk our table occupies. "Colt was struggling. He had been for many years. It started when he was a teenager, around when Alan left. At first, I assumed it was because of the divorce. We never told him why, and I thought his paranoia stemmed from feeling like he didn't have the whole truth. But things continued to get worse and eventually, I realized it wasn't about that. Not entirely.

"I tried to talk to Alan about it once, but he dismissed me as usual. It was the last we spoke, actually. Past that, I tried to get Colt to talk to someone, but he was adamant he didn't need a 'shrink'"—she adds air quotes—"and since he was so close to being on his own, there wasn't a lot I could do."

She shakes her head sadly before continuing.

"He wanted to go into the military, but I don't think he passed the evaluation. He wasn't very open with me after the divorce, but he seemed to become suspicious of me after he moved out. We spoke a few times a year, only when I reached out to him."

For whatever reason, I notice how dry her lips are when they purse. I remember being near dehydration from tears after Nana passed. And also because I was living on coffee alone for a few days.

"I wish I could've convinced him to see someone. He needed help." She averts her gaze, studying the bistro table.

"Was he having hallucinations?"

Her lids droop, and she rubs at a place on her forehead absently. "I'm not sure. Sometimes he would mutter to himself." She gives me a questioning look. "But everyone talks to themselves sometimes, right?"

I recall times that it seemed like he was having a side conversation with someone else.

"Colt's fuse seemed to get shorter and shorter. He was never an especially patient person. He got that from Alan." She wrings her hands on the table. "A few months back, he shoved me into a wall when I suggested, again, that he talk to someone. It was the last time we spoke."

She's sharing so freely, like she hasn't been able to discuss her concerns with anyone. I can't bring myself to interrupt or stop her, even though I can't imagine why she's telling me all of this.

"I don't know what the department has shared with you, but I've been very honest with them that I don't think you were in the wrong. Colt could be downright obsessive about the things he wanted, for whatever reason. If that's what was happening with you, I'm not sure there's anything you could have done to change his mind. I truly hope this investigation is put to rest and you can move on with your life."

I'm not sure she understands what she's asking. This isn't something I can tuck neatly in a box in the closet and forget about. I killed a man. Her son. I shot him as he shoved a knife into my gut, and he bled out on me while I wondered if we were going to die there together in a heap in my grandmother's backyard.

But I share none of that with her. I press my lips together and nod. Because the only thing I can think of that might be worse than living with the guilt and trauma of this for the rest of my life would be doing it behind bars. Alone. Without Sutton, or the support of the amazing people in my life. Of which I have so many more now than I used to.

"I wish it had ended differently," I finally manage. My heart rate picks up. I won't be able to go into detail, and I hope that's not what she wants. I recognize that people need closure in different ways, but I cannot provide that for her. Not those details. "I tried to talk to him, to reason with him, but it sounds like he was struggling with things far outside of my reach. I'm so, so sorry. I waited..."

My throat constricts, and it takes me a long moment to force it open. "I waited until I couldn't anymore. I didn't have a choice."

Tears begin to stream down her cheeks and her hand falls away from the cup. Without thinking, I reach across and place my own on top of hers. I can't take back what happened that night. Even if I wish that I could. But I can look into her eyes and tell her honestly that I'm sorry for her loss, because I am.

I'm sorry for mine, too.

There's an innocence that I didn't know I had that was stolen from me that night.

We stare at each other, silent tears falling from our cheeks onto the weathered bistro table. I can't know if she's being truthful about trying to convince the police department of my honesty, and she can't know that I was acting in self-defense, but somehow we choose a mutual trust. In some way, maybe that heals a tiny part of each of our broken hearts.

"I'm sorry." More tears escape her eyes. "And thank you."

My breathing catches. My mouth opens, but the question won't come out.

"There's an unwritten rule that mothers constantly worry about our children. At least, it seems that way to me. You worry if they'll get hurt, how they'll do in school, if they'll make the right friends. Then you worry if they'll get into a car accident, drink too much at a party, get a girl pregnant. Sometimes you worry they'll hurt themselves." Her breathing catches into a sort of hiccup, and her words slow. "Or someone else. I don't have to worry about him hurting someone anymore." Her hands flash up to cover her face, and her elbows drop to the table as she begins to sob, her body wracked with heaving, disjointed breaths.

Behind her self-imposed shield, more words tumble out. "God, what an awful thing to say about your own child." Her voice breaks and her body shakes harder. "I can't believe I'm relieved. I'm an awful person."

Fishing tissues from my crossbody bag, I pull one out and slide the pack across the table, nudging her elbow with it. Tears track my own cheeks, hot against the crisp air. She peeks through her fingers and takes in my face before accepting.

"Would it be okay if I come to Colt's funeral?"

Melissa dabs at her cheeks and around her eyes. She studies me quietly. "Why would you want to do that?"

She's right to think my offer seems out of left field. A large part of me is sorry for how Colt's life came to an end, even if I'd choose my life over his again if I had to. Yet, a quote that I've heard from Mother Theresa sticks in my head. She said, "If you love until it hurts, there can be no more hurt, only more love." I'm no saint, so my desire is somewhat selfish. I'm hopeful that facing this will provide another way for me to heal, as much as I hope it gives a measure of comfort to Melissa. She seems truly and utterly alone, and that's heartbreaking. So, I channel a bit of Nana's grit and compassion, hoping I can achieve something good for all of us with this one action.

"Colt made some bad choices with dire consequences...but he was still loved. I'd like to show my condolences for his lost life." I tuck my hands into my lap. "I won't come if it will make you uncomfortable, though."

She sniffs. "No, that's fine. You're welcome to come." She folds the tissue and tucks it under the base of her cup. "As it is, I think I'll be the only one there." Her voice breaks and fat tears crest her cheeks again. "It's next Wednesday. At eleven."

"Ok. I'll be there." I hope my tone is reassuring, even though I keep it soft.

She composes herself again. "Thank you for meeting with me."

"I'm glad I did," I say honestly.

She stands, still staying out of sidewalk traffic, and I follow suit. "I'll see you next week."

"Bye, Melissa."

Melissa turns and walks down the sidewalk in the opposite direction. My feet remain planted until she turns into the parking lot, out of sight, before I turn and make my way through Town Square toward my Jeep.

Despite our open conversation, everything in me feels constricted. A new weight sits on my chest. Could I have done more to stop what happened?

At the final corner, a man I would guess to be about ten years older than me reaches the crosswalk at the same time as I do. "Hey there." He grins at me.

I avert my eyes in annoyance. Does this puffy face and presumably red nose scream flirt with me?

"What's a pretty thing like you doing all by yourself?"

Disgusting.

I whip my head in his direction. "Does that really work for you?"

"Pardon?" His grin widens, and I'm positive his phrasing is deliberate and not a normal speech pattern for him. "I'm just saying, a cute thing like you should be locked up tight." I open my mouth to respond when he adds, "I bet you'd be even prettier if you smiled."

He takes a half-step forward and instinctually, I reach for Sutton's gun tucked into the waistband of my pants.

The man's pupils dilate. He freezes and his grin drops, but his brain is obviously malfunctioning because the falter causes an awkward grimace as he stares at my reaching arm.

My hand stills at my back, my fingers flush against the butt of the gun. I realize my reaction too late; my response is to immediately defend myself. I leave my hand where it is. "Why don't you just fuck off." My voice isn't as harsh as I want it to be, but somehow this fucker gets the clue.

His hands raise in supplication. "Just having a little fun." His weight shifts backward as his eyes return to mine, and he begins to back away.

"Well, I'm about to have a little fun if you don't fuck off." I enunciate the last two words, staring him down as he turns to cross the street, repeatedly checking over his shoulder at me.

My heart races in my chest. Was I really going to pull a gun on a guy on a street corner for hitting on me? He was a massive creep, but it didn't warrant my reaction.

I swallow thickly, adjust my sweater, and hurry to my Jeep. I need to get to the ranch.

CHAPTER 19

SUTTON

A sobbing sound draws me from sleep. Although Maci hasn't been sleeping well, she hasn't cried, so the sound is disorienting. "Firecracker?"

I sit up and look around the pitch-black room. She isn't in the bed with me, and even as my eyes adjust, I don't see her on the couch or throughout the room.

Her crying turns to sniffles, and it registers that she's between the bed and the closet. I roll over her side of the bed to slide onto the floor and scoop her into my arms, leaning my back against the bed. She readjusts, straddling me and tucking her arms between us and laying her head against my shoulder. I rock her side to side without saying anything.

Maci continues to draw new feelings out of me that I'm wholly unprepared for. Usually those new things are good. Since the incident with Colt, there have been more I'd rather not deal with. Like being completely useless at the hospital and terrified that I'd lose her. Now it's like a punch to the gut that she's crying on the floor by herself. Why didn't she wake me?

She keeps trying to convince everyone she's fine, but she's struggling. Maybe she admits it even less to herself.

"I got you." My fingers draw up and down her back in the slow, aimless way that she likes. I want her to open up to me, but I don't want to push her. I want her to want to talk to me. In fact, I'm willing to bet she would normally. Something has her really fucked up.

When her breaths even out and she's no longer audibly crying, I press my luck. "Nightmares?"

Her wet cheek presses into my chest as she shakes her head. She pulls back, wiping at my pec, because of course that's her concern, and tucks herself against me again.

Having Maci's skin on mine is like no other. Her body is a balm to my nerves, but not in this way.

"You want to talk about it?"

She takes a deep, shaky breath but holds it at first. "I killed him."

I want to argue, to come to her defense. Even though what she says is true, it's not like she did it on purpose. It's painful not to object. But whatever she's going through, she needs to get it out in the way that she feels it. Later, I can tell her how fucking wrong she is and why it doesn't matter.

"I took his life. He's dead because of me."

My arms tighten around her. I wish I could send my strength straight through our limbs into her. When she doesn't continue after a minute, I respond. "He's dead because of choices he made."

"He was sick."

"Even if that's true, that wasn't your fault." I kiss the top of her head. I don't want to fight with her, but she may need someone to fight with. She's mad at herself, but she needs to get out of her head.

Maybe that means drawing her out to argue with me. She can't wallow in her self-deprecating grief if she's angry with me. "You did what you had to do in the moment."

She sits up, and I'm a little relieved at the fire I see in her as she says, "I could've tried harder to stop him. To talk him down."

"There was no talking him down. His mind was made up when he got there."

"But he didn't have all the information when he showed up. He didn't know about James."

I shake my head. "James had nothing to do with his decision. He was focused on you. On a history that he created in his mind and that you had nothing to do with."

"He didn't deserve to die."

I shrug. "Neither did you. And if it came down to you and him again, I don't know many people who would've made a different call."

"That's not the point. Of course you're going to say that. You love me. You don't want me dead."

"Fuck no, I don't want you dead!" Now I'm the one getting angry. "And I'm pissed you had to make that call. That *you* had to be the one to put that fucker down. I would gladly take that burden from you. I'm sorry. I'm sorry I didn't make it in time. But you made the right decision. You had to. There was no other way."

Silent tears stream down her face.

"I'm sorry," I repeat.

Her cool hands cup my cheeks. I'm mad at myself all over again that she's trying to comfort me.

"I know what you're trying to do." A tiny, sad smile graces her lips. Her thumbs rub back and forth.

I release her and take her hands into my own, kissing them in succession.

"I'm scared." Her voice is small and choked.

"I'm here." I squeeze her hands tighter. "And he's gone."

She swallows hard. "That's not what I mean." Her nostrils flare as she inhales deeply. "I'm scared of who I've become."

153

My head shakes in confusion. "What do you—"

"When Colt came over that night, I waited until the last possible second. Part of me feels like I should've done more. Instead of antagonizing him, I should've tried to really explain my side so he could see that I never wanted to take Alan from him. But the other part of me knows that I couldn't have waited any longer." She slides her hands down and presses them against my chest, steadying herself.

"I warned him. I told him I would shoot. I hoped he would reconsider." Her eyes fall to the floor as she sees images in her mind that I will never bear witness to. "I tried to move slowly so that he wouldn't jump out of fear. The gun slid out of the holster just as he came at me. I took a step back and shot, but it went right because we were both moving. That's when he slammed into me. When he...stabbed me. The gun was squeezed between us, and I was trying to get my hand free when it went off the second time."

It takes effort not to squeeze her tighter in my hands with the force of my anger. It's not directed at her, but all over again I yearn to break something.

"Any twist one way or the other, one second later, and he probably would've gotten me in a completely different spot. We'd probably both be dead, instead." Her eyes come back to mine. "I waited until the last *possible* second. And now, anytime someone so much as looks at me the wrong way, it feels like I'm loaded and ready to go off. I don't think it's a good idea for me to carry for a while."

My heart drops. "I thought it made you feel safer."

She shakes her head and stares at me blankly. "No. I don't trust myself. It's too easy to pull it now."

CHAPTER 20

STEPHANIE

My marriage can be summed up in one word. Apathy.

Sex with Alan is expected, but nothing exciting. His work trips are regular. It doesn't bother me that he's frequently gone; however, it doesn't minimize my anxiety, thanks to the cameras in the house.

Those came after Maci left. I can only imagine the fit she would've thrown over them being installed while she lived with us. They didn't bother me at first. Alan had a point that they were important for safety, especially with me being alone all the time. Not that I anticipated some drastic event to occur.

Soon, he was asking questions. Vague curiosity turned into pointed observations. Things he would have only known by checking the cameras. "I look forward to seeing the fruits of your shopping trip later," or, "Did you even leave the house this weekend?"

All these years, I've tolerated everything. Worked tirelessly to be the perfect wife, if only to avoid more shame over another failed marriage. Suddenly, apathy leaves a bad taste in my mouth.

The moment Alan walks through the door, he resumes his normal routine, but my eyes are finally open. The compliant, perfect, shame-filled wife of the last ten years is gone. She moves to sit on my shoulder, wearing a red dress and horns.

I may not have cameras to study him while he's gone, but there is plenty for me to observe. Starting with the fact that he never brings dirty clothes home.

Alan slips into the shower to "wash off the grime of travel." I meander in our closet. His suitcase is already entirely unpacked. If he had managed all of his own laundry in the years we've been together, him bringing a suitcase full of clean clothes home wouldn't have alerted me. But he hasn't.

If he can't be bothered to do it here, why is he so proactive elsewhere?

Alan's phone glows, perched atop our dresser and plugged into the charger. My heartbeat picks up. I've never gone through his phone. Just thinking about it feels dangerous. Not because of what I may find, but because of what would happen if he discovered me.

Like a summoning beacon, a notification illuminates the screen. On silent feet, I inch closer. His preview setting is off, but the name is clear. *Kathryn.*

Like a geyser, repressed feelings from the years burst through me. *Who the hell is Kathryn?*

The fury cascading through me isn't jealousy over another woman sleeping with my husband. Though it should be. It's the realization that while I've been here playing Suzy Fucking Homemaker, killing myself to be perfect and poised, to avoid more mistakes and shame, and keep my husband happy in every way, that bastard thought he could humiliate me.

Kathryn could be a work associate. Except that I've seen calls and notifications come in on occasion, and the company name always follows the contact name. Alan's extremely detailed in that aspect.

The shower cuts off and I exit the closet, shutting the door completely so it's as I found it.

A shrill beep echoes through the downstairs as the timer for my lasagna rings. It's the perfect excuse to make myself busy in the kitchen. Alan's going to have something to say about the frozen Texas Toast, but it's a comfort I'm indulging in this evening.

His clipped footsteps approach from behind, the flat soles of his house shoes warning of his arrival.

"Feel better?" It's an effort to keep my voice pleasant as I set the salad and plates on the dining table.

Alan seats himself at the head of the table. "Much."

Sitting next to him, I focus on the salad on my plate, applying the perfect amount of dressing to avoid looking too curious. "How was your trip? Productive?"

His eyes raise to my face while I feign distraction over a large piece of lettuce. Hot fear creeps up from my chest into my neck, and I force it back, worried mostly about the possibility of a telling rouge on my skin. After a moment of silent observation, he says, "It was. Did you keep yourself busy while I was away?"

"Mainly laundry and finding homes for the items I brought from Mother's house." Those things are true, which allows me to look him in the eye.

He lifts his chin in acknowledgement.

We eat quietly for a few minutes, until a question from him cuts through the tension. "Will you be visiting again soon?"

The muscles in my torso tighten, as if bracing for impact. "I don't think so."

"Have you made a decision about contesting the will like we discussed?" This question comes faster, as if it was on the tip of his tongue.

"I haven't." My eyes scan the dining room. "I like our life here in Dallas, don't you? I don't see a reason to worry about the house." I try to keep my face soft when I look back at him.

He doesn't return the attempt. His mouth is tight and he's gripping his fork with enough force that I'm convinced he'll have indentions on his fingers. "You're the eldest daughter, Stephanie. It stands to reason you would be included in the will."

I don't argue that I am. It's him that's the problem. "Randi will work with me." My words do little to calm him.

His jaw ticks. Something flashes in his eyes and he scoops another bite of lasagna into his mouth. After swallowing, he has a new question. "Have you heard from Maci since we left?"

My eyes dart to him. "I saw her for lunch right after you left for your work trip." It hits me like a freight train that it was the same day of the attack. An event that risked both of our children, but only mine made it through.

He waits, but I offer nothing else. Finally he grits out, "She always seems to be causing trouble. I was sure you would have heard from her by now."

I coat my face in boredom and blink at him. "We don't talk that frequently."

He studies me slowly, and I manage to hold his gaze for a few seconds before looking back to my plate as if it's more interesting than this conversation which has my blood pressure through the roof.

What will he do if he finds out the truth? And how the hell am I getting out of here without him doing just that?

CHAPTER 21

MACI

A faint vibration wakes me. My eyes are heavy and swollen, and my brain is muddled. I roll over in the bed, confused. It's brighter than usual, but I can't figure out the time. The vibrating continues.

A chill creeps over me when I toss the covers back and slide off the side of the large bed. It's one of the most comforting places in my life, and I have no desire to leave it today. The thought of dealing with anything is too much.

My phone ceases movement and I find it tucked into my crossbody bag. The battery is low, and a local number shows for the missed call. My caller ID suggests it may be Bull Creek Police Department.

Fabulous.

First, I need coffee. And food. I'm starving.

Plus, I highly doubt whatever Detective Porter wants will change in the next thirty minutes. I shove the charger into the port on my bedside table and notice a prepared mug of coffee. It brings a smile to my lips, but it's cold, and I'm annoyed with myself for sleeping so long. I leave the phone to charge while I shower and prepare for the day. The mood-boosting playlist I blare while I'm getting ready does nothing to help my attitude.

For the first time ever, no one is inside when I enter The Big House to replace my cold coffee. My skin crawls from the absence, even though I don't have the bandwidth to speak with anyone. The sink drips repetitively while I fill my mug, setting my teeth on edge. Every single sensation feels overwhelming.

I have to get out of here.

I may have gone overboard with the caramel creamer this morning. I nearly get a cavity from my first sip and shake my head at myself as I exit onto the front porch.

Thankfully, the keys are in the Defender. I start it up, heading to a familiar place on the ranch, if only to be alone for a little longer to wallow in my terrible mood. Then I'll pick myself up and carry on with life, because that's how the world works.

The blind Sutton took me to not long ago is untouched, as far as I can tell. Instead of going inside it, I find an area between the off-road vehicle and the structure that looks safe enough for sitting. I lie back, staring up the sky. The day is overcast and I study the thick clouds floating through my vision.

I lose track of time, just enjoying being grounded with nature and clearing my mind. The tall grass sings like a rain stick in the breeze, and my body begins to chill. I'm about to return the detective's call when Sutton's voice breaks through the trees, calling to the ranch hands. Their responses mingle together and I enjoy being a hidden observer for a moment.

The grass rustles and a horse approaches. Someone jumps down, but I don't need to see to know it's him. How he found me, or why, I don't know.

I lie unmoving, scanning the vicinity, when he comes into view. He smiles softly down at me from near my feet. His top button is undone, white shirt peeking out, with his hat low over his eyes. I want him to take me right here in this space, love away all that eats at me from the inside.

"Hi," I whisper.

"Hi, yourself," he says, dropping to one knee when he's reached my waist. "You hunting something?"

My mouth tips up on one side. "More like avoiding what's hunting me."

He sits, stretching out a leg and keeping the other bent, where he rests an arm. "And what would that be?"

"Guilt. Despair."

His warm hand brushes loose hair from my face and I lean toward his touch as he starts speaking.

"When I was younger, I had this friend—we were in peewee baseball together—and we were five so we were best friends for life, and nothing could ever separate us. Except he had to move."

I push to sitting, curious about this new detail he's sharing.

"It was the end of the world. The apocalypse. I'd never have another best friend again." He grins at me. "But Mama, she told me, 'Everyone has a purpose in your life. Some are meant to give you something, some are meant to teach you something, and some are meant to take something you don't need anymore. Some stay for a lifetime and some are only around for a season.'"

He smiles at me, his hand infusing warmth into my face as he cups my cheek and drags his thumb back and forth along my jaw. "It's like that. Those feelings are part of you for a reason, but that doesn't mean you have to hold onto them forever."

Warm tears crest my lashes, and I laugh through them. "You and your mom always have a way of saying just the right thing."

"Do we?" I appreciate that he's surprised by my comment. "Must be a learned trait. She always knows just what to say to me."

I wipe my eyes.

Sutton's hand slides into my hair. He grips my neck possessively and pulls me forward for a searing kiss. "You are too good to hold onto those things. The only thing you need to hold onto every day is love. And if you can't feel enough, then I'm not doing my job, and I'll have to show you more."

I smile against his warm lips. "I always feel your love."

His voice is a whisper. "Good."

I press onto my knees, and his hand falls from my hair. "Maybe I could use a *little* more showing."

"Oh yeah?" His words barely precede me pushing him to sit and straddling him.

"Mmhmm." The vibration of sound travels through my lips into his neck as I kiss him with an open mouth.

He groans quietly, acutely aware of the rest of the team somewhere in the trees, and grips my ass with a firm hand. "As much as I would love to show you just how much," he starts to punctuate his words with kisses of his own against my neck, "I don't think that's why you're out here."

A dismissive grunt is the only response I give him as I press back, placing my hands firmly on his chest. There's too much love pouring out of him. Even though that's exactly what we're discussing, emotions are what I'm trying to avoid. I'd much rather deal in a carnal connection with him at this moment.

"I know what you're doing." His voice is low.

I don't bother hiding it.

"You wanna ride the cowboy? I'm yours. Every fucking day. But you have to make the call, Firecracker. You can't avoid what's going on outside this ranch."

I huff and kiss the corner of his mouth sweetly. "Fine. But I'm not gonna like it."

He grins before shoving off the ground. "You want me to stick around?"

I shake my head. "No. I'll be a good girl and call."

I throw myself back onto the grass and wait until the rustle from Sutton and Johnny Walker leaving has ceased before calling Detective Porter back. He's left his direct number and picks up on the second ring.

"Detective Porter." His greeting is just as blasé as the rest of him.

"Detective Porter, this is Maci McCullough."

"Yes. Thank you for calling."

I throw an arm over my face, blocking out the clouds. *Like I have a choice.*

He continues. "I have a few follow-up questions. I don't need you to come to the station yet, but I did want to touch base with you."

My muscles tense. I'm regretting the choice not to hire an attorney again. Maybe Hank has some options.

"After we last spoke, I spoke with Colt's father." He pauses as if I'm going to respond in a specific way.

Instead, I close my eyes, willing my body to relax into the cool grass and ignore the fury coursing through my veins.

"He had a different take on things and shared an older incident with us. Said you pulled a knife on him."

My emotions battle amongst themselves, trying to see if rage or defeat is going to come out on top. I can't believe after everything that he's done, everything I've done to distance myself from him and his abusive tendencies, this may be the story that does me in.

"Do you have anything to say about that?"

Exhaling heavily, I nod to no one, my hair tangling in the grass. "Sure. I'll explain."

Detective Porter's pen clicks.

"Alan made a point to remove any autonomy from me that he could. As a teenager, he constantly made remarks about my clothing, hobbies, dates.

Looking back, he was highly inappropriate, but at the time I thought he was just being an asshole."

"Uh uh." He doesn't sound convinced, but I'm not done.

"He and my mother were both dismissive about anything emotional, not that I came to them with much. He always wanted gratitude where it wasn't warranted. Wanted congratulations when he hadn't earned it. Everything was about image." I jump off the ground, pacing. "The night he's referring to was not long after I turned eighteen, as you said. In fact, I had about three weeks of high school left until graduation."

"He said it was summer."

"I'm not going to argue the seasons with him. It was the last week of April."

"Do you remember the date?" he presses.

"No, not that I see how it matters. But it was a Friday, if that helps."

"Friday. Got it."

"I had plans to go out. Alan had been extra pissed for days. For once, I don't think it had anything to do with me. I just took the brunt. Just before I planned to leave, Alan waltzed into the kitchen where I was. He tried to give me a curfew for an earlier time than I wanted, which I had already worked out with my mother. It wasn't a significant event, honestly."

"Go on." Detective Porter's tone is neutral.

"I argued the time. He got agitated quickly and crowded me into a corner. I told him that I was an adult and that I could stay out later than whatever time he was insisting on. He grabbed my face with his hand and told me that if I was living in his house, it was by his rules. The knife was something I always carried on me, and I pulled it out without thinking. It pressed into the fabric of his pants at his hip. I doubt it did any damage."

"You don't know?"

"I didn't stick around. When he let go of me, I grabbed a bag of clothes and left."

"Were you injured?"

"I had bruises on my face." I recall trying to hide the marks on my face with makeup so no one at school would see, how the flesh of my cheeks had been pressed hard against my teeth, causing them to be tender for several days as they healed.

"Did you report this?"

I sigh. "No. I was young and just wanted to get away."

"Ok. Where'd the knife come from?"

"It was my grandmother's. Well, I found it in her garage." I still have the knife in one of my camera cases.

"Was anyone else there that night? Your mother?"

Sliding into the seat of the Defender, I press my fingers to my temple to stave off the oncoming headache. "No. She arrived after. I called and told her what happened, and he told her his side when she got there."

He's quiet for a few seconds. "Alright. I don't have anything else for now. If I need anything, I'll give you a call."

Despite his neutral tone, our call leaves me feeling defeated. "Ok."

"Have a good day, Maci." He hangs up.

CHAPTER 22

MACI

I question my decision to come here as I stare at the closed chain-link fence. Anxiety turns my stomach. Beyond the gate is a large, black metal building with cedar post columns. It's an attractive mix of rustic and industrial construction. Motorcycles fill the open space in front of it, some covered by a structure similar to a carport.

A man wearing the club cut saunters up to the gate. I've seen him riding with James and the others, and he was one keeping tabs when James came for a visit.

My window whirs its descent and I tip my head out. "Hey. I'm here to see James." His eyebrow quirks. "Maci," I add. I have no idea if that's going to help me or not in terms of getting in.

The man's eyebrows shoot up, and he presses some buttons on a keypad nearby. The gate rattles as it slides open, and the man gestures to a space near the front door for me to park.

A cold breeze greets me as I hop down from the Jeep. The man who let me in yells something through the front door, held open. He turns back to me. "Come on in."

When I get close, he extends a hand. "Hawk."

Hawk, the Falcon. I don't ask how that works or which came first.

"Nice to meet you." I don't ask if it's his given name or not. His handshake is pleasant enough, and he waits for me to enter the building before following me in. Another twenty or so men are spread out in the large, open area, seated at round wooden tables with well-crafted leather and wood chairs. There are more people here than I would expect on a Monday afternoon.

A long bar with a glossy top is situated on the entrance wall, and a woman with shiny auburn hair stands behind it. She peers at me suspiciously. I brush it off. She can be territorial if it suits her.

On the left are a couple of pool tables. A few guys continue chatting, but I've definitely drawn attention to myself. I wonder if this is a men-only club.

Aside from their vests, they wear an array of clothing. Dark jeans, light jeans, button ups, tees. Some wear caps or bandanas.

Like outside, the inside of the building is a mix of sharp, dark metals, next to unblemished, well-cut wood. On the back wall is a set of French doors, cased in charred wood. The style is beautifully distressed. It's more stylish than I would expect for a bunch of guys who ride motorcycles.

Near the French doors is a staircase which leads up to the next level. It's fully exposed along the front except for a narrow railing. My eyes catch on a pair of riding boots and legs descending from above. James comes into view, and a smile automatically spreads across my face.

His eyes light upon landing on me. "Gracie, I'm glad you're here." He tips his chin down at Hawk in acknowledgment. It's a gesture that's becoming familiar for him. "Thank you."

"You bet, Prez."

"Thanks." I give Hawk a sideways glance and make my way across the floor to where James reaches the bottom of the stairs.

He opens his arms subtly for me and I lean in for a short hug. Physical affection doesn't always come naturally to me, but James' arms encase me in a comforting way, even if I'm a little stiff at the newness of it all. When I step back, his hands rest on my shoulders and he looks me over. "You look good, lass."

I don't have to come up with a polite remark as he releases me and opens one side of the French doors. He gestures inside and waits for me to enter before following and closing the door behind us.

Truthfully, I'm not sure what I'm expecting from this visit, but a part of me hopes to learn something about James by visiting a place he frequents.

"How are you?" My question comes out more abrupt than I'd like.

He turns to me with a knowing look and sits at the head of a long table. The top is a full slab of wood, charred and glazed like the other pieces I've seen. A gavel sits near his chair, a combination of dark leather and styled wood, matching the surroundings.

"Do you have an interior designer?"

He smiles. "Only me."

My eyes widen. "You designed all this?"

How are the men in my life so creative, design-wise? I think of Sutton's massive cedar post bedframe with its footboard of entangled branches. Maybe it's fitting, since I'm a photographer.

"Don't sound so surprised. It's my home; it should feel as such." He motions for me to sit in a chair at the right of the table.

A new cloud of anxiety swirls around me. It feels both formal and familial to take a seat here. Whose chair is this normally?

I sit anyway. "You live here?"

"Aye." He pauses, studying my face. "After Stephanie left, I didn't want to be in the house we shared. It didn't matter that it was mine before her. It didn't feel like home without the two of you in it. So, I started on this place."

I'm surprised at his emotional admission. "It's beautiful."

He dips his chin in thanks. "That's not why you came, though." He holds my gaze.

"I don't know why I came. I know that probably sounds awful." He makes a dismissive face at my comment. "Everything in my life feels new, up in the air, in limbo. I'm not really sure. I know we don't have memories—well, I don't have memories—but..." My voice trails off. I have no clue what I'm trying to say or why, so how can I possibly explain that to him?

"You don't need a reason to be here, Gracie." I warm again at his nickname for me. "If you need to get away and come here, you'll always be welcome. If you want answers on something, I can only provide limited information, but I'll try. And if you need help, consider it done."

I swallow thickly. It feels so odd that a man I barely know has embraced me so willingly and openly, has invited me into his home and offered me sanctuary, when the mother who raised me struggles to let me in or be emotionally available. The person who stole me away in the night to protect me is more distant than the man she was trying to protect me from.

"Stephanie will be in town for a while," I blurt. One of his eyebrows lifts in response. "I let her know what happened with Colt. She's leaving Alan, her husband." Adrenaline surges through me. "It turns out he's Colt's father."

James shifts casually in his chair and lays his hands in his lap. "That's a hard situation."

I don't dwell. "She's going to be moving into Nana's house temporarily."

"And how will that affect you?" His voice turns harder. Was that intentional?

169

"Me? Well, I have plans for the house. Business plans. A bed and breakfast and a photography studio. But Stephanie and I don't really see eye to eye on much. I'll probably lay low until she's settled somewhere." I chew my cheek in contemplation.

He crosses his arms and narrows his gaze. "Is she aware of your plans for the house?" There's a pleasing cadence to his phrasing.

I shake my head. "No. I didn't tell her."

"Why?" His question is less curious, more pointed.

A heavy sigh leaves me. "I choose my battles. Some things are easier not to discuss if I don't really have a need. My grandmother stipulated in the will that my aunt have full control of the house and everything in it while Stephanie is married to Alan. Things were pretty tense between us after the lunch you saw, and the conversation with my aunt Randi to discuss my plan happened shortly after. Even if I had wanted to tell her, everything went sideways after that."

"You didn't plan to tell her."

"It's not worth the headache of her knowing beforehand."

His full lips purse, and he strokes his trimmed beard. "Because she'd try to keep it from you if she could?"

I lever my head side-to-side. "Not so much that she'll try to keep it from me, but she can be overcautious and put her foot down when she thinks she's in the right. She doesn't actually have any power over it at this point, but that doesn't mean she wouldn't be annoying about it given the opportunity."

"Do you think she'll move on quickly if she doesn't know your plans?" I'm surprised that he's so concerned about this, but I enjoy listening to him talk. "Say she'll decide to settle here instead."

I shake my head vigorously. "No. She's said our lives aren't here. I can't imagine her staying."

He studies me for a moment, pinning me with another pointed look. "What if she decides it's time to smooth things over with her daughter? You did have a rough go of it lately, even if you handled it on your own. She's still your mam."

My stomach tightens. "I'm not holding my breath."

"Do you want her to stay?"

"Every daughter wants to have a strong relationship with their mother. Right? I'll always wonder why things couldn't be better between us, but here we are. And if her being here adds to my continual stress, then no, I don't want her to stay. In fact, I was fully prepared to go no-contact with her prior to Nana's passing."

He bobs his head slowly several times without responding, mulling over my words. "How's the rancher?"

I smile. "He's good. He's been very attentive."

"You like the ranch?"

"I'm getting to know it. But yes, in theory."

"Good." His eyes remain soft as he lets the quiet linger after his statement.

I take a deep breath. "Actually, there is one thing I want to talk to you about."

"Oh?" His face remains passive.

"Colt. Well, his funeral." I hesitate, unsure of how he's going to react.

James stares at me without speaking. I don't know what to make of his tight expression. His emotions are always so composed. Unlike my mother, who does it to present something perfect, I get the impression he wants to appear open, receptive, even if what he's thinking is not so much. I'm still learning his tells. Though if he didn't like something, I think I'd know.

171

"I spoke with his mother. She hinted that he may have had a mental disorder. Nothing was ever diagnosed, but she described him as frequently paranoid and increasingly aggressive."

After a moment he says, "He'd not been with the club long, so I didn't have a chance to observe if that's accurate."

"I didn't know him long either." My eyes fall to the floor. "Anyway, I'm going to be attending his service."

"Do you think that's a good idea?"

I smile. "He's already dead. He can't hurt me now."

He smirks. "Not what I meant. I mean his Da. Won't he be there?"

"Yes. I suppose he will." A challenging smile graces my lips. "Alan's felt the end of my blade. I'm not worried about him."

James tilts his head gently in disagreement. "I wouldn't be so quick to judge. You took him on as a teenager. One who hadn't killed his only kin. He likely won't react that way he used to."

I frown at the blunt way he addresses what happened with Colt. Not that it's accusatory. Just uncomfortable.

"I'll come," he says plainly.

My heart rate kicks up at his speedy decision. "Really?"

"Aye. I'll not let my daughter go marching into the funeral of the man she killed, with his very angry kin, unprotected."

An unfamiliar tingle coats my skin, and my cheeks heat.

He stands. "Let's show you around, in case you care to spend any amount of time here."

There are more men filling the main room compared to a few minutes ago. It's nearing dinner, but it appears most are drinking their meal.

"Hey! Maci!" A familiar voice catches my attention, and I snap my head its direction to find Pete walking over from one of the pool tables.

172

"Pete, how are you?" I force a pleasant smile. As Colt's friend, I'm not sure what he thinks of the situation.

He shuffles. "Heard what happened with Colt. They're really taking this seriously. You doing ok?"

I nod. "Yeah, thanks." My fingers are drawn toward the scar on my side, but I drop my hand. I'm not sure how much they know, and I'm not interested in getting into the details.

Pete's eyes drop to my side, and his face softens as his gaze returns to me.

"All good," I press.

"Prez." Pete nods at James.

My father's eyes linger on him, not unlike the way they studied Colt the night we met at the bar. He finally nods, and I take in the rest of the room. Several people sneak glances our way.

James clears his throat, chatter dying down around us. "Listen up. I'm going to say this once and only once." He looks around the room with a dark gaze. "This is Maci. She's my daughter. Nobody fucks with her, or I'll castrate you on the spot." His bright green eyes land on Pete.

I should be annoyed that he announced our connection without asking, but I'm unbothered. Murmured agreement travels through the room. Pete stares at me bewildered, while James waits for him to nod agreement.

A brighter patch on Pete's leather cut draws my attention. It has a freshness to it that some of the others lack. Where Prospect used to be, a Member patch has replaced it.

Hawk approaches from James' other side. I study him closer this time. He sports a Vice President patch, among others that I largely ignore. He's the only one that doesn't seem surprised by the new information.

"You met Hawk." James acknowledges his presence before addressing him directly.

The majority of the group seems to be older than Pete and me, though they vary in age somewhat, aside from one guy sitting alone at the bar chatting with the bartender.

James looks the same direction I have. "That's Ginger." He motions to the woman behind the bar. Her greeting is stiffer than the others, only acknowledging me with a glance. James doesn't bother introducing the rest, and I wonder if it's because there are so many or some other reason.

Slowly, our observers return to their conversations. James gestures to the stairs. "Upstairs are a few rooms with beds. Occasionally the guys will stay over, but I suggest staying out of that area, lest you find something you aren't looking for." He grins.

I laugh. "Noted."

His smile remains wide another moment before he continues. "I have private quarters on the third floor. You ever need to get away, you head up there." I don't know what I could need to get away from that would drive me here for refuge, but I nod in acknowledgement.

"I'll let Petey show you around outside." He turns to Pete. "Church in ten."

My brows furrow.

"Proud of you, Gracie." James winks at me and turns to talk quietly with Hawk.

I turn to Pete. "Church?"

"Yeah. It's club meeting lingo. It was already planned; that's why there are so many people here. Buuut, after the news he just shared, I'm thinking he'll have more to go over."

I shrug. "Not much to share, honestly."

Pete gives me a skeptical look. "You need a drink?"

"Sure."

He heads toward to the front door by way of the bar. We stop at the glossy bar top and the lone man there salutes me with his beer.

I offer a friendly, "Hey."

"McCoy," is all he says. His curt speech reminds me of Colt, only this guy has the bad-boy look in spades.

"Nice to meet you."

Ginger leans against the bar with a less-than-hospitable look. I don't know what her damn problem is. It's already been made abundantly clear why I'm here. What could she possibly have a problem with? "What can I getcha, Mouse?"

My temper flares.

"Don't be stupid, Ginger," Pete says from behind me. McCoy's attention doesn't leave us.

"Do I look meek to you?" I cock my head.

"That's not what she means," Pete grumbles.

I lean both hands onto the bar and press my face closer to hers. "Well, why don't you tell me what you mean, *Ginger*."

She stands upright and crosses her arms. "I don't care if you're some little runaway. This isn't your home."

I laugh. "I'm not a runaway. I don't know what your problem is, but if you're worried that I'm going to stop you from fucking my dad, then reel it in. I don't care who you, or he, bangs."

Ginger's face turns a deep shade of red and her smug look falters.

"And for the record, I'm no fucking mouse. James' support or not, you'll meet claws if you come at me."

Pete wraps an arm around my waist from behind, pulling me toward the front door. "Come on, Maci."

I hold Ginger's eyes until they search for my father. James watches intently, though he doesn't say anything.

McCoy lets out a low whistle as we walk by. "Well, you can certainly see the Irish fire in that one." He takes another long pull from his beer.

Outside, Pete releases me at the same time I shove away from him. "You good?" He studies my face, waiting.

I just stare at him. He continues to wait with a pointed look.

Releasing a huge breath, I scan the lot. "Ok, so maybe I overreacted a little bit."

His eyebrows raise slightly. "I mean, I like a good cat fight, but I don't want to see you tussle with Ginger." He puts a hand up. "It's not that I don't think you can handle your own. In fact, I know you can. But I need you to put in a good word for me with Leah, and I need James to let me stick around, so keeping you out of drama is going to be a priority."

"I don't need you to keep me out of drama." I cross my arms. I don't address the Leah bit, even though I remember his puppy dog eyes when we left that night. "Just tell me what that comment was."

"A house mouse." He shifts back and forth on his feet, rubbing the top of his backward cap with a hand. "She was just being a bitch."

I say nothing, and he eventually continues. "It's a term sometimes used for young runaways. They want a bad boy and find their way to MC clubhouses. Some stick around for work, some stick around for dick."

I roll my eyes and shake my head, my blood reheating angrily.

"She's not fucking James," he continues. I don't look at him. "She probably *would*, given the chance, but she's not his type. Come to think of it, I don't actually know if he has a type."

I hold a hand up by my face to stop him talking and figuratively push away the unwanted details. "It doesn't matter. I don't need or want to know about his sex life. We've barely met each other, and I'm just trying to see if we can have a real relationship."

"That explains why you two didn't interact at The Spur that night."

That night. The night I met Colt. A man I didn't realize was my stepbrother. The same night I met James, who I didn't know was my father. I snort. This is all too much.

"Also, you wanna tell me why you're carrying?" He crosses his arms.

I have half a mind not to respond. "How do you know I'm carrying?"

His mouth tips up on one side and he gestures to my long-sleeved shirt. "That's not as loose as you think it is. And I felt it when I pulled you away from the bar."

I close my eyes. "Habit."

We stare at each other for a moment. "I had to talk to the detective. About you," he adds, like I don't know what he means.

"You don't have to tell me." I look into the parking lot. A few stragglers hurry into the building.

"I didn't lie. I told them what I knew. Which is very little, because frankly, Colt didn't tell me shit. But I do know he was obsessed with you." He smirks. "And it might get me punched saying so, but as hot as you are, it's not surprising. But still not his style."

He waits quietly for me to say something.

"Ok, that wasn't appropriate, I just mean—"

"I know what you mean," I cut him off. Too much from the last few weeks pummels into me. "I gotta go. I'll talk to you later."

"See you around." He gives a small wave as I hurry back to the Jeep. Despite the space here, I need the open skies of the ranch. Everything is closing in on me.

CHAPTER 23

SUTTON

Maci's Jeep throws a shit ton of dust up behind her as she speeds up the driveway and parks. She slams her door hard enough that the Jeep rocks side to side. Her steps are heavy, stomping around the corner, and she misses me as I come out of The Big House.

Guess that soreness is wearing off.

I don't bother calling after her. I'm actually a little pleased to see some fire in her. She's been so stoic since everything with Colt. Unless she's trying to jump me.

The door closes loudly behind her, and I throw it open again almost immediately.

She jolts in the hallway where she's sliding out of her shoes. "Oh! I didn't know you were there."

"I bet not." I grin. "Who pissed in your Cheerios this morning?"

She tilts her head and gives me an exasperated look. "I don't know if going to the MC was the best idea."

My brows tighten. "Why? James say something?"

"No." She shakes her head and backs into the bedroom, apparently unaware of the effect she has on me as she inadvertently leads me in. "Actually, he seems very welcoming and supportive. It's a little surreal."

When she doesn't continue, I prod further. "Then?"

178

"The bartender."

"The bartender?"

She throws herself onto the couch and pins me with an annoyed look. I slide down next to her and pull her legs atop mine, beginning to rub her calves. "Ginger. I don't know. She made some stupid comment about me being a House Mouse."

"Come again?"

"A runaway?" She sounds as confused as me. "I don't know. Pete said it didn't fit. I mean, obviously it doesn't fit. She probably felt threatened." She shrugs, but it's not as dismissive as she's going for.

I consider what she's said. "I'm going to guess you didn't let her have the last word."

Her cheeks redden, but her eyes have a wicked gleam and a smirk tugs at her lips. "Maybe I did, maybe I didn't."

I squeeze her thigh. "Damn. Wish I could've been a fly on the wall." A sheepish giggle escapes her, and I'm proud of the small victory.

Her head falls backward onto the arm of the couch. "How's everything going here?"

"Buttery smooth."

Her cool fingers slip into mine on her leg. "That good, huh?"

"Yep. In fact, I have some time this afternoon. If you're up for it, I want to give you a lay of the land here. It'll be helpful if you start to get a feel for what's around, especially with the expansion coming up."

She wipes her face blank for a split second before dropping her feet onto the floor and sitting forward in a swift motion. "Sure. Let me put my boots on."

Her sudden mood change has me on alert.

"Do you ride?"

A coy smile greets me over her shoulder.

"I walked right into that one." Along with shoving everything under a rug, I suspect she'd use sex to avoid all the emotions whipping around inside her these last few days, even ignoring her injury, if I gave her the opportunity. "Have you ridden horses?"

She pretends to study her socks intently as she puts them on, avoiding eye contact. "Not in a while. Izzy's family has horses, and I rode with her a few times when we were younger."

"Are you nervous?"

She meets my gaze. "I'm a little rusty, but I'm not nervous about the horses. I understand bits and pieces about animals and ranches. I just want to make sure I soak it all in." She heads for the hallway where all the boots are.

I snake one arm out and pull her flush against my body. Damn, she feels good like that.

"No one is judging you here. Not about ranch life or anything else." She softens in my arms, and I dust her face and mouth with gentle, chaste kisses. "Even if you decide you don't want to participate in what goes on here, I won't be upset with you."

Her eyes well and she nods with a sad smile.

"Come on. I have someone I want you to meet."

"Ok, let me just grab my camera."

Maci's quiet while we drive the Defender to the stables. Her lips purse thoughtfully and she gives me a curious look. "Did you forget I know Johnny Walker?"

I shake my head, smiling. "Not Johnny Walker."

I round the front and open her door. "Look at you being a good girl and waiting patiently." Her pupils expand and a gorgeous blush rushes into her neck and face.

Fuck.

Keeping my hands off of her has only been manageable because the prospect of hurting her is unfathomable. Knowing she's healing well causes my desire to crest.

"I'm always a good girl." She holds my gaze boldly.

Tucking my head into her hair, I nuzzle her neck before placing a long kiss below her jaw. "Yes, you are."

Her sharp inhale makes my cock jump, and I smirk against her skin. She smells like my body wash, causing a primal pleasure at her being somehow marked as mine, but I also miss her spicy cinnamon scent.

Tangling my fingers with hers, I lead her into the stables. The last stall houses the horse I want her to meet. "This is Veda."

Awestruck eyes fly to me and back to the painted horse. Veda's coat is a mix of the darkest walnut and pure white, crafted artfully over her strong body.

"Veda?" She studies the horse, transfixed, but I don't miss the curiosity around the name.

"Mama named her," I confirm.

Veda's head swings toward her at the stable door. Maci rubs the dark muzzle confidently. "That doesn't sound much like Daisy."

She's right. Mama naming animals has about as much of a pattern to it as if I tried my hand at her crocheting. "Apparently it means wise. Don't ask me how she comes up with these things."

Maci laughs, and I can see the other side of this darkness that we're in. That one sound reminds me that there's a way through all of the bullshit; we just have to get there together.

"You wanna ride her?"

Maci talks to Veda instead of me. "What do you think, Veda? Want to take me for a spin?" She pulls her hand back from rubbing and Veda nudges forward, seeking contact again. There's only a hint of hesitation on Maci's face.

"She's really calm. A sweet girl." I wrap an arm around Maci's waist, tucking her against me.

"Okay." I hardly hear her.

As we prep the horses for the ride, I talk Maci through the process of saddling. She rubs her free hand over Veda as she brushes and watches intently at everything I tell her about getting the saddle on right.

"You ready?" I press my front to Maci's back, setting my hands on her hips. "I'll give you a boost."

She smirks over her shoulder. "Don't think I can do it?"

Shifting my mouth close to her ear, I lower my voice. "I'm confident you can do it. Just like you can do anything you set your mind to. I just want to touch you, Firecracker. That ok?"

Her hips shift backward the slightest bit. "That all?"

I kiss the crook of her neck. "For now." My grip tightens on her waist. "Ready?"

She nods, puts her left leg into the stirrup and shifts, while I help lift her sweet ass onto Veda. I don't miss her wince as she rights herself.

"You good? If you're not ready, we don't have to go out yet."

She shakes her head quickly. "No, I'm fine. I'm sore still, but I'm okay."

I know better than to think Maci will be forthcoming with me, so I study her a few seconds longer to assess for myself. She has more tells than she thinks. Her head drops over to one side and she pins me with a sassy look.

Fine. She can be sore then.

I mount Johnny Walker and we head out. Maci rides quietly next to me, listening to everything I tell her like there's a test. She asks about all of the structures we come across, studying the animals and generally enjoying the ride.

Some might think she's shy with the way she can fall into quiet so easily, but I don't think there's ever a time where she's not in her head. Thinking, creating, analyzing.

Periodically, she lifts the camera and takes photos. Shots of the herd, the landscape, me—though I try to ignore the last part.

I decide to finish our tour by bringing her to our future home site. She perks up as soon as we pass the fence line, but I can practically hear her wheels turning.

"What's going on in that pretty head?"

She smiles softly at me. "I'm wondering about something, but I'm almost afraid to bring it up."

"Because of me?"

"No. I don't want to manifest it."

I have a feeling I won't like where this is going. "That's not quite how that works. What's up?"

Her hands tighten on the reins and Veda bobs her head.

"Loosen up, Firecracker." Her arms fall into her lap, but the tension still remains. "Do you trust me?"

She peers into my soul as she speaks. "With my life."

"Drop the reins."

Her eyes widen.

I smirk. "Be a good girl and do as I say. Drop the reins." She does, and my cock jumps again. It shouldn't be that fucking sexy for her to obey, but damn if there's anything I can do to make my body react differently. "Now, tell me what the problem is."

I look out over the land and wait for the words to come to her. Veda and Johnny Walker slow and begin to graze in what will someday be our front yard. "What if I'm arrested?"

My head snaps her way. "That's not going to happen."

"You can't just say it and expect it to be true." She's staring into the distance.

"Isn't that what you just said about manifesting?" I stare at her. "Maci."

"Sutton." She turns to hold my stare. "You cannot ignore this any more than I can."

Despite the distance between us, the tension is a connective link. Our shallow breaths are in time. Neither of us speaks at first.

We've touched on this over the last week or so, but we haven't jumped in. Haven't really discussed the hard things. It's like we're about to head into the deep together, and that light that I saw in the stables may not be enough to bring us through the abyss.

I know the stakes are high. It's why I want her to have a lawyer. But it's not lost on me that sometimes the system fails anyway.

We continue to stare.

Finally, she whispers, "I killed someone."

It's easier to defend her when she's worried. My worries are different. "You were defending yourself."

She shakes her head. "It doesn't matter. If the detective disagrees, he'll turn this over to the prosecutor. We need to talk about what happens if they decide to prosecute me." When I still don't speak, she continues. "You weren't there. Detective Porter doesn't believe me."

I drop my head. "I knew we should've gotten you a lawyer."

"I still can. I just hoped that if I was open with them, and with the other reports, they'd see it wasn't malicious."

Frustration rises in me. Maci is so used to doing everything on her own that she won't accept my help, won't see reason. I can't lose her to jail after everything. "They'd be stupid not to see the truth," I tell her. "And I want to get you a lawyer."

"That's not the point. I want to know what you're going to do." Her voice rises with anxiety.

I jump off Johnny Walker and pull Maci off Veda in a flash. Gripping her face between my hands, I speak low. "You're not getting arrested. We're getting you a lawyer and getting this sorted out. And on the very slim, never-going-to-happen, strictly hypothetical chance that you do, I'm going to be with you every step of the way. You're not going to jail, Firecracker. I don't care if I have to blow up the entire fucking building with everyone in it before you get there."

There is no world where Maci being trapped in jail is going to fly.

Her eyes glisten and she nods. "Ok."

She wraps her arms tightly around me, pressing herself against me completely, and I return the action, squeezing her to me like someone is on their way to take her now.

"We need to name this place." Her change of topic catches me off guard.

I lean back to look at her. "It has a name. Strickland Ranch."

She grins. "I don't mean the *whole* place, I mean *this* place." She swings one arm around the expansive area.

"Ah." I take in the secluded space. "What do you have in mind?"

She presses her lips flat. "Just something that represents us and our life. Like Nopal Vista. It's Spanish—"

"I love it," I promise, interrupting her. She doesn't need to finish telling me that nopal is the Spanish word for the prickly pear cactus or that vista means view.

"Yeah? I was just thinking about the one you gifted me from out here. It's not silly?"

"Not at all. I love it." I tip her chin up with a finger and capture her mouth in a firm kiss. Her arms pull back and she slides her hands up my chest, pulling a groan from me. "I've missed you."

Her hands still. "I've been here."

I shake my head. "Carefree you. Present you."

"I see what you mean." She pauses. "I'm not sure I'll ever be exactly her again."

My thumb rubs against her soft cheek. She's so tender, and yet also the strongest woman I've ever known. "That's ok. As long as I get to come with you."

She fists my shirt in both hands, all but dragging me down to her for a heated kiss.

CHAPTER 24

MACI

Gripping Sutton's shirt like my life depends on it, I break our kiss. "Take me home, Cowboy."

The corner of his mouth tips up. "You are home." His thumb rubs along my cheek again.

"Our temporary home, then." My voice is husky.

He kisses me with a hard, closed mouth. "I like the sound of that."

Veda and Johnny Walker graze nearby, and Sutton gives me another boost before climbing astride Johnny. The way his arms tug on the reins, swiftly guiding Johnny Walker where he wants to go, ignites my body in an entirely new way. I know what that feels like. To have his hands be completely in control. My skin tingles at the thought of having them upon me again.

Veda follows suit, though my guiding isn't expert level. As she walks forward, Sutton leans back the slightest bit, looking me over with a wicked grin.

My mouth pulls into a stupid smile, though I have no idea what he's after, and I take him in.

"Want to race?" He only gives me a split second before he squeezes his legs on Johnny and they're off.

What a cheater.

I give a similar squeeze on Veda, but it takes her a moment to get going. I loosen my grip on the reins, grabbing the pommel of the saddle instead, and lean forward, as if she can't hear me sitting upright. "Come on, girl. Don't let me down."

We don't have a chance in hell. With the head start and Johnny Walker's speed, Veda and I come in last place. Sutton is already on the ground and pulls me off Veda in a rush as I round the front of the stables.

Cody picks the perfect time to exit the building. "Hey guys."

"Cody, you mind taking care of Veda and Johnny?" Sutton doesn't take his eyes off me despite his softer-than-usual voice.

Cody looks between us. "Not at all, boss."

"Thanks," I whisper, and we're in the Defender before Cody can respond.

We barely make it through the door when Sutton pins me up against the wall with a hard kiss. We're both kicking out of our boots, trying not to lose connection with our lips and hands.

He manages to get his hat onto the rack, and my hands reach for the hem of my shirt. He covers them with his own.

"Let me."

Another wave of warmth floods me.

He removes my top slowly, admiring me in my bra and jeans before him. His perusal stops on the healing wound on my hip. It's the first day I've left the area free of a bandage.

The muscle is tender from riding, but it feels good to work it out anyway.

All at once, he drops down to his knees, grabbing my hips with his hands, and leans in to kiss the stitched area. The warmth of his lips combined with the tenderness of his touch is oddly erotic, and I lay my hands on his head.

He tucks his thumbs into my jeans and slides them off me before rising. Wetness pools between my legs.

I hardly breathe, entranced as he slowly opens the front of his shirt, button by excruciating button. I don't dare move. The anticipation of what he plans to do is killing me, but I know with one wrong move he'll go back into protector mode.

I may actually die if he stops.

I lick my lips, not taking my eyes off his hands, which remove his undershirt next, leaving his tanned, muscular body on display before me. My hands rise and fall. If I touch him, will he stop?

He moves on to his belt, unbuckling it in the slowest fashion possible. His stormy eyes pin me in place, confidence, seduction, and pure hunger radiating from him.

Finally, his jeans fall to the ground, and I can't take it anymore. I take a tiny step forward. He watches intently but doesn't stop me. My hands travel the planes of his chest, fingers tracing along the muscles, eliciting shivers throughout his body.

His fingers slip under mine and he intertwines them together, pulling them to his mouth, where he kisses my knuckles in succession. When his gaze comes back to mine, there's a sensation that he's going to shatter me and rebuild me anew.

"I know you're healing, and I'm going to take good care of you, but I can't go another day without making love to you, Maci." His declaration has a question mark, as he waits for my approval. As if I could deny him.

I nod with a smile.

With a slight bend, he slides his hands down the backs of my thighs, gripping firmly just above the back of each knee and lifting me off the ground. I wrap my legs around him as he carries me to the bedroom, claiming my mouth in a searing kiss, my hands gripping his neck. Our bodies transfer warmth back and forth. His erection presses against my center, and I'm dying for him to be inside of me. With one hand, he releases the clasp of my bra and I slip it down, tossing it to the side.

Carefully, he lays me back on the bed, looming over me on all fours. The fact that he still has boxer briefs on and I'm in my panties is entirely too much. "Too many clothes," I breathe, and reach for the waistband on him.

He grips my wrist firmly. "Let me take care of you." I nod, my head surrounded again by the ridiculous number of pillows. Something I've grown fond of.

Once he's naked, he slides his fingers into my lacy waistband and slowly lowers the delicate material down my legs. A chill races over my skin as warmth pools in my core. He takes to the bed on his knees, speaking in a low, warm voice that saturates my limbs. "Look at you. All mine."

"Yes."

He leans over me, kissing me deeply before licking and kissing a trail down my body. My deep inhale brings with it the worn leather scent of him. His tongue circles around one pebbled nipple. My back arches, and he bites the nipple between his teeth before soothing it with his tongue. Moving to the other nipple, he follows the same method, biting harder this time. I groan and arch deeper.

A calloused hand grabs each knee, spreading me open before trailing his fingertips along the inside of my thigh. He traces over my pubic bone and rests just above my throbbing center.

"I can't wait to be inside you, but I can't go without a taste."

The anticipation causes my heart rate to skyrocket.

His thumb circles my clit in a whisper and my hips buck. I'm highly combustible in his hands. He always knows just how to touch and tease me to gain the reaction he seeks. A deep chuckle fills the space between us, followed by my heavy breathing. He doesn't relent. "Miss me, Firecracker?"

"Cowboy, what have I told you about teasing?" My hips rock against his hand.

The circling stops. "What are you going to do about it?"

Our push and pull is one of my favorite things about our relationship. Sutton's ability to take my body to places it's never been is in large part because I let him handle me at his discretion. A vulnerability I've never offered to a partner until him.

I prop myself up on my elbows and he eyes me suspiciously. His thumb traces lightly over the sensitive skin surrounding that bundle of nerves, driving me wild. And I let him.

"Nothing."

He tilts his head to one side in question.

"I'm not going to do anything, because I know that you take care of what's yours. You'll do the same with me."

He blows a cool breath at my clit. "Is that so?"

My head falls back between my shoulders at the fiery chill that shoots through me. "Yes. I want you to have your way with me." My core sends down a wave of arousal at my admission. Giving myself to him is a high I never anticipated.

"Fuck." Without another word, he dives into my pussy, licking, kissing, and sucking me into oblivion. My arms give and I fall flat again, my gasping filling through the room. He sucks hard on my clit before pulling back and driving two fingers deep inside me.

His mouth crashes onto mine, claiming and hot, swallowing my cry. Devouring me. Our tongues war and dance, greedy and insatiable. When he finally pulls back so we can breathe, my orgasm has already started to build.

Hot kisses rain down my neck and chest as he makes his way to my breasts, still thrusting into me with his hand. My fingers thread into his hair as he worships each breast.

Soon, my orgasm teases me the same way he does. Rocking against his hand, arching into his mouth, I soak in all the hot and wet sensations driving me to the edge.

He releases my nipple with a stinging bite. "You gonna come for me, Firecracker?"

My eyes pop open and find him. "Yes."

"Good girl." His mouth drags back down my body, licking and sucking hungrily when he reaches the highly sensitive place, still fucking me with his hand. All at once, I come apart, shaking and crying out his name. His appreciative groan against my pussy elongates the orgasm as wave after wave consumes me.

Like before, he slides his fingers gently out of me and places a last kiss on my clit. "I fucking love that." He pins me with his gaze, sucking his fingers slowly into his mouth and offering me a wicked grin.

I rub my legs together, already aching for more.

He leans over, pressing his lips to mine for a few moments, before burying his face in my neck to kiss and lick there. My body still seeks friction, pressing and rolling into him above me.

"Come 'ere." His voice catches as he moves to sit next to me. As I roll onto my hip, he gingerly guides me to straddle his lap. His shaft slides through the aftermath of my orgasm, and I rock my hips to slide over him again.

He grips my face between his hands. Nothing will ever compare to his touch. His lips against mine start out incredibly soft, becoming firmer as the kiss intensifies, and then he breaks it, leaving only a breath between us. "I'm going to show you every day how much you mean to me."

"You already do." An unspoken question lights his face. "It's the little things you do. The cactus on our first date. Making sure I have the right creamer for my coffee. The tire swing. Your ability to read me like a book. You don't have to promise me those things because you do it without thinking."

"I fucking love you, Maci." He bows his head to nip my breast before licking the sensitive spot he created, causing me to squeeze my thighs against him.

When he rights his head, his eyes are soft. A hand snakes between us, dragging his erection against my sensitive flesh in a teasing manner.

"Please..." It's a breath of a word.

"Maci," he says, waiting for my attention. "I'm not wearing a condom."

"I told you, I trust you." My rocking picks up. I need him inside of me.

"We haven't talked about kids." He licks the other nipple, biting gently this time. "Or anything else."

I grab his face with both hands, pulling his gaze to me. "I've never not used a barrier—"

"I'm not asking." His eyes are intense. "I think higher of you than to put me at risk, Firecracker. I'm giving you a chance to ask me."

Oh my God. How does he continue to get better and better?

"What part of I trust you with my life did you not understand?" My hips rock against him again. "And when the time is right, I will give you all the babies you want. For now, I'm on the shot." I press a hard kiss to his mouth. "But if you don't slide that hard fucking cock inside me right now, I will ride you and come like this."

He grins. "Do you eat with that dirty mouth?"

"Oh, do I."

With that, he adjusts the head of his cock at my entrance, and I ease onto him. My head falls back in ecstasy before he's fully in. Once he is, I grip his neck, dragging my thumbs against his jaw.

We build a rhythm together, sweat covering our bodies. I'm pretty sure this was in the to-don't of my discharge instructions after the incident, but I don't care.

"You feel so good wrapped around me." Sutton groans. "The perfect fit."

All my coherent thoughts are gone. I'm all sensation. It's just the feel of him thrusting inside of me, us tangled together, our combined sounds echoing around us.

He looks down to where we connect. "Look at you." No one has ever told me to watch as they fuck me, but when I look down to where we meet, watching as he thrusts into me, my arousal escalates. I'm dancing on the edge. My pace increases in response.

"Fuck, yes. Use me, baby. Let me see you explode all over my cock." His words coupled with him pressing hard against my clit cause me to shatter. I tuck my head against him and he murmurs, "So fucking good," and the sexiest grunt ever fills my ears as his head falls to my shoulder and he finds his release. His fingers dig into me and I'm lost in his heavy breaths, the heat of his exhales against my skin.

As our breathing and heartbeats calm, I pull his face to mine, kissing him hard. "There's something I need to tell you."

"Anything." He kisses me back.

"I'm not very good at sharing."

His responding laugh is the best sound I've ever heard. I grin proudly at him.

CHAPTER 25

STEPHANIE

It takes three glasses of wine and talking myself into it for days before I work up the nerve to check Alan's phone. I wait for him to fall asleep before me. Nearly an hour passes before his breathing becomes even and slow. I ease out of bed and round to his side. His phone lies on the side table, locked. Slowly, and with enough ringing in my ears that it may wake him, I slide his phone under his limp hand for a fingerprint.

The screen comes to life and my heart nearly barrels out of my chest. Rushing into the closet on quiet toes, I slip the door closed. If he catches me using my phone to take photos of his contacts, it's not going to end well.

I've never gone through someone else's phone, but his messages, or lack thereof, are concerning. While my own recent conversations include Randi, Maci, Mother, Alan, committee members, the dentist, bill reminders, and random others, Alan's are scant. My own name and two other women.

After videoing the messages in record speed, I place the phone back on the bedside table. The box for the security system is in our closet, and I'm able to clear the last few minutes of camera footage before slipping back into bed. Thankfully, though there is a camera in the bedroom, there isn't one in the bathroom or closet that I need to worry about.

I don't fall asleep for hours. Between wanting to investigate the messages and worrying that he'll find out what I've done and I won't actually wake up, it's the early hours of the morning before my body relaxes.

Even when I do finally fall asleep, every little sound wakes me. As soon as Alan stirs in the bed, I get up for the day.

He dresses in a dark suit, similar to what he wore to Mother's funeral. He's still not told me about Colt's death.

"You look nice." I run my hand down the soft lapel.

He grips my wrist firmly in one hand. "I'll handle you after I get back."

Handle. He hasn't handled my needs more than a handful of times, accidentally at that, since we've been married. Although, given the circumstances, I'm not sure if that's what he means in this instance.

Pressing my lips out in a soft pout, I nod. "I'm surprised you have a meeting so soon after getting home."

He never does—something else I've observed. He's a creature of habit.

He grunts a response but eyes me over the top of his glasses rim studiously. His brown eyes never did anything for me. Not like the sparkle of James' green. I drop my gaze and turn away. The least interested I seem, the better.

I mill around the house, tidying up things that don't need tidying and staring at the pages of a book I'm not reading, until he finally leaves. He's in a terrible mood and doesn't acknowledge me before he goes.

The moment his Mercedes leaves the drive, I hurry up the stairs to retrieve my phone and shut off the cameras. I've never done it before, because I had nothing to hide, but I've watched him enough times to know how. My frantic heartbeat is almost deafening.

The last time I remember packing this quickly was when James and I eloped.

I choose the largest suitcase and fill it with as many items as I can shove in, including the things I just relocated from Mother's, before grabbing my purse, phone charger, and a file of important documents from a filing cabinet in the office. I'd be surprised if ten minutes go by between Alan leaving and when I hurry out to my car. I don't stop again until I'm at the halfway mark between our house in Dallas and Bull Creek.

I stop at a ridiculously large, busy gas station. Alan and I never stop here. Tucking my car in an inside lane in the middle of the melee, I set the gas to pumping and take my phone with me to the tiny, fenced dog area, sitting on a bench under a tree.

My hands shake as I pull up the photo of Kathryn's number. This could all be a wild goose chase.

Does star sixty-seven still make a number private? I try it anyway when I call.

Her voice is poised, demure, when she answers. "Hello?"

She sounds like me. Is it her natural tone, or an affected one?

"Hello?" Her voice is louder the second time.

"Is this Kathryn?" Somehow, my voice comes out steady.

"Yes? Who's calling?"

What am I risking if I tell her the truth?

Everything. I'm risking everything.

"My name is Stephanie." I wait. "Stephanie Young."

"Young?" She startles. "Do I know you?"

"I think we have someone in common." My anger renews. It's what I need to continue. "Alan."

"Alan?" She falls silent again. I wait. "How do you know Alan?"

"He's my husband," I say, flatly.

"I beg your pardon!" She nearly shrieks through the phone. "Is this a joke?" She's angry. As she should be. He's lied to us both, and for who knows how long.

"I've been married to Alan for ten years."

"We're obviously talking about two different people. I've been married to Alan for six years, and people can't marry more than one person." Her tone indicates that she thinks she's solved our problem.

"Where do you think I got your number from?"

"I—" She falters. "I have no idea where you got my number from."

"Alan Young from Texas is my husband. He's here now."

"Let me talk to him." She almost spits the words.

"He's on his way to a funeral." I think.

"Convenient," she mutters. "Well, no one in Alan's life has passed recently, so we must be talking about different people."

I rattle off his number to her and she quiets. "You sent him a text yesterday to make sure he arrived at the hotel ok. He was showering in our bathroom."

There's silence and then she whispers, "This is insanity."

"The last ten years have been insanity. This is reality." It's now or never. "I'd like to compare some things, if you're comfortable."

"Might as well. I've devoted years to this prick. If you're right, I'm about to burn all of his clothes on the lawn."

Her idea doesn't sound half bad.

CHAPTER 26

MACI

The funeral home parking lot hosts two cars and a truck squished together near the front. However, the entire left side of the lot is overrun with motorcycles.

My voice comes out in a whisper. "They came."

"You didn't think they would?" Sutton's curiosity is genuine.

I shrug. "I think I pictured a handful of them coming, at most. Not a large portion."

Sutton's lips purse, and he surveys the sea of motorcycles.

This is a different location than Nana's funeral, and I'm thankful for that. After everything, I'm not sure I could step foot inside there right now. Not without completely breaking down.

Unlike Nana's funeral, today I do wear black. This isn't a celebration of life. It's a truly somber time, and my heart is broken at what's been lost and why. Not just for my part in it, but for how this all came to be.

Pete stands closest to the front doors. He nods in greeting as we approach. The club members aren't dressed any differently than usual. Jeans and t-shirts, leather cuts. I spot James approaching from the throng. He looks impeccable as always, his black jeans and crisp, white button-up paired with stylish black riding boots.

I smile at him, full of gratitude. Something like affection is there, too. He keeps showing up when I need him, and brick by brick it feels like we're building something.

Sutton and James shake hands, exchanging a cordial greeting. I watch them openly. There's a tension that lingers. Not animosity so much as limited trust.

"Thank you for coming. I didn't expect you to bring everyone." I lean into James' open arms for a short hug, and he kisses my cheek.

"It was their choice." He brushes off the comment.

"I'm going to find Melissa." I gesture to the door with my chin, and James waves me to enter while he stays behind.

The small room is sparsely decorated in dark jewel tones. A standard soundtrack of somber music filters softly through two mounted speakers. In the front row, Melissa sits with her head bowed, and her body shakes with silent sobs.

In this moment, I'm glad we ran into each other at the police department. Our acquaintance is an odd one, considering the circumstances, but no one should have to mourn their son alone. So without hesitation, I walk right up to the front row and sit in the open seat next to her.

Her shoulders continue to quake as I wrap my arms around her. "I'm so, so sorry," I whisper into her hair. This time, my apology isn't for my actions. It's simply a heartfelt reaction to her loss.

Sutton's hand rests on my shoulder, while he remains standing.

I continue to hold her until she dabs at her eyes with a mangled tissue and turns to look at me. Her eyes are swollen and red-rimmed. My arms fall to my lap and I shift back in the seat, creating more space between us.

Melissa lifts her gaze and takes in the room, suddenly filled with people. Her eyes widen and shoot back to me. "Did you do this?"

I can't decipher her tone. "I hope it's ok. My dad is the President of the Falcons, the motorcycle club Colt was a part of. I shared some of his struggles so they would understand that his actions didn't all come from a bad place."

Her lower lip trembles and tears pour over her lashes again. "Thank you."

Heavy tears roll down my own cheeks. "I wish I could do more."

"Will you sit with me?" Her voice is soft, timid. Nothing like the woman I've seen previously who, though grieving, had a certain conviction.

"Sure. If that's ok."

She pats my leg where I sit, and Sutton sits in the seat next to me. His arm drapes behind me, but not in the casual way he usually does. His body is stiff.

Many of the club members take seats throughout the room. I don't miss Hawk standing near the front door with my dad.

My dad. What an odd thought. I said it to Ginger before, but it's starting to feel more casual, natural, to think and say.

The room falls eerily quiet and tension builds. James gives Hawk a pat on the arm as he passes and saunters down the aisle our way. Alone, he maneuvers into the second row, sitting in the chair directly behind mine.

Melissa looks over her shoulder at him, and he nods in greeting.

Her attention draws past him, and I turn to see what's caught her eye.

Alan's glare is already on me as he enters from the double doors. He misses Hawk's gaze narrowing behind him.

My heart pounds in my chest. What information has been shared with him? Not that it matters. He's never needed a reason to hate me.

Like at Nana's funeral, Alan wears a black suit. I inspect him more critically than usual and note the perfect fit of the jacket and the sleek appearance of the pants. It's a beautiful set.

Contrarily, Colt's mom wears a thin, black dress with a shawl over the top. The ends are tattered and the state of the dress hints at being worn many times. I find myself looking for her reaction. After watching him in a mixture of sadness and disgust, she shakes her head and turns forward again, dabbing at her eyes.

Colt's words from Nana's house resurface. His rage over the financial disparity between how Alan lived with Stephanie and me compared to the trailer park that Colt and his mother lived in.

Instead of walking down the middle aisle as we did, Alan skirts along the side of the room farthest from us. If looks could kill, he'd make sure I was six feet under. He's always been less than tolerant of me, but this is a new level of hostility.

He doesn't acknowledge Melissa.

Sutton's arm around my shoulders tightens. Anger sizzles beneath his composed demeanor.

Alan seats himself in the center of the front row on the opposite side of the aisle. The closest club member is about three rows back from him.

An older man in a suit comes in, eliciting everyone's attention. The tension doesn't dissipate as he approaches the podium. He goes through a short service that concludes in a matter of minutes. No one else speaks, and there's hardly a mention of what Colt did with his life. There's just a small photo on the table where his simple gray urn sits.

There's no invitation to a lunch, which isn't surprising, considering this isn't a group that's going to spend any time together.

Colt's mother stays in her seat as Sutton and I rise. Pete nods from two rows back as he exits before us, but James makes his way around to Melissa. He begins to speak, but a different voice breaks the quiet first.

"I can't believe you had the gall to show your face here." Alan stands on the other side of the aisle, his eyes shooting death rays at me. His behavior is different than I've experienced. I'm used to his furious faces, as if his top could actually blow. Today, he seems smug, like he knows something I don't, despite his anger.

James turns and eliminates the space between Alan and him in three long strides. "You don't know me, but that's my daughter, and if you so much as breathe wrong in her direction, you're going to join your son as a pile of ashes." His accent is the thickest I've heard, leading me to believe he tempers it.

Alan's head snaps back and his weight shifts, though to his credit his feet remain planted.

James' voice quiets, but I don't think for one second it's to hide it from anyone. The fury rolling off of him is palpable, and for once, he's actually a little scary. "You're lucky I don't take care of you now. I know you put your hands on my daughter."

I'm rooted in place, silently wondering if Alan's teeth may actually break into pieces like in the cartoons considering how tightly he's gritting them.

Somehow, he has the balls to say, "Maybe someone should've put their hands on her sooner. She's a spoiled brat."

In the time it takes Sutton to jolt, and me to grip his arm to stop him moving, James wraps one hand around Alan's neck and sends him stumbling backward toward the far wall, until they're both pressed tightly to it. His grip doesn't loosen as he squeezes the life from Alan.

It seems no one followed the officiant out, because the Falcons are still scattered around the room, none moving to or away from the situation. Melissa is frozen next to me. She hasn't made a sound the entire time.

James' voice is lethally quiet. I almost miss what comes out between the volume and distance between us. "You're a vile piece of shite. You pick on people to counterbalance your tiny dick. But you will not disrespect my daughter again, or it will be the last thing you do."

Alan's face is turning a deep crimson, and he flounders like a fish in James' grasp, his own hands trying futilely to open my father's hand. The maneuver accentuates the difference in their builds, despite the relatively similar height.

James is unbothered. He continues to hold fast on Alan's neck. After a few long seconds, he asks, "D'you understand?"

Alan's flailing must somehow be affirmation, because James seems to accept whatever it is and releases him. Alan almost falls to the ground but ultimately manages to stay on his feet, using the wall as support.

James turns casually and walks back over to Melissa. He gestures for her to exit before him and she does without question. With a final glance at Alan, whose color is slowly returning to normal as he coughs fitfully, Sutton and I follow after James and Melissa into the parking lot.

The other club members follow suit, then mill around their bikes as the four of us stand together before the left side of the building. The only person to exit after Alan is McCoy. He waits for Alan to get in his car before joining the rest of the group.

James takes the opportunity to speak to Melissa. "I couldn't help but notice that Colt's military time wasn't mentioned today."

Melissa's brows come together and her lips purse in confusion. "Colt wasn't in the military."

"Is that so?" James exchanges a look with Hawk nearby. "It's not a requirement of the club, but many have history in the military. Colt used to talk about it frequently."

Melissa's face softens. "He always wanted to be in the army. A sniper. I don't know for certain, but I think he attempted to enlist and didn't pass the evaluation."

Understanding dawns on James' face. "I see." He touches Melissa's shoulder lightly. "You reach out if we can help you in any way."

The corner of her mouth tugs into a smile. "Thank you. And thank you all for coming." Her eyes well with tears. "I know Colt burned a lot of bridges, but he struggled with his demons."

James continues to look at her softly, though he doesn't say anything else.

She turns to me. "Thank you for coming, Maci. I'm sure this couldn't have been easy for you. I hope the trouble with Alan blows over. Is your mother ok?"

My heart rate picks up. "Yes?"

She lets out an odd sort of chuckle. "She didn't come today, that's why I asked. I don't think it's within Alan's wheelhouse to think about my feelings, so I doubt he asked her not to come for my sake."

I shake my head. "No. Um, they're separated."

Her eyes take on a worried look. "Hopefully she's smarter than me. Maybe she caught on to his secret life sooner than I did."

Sutton's fingers grip my back tighter as I cock my head in question. "I'm sorry, what do you mean, secret life?"

She angles her head toward one shoulder. "He was always on work trips. Never would give me much in the way of details. Always spending money in large amounts."

I think back to the start of Stephanie's marriage to Alan. "You mean gambling?"

"Oh, no, he wasn't into gambling. He had a family in another state," she says adamantly.

My mouth drops open for entirely too long. "He had...wait, you know this with certainty?"

"Oh, sure. I talked to the wife once. When I confronted him about it, he filed for divorce. Said I was delusional." She shrugs. "He was an awful husband. Nothing I did ever made him happy, so I couldn't be bothered to care if he claimed I was delusional. We both knew he was lying."

How the fuck did we miss this?

"Anyway, good luck with everything, Maci." Melissa smiles softly and then walks away.

Sutton rubs his hand up and down my shoulder, trying to comfort me. "You ready?"

He may think I'm close to crumbling with the twists and turns of the day.

James looks between us.

"Yes," I say, distracted.

Sutton tips his chin down at James and leads me to the truck with his arm still tucked around me.

CHAPTER 27

SUTTON

Maci is only quiet for a moment as we pull out of the funeral home parking lot before she starts talking. "I can't believe he had a secret life. Do you think he still does? Do you think Stephanie knows?"

Honestly, I don't know how to answer her. "Maybe? He doesn't strike me as the type to learn his lesson. He didn't even acknowledge Colt's mom."

She stares out the windshield, her hands playing with the hem of her dress.

"You're probably right." Her eyes are vacant, and despite her words, I'm not convinced she's talking to me.

At the red light, I check the rearview mirror out of habit. A dark Mercedes inches closer behind us. The entrance ramp to the highway is on the right, which I normally take for a shortcut out of town. Instead of turning when the light turns green, I test a theory and drive straight, fairly certain the person behind us is none other than Alan.

"Where are you going?" She scans the road before us, trying to find the reason for my alternate route.

"Checking on something." I wink at her for good measure, but it doesn't matter. She knows something is up.

As our truck crosses the overpass, I check the mirror again. Sure enough, Alan is right behind us. I don't know what he's planning, but he's sure as fuck not following us home.

I whip into the next parking lot. He follows suit, but since I know where we're going and he doesn't, I pull a U-y so the truck faces him before he's fully in the parking lot. He realizes his mistake too late.

"What the fuck?" Maci cries. "He followed us?" She turns to me for an answer.

"Seems that way." I give her leg a gentle squeeze. "Wait here."

"Like hell!"

Her door flies open at the same time mine does, but I don't let go of her leg.

"Sutton." Her voice is a mixture of pleading and surprise as she stares as me.

I don't want to do this, but I'm not taking no this time. "For once, please just listen to me. Stay in the truck."

"Sutton." The pleading has intensified, but she's about to give in. Her eyes are concerned, though softer.

I tap under her chin playfully with a knuckle before jumping down from the truck and slamming the door behind me. There's no mirroring sound from her side, and despite her staying put for the moment, I know she's one step from climbing down after me.

Alan steps out of his car quickly and shuts the door to his sedan. To his credit, he comes at me head on. "You can't hide her forever."

I snatch his dress shirt beneath the collar band, crumpling it in my fist and shoving him backward toward his hood. His knees buckle and I pin him in place. "You've been warned already, so you're either really fucking stupid, or really fucking ballsy." I lean closer to him. "But let me be clear. The big Irish guy isn't the only one willing to end your life in a blink."

Alan's smug face doesn't falter. "How romantic. Maci found a dumb redneck who's a killer, just like her." He enunciates the last three words slowly.

She's had enough bullshit trying to process all of this on her own, and we don't need any setbacks from this piece of shit.

"Maybe you aren't aware, but they don't arrest people for self-defense."

Alan's jaw ticks. "We'll see about that. I knew I should've reported her when she stabbed me."

"Oh, give it up!" Maci shouts from the truck, and I toss a look over my shoulder to find her with one foot in the cab and one on the open door, as she leans through the V the two pieces of the truck create. "It was barely a nick and you deserved it! You and Colt clearly needed a lesson in how to handle women."

"Maybe you need a lesson in how I handle women." A dark calmness washes over his face.

"Yeah, see, that sounds like a threat, and that's the kind of thing I won't fucking tolerate." I tighten my grip on his shirt and give a solid shake, his shoulders bouncing off the hood once.

His voice lowers. "When I'm done with her, she won't have a pot to piss in."

"Whatever you say, but if you try to follow us out to my property again, I'll assume you want a tour. And I have to tell you, I have four *really* fucking moody bulls, and a few pigs. And, I don't know if you know this or not"—I pause for dramatic effect—"but pigs will eat *anything*."

I don't want to warn this asshole again. I want to bash his brains into the hood of his own car. Run him over with my truck. I don't want to let him go.

Maci continues to stare her stepfather down.

With a final slam to his hood, I release him and turn to walk away. "If you have anything else to say, it can go through our lawyer."

Before climbing in, I practically shove Maci back into the truck, buckling her seatbelt while she stares wide-eyed at me. Once inside, I whip around Alan getting back into his own vehicle. Whether he understood my threat or not, he doesn't attempt to follow us this time.

CHAPTER 28

MACI

By Monday, my wound is almost completely healed. The skin will never be unblemished again, a reminder of what I fought to keep that night. I haven't made it by Nana's yet, but other things are getting back to normal.

I spend the morning catching up on work and emails and preparing for my holiday mini-sessions in Austin, and decide to wander around the property to take some more photos.

I've always loved family photography, but there's something majestic about photos of the ranch and animals. Aside from a few curious stares, the animals largely ignore me.

Coming up on the backside of the stables, my attention is drawn to Cody and Jason repairing one of the gates. Unlike Sutton, they both wear various ball caps with jeans and their t-shirts most days. I manage to get a few candid shots without them noticing me. Johnny Walker gives me away by sauntering to the fence closest to me. I rub his muzzle. "Hey, boy."

He gives me another solid bump.

Cody perks up at the distraction, waving in my direction. I snap another photo. He has such an innocent disposition, my heart warms at his genial demeanor. I wave back with a smile, just as my phone rings in my back pocket.

Hank.

"Hey, Hank," I say cheerfully.

"Hey, Maci. How are you?" His voice is like smooth waters, calm and unbothered.

"Honestly? Taking it day by day." I hardly know Hank, but he has a way of grounding me and seeing to the truth of things, like Sutton.

"I don't know if I have the right words to make you feel any better, especially given everything that's happened in the last few weeks. But I'm sure whatever you're feeling is natural. Do you have anyone to talk to? Family, at least?"

Johnny Walker blows into my hair as I lean my back against the fence. "Yeah, Liv and Randi. I have some girlfriends and my boyfriend, Sutton. His family is amazing. Actually, that's where I'm staying."

"Good. I'm glad. Speaking of Liv and Randi, I'm calling them next. I need to have you and Liv come by my office to fill out a bank affidavit to distribute the funds allocated to each of you in the will."

"Oh." With everything going on, I'd forgotten about probate. "Sure, I can come by."

"Perfect. Once you do, we'll initiate a wire transfer."

I contemplate briefly. "I didn't pay attention to the amount. Do you think it's enough to retain a lawyer?"

"Well, I can't speak on specific rates, each lawyer is different, but yes, I would think so. Do you need an attorney?"

The weight on my chest has returned. "I've been trying to cooperate with the investigation, but I think I underestimated how long it would go on. I was defending myself, and with the other reports about incidents with Colt, and the fact that he approached me at Nana's, I thought it'd be a done deal."

"Yeah, I can see that. Unfortunately—and fortunately—even in self-defense cases, the department should be conducting a full investigation." He pauses. "I'm sorry this is happening."

I fill my lungs to the point of bursting before releasing my breath. "Yeah...me too. Thanks." Johnny nibbles my hair and I jerk away. When I turn around, Sutton is standing on the other side of the paddock, studying us curiously. I can't tell if it's directed at me or his horse.

"I'll stop by to fill out the form for you. Thanks again, Hank."

"You bet. Bye, Maci."

After hanging up, I pocket my phone and begin to make my way around to the front of the stables. Sutton meets me there.

"You trying to steal my horse from me, Firecracker?" His hands rest on his hips, his head cocked to one side.

I chuckle. "I beg your pardon. I think your horse is after me."

His lips purse. "This seems to be a recurring thing. Pretty soon, I'm going to have to start defending my property."

A startled laugh bursts from me. "So long as we agree that doesn't apply to me."

His eyebrow hitches, but he grins. "Everything ok? I saw you on the phone."

"Oh yeah. Just Hank updating me on probate. I need to stop by his office soon."

He nods and reaches out to pull me closer to him. His voice is low. "Does he have an associate who could represent you?"

"I don't think so. I think he's a junior partner or something, but the firm is all estate lawyers as far as I know. I can ask when I stop by."

Sutton drops his chin, looking pointedly at me. "You can, but will you?"

I stick my tongue out at him. He shakes his head and kisses the top of mine.

My fingers draw on Sutton's bare chest as I study his face. One arm is behind his head and the other is wrapped around me as we come down after a figurative romp in the hay.

His eyes are closed, but I know he's awake.

"Wake me in the morning, Cowboy."

"Hot date?" His voice is playful and croaky as his eyes peel open and he peers at me from the side.

I smack his bare chest and he snatches my hand in his, bringing it up to his mouth to kiss. He may have already had his way with me, but I'm happy to indulge in another round.

"I'm going to Austin tomorrow, remember?"

He says nothing, flipping my hand over and kissing the open palm. My core throbs. This man and his mouth.

"How long will I be without you? Because as I've said, I'm wholly addicted." He scrapes his stubble against the sensitive skin.

I grin against his pec. "I'll be back after dinner."

"Unacceptable." His tone is serious despite the joke.

"Besides the holiday mini-sessions, I'm going to stop by my apartment. I need to get some clothes and check the mail. Organize a few things before the move."

He turns his head my direction. "I don't want you worrying about that. I told you I'd go up there and help you get everything squared away."

I roll my eyes and his grip on my wrist tightens. "Don't sass me, Firecracker."

A huffed laugh bubbles out of me. "I know what you said. And that's fine. It's just a little organizing."

"You're still healing." Before I can argue, he tightens the arm I'm tucked in and slips the other hand to my waist, pulling me atop his body.

"It seems to me you only want to use me for your pleasure." I lean down and dance my lips over his.

His head lifts up from the pillow to get closer. "I distinctly remember you telling me to have my way with you." One hand comes off my waist and he grips the back of my neck, forcing my head down so he can kiss me deeply.

When I pull back, breathless, I barely manage to whisper, "That was a one-time thing."

"Liar." He nips my lip. My hips rock against him instinctively. "You ready for me to light you up again, Firecracker?" His fingers wind through my hair.

"I'm always ready for you." I raise my hips and he reaches between us to guide his shaft through my waiting heat. He slides fully into me before pulling me down for a searing kiss.

My side protests that I've been doing too much lately, but there's no way I'm stopping. Instead, I grind harder as he thrusts deeper, both of us seeking something only the other brings.

The moment our breathing rights after finishing, he scoops me from the bed and carries me into the bathroom as I giggle like an idiot, until he sets me in the shower and turns the spray on.

Chapter 29

Maci

The apartment is cold when I arrive. Figuratively and physically. The air conditioning is still on from when I was here last, and the air is chilly enough that the apartment is in need of some heating. I fiddle with the thermostat and the heater blasts its signature "first use of the season" smell as I meander through the rooms.

If I thought it was weird to be here after Nana passed, it's even more surreal now that I've been staying with Sutton over the last few weeks. There isn't much of my hodge-podge decor that I care to bring. It'd be just as easy to schedule a donation pick-up.

Me:

> **Hey Cowboy, miss you already.**

> **I don't think there's much here for us to grab. I can probably fit it all in the Jeep, honestly.**

The time between my second text and the one Sutton sends is almost non-existent.

Cowboy:

> **Don't even think about it.**

We'll go up soon and get whatever is needed.

Yes sir.

You're getting a spanking when you get home.

Promises, promises.

I keep my promises.

I know.

I'm counting on it.

I look through the cabinets to remind myself of anything important that's here, but there's little with any sentimental value. Instead, I pull out my remaining suitcase and pack it to overflowing with additional clothing and the remaining jewelry that Nana gave me. I shove a bunch of shoes into an oversized, reusable shopping bag and set both items by the front door.

Like Sutton's transition in acquiring more land, my own business has a change to go through. With a little time before I need to leave for today's mini-sessions, I craft an email to my existing clients as well as some social media notices to inform everyone of my relocation.

It may not be anyone's business, but many of my clients have multiple sessions with me throughout the year. Scheduling for the Austin area will have to change somewhat, and I need to make some decisions about what to commit to.

The weather is perfect for photos. I set up at my favorite nature preserve and thank my luck for a rain-free, cool day. There's a tiny building on the property that looks like a mini stone lighthouse. It's sealed shut, but the dark wooden door is the perfect backdrop for the scene I have in mind.

A tiny hook holds a small, lush wreath that I brought, and I add a dark bench with a plaid festive blanket. A few other holiday trinkets get added to the mix, and before long, I've prepared a cozy winter setting. It's important to me that the backdrop is inclusive for various holiday celebrations, and I hope that I've done that justice with the look.

When the first family arrives, it feels like coming home. I get lost in the atmosphere. The click of the shutter is an old friend, the brilliant smiles and laughs of family members a warm embrace. Later I can focus on the logistics of everything, but for now I just enjoy being in the moment.

Despite being just past dinner, it's dark as night when I pull back onto Strickland Ranch. My least favorite thing about moving into winter is the early darkness.

I don't bother unloading anything before heading inside. Sutton will just grumble at me if I do.

As I toe off my boots, the sound of the shower spray greets me in the hall. I undress, tossing my blouse over the lampshade to create a softer glow, and lie on my back across the foot of the bed. I need Sutton's hands on me, our bodies tangled together.

My hand trails up and down my exposed stomach. Goosebumps race over my skin and my nipples harden, the air suddenly feeling cooler against my body. The water cuts off and anticipation builds within me. My core is already throbbing, heat gathering between my legs. You'd think I'm neglected, but the truth is I'll never get enough of Sutton.

The bathroom door swings open and Sutton comes into the room in just a towel. He moves slowly, eyes traveling over my nude body stretched out atop the blankets.

"Are you waiting for something?" An eyebrow arches playfully, and his low voice causes more heat to surge to my center.

"Someone." My voice is only just above a whisper.

He rounds to his side of the bed, where my head rests near the edge, looking at me from above. When he drops his towel, I do my best to hold in a whine. His freshly-showered scent invades my nose as if he released it into the air with his towel. It's so innately *him*, washing me in comfort.

I lift my hand and crook a finger at him, gesturing for him to come closer.

The height of the bed feels intentional, as his cock is almost at the perfect angle to slide into my mouth as he approaches. I reach backward with my hands, gripping his ass to pull us closer together. When he's close enough, I open wide and take him into my mouth.

"Fuck. Your mouth is fucking divine, and this angle is my new favorite." His words seep into my bones as a half moan, half growl.

I hum around him in agreement as he begins to thrust slowly in my mouth. He leans forward, adjusting, and lets out a hiss as his cock slides even farther into my throat.

Taking him farther than before does wicked things to me. Satisfaction at increasing his pleasure is intoxicating, and I suck harder.

"Can't get enough, can you, greedy girl?"

Smiling around him, I push back gently with a hand on his thigh and he pulls out of my mouth with a satisfying pop. "I'll cut this thing off before I share it with anyone else, so yeah, I'm greedy. It's mine."

He guides himself back into my mouth with a dirty grin. "Why, Firecracker, are you objectifying me? Am I just a cock to you?"

I nod as much as I can sucking him off with my head dangling off the side of the bed and he laughs. Again, he leans forward and pushes deeper into my throat. I've never been so turned on giving head before.

One of his hands presses onto the bed and the other, mercifully warm, finds my aching center. He runs his fingers through my gathered arousal, toying with the sensitive skin around my clit before swirling his wet fingers on it. My grateful cry is muffled by his cock deep in my throat, which just draws more moans from me.

The tip of his tongue dragging through my slit causes my hips to jerk. My focus splits between enjoying his thrusting into my mouth and his tongue driving me toward my climax. The wonderful distraction causes my own motions to become somewhat erratic, disjointed pleasured noises to fill my throat.

He groans and shifts an arm under my hips, lifting them off the bed toward him. My feet press flat onto the mattress, shoving my hips farther up to assist. And frankly, because I need his mouth deeper in me. An appreciative vibration travels through my highly sensitive core. I'm not going to last long.

Pulled between the dueling activities, I slide my mouth off his cock. He doubles down his efforts and my nails dig into his thighs as I gasp. His free hand grabs my leg at the knee, forcing me open wider. It's all I need to tumble right over the edge, and I cry out as my orgasm rocks through me.

Sutton doesn't release me as I come down. His attention slows and softens, and I wrap my mouth around him with renewed fervor. One orgasm isn't enough with him. It's only enough to drive me further.

In an instant, he wraps his second arm around my waist and stands fully, hauling me off the bed upside down and pressing me firmly against him, his mouth still on my core. My surprised squeal is muted behind his cock. I grab his shaft with one hand to control the angle and wrap my free arm around his lower back to steady myself. Trusting that he won't drop me doesn't change the nature of our position and natural reactions.

I don't know what to do with my legs and it's somewhat distracting, but Sutton's licking and sucking picks up again, drawing me back in, and I ignore everything else. The blood rushing to my head adds another layer to the multitude of sensations.

Somehow, I bob my head around his cock. He's still not relenting on my pussy, and another orgasm begins to build. My nails dig into his back, and he sets me against the bed, shoulders first, and lowers me down on my back again.

"I'm not done with you," he promises.

"Thank fucking god." I watch as he rounds to my side of the bed, grabbing an ankle and rotating my lower half onto one side.

His warm hand slides up my thigh until he reaches my ass, where he slaps, and I jump. He watches me closely as he does it again.

"Fuck," I pant. How am I even more wet than I was?

His wicked grin returns. "You like that? I told you I was going to spank you because of your sassy fucking mouth."

No one has ever spanked me before. Granted, no one has done a lot of the things that Sutton has done to me, like eating me out while I'm practically on my head. I never thought I'd enjoy spanking. In the abstract, it seemed demeaning, but now I feel the opposite. Empowered and sexy.

"Surprisingly. You're the only man I've ever let hit me."

He laughs. "That's not a hit. It's a love tap."

I chuckle as he climbs onto the bed, resting on his knees. He pumps his cock deliberately, holding my gaze. A blushing heat rises from my chest into my face.

Am I embarrassed or turned on by watching him stroke himself as he looks over me? I settle on highly fucking aroused.

"I may be greedy, but I've been good. Don't tease me."

"You have been good." He scoots closer and guides the tip of his cock through my exposed arousal. With my shoulders mostly flat on the bed and my hips twisted to one side, I can almost seat myself against him as he teases my clit and opening back and forth. When he finally enters me, the fullness is amazing. I never realized how much I hadn't experienced in sex, this partially turned position one of those things, and the angle provides an exquisite reach.

Something like a moaned 'yes' falls from my mouth and I lay my head back.

"You like being my good girl, don't you?"

My head pops back up.

"You're fierce and sassy, but you like it when I tell you what a good listener you are."

He's right. Praise never sounds as good as when it's coming off his lips for me. "When you make it worth my while."

He thrusts into me deeply. "I always make it worth your while."

I groan again. "Except when you tease me."

"Liar." He slams into me again and leans forward, so our mouths are nearly touching. "You fucking love when I tease you. And it's only to repay your own teasing."

"I never tease." My eyes close as I dial into the feel of his cock filling me up over and over. He's become more vocal during sex, and it's something I never knew I needed but enjoy immensely.

He slaps my ass hard, and I'm positive my pussy floods him further in response, squeezing tightly around him. "Oh really? Calling me 'Sir' isn't a tease?"

"Uh-uh." Getting the response out takes entirely too much concentration as I begin to succumb to his treatment of me.

One of his hands slides up the column of my throat and he uses his thumb to press against my jaw, causing me to turn and meet his eyes. He only needs to use tiny, subtle gestures for me to do as he pleases.

His thumb rests against my throat again. Our eyes bore into each other as he continues to pump into me in a slow rhythm. I lean my head back slightly, causing my throat to push farther into his grip. His eyes gleam. "You like my hand around your throat, Firecracker?"

Letting him grip me in a way that's inherently dangerous and trusting him implicitly with my life force is another vulnerability that I never foresaw handing over to someone. How many times has he asked me if I trust him, and how many times have I told him yes? If this isn't the ultimate trust exercise, I don't know what is. But it doesn't feel like work. It feels erotic and even safe.

He studies me with a quirked eyebrow, waiting.

"Yes."

"Good girl." His grip tightens the tiniest bit and I moan again. In a flash, he leans forward, never letting go of my neck, and kisses me deeply. His thrusts pick up pace and intensity.

The completeness of being at Sutton's mercy, coupled with the exquisite way he's thrusting into me causes my orgasm to crash through me in no time, with him spilling into me soon after.

His mouth falls next to my ear and he grunts beautifully. "Fuck." His heavy breaths fill my ear. "Now I need another shower. This time, you're coming with me."

CHAPTER 30

MACI

For the next few days, I lay low at the ranch. Editing and sending proof packages for my holiday mini-sessions only takes me about a day and a half. I spend quite a bit of time with Andi in the kitchen, learning different recipes and even making Nana's chicken noodle soup one night, with molasses cookies for dessert. I'm thankful for these things that tie me to my former self, grounding me.

I also spend a ton of time with Sutton and the horses, learning about the ranch. Veda seems to enjoy our rides and Sutton grumbles every time Johnny Walker nibbles at my hair. Even Daisy makes longer and more frequent appearances around the house.

"It's just because you spoil them with apples and carrots," Sutton says one afternoon as we ride the west side of the property. This is the side that will expand, and Sutton and I are checking an area where he wants to add another herd.

"You know what they say: an apple a day." I grin over at him from atop Veda.

He feigns annoyance and huffs.

"Oh, please. What would you do if your animals hated your girlfriend?"

He purses his lips. "I'm hardly going to make a judgement based on a cow."

"So if Daisy hated me, you wouldn't care." I guide Veda closer to him. Over the additional riding time, I've gotten better at maneuvering and she's gotten used to me so that we're more in sync.

Johnny Walker bobs his head at Veda and shifts closer.

Sutton pins me with a look. "For one, no. I don't care who Daisy likes. And for two, stop controlling both of the horses."

I laugh loudly. "I'm not! All I did was move closer to you. I can't help it if Johnny Walker wants to sow his wild oats with Veda."

"Jesus, Firecracker. He isn't interested in a romp in the hay. He's just used to her."

I grunt in dismissal. "Whatever you say. She's gorgeous, and we all know it."

He rubs a hand across his face.

We ease the horses through a dry creek bed and up onto the other side. The landscape opens up more than any other place I've seen on the ranch.

"Whoa." The land goes far enough to blend into the horizon.

Sutton grins at me. "This is it."

"It's beautiful. How big will the herd be here?"

He pulls Johnny Walker to a stop. "We'll move one of the established herds here. With them being farther out, we'll need cattle that we know do well together. Know their temperament and health histories. The new herd will get started in the pasture closest to home after we isolate them for a bit."

My eyes widen and hold as I consider the work of what he's saying. I perk up. "Wait! Do I get to help with a cattle drive?"

He smirks. "Only if you wear a hat."

"Your hat?" I bounce my eyebrows at him.

"No. Your hat. You wear my hat and we won't get any cattle moved. We'll just spend the day in your favorite deer blind."

I grin wickedly. "Challenge accepted."

"I have an idea." I'm seated on the middle plank of the paddock fence, with my arms and torso draped over the top plank.

Sutton brushes Johnny Walker inside the corral. I've already brushed Veda and given her oats. I think Johnny is perfectly groomed as well, but Sutton is like a boy with his puppy sometimes and doesn't want to stop interacting. It's endearing, and I have no intention of telling him to hurry it along.

"Let's hear it." His voice is gruff, but a smirk plays at his lips. Johnny Walker seems to nod in agreement.

"I think we should shoot a calendar."

Sutton stops moving and he shifts his head to look at me. "Come again?"

I grin. "You know, a calendar. Like they hang on walls in some places. It has the months and days of the year and people write important events in them, so they don't forget."

Like lighting, he reaches out with both hands and grips my boots, teasing that he's going to tip me backward off the fence. I shriek and laugh.

"I know what a calendar is, smart ass. I need you to explain how that has anything to do with this ranch."

"Well..." I lower my voice like I'm telling him a secret. "Some people, women I hear, tend to like when said calendars have sexy fucking men on them."

He grins and continues brushing Johnny.

"Actually, I'd like to get a mix of photos. Stills from around the ranch, action shots of you and the ranch hands, a couple of candid pieces, and a few posed."

The brush pauses again. "Posed."

"Yes, posed. Without shirts, maybe."

This time, he grabs my ankles and jerks me through the fence. I land on my feet, laughing hysterically as his hands hold firm to my waist. His hips press me into the fencing as he crowds over me, gripping the side of my neck with his gloved hand. The worn leather against my skin sends a shot of arousal straight to my core and my skin flushes. "You want me to take my shirt off, and you're going to photograph me so the entire town can see." His voice is incredibly low and quiet.

"I was thinking more like the county."

One eyebrow quirks. "And you're okay with the whole county ogling what's yours?"

I lean up and brush my lips against his. "You're feeling awfully proud of yourself right now, Cowboy."

Without a word, he drops the brush and grips both of my thighs, lifting me off the ground and hoisting me up to his hips. I wrap my legs and arms around him.

"I don't give a shit what any other woman in this county or the whole damn world thinks. As long as your heart calls to mine and your pussy aches for my cock."

"Oh, it aches," I whisper.

"Fucking hell. I'm about to take you in this stable like a wild animal."

Johnny Walker knickers behind him.

"Take me, Cowboy."

His gaze darkens. "Last chance."

"Do your worst."

Quickly shifting his weight, Sutton grips both sides of my hips and pushes me upward, dangling me over his shoulder with a sharp slap to my ass. I yelp.

"You asked for it," he says.

Through my hair I catch him unlatch the lead from Johnny Walker, freeing him to walk around the pen. He then turns and makes a direct line for the office in the stables. The door shuts with a bang and I bite my lip. I have no idea what I'm in for.

There's no heat in here, and the chilly autumn air has easily claimed this space. The lone window is closed, but it doesn't seem especially weather proofed. There's a hint of stale oats and hay, with a side of worn leather that lingers. It reminds me of the first time I rode in Sutton's truck, and desire and comfort battle for control of my body.

He sets me on the desk which, much like the others in the house, has nothing atop it. Convenient. "How wet am I going to find this pussy when I undress you?"

I watch with rapt attention as he pulls his worn gloves off. Who the fuck gets turned on by that? Between the spanking and the gloves, I'm a goner.

"Drenched." I stare directly back at him.

He groans and releases my throat to pull my sweater over my head. My boots come off next, tossed toward the rolling chair but missing completely. Somehow, he manages to rip my jeans and underwear off in one swift motion, which is no small feat considering I chose a pair that, according to Leah, look painted on when worn.

He uses his hand at the base of my throat to press me back into a lying position, his hips situated between my spread legs. Warm fingers grip my inner thighs possessively, opening me to him.

"Look at you. You're fucking soaked."

I'm about to confirm and remind him that I already told him as much, when he leans down with his hand on my throat again and nips my bottom lip. "You're all worked up because I spanked you, huh?"

His behavior is different here in the stables. Primal, like being surrounded by the hay and horse scents unlocks his animalistic side. But I enjoy this side of him, too. I nod as arousal courses through my entire body.

"Words."

"Yes," I breathe. "I like when you spank me."

The chill in the air is causing my bare torso and arms to grow cold. It's a wild opposite to my core, which is warming furiously as it aches for him to bury himself inside me.

"Good girl."

I moan from his praise.

Without warning, he flips me over onto my stomach and gives me another firm smack before rubbing over my ass with his hand. "Fuck, you look good like that."

I arch myself back toward him, pressing off the desk with both hands. "Do it again." I'm almost embarrassed when my voice comes out akin to begging.

Smack.

I'm confident I'm about to start dripping onto the floor, my pussy weeping happily at his powerful hands.

His zipper sliding down breaks the otherwise quiet of the room and he teases my ass with his exposed cock.

"Oh fuck," I whine.

He chuckles. "You ok, Firecracker?"

"Mm mm." I shake my head furiously. "I need you. Please."

One of his hands reaches around my waist, pulling me tighter against him as he continues to tease my backside.

Suddenly, I hear murmurs from outside, growing closer. My body tenses against the desk.

Sutton lines up against my eager opening. He leans down and whispers against my ear, "Oh no, you're not getting out of this," his breath hot against my skin. I whimper against him, fear and excitement battling within.

The voices enter the stable, though I can't be bothered to decipher exactly what's said. My eyes fly to the closed door. I don't know if Sutton locked it behind us.

He slides slowly into me and I stifle a moan.

"Yo! Sutton!" It's Cody.

Sutton pulls back and thrusts into me again. I drop my head against a hand on the desk with a thud.

"Think he's in the office," Cody says to someone else.

"He never uses the office." Wonderful, Jason too.

Jesus Christ. Am I willing to stop if they come in? Probably not. Is he?

I grind my hips against him, almost begging him to move again.

"Busy!" Sutton shouts. "I'll find you in a bit." He pulls out again and slams into me, picking up pace, and I can't stifle the moan this time.

Continuing his movements, he grabs a handful of hair and leans my head back toward him. He growls into my ear, "I told you before, sounds count as sharing, Firecracker."

I don't respond, instead shoving my hips back toward him. He grunts appreciatively. His hand slams hard against my ass again, apparently unconcerned with how far away the ranch hands are, but I squeeze my lips together to hide my pleasured sound.

"You're taking me so well," he says, increasing his force.

My nails scrape the wooden desktop as my fingers uselessly grip at it. Electricity winds itself up my belly as my orgasm builds. Knowingly, one of Sutton's hands slides between my legs, finding my swollen clit.

A wanton moan spills from my lips at the same time that Cody asks through the door, "You want me to put Johnny Walker to pasture?"

Fuck.

"Yep," Sutton calls calmly. Then his whisper teases along my ear, "You were being so good, Firecracker. Now I have to punish you." Before I can react, the hand playing between my legs slaps against my pussy.

I squeak in an effort not to make more noise and he does it again. It's the catalyst that sends me over the edge, and my orgasm rockets through me

"Fuck," I whine, dropping my head and pushing my hips firmly against him.

"Shit." A few thrusts later and Sutton's finding his own release, clenching my hips tightly. He pulls out of me and rolls me over, so I'm perched on the edge of the desk. Tucking himself into his pants, he finds my clothes nearby and begins dragging my panties back up my legs.

I'm ready for him to take me all over again. When my underwear pass my knees, he pauses. "Look at that. Your pussy has a death grip on my cum." He pulls them the rest of the way up and leans in, his lips just shy of touching mine. "That's a good girl. You keep that cum in there and think about what you do to me."

"What about what you do to me?" I ask, pushing to stand.

He smirks. "You can think about that, too." He presses a firm kiss against me.

CHAPTER 31

SUTTON

It's been a while since I've gotten away for a solo whiskey at my favorite restaurant and bar. Maci has plans to meet with her mother today, and I'm getting the ranch hands started on some final projects before I head out to enjoy my whiskey.

"I'm going to run into town in a bit and handle some things, and while I'm there I'm going to pick up materials for a pig enclosure." The four of us stand out front of the stables.

"Say what?" Jason looks at me skeptically.

I grin. "I made a threat, and I might need to make good on it."

"You threatened pigs?" Cody is equally confused.

My chuckle turns into a full belly laugh, and the three ranch hands stare at me with wide eyes and gaping mouths. "I did not threaten pigs. Though, if I'm being honest, their days will be numbered here."

"I'm still not following," Jason says.

I readjust my hat, still smiling. "No need to worry about it. Just know you'll be building the enclosure this afternoon when I get back."

"Whatever you say, boss." They exchange glances again as I head to my truck.

It's an odd feeling to enjoy some peace and also wish it wasn't so peaceful. Maci and I have independent lives, and I think that's important. But it doesn't mean I wouldn't want her with me while I enjoy this whiskey right now.

I'm heading back out to the truck when a familiar voice calls out to me. "Mr. Strickland, how are you?"

I perk up and look left. Detective Porter is almost to the bar and grill entrance. My eyes narrow, and I don't greet him.

"Grabbing a drink?" He smiles, but it doesn't put me at ease.

"Business."

"Good, good. Glad business is good." He shoves his hands into his pockets.

Once again, I fail to respond. I'm not in the mood for small talk with him.

"Got a couple questions. Have a minute?"

"I have an appointment, but I can give you a minute." I widen my stance and cross my arms.

"Wonderful," he says with another useless smile. "How long have you and Ms. McCullough been seeing each other?"

"Long enough."

He doesn't balk. "Did you know Colt Young?"

"Not personally. I witnessed him make Maci uncomfortable at The Spur one night, and saw him hold her against her will on Halloween."

"Shew! That'd make me pretty mad if another man touched my girlfriend."

I blink slowly. "Sorry, what's the question?"

"You ever threaten Colt Young?" His eyes gleam like he's found a thread, but he's so far from the fucking truth.

"Never talked to him. Thirty seconds."

"Whose idea was it?"

"What's that?" He's really bad at this.

"Whose idea was it to lure Colt to the house on Bluebonnet Cove?"

I've never understood smiling angrily until now. It keeps me from grabbing this dumbass by the throat and shaking him. "Let me be really clear, because you seem to be having a hard time with this. Colt attacked Maci at that house, and I didn't make it in time. I wish I had. I would've gladly shot that motherfucker right between the eyes, instead of her having to defend herself." I point a finger at him. "And if you can't say the same about the woman you love, then that says far more about you as a man than Maci as a person."

I drop my hand, and he stares at me so stiffly I'm unsure he's breathing.

"Time's up. Have a good day, Detective."

I've hardly been home ten minutes, delivering a few things to Mama inside, when the house phone rings. I shove the orange juice into the refrigerator as Mama picks up.

"Hello?...Oh. Hi, James." She eyes me.

"She's out." I throw my thumb toward the hall as if she doesn't already know. "He's welcome, but she's having lunch with Stephanie."

Mama repeats the information to James and nods as he responds. "Ok, then. I'll open the gate." She presses the star key and hangs up. "He said he'd talk to you." Her voice is matter-of-fact and she starts moving around the kitchen again, not giving me another thought.

"Wonderful."

That catches her attention. She perks up at the sink. "You don't get along with him?"

I sigh. "It's not that. We haven't had a chance to talk much. It's just tense."

She attempts to hide a smirk. "Seems to me now is as good a time to talk as any." She dares me to argue with a look. "And it's important."

I hang my head and kick my boots against each other. "Yep." I kiss her head and turn to go.

"Sutton," she calls softly, drawing my attention back. "Her building a relationship with him doesn't diminish her feelings for you."

"I know, Mama. It's not that. I just don't know if he's good for her."

"Maybe he's wondering the same thing. You can both be good for her. In your own ways."

I don't respond, just study her sweet face. My lips press together. She always gets right to the root of things. "Thanks, Mama."

The thud of my boots down the hallway grounds me as I head outside to wait for the man who might be my father-in-law soon. If I have my way.

The rumble of his motorcycle cuts through the ranch. Some of the horses nearby pause their grazing. He parks near the front steps, and I make my way down to him.

Maybe he's wondering the same thing.

I offer my hand. "Afternoon."

He shakes it and gives me a nod. "Gracie's out, then."

"Yeah, lunch with her mother." I gesture toward the road that's out of sight. I don't miss that he has his own nickname for her. I can't decide if I like it or not.

His ability to maintain eye contact is a little intense. It strikes me as a habit of someone who often uses a lot of non-verbal communication. "What's your take there?"

I angle my head. "My take on lunch?"

"Aye."

I keep my face slack as I consider his question. Does his history with Stephanie play into this line of questioning? "I'm not sure it's my place—"

"Do you love my daughter?"

My jaw snaps shut at the interruption, and I furrow my brows. "Do I—Yes. I love Maci."

"Do you think you're a worthy partner?"

This conversation has taken a very direct turn. I'm fine with direct. I'm also good with tactful. He doesn't seem concerned with the latter at the moment.

We stare at each other. "Maci deserves the world. I can't give her that. But I can give her a beautiful life here. And I make it my mission every day to try to be worthy of her love."

He dips his chin once. "Then it's your place."

I scrub my neck with a hand. "Okay, then. I think Stephanie's toxic."

His green eyes hold my gaze the same way Maci's do, and I'm starting to soften to their similarities.

"Maci's really good at setting boundaries. She calls Stephanie out on her bullshit and only deals with her when it's a necessity, but it doesn't matter. Even phone conversations drain her. Now, Stephanie's living in the house on Bluebonnet Cove." My hand flies into the air, gesturing into the distance. "Probate's going to be done soon and Maci has plans for the house. Plans that her aunt has agreed to based on what's in the will, but I don't think either of them will push Stephanie out, and *she's* content to do as she damn well pleases."

James is quiet for a long moment. He looks out at the horses. "Why is Gracie meeting with her today?" His use of meeting isn't lost on me. We both know nothing is casual with Stephanie.

"Maci wants to talk to her about Alan and his secret life. See if there's something there. She doesn't get along with her mom, but she doesn't want her to get hurt."

"He hurt them." James looks calm on the surface, but his energy is infectious. A similar thing happened at the funeral. Like water churning beneath a still surface. Maci sometimes talks about the soothing nature of water, but she forgets the destruction flood waters can leave in their wake.

"He's a pretentious asshole." My own anger spikes. "He's put his hands on Maci, and at the very least Stephanie knows. I'm sure he's put his hands on her, too, but she doesn't seem the battered wife."

"Neh." He scoffs. "That's not her way."

I shuffle my boots and kick the gravel. "Do you want to come in?"

An unusual flicker of indecision crosses James' face.

"My dad won't bring a rifle out this time."

We grin at each other.

"Maci and I stay on the backside of the house."

"Aye." He motions for me to lead the way, and I lead him by a half-step around the house.

In my office, I give him a water from the mini fridge, and we sit on opposite sides of a small table on the far side of the room.

"She still beating herself up?"

I kick my ankle up onto my knee. "I think she's coming through. It'll never go away completely, but meeting Melissa was actually helpful to her, in my opinion."

"Don't downplay your part."

My eyes dart to his. "Sir?"

He chuckles. "Don't 'sir' me. Maci relies on you. She's damn strong and I'm wicked proud of her, but that doesn't mean she can do it all on her own. She needs you. You two are like magnets."

It does feel like that sometimes.

"I'm glad she made the call she did." My eyes drop to the floor. "I wish she would've made it sooner. But even more, I wish she didn't have to. I'd have pulled the trigger without hesitation."

James seesaws his head side to side. "You can't know unless you're faced with the decision. She's got a hard exterior, but she wants to do right by people."

I readjust my hat. "Sounds more like you than Stephanie."

James smiles softly. "Gracie's a lot like me. But I suspect she's more like Stephanie than most realize. The struggles with their families, the fierce independence, their take-no-shite attitude. You might not see it that way from Stephanie, but it's there. I guarantee it. Every slight they take is a choice."

I'm starting to see why Maci feels comfortable around James. He's far more intuitive than one would initially think.

"I feel like you need to know something." I don't know if what I'm about to offer up is common decency or some sort of olive branch, but it definitely feels important.

James clasps his hands in his lap.

"Alan tried to follow Maci and me home after the funeral."

His cheek ticks just below his eye.

"I confronted him and told him I'd kill him if he stepped foot out here. But I don't know what his game is."

James nods. "I'm glad you told me."

"I think we share an end goal. I'll continue to keep you in the loop, but I need you to do the same."

There's a hint of a lift at the corner of his mouth. He scratches his upper lip with his thumb nail. "I think you and I will do just fine. I'll tell you everything you need to know, when it comes to Gracie."

A shared understanding weaves its way between us.

I wasn't sure before now, because I'd never heard anything bad about the club, but I know without a doubt that James is involved in some kind of criminal activity.

CHAPTER 32

STEPHANIE

I've been in town for nearly a week before I hear from Maci. Aside from her original call to notify me of the incident at Mother's, this is the first she's reached out. Even considering my call to her about leaving, it's still more than the entire last year.

She wants to "talk" and asked that we meet at the lake. She likely assumes I didn't care enough to ask why we couldn't just meet at Mother's. I'm not dense. I didn't ask where the incident happened with Alan's son, but the backyard looked thoroughly trampled when I arrived.

The lake itself isn't much to write home about. It has a minuscule public park and two boat docks. Thankfully, one has a secondary green space with a bench overlooking the water, where I wait patiently for Maci to arrive.

It's not long before she drops down unceremoniously on the other end of the bench. "Hi."

"Maci." I don't recognize the warmth that fills my voice. Her breath catches. I really have been terrible at showing any affection.

Her nostrils flare and she swallows before responding. "How are you?" The words are timid.

"It's peaceful here." I gesture softly with my chin toward the lake, letting my focus linger on its rippling waters. It reminds me of a story I read as a child about the ripple effect. There's a name for it that eludes me as we sit, but it explores a fictional story about something random and seemingly isolated that occurs, and the ramifications of that tiny incident on a grand scale. Something has caused a ripple in our lives as well, and I believe the ramifications will be more than we could have imagined.

"Bull Creek?"

"The lake." I take in her lovely face. Those piercing green eyes like her father's that haunted me daily. She saw right through me. But I'm there, too. In the strong jawline and cupid's bow of her upper lip paired with the thin lower lip. "Don't you agree?"

Her eyes trail out to the water. The sun is low in the sky and the water sparkles with its reflection. "Yes. It's quiet, serene."

An unfamiliar, genuine smile takes over my face. Lake water doesn't have the same cleansing scent as the salty ocean, but I inhale deeply anyway and shift on the rickety bench, twisting to face Maci better. "I'm glad you chose this place. What's going on?"

"I'm glad you like it here." Her face tightens as she steels herself to talk to me. "The funeral for Colt was last week."

My lips purse.

"Did Alan mention it?"

"No. He arrived as you and I were getting off the phone when I called to tell you I was leaving. Overall, he acted normal. He was a little more tense the morning I left. I believe it was the day of the funeral. He hasn't called since I've been gone." I lift my chin.

"Did you tell him you were leaving?"

"No," I scoff.

Her eyes narrow. "Does he know you've left?"

I swallow. "I don't know how he wouldn't. I've never left without warning before. I'm not sure what to make of the no contact." I leave out the part about the cameras that I shut off.

"Why wouldn't he call?" Maci studies me intently.

I redirect the conversation. "Did something happen?"

She crosses her arms tightly over her chest. "Yes, something happened." Her tone is measured, but anger burns beneath the surface. She's always been this way, almost dancing with the energy writhing inside. "There's a lot we need to discuss, and for once I need you to be open and honest with me."

Turning back to the water, I exhale heavily. She's right, and I want to. I want to fix all that's broken. I also know it's going to be a long, hard road.

"I'm sorry that you looked at me every day and saw my father, but I didn't do that to you. You did. I wish you could've loved me through it." Her hurt words spill out. "I'm sorry that your second husband hated me through no fault of my own. Somehow, I learned to create boundaries, whether or not you two wanted that. I loved you despite my anger. I wish you'd just love me back."

Her admission and coupled accusation stings. "I've always loved you, Maci."

"Well, find a new way to show it. Because it doesn't feel like it." She wipes at her wet face. "Anyway, there's a lot you need to know. I met Alan's ex-wife, Melissa."

Alan only spoke of Melissa a handful of times, while we were dating. She sounded like a troubled woman who needed professional help.

"I can only imagine what you think of her if all you know of her is through Alan's anecdotes. But we need to look past that. Melissa said that Alan had another marriage."

"Before her?" I ask for clarity, but based on recent events, I already know the answer.

Her head shakes. "No. While he was married to her. She claimed to have caught him."

I hadn't made a decision about when or how to much to tell Maci. Knowing these details, now may be better.

"She said the gambling was a lie. His money troubles had to do with the other wife."

I straighten against the bench. "How would that work?"

"I'm not sure exactly. She said the wife was in another state."

Kathryn is in Arizona, but the timeline doesn't fit. "And this was a legal marriage?"

She shrugs, but it's not dismissive. "I really don't know. Did you ever have reason to believe there was someone else?"

I sigh heavily.

"You did," she says, only half-surprised.

I shake my head and lift a hand to stop her spiraling. "I never thought about it. Not until recently."

Maci's head juts forward on her neck. "I'm sorry, what do you mean? Did you think he may be having an affair or not?"

There's that dramatic flair. She really is exhausting sometimes.

Her head cocks in annoyance at me. She's so young still. Untamed. I wonder if she'll soften in time.

"I didn't consider it," I say, staring out into the water again, twenty years of emotions swirling inside. Once again, I question how in the hell I got here. "I didn't pay attention."

"You're telling me you didn't care to know if he was being faithful?" Her tone piques. "Why were you married to him?"

Cool tears drip onto my cheeks, but I ignore them. "I didn't care. I didn't love him; he didn't love me. I couldn't afford to marry for love again."

She gapes, whether at my admission or my emotion, I'm not sure.

"James destroyed me. He was everything to me. The love of my life. When I found out that his past was dangerous, I ran. I didn't think it through. In the moment, I thought I was making the right decision, the safe decision, but I wasn't. It was a mistake." My voice catches, and the dam I've held for so long threatens to break, but now isn't the time.

"I never made the safe decisions. Mother would tell you I was the wild one of Randi and me. I know that seems impossible to you."

She doesn't respond.

"I couldn't bear to tell Mother of the mistake I'd made. Running away to Vegas to marry the love of my life, only to find out he was connected to the mafia." A sardonic laugh breaks free as I continue. "She and Randi *could not* understand why I wouldn't talk through things with him. They adored him. His charm, his accent, his looks. Even if Mother thought I was rash in eloping—and she was fit to be tied when I told her—they were still so fond of him." I close my eyes. "He never came for me, either."

Maci stares at me wordlessly as she processes.

"I spent years trying to be the practiced, responsible person I thought Mother had always wanted me to be. To make up for my stupid decisions. When I met Alan, he offered stability. I didn't need love. I'd had the one great love and ruined it. I wasn't taking that chance again. Mother loathed him, though. She couldn't see it. She wouldn't let James go."

Silence remains unbroken between us for several minutes. Maci's eyes scan the ground, though glazed over.

"He did have an affair." I turn back to her. "Maybe multiple. I don't even know if affair is the right word, but Melissa told the truth. I don't know what she means about the gambling, though."

Maci leans forward. "Wait, he did—wha—" She flubs her words but doesn't attempt to correct them.

"When he arrived after you called about Colt, I started putting things together that I'd noticed through the years. Things I didn't care about enough to consider before, but painted a different story than the one he tells."

Years of being under a figurative microscope make me hesitant to share more, but I know Maci won't let this go without something solid. "I got into his phone." Her eyes bug and her mouth hangs open. "I reached out to a woman he had recent contact with. She claims to be a wife. She was quite stunned to hear that I'm also his wife, but we agreed to speak again."

"So what now?"

"I'm not sure yet."

Maci closes her eyes. "He threatened to sue me."

My head snaps in her direction. "What?"

"He blames me for Colt's death. He never took any responsibility for anything, and apparently, he didn't teach his son to either." She gives me a pointed look. "I don't think the investigation is going how Alan wanted. I can't be sure just yet, but the detective doesn't seem to be sending the case to the prosecutor."

For someone who never spoke of his son, he's acting very strangely. Though, I may know a reason he's even more on edge. "And I didn't contest the will."

Maci nods with a smug look. "And you didn't contest the will. Money-hungry bastard."

She has a point. Winning a civil lawsuit would get him money, which is always at the forefront of his mind. As a partner, I felt it made him responsible. Now it's clear there was far more to it than that.

"Could he actually win a lawsuit?" The words tumble out as I contemplate the situation.

She hesitates. "I think so. If the investigation concludes that I acted in self-defense, I think he could still argue that I acted neglectfully."

Alan has lawyers in his pocket, and I don't know what kind of money I have access to right now to help Maci. "Did you?"

"Are you—"

I press a hand up for her to pause her tirade. "I'm not attacking you, Maci Grace. I'm asking if he has a leg to stand on. Because if there's anything, the *smallest* thing, he'll be like a dog with a bone. He'll bleed you dry."

She's angry but pushes it aside for frustration. "I don't know. And there's nothing to bleed. I don't have anything to give him."

"Except for your inheritance." Not to mention, if she's in cahoots with my sister over Mother's house, Alan will come for it in no time. Fucking bastard.

Maci rubs her face with both hands. "The inheritance may be enough to retain a lawyer, but I don't know that there's as much as he may think."

"What?" I sigh. For all her strengths, this may be the silliest thing I've heard. "You haven't secured a lawyer yet? You need to. And not Mother's handsome estate lawyer, if that's what you're thinking."

She shakes her head through her disgusted tone. "I'll figure it out."

"I guess that means the lawyer's not the boyfriend, then."

She breathes a laugh. "No, he's not the boyfriend."

CHAPTER 33

MACI

At the conclusion of my meeting with Stephanie, she mentions having an appointment somewhere, so I take the opportunity to try to go by Nana's once more. The timing hasn't been right since the last time I made an attempt, and I'm eager to make some progress.

I make it to the end of Bluebonnet Cove again, and even manage to drive all the way into the cul-de-sac, as the pressure on my chest strengthens and my breathing becomes heavy. I can't bring myself to pull up to the driveway though, so I park across the circle.

The trees hide the house and the majority of the yard. A calm breeze blows through and the leaves rustle. Autumn has its own effect here, even if all the trees don't turn and drop their leaves.

Flashes of Colt making his way to me, seen through the flames of the fire I had going, infiltrate my mind. Closing my eyes does nothing to stop them. I want to push them away. To ignore what's happened. But the articles I read in the dining room of The Big House said to let the memories wash over me instead of forcing them out.

His angry eyes will live with me forever. And the grunt when the second round fired.

My stomach turns and I will the contents of my stomach to stay put.

When I've finally settled my mind and emotions, I make my way back to the Strickland Ranch. At some point, I need to loop in Sutton.

CHAPTER 34

SUTTON

When the weekend comes, I'm thankful that things at the ranch have calmed down enough that we can come together for a bonfire. Maci always feels like she's pulling me away from something, and if anything had gone awry she probably would've canceled the whole thing. Hopefully, having friends over will help both of us feel a little more normal and relaxed.

Izzy and Leah show up after dinner, and Nick isn't far behind.

Nick and I head out to Nopal Vista to start up the fire. Either Liv is running late or the ladies are spending an infinite amount of time doing God knows what in my office.

"How are you guys?" Nick asks, taking a swig of his beer, the cooler not far behind him.

I eye him over my beer. I know what he's doing, but I really just want to forget it all tonight. "We're good."

He does his usual stare without speaking.

"There's so much that's happened since the hospital, I wouldn't even know where to begin."

He nods casually, adding a rhythmic motion like he's vibing with the music from the truck. I know better. "You could start at the beginning."

"Yep. I could." Thankfully, the night air is split by Maci's Jeep driving our way from The Big House. "The Callahans coming?"

Nick makes eye contact before shooting his gaze back to the growing fire. "Yeah. They're riding together."

Maybe it's a conflict of interest to have the sheriff and an officer from the city police department out here, but Shane and Casey have been friends of Nick and me since we were kids playing pee wee baseball, and I don't see that changing anytime soon. As it is, it's in the hands of the detectives, and Casey wasn't even involved in the call.

"Good."

Maci's Jeep lights shine through the darkness in the distance, and shortly she pulls up next to my truck. My heart does a fucking somersault when she jumps out. I'm tempted to take her back to the house and tell the others to give us a few minutes. The fact that I won't want to let her go after only a few minutes keeps me from doing just that. Her hair is loose, draped over her shoulders, which are exposed from the soft, too-big sweatshirt she's wearing. It's been cut at the collar and falls teasingly off both sides.

My mouth waters and I'm half hard.

"I'm so fuckin' ready to let loose," Leah says loudly, jumping out the back door. She yanks something out before walking over to us. Nick clocks her movement before turning back to the fire. The busy print of her jeans catches the light, casting odd shadows on her legs as she moves through the high grass, and her bag clicks and clacks from whatever is inside.

Izzy and Liv follow in jeans and sweaters as well. The group of them are done up, considering their casual attire. They are definitely feeling themselves tonight.

Maci makes her way to me, grinning excitedly. "Fire looks good." She makes a show of scanning me slowly. Her eyebrow quirks and her mouth plays at one side. "You okay?"

"Mmhm." I take a swig of my beer, perusing her body.

She leans up for a kiss, which I grant willingly, before I lower my mouth to her ear. "You look fucking edible."

Her face lifts to mine with a sparkle in her eyes and she kisses the corner of my mouth. "Behave."

"I never made that promise," I argue.

She grins playfully at me as she and her friends make their way to the logs Nick and I set up for seating. Their animated chatter fills the night air, and Maci seems happier than she's been in weeks. It's the only thing I want.

"Let's do a round of shots," Leah demands. She pulls a fifth of tequila from her bag.

"Holy shit," Liv pipes up, "how much do you have in there?"

"How do you even carry all of that? It's as big as you." Nick sips his beer as if he didn't just call her out across the fire.

Her attention snaps his way and she works her jaw back and forth. "You aren't the life of the party if you can't carry it." She stands with a sassy flourish and pulls tiny red solo cups from her bag as well.

Liv starts laughing hysterically. "It's like a bag of tricks."

Izzy giggles and bumps into Liv and the two of them fall off the log backward. *Jesus.*

"Did you guys pregame without us?" A chuckle bubbles from my throat.

Maci stares at them with a wide, open-mouthed smile, clearly amused by their antics. "There was no pre-gaming," she says on a laugh.

Leah starts pouring tequila shots and handing them around as another truck pulls into the clearing. This time, the ranch hands step out. Considering my time with the guys over the last few years, and all that we have ahead of us, it doesn't seem right to have a get-together without them joining in. The ranch is their home, and they're our family as much as we are theirs.

Cody and Jason carry another cooler between them and set it near the one Nick and I have stationed away from the fire. Kelly shakes Nick's hand and pulls a beer from the newest cooler.

Maci stalls as Leah shoves a shot cup her way. "This didn't go so well the last time."

Leah grins wickedly. "I'm pretty sure you brought a better cock this time."

"Jesus, Leah!" Izzy's face turns a deep crimson color, and her eyes bounce around us as she rights herself on the log. Liv wears a similar expression and Nick laughs loudly.

Maci's darkening cheeks reflect in the light as she peeks my direction, gauging my response.

I take the few steps over to her, crowding her space and lowering my voice so only she can hear. "Have you been telling your friends about my cock?"

She pins me with a smirk and tips her chin up. "Have you been telling your friends about my pussy?"

I grip her hip deeply with my fingers and she bites her lip appreciatively. "What part of I don't share do you not understand?"

She leans up on her toes. "I've already told you I don't either. Leah's just digging." Her fingers grab my shirt, gripping several buttons as she yanks me. "Now give me a kiss."

"Fuck, I love when you're bossy." My tongue delves into her mouth and she groans into mine.

"I didn't say ride it now," Leah says loudly.

I release Maci's mouth with a smile that mirrors hers.

When everyone has a cup, Leah gets out a half-hearted toast before we all toss our shot back.

Maci grimaces. "Fucking tequila."

"You don't like tequila?" I should know this already, though I know her usual drink of choice is whiskey and Coke.

"Blech. No."

"But you're a good sport!" Leah makes air kisses, pulling something colorful from her bag.

A truck parks at the entrance of the meadow and two doors close before Shane and Casey head our way. Casey was the responding officer when Maci filed the report after Colt busted her window, but she's never met Shane before.

"What's up, man!" Casey yells as he approaches. Greetings go around and Maci introduces Casey to her friends before I introduce Shane to them all.

They're an odd pair for brothers. Casey, despite being nearly thirty, has a baby face void of facial hair. He's average height and build. Next to Shane, he's tiny. Shane even puts Nick's large frame to shame. He's over six feet of bulging muscles. His dark hair, opposite Casey's reddish blonde, is cut short and tucked into a cap tonight, as usual. He looks more like an enforcer than the Sheriff that he is.

Leah smiles at them both and pulls two more solo cups out. "You're behind." She hastily hands one to each of them. "Here, you need these, too." She dangles some of the color before her and I study them, realizing they're some sort of bracelet.

Liv pipes up. "Do these attach to the cups?"

"Yep. Each one has a hole punched already, so you just wind the ring of the bracelet through the hole on the cup and you can hang onto it all night." She's clearly proud.

Shane's face remains stoic, but Casey's eyes jump in surprise before he accepts the token with a grin. His face drops quickly. "Mine's pink."

"You sweet little thing, you," Nick says and snickers.

Casey shoots him a playful glare and says, "Real men wear pink."

"Hear, hear!" Cody shouts and the brothers down their shots.

"Come on, let's dance," Izzy says, standing from her place at a log.

Liv follows. "I'm going to need another shot for that."

"See? It's always the teachers you need to keep an eye on." Leah waggles her eyebrows.

Liv shakes her head, running a hand through her hair and flipping it around nervously.

"I'll adjust the music." Maci turns and hurries over to my truck, unaware of me following her. She flings open the door and leans in, turning up the volume. It's still set on country, blasting a Warren Zeiders song.

I press my hips against her and she startles, before pressing her ass into me and leaning against my chest. "Assuming the position?" I tease.

She laughs. "Am I?"

I palm her ass through the jeans, hardening again. "I can't get enough of you." My lips kiss down her neck to her shoulder and I slip my hands under her sweater.

She jumps. "Your hands are usually warm, but they're fucking freezing." She shivers at the laugh I breathe against her neck, turning in my arms and wrapping her arms around my neck. "We have guests," she chides playfully.

"As the older one, I think I'm supposed to be more mature when it comes to guests."

"See what happens when you think with the wrong head?"

"Firecracker, do not tempt me. Wrong head or not, I will throw your ass in this truck and have my way with you."

She shoves at me with a full laugh. "No you will not, and don't even act like you will."

"Says who?"

"You! We discovered already that I'm not capable of being quiet, and I highly doubt you want any of the men here to hear me."

I'm tired of her practicality. I kiss her hard, gripping her legs and lifting her so I can shove her backward into the driver's seat. She accepts me willingly, moaning quietly and tightening her arms around my neck. I slide her sweater down, exposing a breast and taking her peaked nipple into my mouth.

Her head falls back and her gasp fills the open cab. Swirling my tongue around the nipple grants me another sharp inhale. I grin, nipping the sensitive flesh before covering her up and pulling back. The music drowns her out for now, but she's too responsive to be completely quiet for me.

"You're right. I don't like it when you have to be quiet. I love listening to you fall apart for me." I kiss her on the lips again. "Everything about this smart fucking mouth is mine."

She lifts her head upright, her eyes hooded. "Cowboy," she's almost panting, "that was mean."

"I'm never mean to you." My mouth tugs up on one side.

"Then you're going to have some work to do later, because now I'm wet and aching for you."

I nip her bottom lip. "It's never work with you. Never." This time I kiss her softer. "I'll take very good care of your needy pussy later, when we've finished entertaining our guests that you're concerned with."

She shoves at me again. "I'm getting my camera." Even through my flannel, her cool touch reaches my chest. She stabilizes herself against me as she climbs down from the truck.

At the fire, Leah pours a second round of shots for the women. Casey happily partakes, but I suspect it's less about the drink and more about the company.

Maci's boots shuffle in the grass around us as she makes her way toward her friends across the fire from me, snapping photos. With only the glow of the bonfire to provide light, it seems like she'd have difficulty, but she doesn't seem bothered. The repetitive shutter fades into the background, almost soothing in its presence against the crackle of the fire.

The conversation naturally turns to the expansion of Strickland Ranch and what we have coming up. The ranch hands seem energized talking about what's to come, and the shared excitement is a new kind of win.

A large log in the center of the fire breaks, causing several others to fall in tandem, cracking loudly. Maci jerks violently behind her friends, drawing my attention. Unlike the others, who startle but recover, she stays frozen. The camera is braced stiffly in her hands, her focus glazed over.

I cross the distance between us in quick strides, dropping my bottle into the grass, and lift her up by her thighs to wrap her legs around my waist.

"Hey, hey, hey. Where'd you go?" I keep my voice low, studying her stricken face.

Thankfully, she winds her arms around my neck, keeping the camera firm in one hand.

"I didn't think..." Her voice is quiet and dies off before she finishes her sentence.

"Firecracker," I whisper, "I can't help if you don't talk to me. What happened?"

"I'm sorry. I didn't think about the fire."

I feel like an asshole. Of course the fire would bring back awful memories. "You don't need to apologize. Do we need to call it a night?"

"No!" Her voice comes out hurried and her eyes bore into mine. "No. I can't stop the world from turning."

"You're hardly—"

She presses her free hand to my lips, her fingers cold, and I can't help the fire she starts in me instead. "Life has to go on. The pop caught me off guard, not the flames. It just...brought back memories. I have to work through these things. I'm sorry."

"Stop apologizing." I capture her mouth in a searing kiss. "You have nothing to apologize for. There's no rule about how you need to feel or deal with shit."

A soft smile plays on her lips. "Yes sir."

I slap her ass with one hand, grinning at her. "Don't deflect."

"I just have to make new memories," she says as she starts to unwind her legs from my waist.

"Who says you get to get down?"

"Are you going to hold me all night, Cowboy?" One eyebrow hikes.

"I'm not opposed."

She laughs and pushes at my chest. Reluctantly, I set her on the ground. Her mouth opens to speak.

"Maci, if you're about to apologize, so help me." I don't finish the warning. She snaps her mouth closed with a sheepish smile. Fuck, I love her so damn much it's painful. Every time something scares her and interrupts her otherwise pleasant time, anger surges through me and I want to break something. Preferably her stepfather's face since I can't reach his son.

"You good, honey?" Izzy comes up from the side and reaches for Maci's wrist.

She nods vigorously. "Yep." Using the strap, she hangs the camera from her neck.

She's too good at lying to everyone around her. I stare at her pointedly and she smiles widely in return.

"Come on, Leah's changing the music." Izzy begins to tangle her fingers with Maci's.

"One sec." I pull Maci back to me in a quick motion, keeping my arm tight around her waist and dropping my mouth to her ear. "You can lie to everyone else around you, but you can't lie to me, Firecracker. I see you. You don't have to do this on your own. You don't have to be strong for everyone. But if you insist on faking it for everyone else, please don't fake it with me. Let me be strong for you."

Her body, tense in surprise when I initially grabbed her, softens. She grips my biceps tightly in each hand and looks up at me. "I don't try to hide from you. You're my person. I'm strong for them because the alternative is a lot of questioning that I can't handle. I can only handle healing one mind at a time."

I lean down and kiss her hard. It's all I'm going to get for now, because as usual she's going to sweep this under the rug.

"Maci!" Leah's voice carries across the area. "Dancing time!"

Maci untangles from my arms. Her volume increases. "Go have some fun. Quit worrying about me."

I roll my eyes.

"Oh my God!" she squeals, backing away. "Did you just roll your eyes?"

I move on my feet quickly, faking that I'm going to chase her and eliciting a yelp as she runs off. Leah passes out another round of shots, which most gladly take at this point.

Kelly nods at me as I return to the fire, but once again his eyes hold more understanding than he lets on.

"Just love her through it." His words are an encore of the day in the bunkhouse.

"She's fun." Casey gestures with his beer toward Leah and Nick's eyes whip his way. He bites his tongue and finishes his beer.

I think back to the night at The Spur when I danced with Maci and Leah got too drunk to walk. Nick carried her to the car out of the goodness of his heart, but it's not hard to see that he's keeping an eye on her. Maci told me later that she's concerned about Leah's drinking habits. Addiction runs in the family, and they have their own set of drama going on. I wonder if tonight is adding to all of that. Casey may be happy to match her shot for shot, but Nick at least seems to be more concerned.

All of a sudden, a familiar hip-hop song begins blasting from the truck. Leah screeches something I don't understand and the four women pile into the bed of my truck. The tailgate is down and their bodies sway and bounce to the music. They're definitely going to be feeling this in the morning.

CHAPTER 35

MACI

When I show up to the clubhouse this time, Hawk lets me through the gates right away. He takes a long puff of his cigarette, chatting with another member.

The same parking spot from before is open, and I leave everything in my Jeep aside from my phone, which I shove into my back pocket. Something tells me I don't need any of it inside, nor do I think anyone is going to be rummaging through my stuff. Judging based on James' behavior at the funeral, heads may roll if something like that were to occur.

I still haven't figured out the purpose of the club. They're organized enough, and there's an apparent level of respect, but is that normal in a social club? They don't really come across as hardened criminals.

Then again, I fucked my stepbrother without knowing, and my stepfather apparently has had a secret life for as long as I've known him, so what do I know?

"He's upstairs. You good?" Hawk steps away from his conversation to meet me at the main door as I enter.

"Yeah, I'm good. Thanks." I smile at the man next to him. I hope they don't expect me to learn all their names quickly.

"Maci!" Pete jumps up from a table and makes his way across the room as the door closes behind me. "How are you?"

Pete is such a nice guy. Maybe he let Leah get a little too drunk once, but I can't really fault him since she's grown, too. Still, I don't know why he's so attentive. If it's only because he wants me to put in a good word with her, I need to let him know it's not going to happen.

"Hey Pete, how are you?" I ask as an easy smile forms on my face. He's like sunshine.

"Good. You?"

My tolerance for small talk is limited these days. Everything tends to set me on edge. I miss the Maci of before. "Getting by."

He nods like he understands. He doesn't. Whether or not this group is criminal in nature, I can look into Pete's eyes and see that he's never taken a life. I couldn't say that before, but now I just know.

My jaw slackens. I hadn't considered this about anyone until now.

Movement in my peripheral catches my attention, and my eyes shoot over to the bar where Ginger stares at me in annoyance. McCoy sits at the bar again, nursing a beer, his back to us.

"Prez is upstairs." Pete's voice breaks through my thoughts.

"Thanks." I touch his wrist as I pass, heading directly for the stairs. I bypass the second floor as instructed and head straight for the third. James approaches the top of the steps as I reach them, likely hearing my huffing and heavy footsteps on the solid planks.

"Gracie." His eyes sparkle and he opens his arms again, but today I see something new. Something I didn't pay attention to before. I hug him briefly and take in the space, in an effort to organize my thoughts.

It's a rustic industrial studio, much like the rest of the building. Leather couches, more charred wood tables and chairs, dark pendulum lights, and an open floor plan. Two barn doors rest on a rolling rack on the far side of the room. How unexpected.

"I'm glad you're here."

My eyes return to his. It's there. That hint of something darker. "Have you killed someone before?" I already know the answer, seeing that same thing reflected in my own eyes now. It's like peeking behind the curtain, or visualizing a new color you can't name. It's just a something *else* that's there.

His eyebrows soften, but it's the only hint that I've surprised him. Instead of redirecting the question, or offering for me to sit, he dips his chin once. "Aye. I have."

He gives no additional explanation.

Do I want to know?

I wet my lips and nod.

He arches an eyebrow in question.

I only shake my head. I'm not ready for the details. Maybe he was a soldier at some point. Unlikely, because I suspect Stephanie would've said as much, but once again I'm confronted with the knowledge that she's kept so much from me and knows even less. However, I'm not prepared to shatter what we're building if he's truly a criminal.

And yet, it doesn't seem that simple. I can be labeled a criminal for my choices.

"You staying?" It's as if he wants to confirm that his honesty hasn't altered my opinion of him.

I scan the space again. "Yeah."

He gestures to the couch, and I perch on it stiffly while he sits in a leather wingback chair. These are some of the nicest pieces of furniture in the building, and I see why he has them here.

He draws an ankle up on the opposite knee and rests his hands casually. Aside from the afternoon at the funeral, he's always been so calm and collected. Peaceful even. I'm beginning to dissect these events. Is his calm nature a show?

He wears a couple thick silver rings on each hand. Tattoos peek from under his white dress shirt. My mind is beginning to spiral.

"So, tell me about the club. The Falcons," I finally inquire. He pins me with a pointed look. I hold his gaze, determining how far I want to push. Finally, I add, "It's a social group, right?"

He stares a moment longer before dipping his chin. "Aye. A social club." His head cocks to one side. "We participate in many volunteer events. Funerals for fallen soldiers and veterans, charity events, things of that nature."

I study his face. The set of his bearded jaw, the ease of his gaze. It all seems casual, but the longer I look, the more I see. His secrets are exposed by the way his features resemble my own. We approach the same conclusion together, a silent conversation between us. We're dancing around something here. "Very community-oriented," I summarize.

My chest aches. I don't expect him to be an open book, but I don't know if I can handle another parent who isn't genuine with me.

For now, I'll accept the half-truth he's offering. One day, that may change. "How did Colt play into all of this? Everyone is volunteer basis?"

For a split second, his jaw tightens, but it relaxes as his measured voice pours out. "There's a voting system in the club. Colt's behavior when he was voted in for Prospect was different than at the end." He clasps his fingers together. "Everyone has their role to fulfill."

"And Ginger? What's her role?" I don't actually want to know if he is screwing her, but I do need to know what to expect moving forward.

He smirks. "I saw that spat when you were here last. Seems to me you told her to shut her bake alright."

My eyebrows squeeze together. "Sorry? Shut her...did you say beak?"

He laughs loudly, a huge belly laugh that brings an immediate smile to my face. "Bake. Her mouth."

His clarification only makes me laugh. "That's a new one."

Regaining composure, he adds, "Ginger was the old lady of a former member. He's gone now and she needed work, so the club agreed to let her stick around." He looks me over. "I tend not to interfere with disagreements in the club unless things get too heated. You handled yourself well, but if you don't want to argue, best stay far from her."

"Because she's got a stick up her ass?"

He grins. "Something like that. She's friendly enough with the members, and she doesn't cause a lot of drama in the women, which is good because I've little patience for it. "

I cross my arms. "I make no promises. I won't go out of my way to provoke her, but I'm not backing down if she antagonizes me again."

"And I wouldn't ask you to." He rubs his hand over his leg, contemplating something. "While we're discussing club members, Pete seems keen on you."

I shake my head with a breathy laugh. "No. Pete likes my friend Leah."

"That the wild one that was with you at the bar?"

I scrunch my face. I'm not sure what to think of him noticing her.

He chuckles. "Simmer down. I kept an eye is all."

After a discerning pause, I answer, "Yes, that's Leah. Pete wants me to put in a 'good word' for him." I try to imitate his voice.

James smiles. "And will you?"

It's not that I have a problem with him. She makes her own decisions in that department, and truthfully, I think she'll chew him up and spit him out. He's just too soft. But more than that, I just don't know him well enough to push them together.

"No, I won't."

His eyebrows jump, genuine surprise masking his features.

"She's no good for him. He's too sweet."

He laughs again. "He is a little soft."

"But he's still a nice person."

"A friend?"

I shrug. "Could be."

The topic softens the tension between us and I settle into the couch, asking about Ireland and listening to my father tell me about his home and family growing up. I still get the impression he's withholding things, but I focus on the sweet familial things he shares and imagine the landscape he describes.

At least an hour flies by before I stand to leave.

"You dropped something," James says, following past the couch.

I pat my back pocket, thinking it's my phone, as I turn. Instead, it's my pocketknife which I've started carrying again. Sutton's gun is shelved back in the office case.

"Oh. Thanks." I show him the closed knife in hand before pocketing it. "Pocketknife."

His eyebrows pull together. "Where did you get that?"

"It was in Nana's garage when I was a teenager. I've had it ever since."

He opens his hand, palm up. "May I?"

"Sure." I pull it back out and set it in his hand.

Recognition dawns on his face. "Well, that's interesting," he says, twisting the knife over and then handing it back.

"Is it?"

"I gave that to your mam when we were dating." His eyes crinkle the tiniest bit, the purest joy I've seen from him, as he speaks almost reverently.

I open my mouth on an inhale and look back down to the knife. "This was yours?"

He dips his chin. "Yes. For a time."

What a strange turn of events.

James walks me to the stairs. "Is Stephanie still in town?"

"Yes. I saw her a few days ago."

"Does she have a plan yet?"

I shake my head. "Doesn't seem like she's got anything solid. Sutton and I are moving the rest of my things from my apartment soon, so I think we'll just keep them at the ranch until she's gone."

"Mhm. Ok." He gestures to the stairs. "Drive safe, Gracie."

On my way out, I stop by the bar. Ginger eyes me speculatively as I approach.

I extend my hand over the bar. "I'm Maci."

She sets down the glass she's over-drying. It takes a moment longer, but she accepts my hand and shakes it briefly.

"I was out of line." Her words are mumbled, and I get the impression she's not one to apologize.

I nod. "Yeah. You were. But we all have bad moments, and I didn't exactly react calmly." I smile. "I also plan to be around more. Maybe. Probably. Anyway, clean slate."

One side of her mouth lifts.

"But I also wasn't kidding about the claws. So no more mouse bullshit."

She grins. "You got it."

"See ya, Ginger." I turn to go with a flicked wave.

Just as I reach the door, she speaks. "You really kill Colt?"

I turn to take in her face. We've caught the attention of the few members scattered at the nearest table, one of which is McCoy, who was at the bar before. My eyes catch on his. They don't hold the same question as most of the others. Because he knows my truth, and I know his, too. That tiny thing reflected in his eyes.

I nod and turn back to her. "Yeah. I did. He came for me, and it was me or him."

She nods with a contemplative face. "Glad you made it."

My lungs cease and my head bobs slightly in thanks. I wave and slip out the door.

Chapter 36

Sutton

I 'm not sure what to expect when we arrive at Maci's apartment. She hasn't been messy to live with, but maybe she's still getting comfortable. Her aesthetic could also be completely opposite to mine. Modern, sleek. Then again, I've witnessed her love for woodwork and the way she's designed her rustic backdrops.

It's in a typical cream building with dark faux shutters and about twenty buildings stacked on top of each other, situated on a major intersection in Austin. The noise alone is enough to drive someone insane.

She directs me to a building near the front and seems excited that "her" spot is open, but seems to forget that my truck is wider than her Jeep, so I'm more thankful that the second spot is also open. She claims there isn't much for furniture, but just in case, I spin the truck around and back in.

She lets us in, and I take in the space. I've seen her photos on occasion, when she's editing, but the prints she has on the living room wall are far beyond what I expected. They aren't her family, which is kind of ironic, and they aren't even the same family across the set. Yet, somehow the grouping is cohesive. It's like experiencing the moment with them, while also feeling like they're in their own world.

When Sammi and I were younger, Mama used to make us sit for family photos. Mostly studio ones that came out cheesy and awkward. They hung in the hallway to her and Dad's room. These are nothing like that. They're in living rooms, bedrooms, and green spaces. The people are moving and laughing, interacting in fun and natural ways. A couple have a backdrop, and even though I know she enjoys planning and making them, the ones without are my favorite.

I have a new appreciation for her work and the way she sees things.

"You gonna stand there all day, or you gonna come in?" Maci stands in the middle of the living room with a hand on her hip.

I rub my lips together, suppressing a smirk. "Lead the way, Firecracker."

She gives me an incredibly brief tour of the tiny space. Nothing stands out besides her hung photos. All of the furniture is basic, well-loved, traditional craftsmanship.

"It's cute," I tell her in reference to the apartment, as she scoops some decorations off a side table. "But I don't know how you stand all the noise."

She grins widely. "I'm used to it. Well...I *was* used to it. Now, it feels a little oppressive." Her brows scrunch as if she's remembered something.

"What?"

"I was just thinking how I used to find small-town life oppressive." Her eyes slide over me. "Maybe it's not so bad."

Surprisingly, there's more photography equipment in her closet. Unsurprisingly, she loads that first. Otherwise, it takes us little time to pack up a few boxes of things she wants to keep, as well as the few items left in her closet and bathroom.

The whole scenario has me itching to get our house built like never before. It's like until I had someone to share it with, it didn't matter. Now, I want Maci and I to be comfortable and settled. I want us to start building our new normal, our own little habits and traditions.

"So you just want to get rid of all of this furniture?" There's nothing especially wrong with the pieces, even if they are mismatched.

She shrugs. "I don't have any sentimental reason to hold onto them, and it's not like there's anywhere to put them at Nana's. Or at your house."

"Well, we will have more than a bedroom and office to fill in a few months."

She studies me plainly. "I don't think they fit."

Only about three feet separates us in the living room as we take final stock, but it's too much. I grab a belt loop in each pointer finger and tug her toward me. "And what fits?"

Her grin is salacious. "Are you referring to furniture?" she replies, her voice low.

I chuckle. "I am. Get your mind out of the gutter."

"No fun." Her fingers toy with the hem of my tee. "I guess I thought it would look a lot like what's at your place. Beautiful woodwork, dark leathers, rustic, and...sexy."

My eyebrows jump. "Sexy? Explain."

"Okayyy..." She draws out the word, a blush coating her cheeks as she averts her eyes. "Like the bed, for example. Imagining your hands working to create it—whew!" She fans her face playfully.

A laugh bursts out of me, and I grip her pants tighter as it consumes me. "So I need to make everything for our house?"

"Could you do that?" she asks eagerly.

"The whole house?" I laugh again. "Sure, but it may take a few years considering my lack of free time."

"Ok, so not everything. But at least a few things."

"Yes. I'll make whatever you want." She practically glows in my arms and fuck if I don't fall in love all over again. I capture her mouth in gentle kiss. Her hands slip under my tee.

"Should we give it a send-off?" she asks, returning to her low, seductive tone.

I kiss her again. "You're insatiable."

"I don't think anyone who knows you would blame me." My cheeks burn and her eyes widen again. "Oh my God! You're blushing. Well, shit, that's adorable. I'm definitely letting you fuck me on the couch now."

"Letting me?" I ask, to distract from the rare reaction.

She hikes an eyebrow at me.

It's not like I'll turn her down. The couch isn't the best I've encountered, but having my way with her on it is still enjoyable. Plus, she's loud enough that I'm pretty sure the neighbors get a proper send-off, too.

The drive from Austin is relatively quiet for the first half. Then Maci adjusts in her seat and studies me carefully.

"What is it, Firecracker?" I say through my smirk, squeezing her knee where my hand rests.

"I need to tell you something."

Some men might get nervous over words like that, but I don't. I trust Maci completely. Whatever she's about to tell me isn't going to be a bomb on us; it's just important to her and she's trying to warn me and gauge my response.

I hate that she thinks people won't support her when she shares something big. I try to rectify that every day. It's just going to take time.

"I've been trying exposure therapy on myself."

When she says it that way, it sounds like a trial drug she found on the black market, not a way to heal her mental state. I wonder if she thinks because I'm a rancher that I'll have something against therapy.

"How's it going?"

She picks at her jeans with one hand while tangling her fingers in mine with the other. "Slow." She stares out the windshield.

Maci hasn't been to Ruthie's since the incident with Colt. I've been thinking on how to help, and I have a few ideas. Some are bound to be a little more uncomfortable than others.

"You haven't been to Ruthie's yet," I conclude.

"I sat in the cul-de-sac. I'd like to go onto the property; I just haven't made it that far."

"Do you want me to come with you?" I keep my tone light, even though I only half-expect her to accept my offer.

She chews her lip. "I'm not sure. At some point, probably."

"I already told you, you don't have to do this on your own. And it doesn't have to be me, Firecracker. I know you're trying to protect everyone around you, but you have a lot of people around that want to help."

She nods but doesn't respond, still contemplating as she stares out the window. Admitting her actions to me was probably hard enough. I don't know how hard to push sometimes. Maybe I need the opposite of exposure therapy. What kind of guidance is there for a partner of someone who went through something traumatic?

When we get back to the ranch, I tell Maci to head inside while I store everything in my shop.

She eyes me from the passenger seat. "Are you sure?"

"Would I have asked if I wasn't?"

"Ok, one, it didn't sound like a question." She turns the sass on full volume. "And two, it's my stuff, so I just want to make sure I'm not dumping it on you."

"It's not dumping it on me if I offer. Now get out of here before I give you a spanking for being sassy."

She grins. "Maybe I won't." But she climbs down anyway, giving me one last glance over her shoulder as she rounds the house.

I spend a few minutes clearing space in the shop for Maci's boxes and photography equipment. The shelving in here is plenty for both of us, but I know this will only be a temporary solution. Once Maci is comfortable at Ruthie's again, I'll help her get the garage studio set just how she likes.

On my second trip to unload the truck, Maci rocks in one of the chairs on the front porch, talking on the phone. Her wave is distracted. Instinct has me wanting to jump in, but I give her the space to finish her conversation while I make two more trips.

"Hey, Cowboy," she says coyly, waiting outside the shop as I exit the final time.

"You waiting on something?"

"Someone. I was naughty earlier, and I think I'm supposed to get a spanking."

"If you don't learn your lesson, you may need to experience a whip. We have a couple in the stables." I slide my hands around her waist with a grin.

"Ok, well before you whip out the big guns, I got an odd call while you were gone."

"I'm listening." I grab her around the thighs and throw her over my shoulder. Maci squeals and smacks me on the back.

"I'm serious," she laughs.

"It doesn't sound like it." I'm nearly to the hallway door before she composes herself.

"Stephanie called."

That'll do it. I set her on her feet in front of the door.

"Oh good, you're listening." She grins. "She's leaving Nana's."

"She just got there," I say in confusion.

"Yeah. I know. And she didn't really give me a lot to go on about leaving."

Something seems off. Maci and I stare at each other as if the other holds the answer. "Do you think she's going back to Alan?"

"I don't think so. She seems a little more peaceful away from him. She just said she'd be out of Nana's soon and she wanted me to know."

"Well, that's good, right?"

Maci reaches behind herself for the door handle. "Should be. Just feels weird."

"I know what doesn't feel weird." I crowd her against the door. She releases the handle, a smile tugging at the corners of her mouth as the door falls inward. "About those spankings."

CHAPTER 37

MACI

"Ok, I've got the list, I'll be back in a bit!"

"Thanks, dear." Andi gives me an air kiss on the cheek before I head outside to my Jeep. There are a few last-minute items to grab before the stores are jam-packed with Thanksgiving shoppers.

I don't bother letting the Jeep warm up, but by the time I'm to the front gate, it's blasting warm air into the cab. The wrought iron bars of the gate sport a beautiful script S and swing open easily.

A car is perched on the shoulder near the driveway. I'm on high alert as the driver exits their car, not sure if this person needs help or is here to cause trouble. I roll the window down anyway, determined to floor it, if need be.

A woman in jeans and a sweater walks over. She's carrying paperwork in her hand.

"Do you need some help?" I furrow my brows, taking her in. "Are you lost?"

When she nears my window, she says, "Maci?"

My head pulls back. I don't know this woman. "Yes?"

"Maci McCullough?" she asks again, all business.

Something niggles the back of my head. "...Yes."

"This is a summons. Please sign here in acknowledgment." She shoves half of the stack through my window, continuing to speak rapid-fire style.

"Excuse me?" The words don't make sense as I study it.

A huge X is at the top of the page. "Sign here," she demands, tapping with a pen.

Slowly, I take the pen from her, still not making sense of what I'm reading. I sign my name slower than usual and return the page to her, left with a few sheets in my hand.

She says nothing else before heading back to her car. My eyes dart between her and the paperwork.

Did I really just get served?

I stare at the heading for a while, finally computing that Alan is suing me for the wrongful death of Colt. This can't be happening.

Folding the papers in half, I fling them into the passenger seat and whip around in the street, heading back onto the ranch. I take the drive faster than usual, parking with a lurch and jumping out with the mangled pages.

Andi's head pops out of the kitchen, her lips pursed and brows drawn in confusion. "Did you forget something?" she asks, when she sees me coming up the hall.

"No, someone was waiting for me at the gate." My breathing is shallow as I reach her.

"What? Who?" She looks me over as if the answer is hidden somewhere on me.

I hold the summons up. "A process server. Look at this; I just got served."

She takes a beat to look back and forth between my face and hands several times. Finally, she takes the papers and looks at them. One hand comes to her mouth as she reads silently.

The front door closes hard and both of our heads jerk to find Sutton storming in. "You okay?"

"No, but how did you know I was here?"

"Jason saw you come hauling ass back in the drive and told me. What's going on?" His hackles are raised and he studies me, looking for anything amiss.

"I got served."

His eyes snap wide before narrowing. "By who?" he asks, but it's clear he already knows the answer.

"Alan," I tell him anyway.

He works his jaw back and forth. "That motherfucker."

"Sutton!" Andi's surprised at his quiet words, but fury coats his features. He doesn't acknowledge her. "I'm surprised they came today. I'd think all state employees are off the whole week."

"Apparently not," I mutter.

I pinch the space between my eyes, putting pressure against the place where a headache is forming. "I need to call Hank."

"Hank?" Andi and Sutton ask in unison.

"Yes, Nana's lawyer."

Sutton cocks his head, face shadowed in the dim hall light. "He's an estate lawyer, Maci."

"I know that, but I don't exactly have a defense attorney on retainer!" To his credit, he doesn't seem pissed at my outburst. "Sorry. I know what you're thinking. He can't help. But I don't have another option. Maybe Hank can send something and if Alan sees I do have representation, he'll back off."

Sutton purses his lips before dragging his teeth along the bottom one.

"Out with it," I say, crossing my arms with a sigh.

He shakes his head. "You do what you think is right, Firecracker, but that bastard won't be swayed that easily."

He's right. I know he is. But I have to start somewhere.

I can't believe this is happening.

Sutton kisses my head and turns to go. I don't miss his frustration or the defeated expression on his face, but I don't know what he thinks he can do. All of this because I accepted a stupid drink from a random stranger.

I head outside to sit on the back of the Defender, kicking my feet and raising my face to the low sun, soaking in whatever rays I can. With closed eyes, I enjoy the intermittent breeze kissing my skin periodically. Eventually, I dial Hank.

"Hey, Maci," he says, by way of greeting.

His voice is pleasant, and I can't help but tip a half smile that he can't see. "Hi, Hank."

"You doing okay? I didn't expect to hear from you."

I sigh. "Actually, I'm not. That's why I called."

"How can I help?"

I can't believe I have to say this. I steel my voice before saying, "I need you to represent me as a defense attorney."

There's a long silence that stretches. Understanding must dawn on him because he says, "I think I'm going to need you to elaborate. Is this about the situation at Ruthie's?"

"Yes. Alan is suing me. He's...the victim's father."

He allows quiet to hang for a few more moments. "Maci, I'd love to help you, but I'm not a defense attorney. My specialty is estate law."

"I know, I know. I'm not expecting a miracle."

"I can point you in the right direction. I have a friend from law school that I can share with you. He has a practice in San Antonio."

"Hank, I understand what you're saying, I do." The words catch in my throat. *Why am I fighting this so hard?* "I just want you to help."

"I—" He stops himself. "Maci, I don't think it would be fair to you."

My eyes well and my throat tightens. "I know it doesn't make sense, and I understand the argument. But please. Please." There's more quiet. "Colt's mom doesn't even think I was in the wrong. Surely that has to work to my advantage."

He sighs. "Ok, listen, I'll call my friend and get some information. Then you and I can sit down and discuss the case, and we'll go from there. But if I don't think I can win this, I'm sending you to him. I'm not letting Ruthie's granddaughter go to jail because her prick of a stepfather is a money-hungry bastard."

A wide smile overtakes my mouth. "Ok, totally fair. That's all I'm asking. And it kind of helps that you see him for what he is. He didn't even like Colt. They hadn't spoken in years."

"That's good to know. I'll give you a call tomorrow and we can plan something."

Following my conversation with Hank and the events of the morning, my brain is fried. I need a creative outlet to direct all of my emotions. So, after I finally get to the store, I end up in the barn, sans any animals, painting a four-foot tall gingerbread house.

The Jingle Bell Bash is in two days and I should've started on this sooner, so the urgent distraction is even more helpful given what I'm trying not to think about. I was extremely proud of my Halloween mini-session backdrop. The whimsical, dark lemonade stand was perfect. Having a trailer from the ranch was so fun for the Fall Festival, and my holiday mini-session backdrop turned out beautiful. Oddly, I'm even more ecstatic about this gingerbread house backdrop for photos this week, which is ironic coming from a Halloween superfan.

Once I have the window cut out, I paint the entire piece the perfect shade of brown and leave it to dry.

Sutton told me that Daisy got herself into the hay loft recently. She's so mischievous. I have no idea if that's normal for a cow or not.

I wander the space, finding the stairs she must have used to get into the loft, and make my way up. The thick aroma of hay is a comfort, and I work my way through the bales, positive I'm going to come across a mouse or two, over to a cutout window. How the heck did she get over here? Maybe they moved the hay around after.

Sitting on two stacked bales, I pull out my phone and dial Izzy. It's been too long since we had an honest conversation, and it's time to tell my friends what I'm going through.

"Hi honey," she says cheerfully.

"Hi," I say quietly. "Are you busy?"

"Never too busy for you. Are you ok?" Her voice is soft and soothing. One day, she's going to make a stellar mom.

"Maybe not as much as I've let on."

"Yeah."

"I'm going to add Leah to the call, ok?"

"Of course." She waits while I pause the call and dial Leah, who answers as soon as I've merged the lines.

"Hey, woman," Leah says.

"I have you on three-way."

"Oh, this should be good." As usual, her tart commentary is the opposite of Izzy's calm nature, but they provide a balanced approach that I appreciate. I know what to expect with them.

"How are you two? I miss you."

"Same shit, different day." Leah has a tendency to sweep things under the rug like I do. Things that must be getting more difficult, if her increased drinking is any indication.

"I'm all ears," I promise.

"Oh no, this is about you," she says, deflecting.

"Ok, fine. Next time." I kick my feet against the bales. "I'm sorry I've distanced myself from you guys. I've been trying to deal with everything on my own terms, but I think it's clear that I need more help."

"What can we do?" Izzy asks, immediately.

"It's not any one thing. I actually think it's more about me. I need to be more open and ask for help when I need it."

"Are you having flashbacks?" Leah asks.

"Not exactly. Nightmares. I've been trying to make my way back to Nana's, deal with what happened head on. I found some stuff online about exposure therapy, and since I don't exactly have mental health services, I'm doing what I can to treat it myself."

"Hmm." Izzy's concern is clear. "What are you doing?"

"Gradually revisiting things that trigger me. Physical or emotional. It's a slow process."

"That's okay."

"I just wanted you two to know that I may be reaching out more."

"Anytime," they say in unison, and I smile.

"Talking about it is hard, but maybe just having people around sometimes will help."

"To take your mind off of it," Leah guesses.

"Um no, the opposite actually. Everything I've read says that I need to face everything. Just incrementally."

"Ok, mind on it. Got it." I can hear her grin through the phone.

I breathe a laugh. My friends are just what I need.

CHAPTER 38

MACI

My Jeep clicks and creaks as the engine cools after I park in front of Nana's. It should be quiet with the cab doors still closed, but everything seems so loud.

I'm forcing myself to move forward. I've only managed to get so far as the gravel drive. I'm not even parked as close as usual. Instead, I study the front of the house, even though the real evil happened in the backyard.

There's a rut near the house where the gravel and dirt underneath are displaced, like something was dragged along the area. What could have caused that?

In an effort to get moving, I kick open my door. A cool breeze sweeps into the cab, but I don't get out. I know nothing bad lurks here, but my skin still crawls. It's maddening.

I pull my phone from my back pocket.

Me:

911

Immediately, bubbles appear from both of my friends.

Leah:

Say less.

Where are you?

Nana's

OMW

Same

I'm leaning on the front of the Jeep when my friends arrive one right after the other like it was synchronized.

"What's going on?" Izzy asks, jumping out of her Armada.

I swing an arm at the house. "I came over to get some planning done. But I can't bring myself to go in."

Without speaking, my friends approach from either side and each wraps an arm around my back. It's a different kind of comfort than what Sutton offers, but it's just as welcome.

"Nothing bad happened inside." Leah lays her head on my shoulder.

I tilt mine over to rest on hers. "I know."

"What are you working on today?" Izzy's voice is soft.

"When Liv and Randi were here with me, we went through the rooms and decided what was happening to all of the furniture and belongings. I was going to start organizing things."

Izzy snorts, pulling my attention from the front door. "Sutton doesn't know you're here, does he?" I don't miss her accusatory tone.

"He's not my keeper," I grumble. "And I'm perfectly healed."

Leah snickers, lifting her head. "So that's a no."

I cross my arms over my chest. "Why did I call you two?"

"Because you looove us," Leah coos, then grins and kisses me on the cheek.

I shove her shoulder playfully. "If you're going to annoy me, I'm going to put you to work."

"Fair," Izzy says at the same time Leah says, "Let's go," and pretends to turn for her Acura. We all burst into laughter and the tension of the moment is broken.

"Thank you for coming."

"You don't even have to ask. Now, let's get this show on the road." Izzy rubs my back and then heads up the stairs.

"Actually," I shuffle on my feet, "I think I want to start in the backyard."

She turns and presses her lips together to hide her surprise. "Ok, honey."

The three of us make our way around the house and descend the gentle slope. It's cast in early afternoon shadows by the trees and house. Every muscle in me is taut, and my jaw hurts from clenching. I work to shake out my tight fists.

Izzy, Leah, and I are about ten feet from the fire pit when I stop walking. My friends silently press their bodies shoulder to shoulder with me.

"It's the first time I've been here since I...since I killed Colt."

Izzy tries to hide her intake of breath, but I don't miss it. Saying out loud to my best friends that I took someone's life is almost shameful. My eyes burn, and no amount of blinking will clear the tears.

How do I put into words that the memories are not the only thing in my mind to haunt me? That I know I'm different than I was before Colt showed up that night. Different than I would have been if he'd backed off, listened to me, turned and gone. "I'm not the same."

"We all change." Izzy is quick to quiet my nerves, but this time she can't. Acknowledging the change in me is how I have to move forward.

For weeks, I've been hoping that one day I won't wake up and hate the choice I had to make. But I did make it. And I'm glad, because I want to be here. I want this life with these people. So I have to start being honest about the decision I made to keep building that life, to become Maci 2.0. And I have to get everyone around me to that place, too.

"Yes, we all change. But not this way." My hands reach out on either side, finding theirs and winding my fingers with theirs. "I have to be honest about what happened, and you have to be honest about accepting it. About accepting me."

I look between them, speaking slowly. "I am not the same."

Izzy's eyes well and her nose reddens while Leah's grip on my hand strengthens.

"No one is asking the hard questions. You're all walking around me like I'm breakable. I'm not."

Again, Izzy's mouth opens to protest, and I cock my head to one side, quieting her. "Colt walked into this yard intent on killing me. No amount of talking was going to sway him, no matter how wrong he was. He wouldn't see reason." In some ways, this conversation mirrors one I had with Melissa not long after the incident. The difference isn't in what happened or what I'm saying, so much as my conviction in it. There's no break in my voice or stilted breaths to contend with. "I waited until I couldn't, but when push came to shove, I chose my life over his. A part of me knew when he got here that only one of us was leaving in one piece."

I squeeze their hands in three quick bursts.

"You should plant something where it happened." Leah finally speaks.

Izzy and I both turn her way.

"Something that symbolizes the new you." Her lips turn up gently. "Sure, you can create new memories, but the memory of what happened isn't going away. So give it a physical symbol, something that shows the beauty of what's left when the smoke clears."

"Jesus, you're so hot when you're deep," Izzy says, right before the three of us burst into laughter.

"You may be onto something," I say, after I've composed myself.

"Ok, well, all that deep thinking made me hungry, so let's get this show on the road and get something to eat." Leah bounces her eyebrows at us.

Her attempt to diffuse our attention from the depth she hides doesn't go unnoticed. "Yes ma'am." I salute her. "We should be able to knock it out fairly quickly."

The three of us make our way back to the front of the house.

"You're going to let us do all the lifting, right?" Izzy says as I unlock the front door.

"Yep." My response is too quick, and Leah snorts.

As predicted, it takes us little time to box up the items that are going to be leaving. We move the awful chair from the loft into the living room for easier pickup, along with a few boxes of decor. The majority of the kitchen items are going to stay on for the bed and breakfast, but I box up a few pieces that I want to keep personally.

My phone rings just before we get into the keepsake items. I answer without checking the caller ID.

"This is Maci."

"Hello, my sweet niece. What are you doing?" Randi's happy voice greets me unexpectedly.

"Hi! Actually, Leah, Izzy and I are at Nana's, organizing some things for pickup."

"Oh. Yeah, we don't have long now, and that should all be done," she says as an afterthought.

"I wasn't going to get into Nana's room without you and Liv. The last thing I planned to do today was move some of the personal items out of the guest rooms. Maybe into the garage for now? We need to go through them, but I don't know when we'll be ready, and I don't want them to be messed with by anyone coming through here."

Izzy and Leah stand in the foyer, waiting for direction from me.

"Oh, honey, don't worry about that today," Randi says. "We can do that with you, too. Even if we aren't ready to go through them in detail, no one is going to be in there for weeks. You don't have to do it all."

I exhale a heavy breath. "You're right. We should do it together."

"Yes. Now for the reason for my call. This whole time I assumed you were probably going to be with Sutton's family for Thanksgiving. You are, right? Because all of a sudden, I thought maybe you were going to be alone or something and then worried I should've invited you to spend the day with me and Liv." She spills all the words out as quickly as she can, not giving me a chance to respond until she's taken a huge breath.

"Yes, I'm going to be with Sutton. In fact, you and Liv are welcome to stop by. Andi has planned to feed the entire city of Bull Creek, so there will be way more than we can eat. Plus, Izzy and Leah are coming by at some point, and my dad might even come by."

"Your—" Randi's surprise is loud, even though her voice isn't. "You're calling him 'Dad'?"

My cheeks heat and I'm glad that she can't see me, even though Leah and Izzy's eyes are still glued to me. "No, I'm not *calling* him 'Dad,' I was just referencing him that way. He is my dad. But no, I'm not ready for that just yet."

Her relieved breath comes through the line. Then she says, "Ok, well, we'll try to stop by. Are you sure it won't be awkward? I haven't seen James in over twenty years."

"You mean more awkward than your dad showing up on your late grandmother's porch unannounced and unexpected, to let you know that he is your father and has ties to criminal activity—however loose they may be—and that your mom stole you away in the night?" My own words come out in one long breath.

"Jeez, trauma dump," Leah mutters. Izzy elbows her despite her own grin.

"Well, when you put it that way." Randi lets out a nervous laugh. "Ok. We'll come by."

"Perfect. I love you. I'll see you soon."

"Love you, too, sweetheart."

Randi hangs up and I turn to my friends. "I guess we're done for the day. Thanks for helping. And for letting me trauma dump." I grin widely at Leah, who waves a hand at me in a faux exaggerated dismissive gesture.

I flip off the living room light. Izzy opens the front door, and they make their way onto the front porch as I follow and close up.

"I can do one better than that." Leah wags her phone at me as I turn. The screen is black, so I'm not sure what she's talking about.

"You're giving her your phone?" Izzy purses her lips.

"Nope. I found your phoenix tree." Leah directs her response to me.

"My..." My brows scrunch firmly together. "I have no idea what you're talking about."

She lifts her chin haughtily and flips her wild, dark hair off one shoulder. "Royal Poinciana, or the Flame Tree. I found where to get one here in town.

It's perfect for symbolizing your transformation. Look." She passes the phone in front of her face to unlock it and hands it to me.

An image of a tree with bold red flowers fills the screen. It's reminiscent of a crape myrtle, but the flowers sprout off in long limbs of nearly two feet, drawing you in to its vibrant blooms. It has quite an impact.

"It's lovely," I say, handing the phone to Izzy. "I'll think about it."

Leah reaches her arms to me as mine come to her and we hug each other tightly. A moment later, one of Izzy's arms wraps around my back as she hugs us in an outer layer.

"You two are the absolute best. I love you so much."

"Ok, but last time you said that near this porch, bad things happened after, so..." Leah pushes back and creates an X with her two pointer fingers.

"Your timing can be so damn awful," Izzy says, cackling.

I can't help but laugh either. Ill-timed or not, I have to go on living my life. I won't be sorry for being here and for choosing me.

CHAPTER 39

MACI

My meeting with Hank can't come soon enough. Thankfully, the Wednesday before Thanksgiving, he comes out to the ranch so we can discuss what's going on and Sutton can be a part of the conversation. I told him Sutton didn't have to, but he was having no part of that option.

"How are you?" Hank asks, after sitting in one of the dining table chairs.

Sutton and I have taken up our usual places. Sutton's warm hand rubs my leg in a soothing pattern.

"Truthfully?" I ask, continuing without waiting for a response. "Stressed. I need this done yesterday."

Hank rubs his smooth chin. "I told you I'd see what I could do, and I will, but you know I'll be honest with you about the outlook, too."

Hank has always felt steady to me, and I appreciate his honesty, but right now I just want to hear that he can get this thrown out or something.

"Alright, first things first. I've requested documents from the police department. Alan's lawyer has probably already done that as well, or he wouldn't have agreed to the case. In theory, at least. Once I read through it all, I'll have a clear idea of what's beneficial to us."

The tension coiled inside me eases minutely. I know everyone thinks Hank is the wrong choice as a defense attorney, considering this is so far from his specialty, but I'm following my gut on this.

"In the meantime, we're going to respond to the notice. I'll handle that part." He looks between Sutton and me before continuing. "I'm going to assume we need to hit him hard. It doesn't sound like he's going to respond to anything less. Like logic and reason." He smirks, and I'm reminded of the morning in Nana's kitchen when he tried to soften the somber mood.

Sutton shifts in his chair. "What happens if you can't convince him to drop this?"

"Scheduling will happen. We wouldn't have a meeting with them for months. We can attempt mediation in hopes of convincing them to drop the case or settling."

"I'm not paying him a fucking dime." Hot fury floods my veins.

Hank doesn't seem bothered by my interruption. "If all else fails, we'll be going to trial. There will be a period of discovery when we'll share information so that we understand what they intend to use against you, and vice versa."

"How long is that?" Sutton asks, leaning forward in his seat.

"All in all, we could be looking at eighteen months or more. Years." Hank's face is tight.

"Years?" I exclaim, almost jumping out of my seat. Despair threatens to consume me. The idea of being trapped in dealings with Alan, reliving that horrid night and the past ten years of my life with his narcissistic ass, has me about to implode. "I can't go on like this for years, Hank!"

"Maci." Sutton's voice is soothing as he presses his hand firmer to my leg. His comforting nature isn't working.

"I'm being honest with you about the situation, Maci. I'm not going to sugar-coat this. At any point." Hank's voice is calm despite the seriousness of what he's saying. "That doesn't mean it *will* last all that time. Alan strikes me as wanting immediate wins. I don't think he'll want to be dragging this on for years either. If I can't see a win, I'm directing you to someone else."

My head falls forward and I rub my hand over my face. "I appreciate your honesty. I want it. I can't have this, or him and all of his secrets, hanging over my head for years." I sit up with a sigh.

His brows furrow. "Secrets?"

"Apparently, he has a secret life. At least, potentially. It all sounds like something out of a movie, but Melissa, his ex-wife, said she found out about it and Stephanie confirmed."

Hank leans forward minutely. "Secret life," he repeats.

"Yeah. You know, multiple families in different states," Sutton says.

"Not legally, though." Hank's eyes bounce between us, like he's on the hunt.

I shrug. "I doubt it. There's no way to get multiple marriage licenses, right?"

"Not legally," he repeats. His face relaxes a bit, and the corner of his mouth hints at a smile.

Sutton and I both stare at him.

"Maci, you kind of buried the lead on this one."

"Did I?" I'm not sure how I could have. Alan is a grade-A prick, but I don't see how it's relevant.

"Yes. If he has marriage licenses in multiple states, that's bigamy. It's a felony. We can absolutely use that to our advantage in getting him to drop this case."

My eyes bug. "So, how do we find out?"

"I'll do some digging. Does your mom have any information on this?"

"I know she's been in touch with another wife. I'll get more details from her if I can. I'm sure Melissa would be willing to share what she knows, too."

"Perfect. Get what you can. It's more likely that he has aliases, so work on names. His or potential partners, cities, anything. In the meantime, I'll send our response and get started going through whatever documentation I can get my hands on. We're going to fight this with everything we've got," he says confidently as he stands.

"Thank you, Hank." An uncharacteristic urge to hug him surfaces, but I refrain. "I know this is a gamble, but I appreciate everything you're doing."

He smiles. "I'll be in touch soon. Reach out once you know something."

"Thank you." Sutton extends a hand. He may not think Hank is the right person for the role, but I'm appreciative that he's behind me on this.

I leave Sutton in the dining room and walk Hank out. When I return, he wraps me in his arms. "We're gonna beat this, Firecracker. Come hell or high water."

"I'm not sure how much further into hell I can go," I say into his chest. It's only a half-joke.

Chapter 40

Sutton

"Do you trust me?"

Maci stares back at me from the passenger seat. It's hard to hide the nerves racing through me. I need to do this for her, but I also need her to be comfortable. I rake a hand through my hair. I should've worn my hat.

"Of course I trust you." A soft smile plays on her lips, and I reach across the console to squeeze her leg so I don't take her back inside. Her hand drapes over mine, her skin cold to the touch, soothing. I hope to return the sentiment tonight.

She doesn't ask about our destination, which I appreciate, because I don't want her amped before we get there. It's not like I can hide where we're going, though. As soon as we head out the opposite side of town, her leg starts bouncing in the seat. I give her another gentle squeeze, which she returns with her hand. Her leg stops bouncing, but she stares silently out the window, lost in her own head.

Maci's been trying to increase her exposure at Ruthie's. If she ever plans to move forward, she has to face that demon down. While she managed to visit during the day with her friends, I know there's more that needs to be done. A night that needs to be erased, and a place that needs to be reclaimed.

Even more, I want her to be sure she wants to be on the ranch with me. She can't be sure if she doesn't have all of her choices completely available to her before she decides. So having Ruthie's house feel accessible to her is paramount to us moving forward together, and with our independent career endeavors.

Nothing looks especially different. At least, not to me. I don't know what she sees. We remain silent after parking. Her gaze is trained on the backyard, only a portion of which is visible from here.

I don't bother with words as I get out of the truck. A familiar soft blanket is tucked beneath the backseat, and it comes along with me to get Maci from the passenger side. Once she climbs down, she wraps her arms around my waist, leaning against me. I bring my arm around her, trailing my fingers over the scar hidden beneath her shirt. She doesn't know it yet, but I aim to remove every horrible memory she has of this yard.

Colt stole something from her that night. Something intangible. And I'm going to give it back to her. This yard, this place, this life, every piece of it belongs to her. I won't let her go another day with her feeling like this part of her life is unreachable.

I tilt my head down. "I know you trust me...but if at any point this is too much, just say the word." She bobs her head, still tucked against my sternum. "I'm only trying to help." The last few words are quieter. A promise.

Her head tilts up and her bright green eyes find mine. "I know."

"I love you," I say, ready to show her how much.

"I love you."

Releasing her hip, I tangle our fingers together, a physical representation of the link between us. She follows easily when I give a soft tug. Her steps slow the closer we get to the fire pit. I release her hand and lay out the flannel blanket. She takes in the metal pit with furrowed brows.

"What?"

"There's fresh wood." She glances at me questioningly.

"Yes." I wait for her to say more, but she doesn't. I make quick work of getting the blaze going. The temperature has been mild today, but it's dropping faster as darkness comes on quickly.

A shiver races through her body. I rub up and down her arms to create friction, then using a finger, tip her chin my direction and kiss her firmly. Her lips are warm and soft and she lets out a tiny moan. Good. She needs pleasure here.

I sit on the blanket with my legs spread and motion for her to lean against me. She shifts back and forth on her feet, but I don't take the hesitation personally. Eventually, she sits between my legs and leans back, facing into the yard.

Slowly, her body softens into me as I play with the hair draped over her shoulder. When Maci leans into one arm, looking up at me, I press a kiss to her lips which she returns hungrily.

"This place is yours." I kiss her again, harder, to make my point. "This night is about you. About reclaiming what was taken." With one hand, I begin unbuttoning her shirt from the top down. Her surprised gaze falls to my hand, but when I lean in to kiss her again, she concedes.

When her shirt is completely unbuttoned, I shift my weight, guiding her with the arm she's leaned against so she leans back onto the blanket. I drag a finger along her collarbone and down between her breasts, shifting the shirt off of her left side to expose her new scar. Her body tenses. It's become a habit to press my lips against the marred skin, but it doesn't stop a tiny gasp from leaving her.

"This is a part of you." I look up at her without moving from her hip, caged over her body. "If we're being honest, every part of you is mine," I add, giving her a sideways smirk. Fuck, I love when she grins like that at me. "But this," I say, leaning forward to trail the scar with my mouth, brushing over it without stopping. "This is yours. It's a symbol of your fierce nature, your strength, your determination. You are not a victim. You are a survivor. And you are fucking amazing."

A tear falls from her eye, dropping off the side of her face to the blanket. She nods.

I hum against her hip. I love the way her back arches into me and she groans as I kiss my way over to her belly button, leading up to her chest and then her mouth. She opens willingly and I swipe my tongue against hers. Her hands are even colder than before when she places them on each side of my face, deepening the kiss.

Maci fits against me perfectly, and when I lean her forward, reaching around to help remove her open shirt, she showers my neck and chest with hot kisses, threatening to derail my plan. I take the opportunity to unclasp her bra and toss it aside.

"Don't burn it," she breathes against my neck.

"Fuck it. I'll buy you a new one."

Her laugh is magical. It soothes me when I'm the one trying to soothe her.

I need to be able to help her. If in some way I'm able to help her feel whole again, then maybe she'll have an inkling of how much I love her. How much I need her. And how much I fucking want her.

Naked from the waist up, she falls back onto the blanket. She's a vision. Her dark brown hair splays around her as if it was meticulously placed. Her eyes and mouth are hungry, and I harden immediately. I can't take my eyes off her, throwing my own flannel and undershirt into the grass behind me.

"Oh, sure. *Those* can't be replaced so don't burn *them*."

That fucking mouth.

My hands fall to either side of her head, missing her hair as I lean over her. I let my words come out low, despite being alone. "I'll burn this whole damn world down if it means keeping you."

"I'm not going anywhere," she says softly.

I kiss her lips. "No, you're not."

Slowly, I explore every inch of her exposed skin with my mouth. One hand roams over her body, a partner to my mouth. I twirl a tight, hardened nipple in my fingers, my tongue dancing over the other. Her quiet moan makes my cock jump in my jeans again.

Before traveling farther south, I show the other nipple the same affection with my tongue. Maci's hands grip my hair fiercely.

The button of her jeans pops free easily and I slip a hand inside. She's already soaked, and her moan deepens as I rub my hand over her. I nibble her breast before pulling away, leaning back to work her pants down.

"I have to be honest." I don't look at her, but I can feel her body tighten. "I am being a *little* selfish."

"Oh?"

Flinging the jeans behind me, I find her eyes. "Yes. I'm going to make you see stars. The ones above us and more. But I absolutely have to have a taste before I fuck your needy pussy."

Her legs clench. "I don't think you understand what 'selfish' means then." She pulls her lip between her teeth, and my dick hurts from how hard it's pushing against my zipper.

My hands slip between her knees, pressing her legs open and exposing the extent of her arousal to me. "No? It doesn't mean I'm going to devour you strictly for my own pleasure?"

Her hips buck gently and I grip her thighs, pinning her place. She moans again. "Mutually beneficial is what I would call it."

"Whatever you say, Firecracker. I just know I'm about to have the best dessert ever." I position myself between her legs, kissing along one thigh as I slowly make my way higher.

She stretches to get my face closer to where she wants, but I still.

"Better than cheesecake?" she asks.

"Fuck cheesecake." I bite her inner thigh and she lets out a yip. My attention falls on the other leg as I drag my tongue up her thigh. I'm not sure who I'm torturing more, me or her.

Goosebumps coat her skin as I reach her center, and I know she's dying for me to taste her as much as I am. I look her over, gripping a thigh in each arm. Her head is thrown back in anticipated pleasure. A cool breeze blows over my back. I wait.

Her head comes off the blanket as she looks at me expectantly. "Cowboy, what are you doing?"

"Eating with my eyes, first."

She grins. "Well, your dessert is getting cold, and this one is best served hot."

I raise my eyebrow at her in challenge and brush the tip of my tongue over her clit. She jerks her hips. "I think it's you who's doing the serving."

I half expect her to have another retort, but she falls back with a groan. This time, I drag my tongue fully up her drenched center, equally turned on by her taste and her sounds.

As I continue my slow feast on her, her hips rock into me, trying to control her pleasure. Her hands come to her breasts, twisting and tugging at her peaked nipples. Watching her touching herself, adding to her pleasure, does things to me. She's intoxicating. I told her once I was becoming addicted to her, and it's true. I can never have enough of her. Of this. Of us.

I'd love nothing more than to lie here worshipping her all night, but her movements are becoming more insistent. One hand releases a breast as she latches onto my hair with her fingers, her nails scraping passionately against my scalp. I pick up my pace, devouring her faster, never taking my eyes off her.

I may or may not release an appreciative groan. Watching her come undone is my favorite sight.

Her back arches beautifully in the firelight, right before she gasps. My name on her lips only spurs me to lick and suck harder. I'm not releasing her until she pushes me away. There's no better sound in the world. Though, hearing her confessing her love for me might tie.

My eyes are still laser-focused on her, my tongue slowly lapping up the fruit of my labor, when her head pops up and her eyes find mine. She smiles widely and says playfully, "Your work is done."

I trail the tip of my tongue softly through her sensitive flesh, watching her intently and the way her eyes threaten to roll back again, to prove my point. "My work is never done. And I'm far from finished with you."

"I hope you never finish with me." Her voice is softer, her face relaxed, as she looks over me tucked between her thighs. I'd die right here, given the chance.

"Never." I nip her inner thigh with my teeth, eliciting another yelp. A chuckle vibrates my chest. "Are you crazy? I'm not sharing this delicacy with anyone."

She laughs heartily.

I kiss my way back up her body to her mouth, letting her taste herself on my tongue. She moans into me. Ever since the first time I did it, when I saw the spark in her eye, I make sure to share with her. "You like how you taste, Firecracker?"

Her reddened cheeks are muted in the low light. "It's different. But that's not why I moaned." My lips find their way along her jaw to her neck. How can every part of her be so delicious?

"Mmm. Why then?"

Her hips rock against my leg between her thighs. "Your jeans feel delicious against my pussy."

"Firecracker. Your dirty mouth is doing things to me."

She hikes an eyebrow. "Not yet."

I shake my head to rid the vision of her mouth full of my cock. She's glorious on her knees for me, and that is a distraction I do not need. Instead, I press my thigh harder against her core and I'm rewarded with another sexy moan. She grinds against me. "Fuck, I love watching you take what you need. Pleasure looks good on you."

She smiles. "Feels good. But you feel better."

"You want to feel me, Firecracker?" I pause. She only nods back. "Words, Maci." I don't actually care if she asks for what she wants, but it does something to her when I tell her to say what she wants. Hearing her put it to words is fucking hot, too.

"Yes. I need to feel you."

"Need?" Even teasing, I'm already pulling back to unbutton my pants and drop them from my hips.

"Yes. It's kind of an addiction." She grins, and I laugh at her use of my words.

"I'm happy to give you a fix." I nuzzle into her neck as my cock slides between her legs, immediately covered in her arousal. "You feel so damn good."

"You're telling me," she murmurs. "Fuck me, Cowboy."

I bit her gently. "So demanding."

"Will you deny me?" Her eyes are closed, face turned away, granting me easy access to her tender skin.

I stare at her for a moment. "Never."

"Good." She lifts her hips and drags herself against me, groaning happily before addressing me in a low voice. "Sutton."

I pull back and look at her. Aside from when she cries out my name, she doesn't use it often unless it's important.

Her eyes pierce mine. "Don't be gentle with me."

My brows furrow.

"Here," she says, swallowing thickly. "In this place. I need you to consume me, make me yours, completely."

"You're already completely mine." I know what she's asking. The pain and trauma here have to be outdone by a finality. She continues to stare at me, waiting for an appropriate response. Her mouth is tight and her eyes intense as she breathes heavily.

I stare back at her, seeing the knife sticking out of her abdomen and listening to her beg me to remove it. Maybe we both have shit to work through here.

"Maci, you are mine. If you need me to possess you here, I will, but it doesn't matter where we are, no one is taking you from me."

Her eyes well again and she nods vigorously.

"Are you ready?"

"Yes."

I shift my weight and position myself to enter her. Before I move, I tuck my mouth against her ear. "I meant what I said. If at any moment this is too much, all you have to say is stop and we're gone."

"Don't stop," she orders, just above a whisper.

I thrust into her fully and she cries out. I've never been more in tune with anyone in my life. Her arms wrap around me and she grips my shoulder blades with her nails. I will let her tear me to shreds, take any pain she wants to dole out if it helps her. Focused on her breathing and the way she's clutching me tightly, I pull back and thrust into her again. She hisses a "yes" against me and I give in to her desires.

This isn't like the other times we've been together. It's not playful, or sweet, or lustful. It's a deep need to feel a permanent connection, a desire to feel tethered to someone on a primal level. She needs to override every bad thing that happened here and know that when the world is crumbling, she still belongs to someone. And I need her to know that I would willingly walk through hell with her.

Our pace quickens as we move together. Our mingled sounds drift up to the star-filled sky. In this moment, no one else on earth exists. We're just two beings in the wild world with a crackling fire as our soundtrack.

She grips me tighter as her orgasm bursts through her.

"That's it. Give it to me. Everything you're feeling now is me. Inside you. Around you. It's all me."

My name falls off her lips. "I love you," she whispers.

That's all I need to spill inside her. To claim every part of her, inside and out. Our bodies wrap tightly together as my heart beats furiously against hers and my own release barrels through me.

Maci will be my wife one day. But this night will also be as fundamentally important as that. Overcoming hell and claiming each other and our happiness where so much was taken that night. This place and this life is ours.

CHAPTER 41

MACI

Trusting Sutton comes naturally. Even the first time he asked me on the dance floor, when I was hesitant to give the true answer, I've always trusted him. Letting him lead tonight, to bring me back to the scene that's replayed in my sleep for weeks, may not have been easy, but it was never something I doubted.

Time and again, he has proven that he's going to be there for me. Part of him is holding on to some idea that he needed to be there that night. Maybe he's trying to make up for that somehow, but he doesn't need to.

We lay on the blanket, a tangle of limbs, with a cooling sweat coating our skin. His fingers trace absent-minded circles on my shoulder as I press against him. It reminds me of the night he brought me cheesecake and we rocked on the porch swing here. It's been mere weeks since then, and in some ways seems so long ago.

Peace shrouds me in a way I haven't known for a while. My eyes flutter closed.

"Thank you for doing this. I've been trying to do it on my own and I've only gotten so far. Coming with Izzy and Leah during the day was a start, but being here at night, with you...it's more helpful than you know. I can't say I'll never have a bad thought here, but this space feels more like mine again."

Sutton kisses my head. His fingers dance over my shoulder. "That's all I want."

Gravel crunches on the drive. Sutton's fingers halt, and I hold my breath. A door slams.

Both of our heads pop up and dread washes over me. "Fuck. It's Stephanie."

"Perfect." Sutton's mutter is muffled by our movement to gather our clothes. We dress quickly.

"Who's there?" Stephanie's curt voice calls from near the edge of the house. The glow of the fire barely reaches her. Her blonde hair is pulled into a seamless bun, and she wears a stylish blouse with tapered pants.

"It's me," I say firmly, letting my sure voice carry through the backyard.

"Maci?" She doesn't wait for a response before venturing closer to us. "What on earth—" Her words cease when she realizes I'm not alone. She pauses halfway between the house and the firepit. I adjust my shirt, as Sutton buttons his pants.

My fingers tangle in my hair, running a hand through what I imagine is a very clearly just-been-fucked look. She looks between us and her face hardens. There isn't a single thing she could say to me right now to ruin what just happened. "This is Sutton, my boyfriend."

"Ma'am," Sutton says as he waves politely enough, but his posture is stiff. He grabs the blanket and folds it loosely to avoid eye contact with my mother.

"I can't imagine why you think acting like a couple of hormonal teenagers is appropriate." She pins me with a disgusted look.

A breathy laugh forces itself out of me. "Sex isn't reserved for beds. And I'm willing to bet at one point you agreed."

"Maci Grace." She hisses my name. If she thinks she can embarrass me, she's forgotten who I am.

Sutton's hand is warm when I tuck mine into his. I give him a gentle pull and we meet my mother where she stands. "I didn't realize you were still in town. We'll get out of your way."

"I left a few things." Her lips are tight.

Sutton, now leading me, slows his steps. I turn over my shoulder. "We need to talk about the information Mr. Campbell needs. In the light of day. Have a good night."

At the truck, Sutton opens my door and helps me in, closing it behind me quietly. He throws the blanket into the backseat when he slides in from the driver's side. For a moment, we sit in silence, while he fails to start the truck or say anything.

"Cowboy?"

He fiddles with the keys before looking over at me.

"Are you ok? Did she embarrass you?"

His chuckle is sarcastic. "I'm not afraid of her. There were just some things I didn't like back there."

My eyebrows scrunch together. "I don't—"

"I don't like that she tries to make you smaller. I don't like that I'm not sure what I can and can't say to her. She's your mother, so I know I need to respect her, but I want to build a life with you, and I have no intention of allowing her to talk to you like that for the rest of our lives."

I can't help the smile that crosses my face and the way my heart rate speeds up. "I wouldn't dare censor you, Cowboy. And that was hardly her worst. In truth, I think the last few weeks have been a little eye-opening for her because I haven't stayed quiet like I used to." I reach across the console and place my hand over his. "You say whatever you feel is necessary, but you don't have to fight my battles for me."

He worries his lip. "I don't like being called your boyfriend. Boyfriend feels so temporary. What I feel for you isn't temporary. I told you, I'm building a life with you." He flips his hand over under mine, twisting our fingers together.

"Boyfriend was the best option I had. You're more than a friend, but it's not like we're engaged. I wasn't trying to slight you."

His pouty smile is a little youthful and a little thoughtful. "I know you weren't. I didn't take it that way. I just want more."

"You can have everything." My blush is overtaken by my desire to climb into his lap, and he reflects my hunger with his intense eyes.

CHAPTER 42

SUTTON

I'm on the front porch of The Big House, rocking in one of the chairs, when the ranch hands head my way for breakfast.

"Morning boss." Cody smiles. He's the morning person of the group.

"Morning, Cody." I grin and stand. "Kelly, hang back a minute?"

Kelly nods in acknowledgment while Jason and Cody slip inside. "Everything good?"

"Yeah, no problems here." I shove my hands into my pockets. I could have this conversation inside or in any office around here, but there's no reason to. We're not that formal now, and I'm not about to change that. "Anything you guys need?"

He shakes his head. "No, we're good."

"Good. Well, I spoke with Dad and Terrence separately this morning. We're still a go for paperwork in January, and I'm going to be meeting with a few people from Terrence's team who want to stay on if it's a fit. I think we look good on our side. I also know that this expansion is going to come right around when we're turning bulls out."

"Yep, that's true. We'll manage. Don't worry."

"I feel better knowing you're confident with everything. That's why I wanted to talk with you. I told you guys that I needed to be looking at who could take on a bigger role. I'd like to extend a formal offer for you to manage

310

the cattle operation. It'll come with a salary increase and additional perks. I recognize the headache it is, and I haven't taken the decision lightly. That's if you want it."

Kelly bobs his head in an exaggerated fashion. "Yes, sir. I appreciate it. Strickland Ranch has become home to me, and I'm eager to see it grow."

"You deserve it. And I think it'll make Jason and Cody more comfortable that way, too."

"I agree."

"I'll write up everything and have it to you this afternoon. I want you to take the time to look it over and get back to me with any counteroffers."

Kelly's eyebrows scrunch. "I don't know what you plan to offer, but I've known you long enough to know you're not going to screw me."

My mouth tugs into a wide smile. "Still. This is my legacy, and we're in a period of transition. I want you to grow with us and be compensated for the additional work and hours."

"You got it."

I motion to the door. "Sorry to keep you from breakfast."

"No apologies necessary. Thank you." He extends a hand that I shake willingly.

"I'll meet you guys out there in just a bit."

I've just finished drafting paperwork for Kelly when my cell rings on the desk. It's Jason, which is odd because the guys hardly ever call me when I'm not around.

"Hey, Jason. Everything ok?"

"Uh, yeah," he says, sounding confused. "Were you serious about pigs? Because some guy is here with two big-ass hogs in a truck."

I grin. "Yep. Might add more, too."

"Uh. Ok. Cool. So..." He lets the last word trail off instead of asking a question.

"Have him pull up to the enclosure. Shouldn't take more than the four of you to get them in there." I laugh at their expense.

His confusion turns to concern. "You got it, boss." As he pulls the phone from his ear, I hear, "Just when I feel like I'm getting somewhere with the cattle," and the call cuts off.

Deep into the afternoon, I decide to take Maci on a short tour of Terrence's property. We cut through the gate on the west side of Strickland Ranch, which enters near the front corral.

Terrence waves from the back end of a long trailer attached to a truck. They're loading horses. "Hey there," he says with a smile.

I pull the Defender up alongside him and we climb out. As Maci rounds the front of the vehicle, I wrap an arm around her and tuck my face into her hair. "You're getting punished for that later. You know better than to touch the door."

Her face reddens before she can hide it.

"Terrence, this is Maci. Maci, Terrence."

Terrence extends a gloved hand, which she shakes. "Nice to meet ya," he says, grinning again. "You two getting ready for the big move?"

Maci smiles pleasantly.

I nod. "We are. I'm just giving Maci a quick tour over here, like I mentioned, and we'll be out of the way."

"You're no bother to us." He waves a dismissive hand. "The main house is open if you want to take a peek." He bounces an eyebrow at Maci. "You're welcome to check anything else."

"Thanks." She smiles, and her eyes fall to the horses.

Terrence and I exchange a few more words before we wish him well and head off. This time, Maci waits for me to open the door for her.

"Good girl," I say into her ear before she sits.

She exhales audibly and falls into the seat.

Today, I focus on showing her the buildings. Corrals and stables up front, along with two large open arenas. Kelly previously mentioned using them for events, and I agree it's a good use of what's already here.

"I love these." Maci gestures to the first arena, raising her voice over the yell of the engine. "Didn't you say Kelly thought they could be repurposed?" Her green eyes meet mine, and I'm captivated by the spark there. When she's brainstorming and creative, there's so much life in her. I want to see it all the time.

"Yeah. Actually, I've decided to have him take my role on."

"I think that's a great idea."

"I'd love for you to sit down with me and the ranch hands, especially Kelly, and talk about some ideas. I think you and Kelly would be a great team."

She smiles widely, but I don't miss the hint of surprise cross her face. "I'd love to."

A strong satisfaction coats my insides. Building this legacy with Maci is immensely gratifying, and I'm excited to see where it all goes.

After the buildings toward the front of the property, I drive Maci to the main house. Unlike The Big House, which is a painted blue wood, the main house here has a limestone facade, complimented by thick, sealed cedar posts, giving it the feel of a lodge.

"It's like a lodge, isn't it?" she asks, echoing my thoughts.

I grin. "Yeah."

"The Big House, and the Lodge." She smiles as I pull the Defender to a stop. I open the door and take her hand, leading her up the front steps to the massive, wooden double doors. The handles are made of intertwined antlers.

Inside, the foyer leads into an open-concept floor plan. The lodge atmosphere carries, with lots of wood and taxidermy animals. There's an industrial undertone to contrast it, mainly in the expansive kitchen with stainless-steel features.

"Wow, this would be great for entertaining!" Maci turns to me brightly. "You wouldn't need to build small houses here if you use this space for lodging. This is gorgeous."

Once again, I'm enamored with her glow. I can only smile in return.

"Is that your plan for it?" she asks.

I nod. "We haven't finalized anything, but that makes the most sense to me, too."

She releases my hand, making her way deeper into the kitchen. "Can you imagine cooking in here? Would your mom cook in here?"

I shrug. "Maybe? I think she likes her setup, but if we take on something with guests, she's going to need a bigger setup. And this would be closer. So, either she'd need to come here, or we'd need to hire someone."

We meander through the rooms, many of them themed, all of them complete with rustic decor. Then we make our way back out to the Defender and I head to the smaller house on the property.

"This is pretty," Maci says. Unlike the massive lodge, this home has the look of a secluded cabin. "What's this for?"

"Actually, I plan to offer it to Kelly."

Maci looks proudly at me. "I think that's great."

Our boots echo on the stairs as we ascend, and the scent of honeysuckle invades my nose from a large bush on the far end of the porch. I shove open the front door, which leads into a cozy living room, complete with full-grain leather couches and a massive built-in television. There are three moderately-sized bedrooms and an updated kitchen.

Once we've walked through the rooms, Maci smiles at me in the living room again. "I think this is perfect for a Ranch Manager house. It's a great perk to the role, and it will give him some privacy." As an afterthought, she asks, "Is he seeing anyone?"

I shake my head. "No. But those are the same thoughts I have. He deserves some space to himself, especially as he takes on more responsibility. We won't be able to increase his salary significantly right away, so I'm hoping some additional perks will offset it."

Maci threads her fingers with mine and leans up on her toes to kiss me. "I think he'll appreciate it."

CHAPTER 43

MACI

A ndi must have the largest turkey in the county prepped for Thanksgiving lunch. For the first time in our relationship, I leave Sutton sleeping in the bed and rise first. It's easier said than done though, because when I move to climb out of the bed, his warm arm wraps tighter around my waist and he drags me backward into his chest. I'd love to spend the entire day wrapped up in him in this bed, but for once I'm on a Stephanie-like track, concerned with the responsibilities of the day. I twist in his arms, pressing a kiss to his soft mouth, and extricate myself from his comforting embrace.

I shower quickly and slip into The Big House, where Andi and I meet in the kitchen as if it were synchronized.

"Good morning, sweetheart." Her floral nightgown hangs to her ankles, her hair still wrapped in heatless curlers. She's so adorable my chest threatens to burst.

"Good morning. Happy Thanksgiving." Without discussing it, I swing the fridge door open wide and we reach in together to pull out the massive bird.

We made an extensive game plan yesterday to make sure all the sides would be ready in time for the big meal. Considering all of the cooking Andi does, I'm a little surprised she doesn't have a double oven. I wonder if she's going to fully embrace the kitchen at The Lodge or keep it small here moving forward.

Along with the Stricklands and the ranch hands, Sammi arrived last night with her family. Randi and Liv will be joining us, and my friends will be dropping in after their own family events. Sutton mentioned that his friends often stop by at some point, as well. I even made a point to invite James, though it sounds like the club has their own event that takes place each year.

I still think Andi is prepping for a small army, but better safe than sorry, as Nana always said.

Working these last few weeks in the kitchen with Andi has been a balm for my heart. In some ways, she's the person who's kept me rooted in the familiar, providing me with a link to who I was before I took someone's life, tethering me to the person I loved the most in the world.

I have so much to be thankful for today, and none of it is lost on me.

Once the turkey is in the oven, Andi sneaks back to her bedroom to finish getting ready and I rush through the crisp fall air back to the bed with Sutton. The covers are at his waist, his torso and arms on full display, and my mouth waters.

This amazing man is all mine.

Did you know the gate is open?

> **We're pulling in.**

> **Oh, by the way, we have Banana and Roman.**

> Me:
> **Yes. And that's fine.**

"They here?" Sutton readjusts his hat and stands from the couch in his room. We snuck away for a make-out session a few minutes ago, only to be interrupted by my ass vibrating.

"Yes." I take his outstretched hand. "They brought Leah's niece and nephew."

He dips his chin. "Ok. They're little like Vivi, right?"

I grin at his nickname for his niece. "Banana is a little bit older, not quite two. Roman is four."

He scans the couch absently, searching for something.

"They're pulling in now."

Distractedly, he leans down and kisses me once more. "Ok. But did you say banana?"

"Oh. Yes, I did. Banana is Leah's nickname for her niece. Savannah." I lead the way out of the hall.

We make it to the front of the house as Leah pulls her car in. Izzy and Leah wave our direction, each opening a rear door. Roman pops out of the passenger side, almost shoving Izzy out of the way.

"Maci!" He barrels toward me, and I squat to grab him, realizing too late that while I'm healing well, I haven't taken a forty-pound, full-speed preschooler to the gut in a while. Roman hits me like a rocket, and I attempt to stand to counterbalance.

I'm definitely going over.

Sutton's arm wraps around my waist and I manage to plant my feet as Roman throws his tiny arms around my neck, trying to squeeze the life out of me.

"Hey bud, how are you?" I give him a gentle squeeze and he lets go.

"Happy Tanksgiving." He beams at me.

"Happy Thanksgiving. Did you eat a lot of turkey at your Mimi's?"

He grimaces. "Yuck. No. But I did eat mashed 'totaes. And cramberry sauce."

I return the disgusted face. "Better you than me. That stuff is nasty."

He giggles adorably, while Izzy and Leah approach from behind. Savannah is tucked into Leah's shoulder. Taking the opportunity to set him down, I nod to Sutton beside me. "This is my boyfriend, Sutton. This is his house."

"Hi." Roman's little voice is strong.

Sutton squats and offers Roman a hand. "Hey man, nice to meet you."

Roman's face lights up and he shakes Sutton's hand. "Are doze your horses by the gate?" He looks over his shoulder toward the road.

"Yep. You like horses?"

"Yes!" He bounces a little in his sneakers.

"Happy Thanksgiving, honey," Izzy says, wrapping her arms around me. I return her hug and give Leah a side hug.

"Banana fall asleep?"

Leah grins. "Yeah. Sorry we didn't tell you sooner that they were coming. Lily kind of dropped them on me with some B.S. about working tonight."

"That's ok. I've missed them."

Sutton stands fully. "Happy Thanksgiving."

"Oh, come here," Izzy says with a laugh, and reaches up to hug Sutton around his neck.

He leans down and wraps an arm around her briefly.

"Can we see 'em?" Roman looks between the adults.

"Who, bud?" Leah ruffles his dark hair.

"Da horses!"

Izzy's eyebrows jump.

"I don't mind taking him down there." Sutton's offer comes with the silent caveat that Leah okays it, and he waits.

"Well, hell yeah. Let's go." Leah gestures for him to lead the way.

He pauses. "Do you want to take the truck? I can lay the tailgate down. It's a short drive, but it's a longer walk with a sleeping toddler."

Leah smiles. "That's probably smarter."

Sutton drives while Izzy, Leah, and I ride on the open tailgate. Savannah is still passed out against Leah, while Roman stays tucked between my legs with my arms wrapped around his tiny body. I barely set him on the ground before he makes a beeline for the paddock fence, jumping onto the middle plank and draping his arms over the top.

"Look at dat one!" Roman points excitedly to Johnny Walker on the far side. Dusty, Michael's horse, and Veda graze closer to the driveway. Boots is farther out in the pasture.

We make our way toward them and Sutton climbs quickly over the fence instead of opening the perfectly good gate right next to where we stand. He makes a clicking sound in the side of his mouth and Johnny Walker heads our direction.

"He's coming!" Roman's shriek only increases my own excitement. Seeing things through the eyes of a child gives them such a magical perspective.

"You want to ride him?" Sutton looks over his shoulder at Roman.

Savannah begins to stir, and Leah talks to her quietly.

"Oh, can I?" Roman hardly gets the question out to Sutton before he jumps off the fence and bounces in front of Leah. "Can I please? Please, please, please?"

"Yes, silly." She ruffles his hair again. His eyes are wild with glee and he spins in a few circles before he manages to right his body and run back to the fence.

Sutton guides Roman through the lower two planks of the fencing and gives him some rules about behavior around the horses. Roman is transfixed, wholly focused on Sutton and the words rolling off his tongue. I understand the draw.

In the abstract, I promised Sutton children without a second thought. I've always seen myself as having children at some point and if he wants them, too, great. But now, watching him talk to Roman like he's more than a random four-year-old who turned up on his property, the care and respect that he's giving him? I know without a doubt that he's the perfect father for my future children. Is there anything he does wrong?

"Have you two talked about kids?" Izzy speaks from between me and Leah, as if reading my thoughts.

"Somewhat. Why?"

"Because she's worried she got knocked up just by watching him." Leah snickers at herself.

I laugh, and Izzy's face turns a deep pink. "That's not why I asked."

"Whatever," Leah says. Savannah sits upright in her arms. "If contact pregnancy was a thing, I'd have it."

She's unashamed at ogling my boyfriend and I can't even be mad because he's a dream, and I hardly expect her to make a move.

"Horse," Savannah says, pointing with a tiny finger.

Sutton walks Johnny Walker around the pen with Roman in the saddle. He holds the pommel like a happy prince, waving down at us with a glow like the horse belongs to him.

On the second pass, Sutton winks at me and then his eyes dart to one side. I follow his gaze to Savannah. "Roman!" she yells loudly.

Roman grins and waves at her proudly.

"Me! Me!" Savannah cries, bouncing in Leah's arms.

Sutton guides them all our way. "You want to ride?"

Leah doesn't seem bothered, but I'm wondering how small is too small to ride a horse.

Savannah finally notices Sutton and reaches eagerly with both hands.

"Let's let your sister have a turn," Sutton tells Roman. Roman agrees, thankfully, and Sutton lifts him off Johnny and helps him back through the fence. Then, he mounts Johnny Walker in one swift motion before lining him up tightly along he fence.

Savannah's arms are still outstretched, oddly comfortable with going to a stranger, and Leah lifts her up to Sutton. He grips her with two hands as he pulls her up, turning her around so she's facing forward, and setting her in front of him in the saddle.

A large hand rests around her belly and he tells her to hold onto the pommel. Her grip is loose and her grin is huge, twinkling eyes taking in the horse and us watching her. Sutton walks them slowly in a small circle. Savannah's high-pitch giggle is infectious, and soon everyone outside the fence is beaming and laughing with her.

"Isn't it fun, Banana?" Roman yells from next to us. She nods enthusiastically, doing little to hold on, but Sutton's grip is sure.

When Johnny Walker comes to stand before us again, Sutton leans down to whisper something in Banana's ear. Her tiny finger finds its way into her mouth, where she nibbles on it nervously while nodding at whatever was asked.

Leah ducks through the fence and takes Savannah as Sutton passes her down. He turns, speaking to Roman and ignoring the rest of us. "Come on." His head jerks toward the attached stables and he takes Savannah back from Leah.

Roman zips through the fence, careful of Johnny Walker standing close by, and hurries to Sutton, grasping his free hand without prompting.

"Who knew the cowboy was a baby whisperer?" Leah mutters. My heart is doing stupid somersaults again, and I can't bring myself to respond.

"No shit," Izzy says. She reaches over to Johnny, rubbing his muzzle.

The trio returns, Savannah still in one of Sutton's arms, and Roman carries a handful of carrots. Sutton talks Roman through offering a carrot safely to Johnny Walker as Savannah shouts, "Me! Me!"

She bursts into laughter as Sutton tickles her round tummy and talks quietly to her. As if to steady herself, she grips his face between her tiny hands and he smiles widely.

Fuck. I think my ovaries are in hyperdrive.

Chapter 44

Maci

It's dark before Izzy and Leah leave, two sleepy-eyed kids in tow. Leah's niece and nephew have always been special to me, but today they pulled out a side of Sutton I wasn't expecting. At least not yet.

The thought seems to draw him to me, and his warm arms wrap around me from behind as I watch my friends' taillights disappear in the driveway.

"What do you think about sleeping under the stars?" His voice is low and questioning in my ear.

I groan and press my body deeper against him. "Anywhere you are is where I want to be."

"I'm serious. I'll throw a blow-up mattress into the truck bed and we'll sleep at Nopal Vista."

Hearing the name tumble off his lips lights me on fire. His arms loosen but don't let go as I twist to look up at him. "Yes."

His lips are warm, especially compared to the cool November air, as he presses a soft kiss to my own. I've felt gratitude in massive waves today, but my thanks for this man are never-ending.

"I'll be right back." He kisses me again and heads back into the main house before returning with a large beige bag thrown over a shoulder and several comforters trapped under the other arm.

I extend my hands for a comforter, but he only arches an eyebrow at me.

"And you call me a stubborn ass."

He slaps my ass as I crest the top stairs.

"Hey!" I call over my shoulder with a laugh.

"It's a love tap." His laugh is young and free. I never want this night to end.

In the meadow, Sutton parks facing out from where the house will sit one day. A small battery-operated unit blows up the massive air mattress he throws into the back of the truck. I can only hear it, not see, because obviously I'm not allowed to get out of the truck until he comes to get me. I snort at the thought.

I wonder if he realizes he's turning me into a passenger princess. A girl could get used to letting someone else do all the work. Actually, I don't think I'm capable.

Finally, he opens my door. "You been feeling better, yeah?"

My brows furrow. "Yeah..."

"Good." He leans in and unclips my buckle.

I open my mouth to inquire just what's going on when he grabs me on either side of my waist, pulling me out of the open door. My hands reach to brace on his shoulders, but he throws me over his shoulder, causing me to squeal.

"I never realized how much I'd love that," he chuckles, the sound vibrating his chest.

Blood rushes to my head and I grip his cool jacket with both hands. "Hauling me around like a bale of hay?"

He laughs louder. "Have you seen anyone haul hay here?"

"That's. Not. The point," I grunt into his back.

Sutton sits me upright in a whoosh and lands me on the open tailgate. My head spins as the blood rushes back into my body.

"Listening to you squeal." His arms cage me in on either side.

I can't be sure, but I think I feel my pupils dilate as I take him in standing in the dark, lit from behind by the semi-covered moon.

"Oh?" My voice is breathless, and I don't try for more. His effect on me is always instantaneous—his hold on my arousal, as much as his grasp on my emotions.

His lips brush mine teasingly. "Yeah, oh. I'm a fan of all the sounds you make." I'm chasing after him when he pulls back.

"I see."

"You know, I thought I was becoming addicted to you."

I swallow. "I remember. Did you get yourself in check?"

"Never." His nose drags along my jaw and into my loose hair. "In fact, I think it's much worse than I thought."

I try for "oh no" but all that comes out is a breathy "ohhh" as my body stills, afraid that if I move too much he'll pull back again.

"I warned you about sharing. And you've been such a good girl," he breathes, tickling my ear. "But it's getting worse. I don't even like sharing you with family."

"Good thing I don't want to sleep with them."

He pulls back and grabs my jaw in the crook of his hand in a flash. "Not funny, Firecracker." There's mirth in his stormy eyes, though.

"I thought it was pretty funny," I challenge.

He closes his eyes briefly. "You're always trying to set me off."

"Yes. Because I love every part of you. Even that beast you keep locked inside."

He grins. "I'm not a beast."

I lean back. He's getting away with too much teasing, and I'm taking matters into my own hands. "You're right." I feign boredom and sigh. "You're really kind of a fuddy duddy."

He belly laughs, and I can't help the wide smile that splits my face. "A fuddy duddy?" His laughing strengthens.

Pride fills me. "Yep. Such a boring gentleman."

He leans in so his breath skates over my lips again, but he doesn't break eye contact. "Is that why you call me 'Sir'?"

"It's the respectable thing to do with your elders." The challenge has left my voice, but I manage to maintain his stare.

"You're such a brat." He removes his hands from the truck bed. "That's alright. I owe you one."

"One what?" Confusion overtakes my playfulness.

His hands land on my hips. "I told you I was going to watch you come apart under the stars out here, and I'm going to make good on that promise." My mouth drops open and he follows up with, "Because us fuddy duddies keep our word."

And with that, he launches me onto his shoulder again, eliciting another surprised squeal. His grip on my thighs is sure, and he grabs the frame of the truck bed with his free hand, climbing swiftly into the back.

"I have another idea."

"Regarding?" Sutton's fingers stroke my shoulder. We're loosely tucked under the comforters he brought, gazing at the star-filled sky in our afterglow.

"The ranch," I say matter-of-factly.

"This should be good. A wet T-shirt contest?"

"What?" Laughter bursts out of me.

"Well, last time you said me and all the guys should pose nude for a calendar."

"Oh my God, I did not say nude! I said maybe without shirts." I continue to laugh, shaking against his warm body. "Why would I submit for the objectification of women's bodies?"

"Only men's bodies, then."

"Absolutely."

His hand drops from my shoulder to tickle my waist. "You just want to show off what you have."

I squirm and wiggle until my laughter causes tears.

"Ok, so then what's the big plan?"

"A haunted house." His fingers resume trailing over my skin, and I take his silence as cue enough to continue. "With everything going on, you haven't been subjected to my insane love for Halloween yet, so this probably seems out of left field. But I think a creepy-ass haunted house would be amazing out here."

"Mmhmm," he hums neutrally, encouragement enough for me to continue.

"We'd get volunteer actors. I'm sure there are people in the community, and we can source the community colleges nearby, too. We could have set dates, like only Fridays and Saturdays in October. The structures would be permanent and we could repurpose them, if we want, during the other months."

"October is a pretty busy month for the ranch. I don't know if we need to add to that," he says with a hint of reservation.

I'm not put off by his thoughts, instead pushing harder. "All you're doing is adding to it. You're adding four times as much busy as you have now."

"That's fair."

"I think you're under the impression that you're going to need to oversee everything that happens. And on a big-picture scale, you are. But you're going to have to get comfortable delegating," I tell him pointedly.

"Says the woman who's always trying to shoo me out to work." He kisses the top of my head.

"I just don't like being in the way."

Like lightning, he readjusts his grip and pulls me atop him again. "Would you stop that? You're not *in* the way. You are the only way. The only path I care about is the one where you are." He reaches up to run his fingers through my loose hair, but they tangle near my ear and I snicker. He doesn't acknowledge either.

"I used to think that expanding was only about what was best for Strickland Ranch. The legacy. I wanted to make my parents proud."

I quiet to take in the seriousness of what he's sharing.

"Now I know it's not just that. I still want those things. I want to do everything in my power to keep Strickland Ranch thriving and growing. But I also want to build a life with you. So only the things that make that a possibility matter to me."

I lean down and press a tender kiss to his lips. "Fine. I am the way." I grin against his mouth and his lifts into a returning smile.

"Fuck, I love you."

My heart tips over itself. "I love hearing you say that."

He lifts his head up, pulling me tighter against him, and growling repeatedly in my ear, "I love you, I love you, I love you."

I giggle as he rolls us over, sliding his growing erection between my legs again. "Show me again," I whisper.

CHAPTER 45

STEPHANIE

Nothing in my life looks the way it used to. In some ways, I've been living in limbo for twenty years. The days I've spent at Mother's have been quiet. Quiet sorrow, quiet rage, quiet shame.

Kathryn and I spoke once more after our initial conversation. We shared details about our lives with Alan and discovered that we have too much in common to be coincidence. Oldest daughters of widowed mothers, families with land or assumed assets to be inherited, mothers to daughters not sons, and absent ex-husbands. We also have similar features, including our blonde hair and blue eyes.

I haven't figured out what it all means, aside from Alan being a controlling, psychotic bigamist.

After finding Maci and her boyfriend postcoital in the yard, I've not heard from her. I know she was surprised at my leaving abruptly, but I could hardly tell her what happened when James came by. It will only solidify her animosity toward me.

It's not until Thanksgiving when I'm at my short-term rental enjoying a bottle of wine and a charcuterie tray that I begin to contemplate what I'm going to do with my newfound information. I still haven't heard from Alan. Given what I've gleaned from Maci and Kathryn recently, my body tingles on and off like a live wire.

Alan has to be in control. He made a choice not to tell me about Colt, and now he hasn't called me even though he *must* know I've left. It's all indicative of a plan. So what is it?

Even after ten years with him, I still can't anticipate his moves. Frustration fuels my focused thoughts today.

That's ok. I have a plan, too.

Someone starts screaming, waking me. I jerk upright, finding myself still on the couch in my rental. The incessant noise isn't a person, but my phone wailing on the kitchen island. I stumble to it, courtesy of my second bottle of wine.

"Hello?" I've never sounded this rough in my life.

"Mrs. Young, this is AYT Security. We received a fire alert. Do you need us to dispatch the fire department?"

Blinking to clear my blurry vision, I press a hand against the cool counter to maintain my balance. "I beg your pardon?"

"Ma'am, is your house on fire?" There's an urgency to the man's voice.

"Fire?" I scan the kitchen and living room. "No, I—Wait." My brain catches up faster than my vision. "AYT? Is this about the house in Dallas?"

"Yes ma'am. Is your house on fire?"

"I'm not there. I'm in San Antonio."

"Is anyone else at the house?" he asks, his tone remaining calm and insistent. This is exactly why my number is the primary, because I'm usually the one there. For once, I'm not.

"I don't know. My husband might be there."

"I'll dispatch the fire department immediately."

"Thank you." I hang up before the man says anything else, dialing Alan. I haven't decided if I care if he burns to a crisp inside the house or not, but auto-pilot directs my actions.

The phone rings three times before he answers. "Did your daughter try to burn my fucking house down, Stephanie?"

His question catches me off-guard, but I don't have a chance to respond before he continues in a condescending tone. "She and her boyfriend threatened me, you know. If she thought I was going to sue her for every penny she has before, she's in deep fucking water now."

I open my mouth to respond, but he continues to spit anger down the line. I'm not convinced he even knows or cares if I'm still on the phone. "She's going to jail, Stephanie. That little slut is going to jail. Murder. Arson. The judge will throw the book at her. She'll never see the light of day again."

Alan's always had high standards for Maci, commented on her clothing choices, how much time she spent out, her attitude. But he's never said such a disgusting thing about her. Not to me. Even the night they argued in our kitchen and she pulled a knife on him, he still pushed for the police and talked about her needing psychiatric help. Never something like this.

"I could have died! I probably have lung damage from smoke inhalation!" He's roaring now. "It's nothing but sticks now, Stephanie. There's nothing left!"

Serves him right.

I wonder briefly if Kathryn did, in fact, burn his clothes? Has she kept our conversation under wraps?

Suddenly, the last ten years of bullshit that I've put up with rains down on me.

"You stupid prick. You have no idea what you've started. It's too bad you didn't burn to death in that house. You think this isn't over because you're not done with Maci? No. This isn't over because I'm not done with you."

I hang up before he can respond. I'd much rather he were bacon right now.

CHAPTER 46

MACI

"You guys are coming today right? I *have* to get photos of Vivi in front of the gingerbread house."

Sammi and I are seated in The Big House living room, with Viviane playing on the floor. She stands and walks along the edge of the couch between the two of us every few minutes before finding a toy to distract herself with.

Sutton is with the ranch hands and Justin is taking the opportunity to sleep in.

"So you picked up my brother's nickname for her," Sammi says to me with a grin. Their faces are strikingly similar, and also completely different.

My cheeks heat. "I guess I did."

"We'll try to stop by. We're supposed to drop by some friends of ours today, too." Viviane stands again, finding her mom with a toothy grin, and Sammi brushes her dark hair from her eyes.

Andi pads in from the kitchen with coffee in hand, tucking herself onto her chair under the reading lamp.

"You want to sit with Memaw?" she coos down at Viviane.

Viviane looks up at her with a smile but goes back to banging her toys together.

My phone rings and I'm surprised to see Stephanie's name. I wish I had a clearer idea of where things stand with us, but that hasn't happened yet. We do need to discuss Alan, though. "Sorry, I need to take this."

Sammi and Andi wave me off and I answer the phone as I head down the hallway to the front door. "Good morning."

"Maci, where are you?" Stephanie's voice is tight, but in a different way than usual. She's not quite breathless but obviously concerned.

"I'm at Sutton's ranch." My tone is questioning, and I look around the acreage for a sign of something.

"It's safe there?"

My heart immediately starts thudding faster in my chest, the volume increasing in my ears. "Why wouldn't it be?"

"Do you know anything about Alan's house?"

"Alan's—Okay, I have no idea what you're talking about." Now I know how she feels when I drag things out.

"The house in Dallas burned down last night," she says flatly. "The alarm company called me because our fire alarms were going off. When I called Alan to see if he was at the house, he blamed you."

"Me? I was here all day. There are over a dozen people who can swear to that, if it comes down to it." This is a new level of insanity even for him. I start walking without a clear destination in mind. "Oh no, what about the things you took from Nana's?"

"I have them with me. I brought everything when I left."

That's a small relief. "Where are you?"

"I'm in San Antonio. At my rental."

"Your rental?" Stephanie was extremely vague in her conversation to let me know she was leaving Nana's. I knew she'd be in San Antonio, but nothing more than that.

"It's temporary."

I purse my lips.

"Anyway, Alan threatened to point the finger at you for the fire. So just be prepared for that. That's not the only reason I called. I spoke to Kathryn, Alan's other wife."

"Fabulous. Did you get names or anything? I need to put a stop to the lawsuit soon."

"Do you have a pen?"

"No, but I can put a note in my phone." I quickly set the audio to speakerphone and open the application on my phone to jot the details down.

She rattles off the information quickly as I continue walking toward the stables. It's not muscle memory just yet, but thankfully the fence line provides an easy guide and my feet make quick work of the path.

"Thank you. I don't know what will come of this, but my lawyer seems to think it will be helpful."

"I hope so." Stephanie's voice is earnest. "I don't know how else I can help you right now. I'm sorry." Her voice seems to stick. "I'm sorry I didn't believe you when you were younger. That I didn't call Alan out for who he is. He's not all to blame for the state of our relationship. I know that."

I stop walking and stare at my phone, not taking it off speaker.

"There's a lot of years' worth of shit to go through," she continues. My head pulls back and my eyes widen. Stephanie hardly ever curses. "If you're willing, I'd like to give it a try. It's okay if you need time."

I've never been speechless before. I stare at the phone like an idiot, my mouth opening and closing the tiniest amount but not formulating any words.

"Maci?"

"I'm here. I…" What do I even want? Sure, I want a mother who cares. She's right that we have a lot to wade through, and I have no idea where it will get us. If the last two months have taught me anything, it's that we have to grab life by the horns while we can, because you never know when it will be too late. "I agree, it's not going to be easy. I'm willing to try, if you are."

There's a tiny sniff from the speaker. "Ok. That sounds lovely. Please keep me updated on what your lawyer says."

"Ok. I will."

"Thank you."

Our phone conversations usually end abruptly. Instead, this one is dragging on in an awkward fashion. "Talk to you soon."

"Bye." She finally hangs up.

Veda whinnies at me from the pasture. I lean against the fence, dialing Hank. Veda heads my direction as he answers. I run through the details that Stephanie gave me.

I'm breathless by the end, though there isn't a ton to share. "Is this enough? Is it even helpful?"

"Everything is helpful. You're going to The Jingle Bell Bash today, right?"

"Yes."

"Good. Let me get working on this, go have some fun, and I'll follow up when I have more information. We're on the right track, Maci. So far, there's nothing in what the police department sent over that proves anything malicious or neglectful on your part. That's likely why the detective didn't send it to the prosecutor."

His words have minimal effect in relieving the pressure in my chest. "Okay. I'll try. Thank you, Hank."

"You're welcome, Maci. Have a good weekend."

"You, too." He hangs up, and I tap the phone against my mouth in silent contemplation. Who would've thought I'd be twenty-four years old wondering if I'm going to be arrested, or sued for everything I'm worth?

The Jingle Bell Bash is a gorgeous event. Whether it falls on a warm autumn day or an icy one, the committee has always done a good job of instilling the festive spirit of the period they're trying to recreate.

My photo area isn't the same as the Fall Festival. I'm stationed on the opposite direction of Town Square this time. Andi, Sutton, and I ride together, unloading Andi's necessities first and then getting my props in place.

I'm not sure what to expect today. Santa pictures are a given at the event, but I'm not involved in that. Instead, my gingerbread house and I will be celebrating a different holiday spirit.

Despite knowing Colt won't show up this year, Sutton refuses to leave my side. I don't know what he's going to do for the four hours I'm scheduled to be here, but he refused to hear reason and told me not to worry about him.

Fine. Let him stand guard if he feels better for it. He seems to need that reassurance.

The kids are jazzed up on hot chocolate and funnel cakes when they come through my line. Parents seem a little less frazzled than the Santa line, but there's obvious expectation for cute holiday photos. I treat them all like extended family, hyping them up and hugging them when the mood feels right as they make sweet and silly faces in front of the child-sized backdrop.

The temperature is dropping quickly as we near dusk, and my hands are freezing, being exposed to the cold for so long. In between families, which have kept me unexpectedly busy, I rub my hands together for some friction. Sutton appears out of nowhere.

"Cold?" He grabs both of my hands in his.

My stupid heart flutters again. When is it going to stop that? His look is so intense that I blush in the crowd.

He presses his lips to my hands. "How does some hot chocolate sound?"

"Amazing." Somehow I manage not to jump up and down, but he clocks my excitement. I rise up on the balls of my feet, kissing his lips.

"Firecracker," he stage-whispers, scanning the space in a faux attempt at secrecy, "did you just kiss me in front of all of these people?"

I throw my head back and laugh. "Is that such a surprise?"

"A welcomed one. Our last event like this, things were so cut and dry. At least, for you." He winks.

I lean up and kiss him again. "To make up for last time." I smile against his lips before settling onto my feet again.

"I'll be back." He disappears into the growing crowd toward The Jim-Dandy where Melissa and I met previously. I'm so glad he knows where the best hot chocolate is.

The next family signs in at the table, which is even bigger since the last event. I'm nearly out of cards and make a mental note to order more soon. Maybe relocating here won't be such a hit on my business after all.

"Hi, I'm Maci."

The mom smiles. "I'm Candy—no joke." I grin as she continues. "I'm Cody's sister." I don't have a chance to consider who she's referring to. "He works at the ranch with Sutton."

"Yes. We love him." My skin is on fire. I don't know what anyone knows or how to refer to them.

Her smile doesn't falter. "Well, he has good things to say about you. He and the other hands were talking about your work last weekend and he told me I *had* to come over with the kids."

"Oh, wow. That's so kind of him."

Her eyes flit to her husband, managing their toddler as she continues to bounce their newborn, and back to me. "He mentioned you had an accident recently. Are you healed ok?"

My familiar perma-smile adheres to my face. "I am. Thank you. Why don't we get you all on this bench in front of the gingerbread house?" I gesture to the backdrop. "Then we can situate the babies in the windows."

"That sounds adorable." She beams.

I jump into work mode, urging them to get situated to avoid discussing myself. I'm trying to push my usual "stupid small town" thought from my mind, but given the circumstances, it's swirling back there waiting to be let in.

Cody's family precedes the last family, and then I start closing up. The timing couldn't be better, because we barely managed with the light we had and it's darkening quickly.

"Look at you, playing sweet with the locals." An evil chill races down my spine at Alan's voice.

I whip around to find him only a few feet away. "You've got to be kidding. Are you stalking me? Like father, like son, I guess." I can't help the words as they tumble from my mouth.

"I doubt my son was stalking you. You probably lured him over with one of your slutty outfits and then killed him."

Disgust wages war inside, but what comes out of me is villainous. "Ah, yes. The black widow. She eats the male after they fuck, right?"

His eyes bulge, and he steps forward hastily.

I hold up a finger in his face as he closes in, wagging it back and forth. "Ah-ah. Do you remember what happened last time you came at me?"

Though he pauses, he doesn't look any calmer.

I smirk. "Little secret? I found out that knife I stuck you with was my father's. How ironic that you can't manage to parent any child you've known, and mine managed to save me even though he was never around."

"'Save' is quite the exaggeration. Still have a feel for theatrics, I see."

This time, I step forward. "Did you not put your fucking hands on me when I was a teenager, and did I not stop you?"

A street light flickers to life behind me. The area I'm stationed in has all but cleared out. Ice sculpting is scheduled to start in minutes, and it draws the largest crowd each year. Anyone in this area is lost in happy chatter as they hurry by. "Don't test me."

"Do you think I'm afraid of a slut?" He practically spits his anger on me. "My son wasn't all there, according to his mother. I doubt he could've defended himself well."

He shifts his weight as if to step closer again. I slip the same knife from my back pocket and flick it open. Alan's eyes widen when I press the tip to his stomach, but suspiciously he doesn't move.

"Your son stabbed me." My voice is a lethal whisper. "I've watched enough crime dramas to know it's pseudo penetration. So, I'm pretty certain he wanted to screw me again, but we both knew he couldn't get me off by that point."

"Are you saying you want to fuck me?" He seems proud of the comment.

I grin. "No, thanks. Colt's premeditated plan to gut me isn't exactly the same as me defending myself with a pocketknife. Again. But nice try."

I press harder into his gut. "Besides. Did you know that cock size is hereditary? So are kinks. So *I* think that you also have only a moderate dick, and probably suck in bed."

His jaw clenches so hard, I'm surprised I can't hear his teeth grinding.

"Sucks for my mother." I let out a sarcastic laugh. "I could never. Because, I'm a slut. Right?" He doesn't respond, but he doesn't need to. "Well, guess what? I'm a slut who doesn't fuck around anymore. So if *you* decide to fuck around, you're going to find out what your son did, and that's that I don't bluff." I press firmer with the knife to drive the point home. Thanks to his lightweight jacket, I doubt my small knife is inciting any pain. But I'm fully prepared to shove with all my might if necessary.

He swallows and backs up. "You're ruined. The prosecutor may not want to go after you, but a judge is going to see right through you in civil court. Especially after I tell them you burned my house down. You're mine."

"I hope you have *all* your ducks in a row, Alan, because police reports show that Colt was a ticking time bomb and a stalker. And I have no idea what fire you're talking about, but it will be a cold day in hell before you can prove something that didn't happen."

He gives me a sharp look before turning and walking off angrily into the dark.

I'm still standing with the knife in hand when Sutton comes back with hot chocolate. "Maci?"

I don't respond at first as he approaches from behind. He rounds to my front and his eyes widen as he takes in the blade. "What the fuck? Maci?"

"Take it," I say, waving the blade in a small motion. I open the other for a hot chocolate and he makes the exchange quickly, before handing me the second drink. He shoves the closed knife into a pocket.

"What the hell is going on?" He ducks his head to get closer to me, gripping my face gently in his hands and studying my glazed look.

"Alan."

His eyes dart around, and I blink.

"No, he's gone. He was here." I extend one arm and he takes the hot chocolate absently.

"Did he come at you?"

"Sort of." I sip my drink in an attempt to warm myself from the inside out. "Yes."

"I'm going to fucking kill him." Sutton's words almost hiss out of his mouth and jar me from my thoughts. "He's going to be the first animal we go after on our new guided hunts. Archery, not rifle. And then, I'm going to hang him by his fucking feet and let him bleed out like any other animal, before I gut him and feed him to the fucking pigs."

"No, you're not." I can't decide how serious I think he is, but like an idiot I smile softly anyway. With my free hand, I reach inside his jacket, wrapping my arm around his middle and pulling us tightly together. "We're going to get through this the right way. I cannot have you in jail."

His stormy blue eyes take me in, a new kind of intensity brewing within them, as I set my chin on his chest and look up at him. His lips are warm on my forehead.

"Maci, I need you to understand how serious I am. I made a promise, and I keep them."

"I know how serious you are, and I love you for it. But he's gone. I'll call Detective Porter and let him know what happened." I don't give voice to my inner question: how long is he gone? Are we *both* going to be facing murder charges soon?

CHAPTER 47

MACI

Sutton has just finished showing me all of my photography equipment in his shop when my phone rings from Hank's call.

"Hi, Hank." My greeting is lackluster—not rude, but nothing like my usual chipper tone with him. "You're on speaker."

In comparison, his enthusiastic greeting is even more lively than usual. "Hey, Maci. Hey, Sutton. How are you?"

"Truthfully?" I don't give Hank a chance to respond before I continue. "My anxiety is through the roof. Alan is following me. I can't live like this, Hank. You have to get him to drop this suit."

"What do you mean, following you?" Hank asks, unamused.

"He attempted to follow us after the funeral," Sutton tells him. "And he showed up at the Jingle Bell Bash."

"Did he approach you?"

"Yes." I bring the phone closer to me, like I'm about to share a secret, but my volume doesn't decrease. "And I don't respond the same as I used to. My gut reaction is self-defense. *Offense* even. I pulled a knife on him."

Part of me is wishing we had this conversation face to face. Is Hank rethinking helping me? Thinking he needs to increase his fees? *Oh my God, I didn't even ask what he charges.*

"He didn't call the police?" Hank's skeptical question interrupts my thoughts.

"He left. I called Detective Porter and let him know, but he's not as invested as he needs to be. I'm sure Alan will try to use the situation to his advantage, even though he started it."

"And no one saw these events? Surely there were witnesses at the bash."

"No. It was dark and there were hardly any people in my area because it was time for ice sculpting."

Sutton speaks up. "The cameras at the shopping center heading out of town may have caught something. But only our argument, not the following. I'll look like the aggressor on that one."

Hank hums in thought. "Ok, well let's hope we don't have to get into all that. I got a hit based on the info you gave me."

Adrenaline surges through my veins. I don't dare interrupt.

"It turns out Alan has active marriage licenses in three states."

"Three?" The word slips out in surprise. "Sorry, continue."

Even through the phone, I can hear the smile that tilts Hank's mouth and affects his speech. "One of the marriages is using an alias. We were able to find it based on information he gave the police department."

"So now what?" Sutton leans closer to me over the console.

"Two of the marriages would likely be deemed invalid. The only legal one currently is to Stephanie. However, he's participating in bigamy, which is a felony. My recommendation would be to submit our findings to Alan's lawyer. Notify them that we plan to share with the district attorney."

I don't miss the gleam in Sutton's eyes, the hidden joy. His response to Hank's suggestion adds to my own positive feelings.

"We'll offer to withhold the information on the understanding of him dropping the case. I'll also prepare documents that state if Alan decides to try this again later, we'll immediately send documentation to the District Attorney."

"Will that work?"

"If he gets slapped with a third-degree felony, he could be looking at ten years in prison in addition to fines. I think he will reconsider."

It may not be a life sentence, but picturing Alan in an orange jumpsuit without any control over his own life is immensely satisfying. He'd never allow that to happen. "Do it."

"You got it. We've got him, Maci. Give it a day or so and I bet we'll have word from his attorney that they're dropping the suit."

Once again, I want to throw my arms around Hank's neck. "I was right before. We don't deserve you."

"There's nothing to deserve," he says through a chuckle. "Do you want Stephanie to be included in the documentation? Alan may require it. She has intimate knowledge of his life and may be able to access more than what we have initially."

Sutton's eyebrows rise at me in question.

"I don't know. I'm not sure how she planned to use the knowledge. Let's move forward as is. If he requests it, then I'll talk to her."

"You got it. Talk to you soon, Maci."

"Bye, Hank. Thank you." A cautious relief washes over me. I'm finally seeing the light at the end of the tunnel.

"Thanks, Hank," Sutton says from next to me.

"Bye guys." Hank hangs up.

Sutton and I stare at each other quietly for a few seconds, then he speaks softly. "Almost done, Firecracker."

CHAPTER 48

MACI

After talking to Hank on Saturday, I try to keep busy. Sutton and the crew have a full day of deworming and weighing calves. He offered for me to help, and it's not that I don't want to, but my mind is busy with anxiety. Not wanting to distract my favorite comforting man, I decide to visit my second-favorite.

It's a weird thing to think that James has become so important to me in such a short time, but he offers a sense of peace that I could use now.

A member I don't recognize waves me in at the gate, and I park in what's becoming my usual spot.

McCoy pushes the front door open on his way out as I enter. My eyes catch on his bandaged hand. He only tips his head at me in greeting. Unlike many of the others, he never looks at me with interest of any sort. Some seem curious, likely at my being the President's daughter. Pete always seems happy to see me. My dad and Hawk tend to look at me with a familial feel. But McCoy just watches; there's nothing else there.

"Hey," I say quietly, as he walks out and I walk in. I turn back toward him. "Everything ok?"

He stops walking and stares at me from the sidewalk, the door still held open between us.

"Your hand," I clarify, moving my own briefly in his direction.

"Yep." His casual response doesn't translate to a softness in his eyes, and I continue to study him for an indication of what happened. It's not actually my business, but his usual laid-back personality has been replaced with something falsely indifferent, stiff, leading me to believe he's actually hiding something.

I'm not sure why an injury would even matter. Unless he's embarrassed as to how he got it.

"Just a little barbecue accident." His entire persona changes after he speaks. He lifts the wrapped hand to waist level and laughs sardonically. "That's why I don't cook."

His following smile doesn't feel natural. "See ya, Maci." He waves with the good hand and lets the door fall closed.

Why can't I picture McCoy barbecuing?

"Hey Maci," Ginger calls from behind me.

I turn and wave at her behind the bar.

"James isn't here."

"Oh." I make my way her direction and plop down in one of the chairs stationed at her bar.

"Everything ok?" She doesn't have the soft voice of Izzy, or the playful voice of Leah, but she seems genuine in her care. Which is odd, considering our start.

The corner of my mouth tips up.

"I think I'm just...tired. You know, when your brain, your body, even your bones are tired?"

She pours a whiskey and soda and slides the glass to me. "You're welcome to sit here and relax for as long as you need."

Are we building a friendship? I guess stranger things have happened.

"Thanks." I sip the drink and settle in for a while.

Sutton and I have rearranged the office to butt the desk and small table against each other, spreading out maps of both properties side by side.

Looking at the little buildings dotting both adds a new perspective to what's in process. Sutton draws a blue shape akin to a rectangle around The Big House and the area surrounding it that he plans to make more personal for his parents. This includes the existing garden and the new pig pen.

"Are you sure they want Oinks and Snorts to stay there?" I press a finger to where the new addition is.

Sutton gives me a puzzled look. "Who?"

"Oinks and Snorts. The hogs."

He blinks. "And you have shit to say about Mama naming things." His face softens. "Yeah. They're good there for now."

He outlines the area for Nopal Vista in green. It's more square and includes a section of the hidden creek.

I pull up one of the chairs and he makes a colorful representation of the various categories on the ranch and anything that's fairly permanent. Then he follows up with pencil sketches.

"Your haunted house could go here." Using the pencil as a pointer, he taps a square with a pumpkin in it on the northwest side of the new property. "There're additional entrances here and here," the pencil taps, "so we can avoid everyone coming through the more private areas."

"It's not my haunted house." The flush is leaving my cheeks.

His signature hidden smirk plays on his lips. "Yes it is. I'm even going to put a big-ass sign that says Maci's Slaughterhouse on it."

My mouth falls open and the heat returns as quickly as it vanished. "You won't."

He laughs. Then he goes about penciling in all the other ideas that have come up.

"Is this how you plan the pieces you craft?"

"I do a little sketch. Nothing crazy." He pretends to focus on the map, but his reddening cheeks give him away.

"You look a little flushed. Need some fresh air?"

The pencil hits the desk with a smack. "Great idea. I'm starving."

Before I can stand, he cages me into the chair I'm sitting in. "Grab the Defender and meet me at the front." He punctuates his request with a hard kiss, then leaves before I can stand.

The day is gorgeous and chilly, just how I like it. I tug my boots on and head out to find the keys in the Defender. Just as I'm pulling up to the front porch, Sutton opens the front door and comes out with an insulated bag.

"What's this?" I slide into the passenger side.

"Lunch." He tucks the overstuffed bag in the floorboard and climbs into the driver's seat. We head in the direction of Nopal Vista.

We talked over moving into The Lodge until our house is built, but decided not to. We'll focus on getting it ready for guests, instead. Michael and Andi don't bother us at The Big House, and the walls are surprisingly thick, giving us at least the illusion of being secluded for a few more months.

I love that we already spend so much time where we'll be permanently, though. Building these memories from the literal ground up.

Together, we spread a comforter where the house will go, and Sutton starts removing food from the bag.

"Looks like a celebration." I sink down to the blanket.

"Just lunch with my favorite person."

My heart trips over itself right as my phone rings. "Wonder who that could be." I yank it out. "It's Hank."

Our eyes lock. He doesn't have news already, right? Maybe Alan told him to fuck off.

"Hi, Hank." I wish my voice came out stronger. I can't help but anticipate the worst.

"Hey, Maci." His tone is neutral.

"Should I put you on speaker?"

"Sure, if you want."

I press the button. "Go ahead."

"Well, I have news. Alan's lawyer called me just a few minutes ago." Again, his tone gives nothing away. It's not usually his style, and I'm wondering if he's trying to calm me before he tells me I'm screwed.

"Alan has agreed to drop the civil lawsuit, with the counter request of all parties signing an NDA."

"Who are 'all parties'?" I chew my lip.

"You, Sutton, and Stephanie."

"So, we could never use the bigamy." Sutton studies the phone.

"Correct. Contractually, he would sign agreeing to drop any claims and refrain from filing anything new. Everyone else would sign not to pursue the bigamy or share any knowledge surrounding it."

"Is that legal?" Sutton presses.

"People agree not to share all kinds of learned information," Hank says. "It's up to you, though."

Sutton's eyes bore into mine with a new hunger. We're both so ready to be past this.

"Tell the lawyer we'll do it. But I have my own requests. Alan has to also agree to give Stephanie an uncontested divorce. And she gets any insurance money from the house."

Sutton smiles wickedly at me.

"The house?" Hank asks.

"Alan's house burned down on Thanksgiving."

"Oh, shit. He's just taking it left and right." Hank sounds more impressed than concerned. "Ok, I'll let you know if there's a problem. Otherwise, we'll sign later this week."

"Thanks, Hank." I end the call and practically jump into Sutton's lap.

He willingly pulls me to straddle his outstretched legs.

"Now we have something to celebrate."

He kisses me softly. "Every day with you is a day to celebrate."

"Well, it looks like you're going to be packing a lot of fancy lunches, because I'm not going anywhere." I grab his hat and place it on my head.

"Excuse me, Firecracker. But there's a rule about wearing the hat."

"Does it have to do with breaking in this land?" I bounce my eyebrows at him.

"It does. Now, would you like to fulfill the requirement before or after dessert?" His eyes flash.

My face falls slightly. "I'm usually dessert."

He grins. "I have a sweet tooth. I'll have two." He reaches into the bottom of the insulated bag and pulls out a tiny cheesecake.

"Cheesecake! I'm feeling spoiled, Cowboy."

"I intend to spoil you any day I can."

I take the cheesecake tray and set it aside. "That's for later." My fingers thread into his hair and I pull him tightly to me for a hard kiss. "First, we break in the land. Then, cheesecake. Then, I have to give you a really long honey-do list for the house."

"The house that's not built?" he says against my lips.

"Yes. It's like an unwritten rule. You need to have never-ending tasks."

He snickers. "I already do. But that's fine. As long as you're on the list."

"Every day, sir. Every day."

Epilogue

Maci

Christmas morning arrives in no time. With the NDA completed with Alan, paperwork finalized for Nana's, and things on track for Strickland Ranch's expansion, it finally feels like the right time to take a short vacation to visit Sutton's sister and family in the Dallas–Fort Worth area.

They have a two-story home in the suburbs with a perfect yard, a community playground, and a neighborhood pool. A lovely place to live. But it solidifies that I found my home.

The area here is friendly but loud. You can't see the stars for miles without interruption. There's no babbling creek in the backyard or the calming scent of mesquite and cedar. I can't wait to get home.

The only person I share this with is Sutton on Christmas morning. "Your family is amazing. I adore your sister."

"They feel the same," he says quietly, kissing the top of my head.

I snuggle tighter into his bare chest, and his arms tighten around me. Our breathing has finally returned to normal after the best, albeit the quietest, Christmas morning sex I've ever had.

"I still can't wait to be home," I add.

"I know what you mean."

A knock comes to the door. "Wakey wakey, sleepy heads." Sammi's sweet voice greets us from the other side.

"Be out in a minute," Sutton calls.

We dress quickly, in matching Christmas pajamas per his mother's request, and join the others in the living room. Nine-month-old Viviane is already playing with new toys on the plush carpet before the tree. The number of gifts surrounding it is insanity, and I haven't figured out how they managed to keep her from getting into anything. There's no gate stopping her. She just avoids all the brightly wrapped gifts of her own volition.

Truth be told, she's the most beautiful child I've ever laid eyes on. Truer, she carries so many of the Strickland genes that I'm almost eager to pop a bun in the oven.

Andi makes a pancake breakfast, and we eat on the couches in the living room.

"You sure do look festive in those pajamas," I tell Michael with a wink.

"Now, Maci, I thought we had an understanding. I don't pick on you, you don't pick on me." He winks back.

I throw my head back and laugh.

As usual, I clean up the dishes with Andi. And like another day not too long ago, I lean into her and whisper, "Thank you for letting me come to your family Christmas."

"I told you before, honey, you don't need to say thank you. At this point, I'd have a hard time picking Sutton over you." She kisses me on the cheek before heading back into the living room.

Sutton and I exchanged gifts last night. An agreement we made about doing things privately. I got him a sketch set for all the woodworking designs he's going to be coming up with, as a starter. But he preferred the album of boudoir photos I put together for him. Taking my own photos was challenging, and it was my first time using a remote shutter.

"This is my favorite," he told me after looking his fill, and he flipped back to one of me arched over a chaise longue, with my new scar on full display. His finger rested below it on the photo.

He got me a perfectly sized Stetson, as promised a few weeks ago. I may or may not have worn only that for playtime last night.

A few other gifts get passed around now, mainly between the Stricklands and Sammi's family. Sutton and I watch, standing behind the living room couch. Viviane claps happily every time someone tears paper, and my cheeks ache from my wide smile.

As the gift-giving finishes, Sutton wraps his arms around me. It's a habit for him to tuck them under mine, so my hands fall over his. I'm surprised to find something occupying his hands this time.

I look down to find a tiny velvet box, navy in color. I dart my eyes up to him.

He speaks softly. "I know we said no gifts today. But I have one more. It's a small one."

"What's that?" Sammi says, noticing our interaction.

"No fair. You always want to one-up me." My body heats from the center out and my face burns.

He smiles. "Never. You got me two. I owed you one."

He loosens his arms enough for me to remove the box from his hands and bring it closer to inspect. The case pops loudly when I lift the lid, and the room goes silent, except for my gasp.

A tiny gold band holds a cluster of stones. It's obviously antique. It catches all the light in the room, reflecting back at me in a beautiful display.

"It was my grandmother's."

"Sutton," I whisper.

He turns me in his arms, so we're both sideways to the back of the couch, facing each other. Intense gazes bore into us. Andi sniffles.

Sutton drops to one knee. "Maci, you are the part of me I never knew was missing. It doesn't matter how short a time we've known each other. I know you like your coffee sweet and your alcohol strong. I know there's no stopping you from dancing when Copperhead Road comes on a crowded dance floor, and that you're just as happy dancing to the crickets singing in an empty pasture. I know how strong you are facing down your demons. How you press this spot right here on your eyebrow when you're frustrated." He traces an imaginary line through his brow bone, as if replicating my own.

"But there are still things I don't know," he continues. "I don't know what you'll look like walking toward me on our wedding day, or how you'll glow when you're carrying our child. I don't know what lullabies you'll sing to a sleepless baby, or how you'll dance when they walk for the first time. But I want to. I want to know all of those things and more. I want to walk with you through this life. I don't care about sickness and health. I'm going to be here to face all of your darkest demons, and to watch you fly when you achieve your biggest dream. I love you. Will you marry me?"

"Oh my God," Sammi whimpers through tears.

"Yes," I say, leaning down to kiss him with the box tucked between us. Salty tears slip between our lips, brought on by his beautiful vision of our life together.

He stands, removing the ring from the box, which he tosses playfully. It falls over the couch and tumbles to the living room floor. Viviane picks it up happily. I giggle and Sutton places the ring on my fourth finger.

"Do you think this is clear enough that you're mine, or should I tattoo my name on your foot?"

I laugh wildly. "No one is tattooing my foot." I kiss him. "I love you."

I study the ring and he rubs my back with his hands. "Rainbow Connection." I lift my eyes.

"What?" His eyebrows dip briefly.

My lips press the corner of his mouth. "The lullaby."

His eyes light up in understanding, and he grips my cheeks firmly with both hands. "Fuck, I love you."

Epilogue II

Sutton

My eyes track Oinks and Snorts in their pen behind my parents' house. It's a bit of a shame they didn't get to have any fun with a certain stepfather. I don't think I'll have to work hard to convince Maci to move all four of the pigs closer to us once the house is finished. Just in case.

Voices swirl happily throughout the house. In less than an hour, Maci will be my wife. Spring is blooming on the ranch as much as it does in the hill country, and the homesite is beautifully prepped for our big day thanks to Maci, our friends, and our family.

I don't need the piece of paper. I only need her with me forever.

James approaches from the living room, following my eyes out the dining room window before turning to me. Somehow, we've managed to include all the immediate family without too much drama so far, even if James does also bring a small entourage with him.

He extends his closed fist and I open my hand, wondering what he has. He drops something heavy into my palm and tucks his hand back into his suit pocket.

Two black rectangular magnets sit attached, staring back at me.

Magnets.

"Like you two," he says, making his eyebrows jump once. My eyes meet his and he stares back with his usual intensity. "I think it goes without saying that if you hurt my daughter, I'll kill you."

For all the way we've come over the months, I've never had any reason to fear James and I still don't, but it's the first time I think I could.

He grins. "Not that you have anything to worry about."

I smile softly. "I'm glad I'll never be on your bad side."

"Oh?"

"No. Just like I told you at the ranch months ago, I plan to spend every day proving that I'm worthy of Maci's love. No matter what comes, I'm fully prepared for the fallout."

Maci's legs drape over mine on our porch swing. It was the first item she asked me to build once the house was done, and a strong choice because we spend nearly every evening here when time allows. Spring showers turned into summer thunderstorms, much like tonight as lightning cracks across the indigo sky.

An empty dessert plate sets on the wine barrel table next to us, once hosting a slice of homemade cheesecake.

"I decided today what the next piece is that I want you build for the house." Maci's voice is soft and her eyes are filled with wonder as she studies me, leaned against the arm of the swing.

"Oh?" I hike an eyebrow at her and hide a smirk. The swing and the matching wine barrel side tables were easy. I know she has a dining room set on her mind, but she hasn't given me a lot to go on yet.

She pulls her bottom lip into her mouth with her teeth, and her cheeks blush. I'll never tire of that look. Aside from earning her love daily, I make it my mission to cause her to blush as frequently as possible.

Sitting upright, she draws her legs back. I miss her warmth already.

Her chest rises and falls deeply, and I know this must be a significant piece, the way she's drawing it out.

"So?" I press, hitching my hips to the side to face her better.

"A cradle."

My brows furrow for one second while I process. "Firecracker, are you serious?" I reach for her with both hands, lifting her to straddle my legs and studying her face more closely.

She nods sheepishly.

My eyes drop to her torso, on delicious display in her snug lace tank top. One palm lays across her abdomen, pouring my love toward our growing baby. My throat clogs uncharacteristically. Only seeing Maci walking toward me in her vintage gown on our wedding day has even brought me as much joy as this.

"I found out today," she whispers, placing a cool hand over mine. "But I had a dream earlier this week. I think it's a boy."

I take in her stunning face, perfectly aglow, and for the first time that I can ever remember, wetness tracks down my cheeks.

Her own tears shine back at me in the limited light from the front window.

"You can't know that already," I say, more in awe than argument.

She smiles. "I can't. It's just a feeling."

"A boy," I whisper. "A cradle." We stare at each other in a short silence, a myriad of emotions dancing between us. "You're going to be an amazing mother."

More fat tears fall from her eyes. "And you're going to be an amazing father." She grips my face in her hands and kisses me deeply, our salty tears mingling between us.

Every day with her only gets better. Only lets in more love. And now, we get to grow our family together on this stunning piece of land where we're building our life together.

Thank You For Reading!

Maci and Sutton are so important to me, as a bit of my own origin story. I truly hope you enjoyed their books. Would you consider taking a minute to post a review on your favorite site? A few words and a star rating go a long way!

Stay updated and enjoy bonus content (including a bonus chapter from James' POV) by subscribing to Amanda's newsletter.

Also by Amanda Marquardt
The Fallout Duet
When Sparks Fly

When the Smoke Clears
Bull Creek Series
A Penny For Your Thoughts

Book Two – Coming 2026
Falcons MC
Untamed – Coming 2026

ACKNOWLEDGEMENTS

I can't be the only one who starts thinking about all of the people they want to say 'thank you' to during the drafting process. There are so many individuals I have to express gratitude to, without whom this book would not be here!

Tabitha & Chloe, you two probably don't realize how incredibly important and valuable you are to me. Your continued love for these characters, and interest in the process and behind-the-scenes, all of your support of my writing and myself, was more inspiring than I can put into words. You two were able to see the characters exactly as I felt them and our discussions about my books, and the industry as a whole, were so crucial to this process that I can't imagine achieving the same book without them. Thank you, friends.

My editor, Megan. I've said it before, and I'll say it again, your perspective is always so valuable to me. Your advice and input has been instrumental in helping me achieve what I wanted with this book. You're stuck with me forever, and I can't wait to read your own work!

My cover designer, KBG Designs. Thank you for another amazing process. You pushed me when I didn't think I needed it, and dealt with my back and forth, again.

My teams! I started this series with a few amazing beta readers, and we're completing the duet with alpha, beta, street, and ARC teams. I couldn't have imagined the growth from book one to book two, and your support and love is so appreciated! I'm thankful for each and every one of you! Thank you for dedicating your love and attention to this story. It's so much better because of you.

My family. My husband, the non-reader, you are so incredibly supportive. A true cheerleader who doesn't fully understand the process. I love you. My children who are learning to balance this life alongside me. Thank you for your love and support. Your excitement and pride over this work makes it more fulfilling than I could have imagined. I hope you always choose to go after your dreams.

To all the readers, thank you for taking a chance on a debut author! Your messages with love (and panic) over these characters and their story has been so validating and heartwarming. I've loved hearing how you connected to When Sparks Fly and I thank you for completing the duet with us. I can't wait to share the rest of the stories with you!

ABOUT THE AUTHOR

Amanda Marquardt is a native Texan, wife, and mother of four. She considers herself a chaos coordinator, taking on more tasks than she can manage and setting nearly impossible deadlines for herself. Her days consist of lots of caffeine, sometimes equal amounts of wine, and minimal sleep. When not homeschooling or writing, she can be found spending time with her family or reading.

To stay updated on upcoming releases and access exclusive content, visit amandamarquardt.beehiiv.com or subscribe to Amanda's newsletter.